AUTUMN WIND

"Come," Fireheart said, "let us swim."

Joanna was reluctant to move. She was supremely conscious of him as a man. Her body pulsated with life at his nearness, and she was embarrassed. She wondered how she could swim without revealing more skin. "Close your eyes," she said.

He looked amused. "When you were a child, you showed your breasts."

She felt herself flush. "I'm not a child anymore."

"Kihiila," he agreed with such meaning in his tone. "Come, Autumn Wind, be Lenape again."

His words and tone enticed her. The air was warm, but the little bumps rose on her skin. She caught Fireheart's gaze, was unable to release it. It was dark, but she could make out the planes of his face in the shadow. There was enough light to see the glistening of his dark eyes.

Then she was facing him in the water, and his hands fastened on her waist, drawing her close. To her shock, she felt his lips on her mouth. She had no time to utter a word; her head spun and her body pulsed with wild sensation.

Joanna moaned softly as he raised his head and shifted his hands to cup her face.

"Autumn Wind," he murmured.

"Fireheart."

She was drawn to him as she'd never before been attracted to another. The awkwardness between them was gone. They were man and woman. Fireheart and Autumn Wind ... alone together in the night ... and wanting.

Books by Candace McCarthy

WILD INNOCENCE
SWEET POSSESSION
WHITE BEAR'S WOMAN
IRISH LINEN
HEAVEN'S FIRE
SEA MISTRESS
RAPTURE'S BETRAYAL
WARRIOR'S CARESS
SMUGGLER'S WOMAN

With stories in these collections:

IRISH ENCHANTMENT
BABY IN A BASKET
AFFAIRS OF THE HEART

Published by Zebra Books

FIREHEART

Candace
McCarthy

Zebra Books
Kensington Publishing Corp.
http://www.zebrabooks.com

ZEBRA BOOKS are published by

Kensington Publishing Corp.
850 Third Avenue
New York, NY 10022

First Printing: June, 2000
10 9 8 7 6 5 4 3 2 1

Printed in the United States of America

For Mom, who has always been there for me . . . for your love, friendship, and support. Thanks. I love you.

Prologue

Little River Town—a Lenni Lenape village
Pennsylvania
August 1720

Mary Littleton stood at the door of her wigwam, watching the children at play in the village yard. It was a beautiful hot summer's day. The shade from the trees above kept out most of the sun's heat. A light breeze lowered the humidity in the air and tossed about the scent of meat roasting on someone's cook-fire.

Mary smiled as childish laughter rang out, followed by giggles. Dogs barked as they ran about the compound, egged on by a group of young boys at play. A woman sat outside the neighboring wigwam, weaving a basket while her young son sat on a mat beside her, munching contentedly on a piece of dried venison. Next door, a young warrior crouched before his lodge, sharpening an arrowhead, glancing up often to grin at the children's antics.

Behind Mary, her husband, Rising Bird, slept on

their sleeping mat undisturbed by the noise. He'd been gone for a week, and his journey had tired him. His return last night, long after the village had retired, had surprised her. There'd been little sleep between them as they'd held and stroked each other until their soft cries filled the dawn of the new day.

A young blonde girl came out of Woman with Eyes of Hawk's wigwam across the way, capturing Mary's attention. At fourteen, her cousin Joanna Neville was a lovely child with red-gold hair, smooth skin, and eyes of bright forest-green. She was blossoming into a woman, and Mary felt more than a moment's concern when she realized that the young braves within the village had noticed the changes, too.

How long had it been since she had brought Joanna here to the Lenni Lenape village to live? Nine years, since the death of the girl's mother, her own beloved Aunt Elizabeth?

Mary frowned as she followed Joanna's progress across the compound. Her young cousin appeared to be conscious of her own beauty as she sauntered across the yard with her hair loose about her shoulders and her only article of clothing a doeskin kilt about her slim hips. She wore a necklace of copper beads and animal teeth, and she had darkened her cheeks and lips with red berry juice.

Mary's discomfort grew as Joanna paused as if posing. The girl stood for a moment with her back straight and her chest thrust forward as if to draw attention to her young, firm breasts before she continued across the yard. It wasn't that Joanna was promiscuous, or wore any less clothing than the other Indian females. Mary's concern lay with Joanna's spirited nature. After years of life among the Lenape, she feared that Joanna no longer knew what was proper behavior in the English culture, her birthright. It was something that had begun to worry Mary since she'd received the letter from Joanna's uncle.

What if fate took Joanna away from them? Had she done her young cousin a disservice by introducing her to village life?

It wasn't the first time that Mary had suffered doubts. She'd struggled with the concern before, but in the past she'd been able to push that worry aside with the knowledge that the child was clearly happy here. The letter from Roderick Neville in England was forcing Mary to reevaluate the child's upbringing. She had a decision to make, and she wasn't certain what to do.

Joanna changed direction as if to walk intentionally past a group of young Lenni Lenape braves. Mary scowled. Was Joanna teasing those boys?

Tossing her blonde hair back with a sweep of her hand, Joanna rewarded several young men with a flirtatious smile. All of the boys widened their eyes, but one. Mary felt a stirring of unease as she saw the way Broken Bow studied her young cousin.

Her gaze then fell on another boy, much younger than Broken Bow, and Mary's expression softened. Yellow Deer adored Joanna, but her cousin had no interest in the brave. He was the youngest of the group and apparently not worthy of her note. Yellow Deer was a kind boy who gazed at Joanna with longing, not with the gleam of boyhood lust.

Mary sighed. Why couldn't Joanna be interested in Yellow Deer? Perhaps then, she wouldn't worry so much about the girl.

Broken Bow's eyes never left Joanna as the girl moved on and then stopped to chat with her best friend Little Blossom. Mary made a silent vow to speak with her cousin about the dangers of young males with more on their minds than friendship.

What should I do? Mary wondered. She loved her life with the Indians. She had come to them as a captive in trade. Terrified, she had wanted only to escape until the Lenape people had charmed her, treating her kindly when she expected to be tortured, or worse. The one time she'd tried to escape, she'd been found and brought back by Rising Bird who had faced her not with anger, as Mary had expected, but with kindness. She had quickly learned that peace and serenity were a way of life for these Indian people.

Later, Mary had married Rising Bird, and she had lived with her husband now for over ten years. She'd never once regretted giving up her former English life. Happy and at peace here, she'd wanted the same for Joanna.

But had that been fair to her young cousin? Joanna had been only a child when Mary had brought her to the village, while she herself had been a full-grown woman. Joanna had gone blindly where she was told, while Mary had chosen her life's direction.

Joanna followed Little Blossom into a wigwam, and Mary turned from the doorway, allowing the door flap made from deerskin to fall, shutting her inside.

Joanna was a good girl, and Mary loved her. *I'm really concerned about Roderick Neville's letter, not her behavior.* The man wanted to see his niece. *He says he wants to make Joanna heiress to his estate. But how can I make a decision that might force us to lose her?* Mary wondered.

She didn't want Joanna to go to England. But what if it was the best thing for her cousin?

She wanted to be selfish and make Joanna stay, but then she would be guilty of keeping Joanna from her inheritance. And how could she deny the child her birthright?

In England, Joanna could be educated, have beautiful clothes and fine surroundings. And then there was the fact of her uncle, brother to Joanna's beloved father. Didn't Joanna have the right to meet the rest of her family?

Mary's first notion upon receiving Roderick Neville's missive was to destroy it. She couldn't bear the thought of letting Joanna go. After raising the girl, she regarded Joanna more as a daughter than a cousin.

England was such a long journey by ship. How could she not be concerned about the girl?

Mary had worried for two days now. She hadn't told Joanna about her uncle's letter. She'd wanted to discuss the matter with her husband first. Rising Bird would know what to do.

She lay down next to her husband, snuggling close for comfort, and attempted to put Roderick Neville's missive from her mind. She would talk with Rising Bird later when he was well-rested. Then she must decide what was best for Joanna.

Chapter 1

*Neville Manor—an estate just outside London, England
March 1727*

"Joanna?"

Joanna glanced up from her cousin's letter to gaze sightlessly at her neighbor and friend, her green eyes glistening from emotional pain.

"Are you all right?" John Burton asked with concern. "You seem troubled." The young man frowned as he approached.

She gave him a smile as she carefully folded the missive. "I'm fine." When John slipped his arm around her shoulders, she fought the urge to pull away. John was a handsome man with a magnificent physique and beautiful blue eyes.

Today, John looked splendid in his navy long coat with vest over a white linen shirt. His white stockings made a nice contrast with his matching navy knee breeches, and the silver buckles on his shoes had been polished to a high shine. On his head, a cocked hat sat on his powdered wig in which the hair had been pulled back and secured with a white ribbon at his nape.

John Burton was the kindest man she knew in England. When John had first visited Neville Manor, it had become clear to Joanna that even her uncle had approved of the young man . . . a fact that might have made Joanna dislike John immediately if it were not for his winning charm.

John wanted to be more than her friend, but Joanna couldn't envision him as her husband or lover. If her uncle had still been alive, he would have been pushing John's suit.

Uncle Roderick is dead, she thought. *I don't have to please him or anyone but myself.*

Joanna feared that John was longing to propose to her, and that their friendship would be over after she rejected him. She didn't love John. Marriage might be the best thing for her, she mused, but she wouldn't marry without love, not even for the sake of Neville Manor. Neville Manor was her late uncle's estate, now her inheritance. It was a beautiful place, but it held only bad memories for her. She had never been happy here.

Joanna moved to the window to gaze out over the manicured lawn and garden. The grass was a vast carpet of bright green. The flowers were in full bloom, a riotous splash of spring color, but the sight gave her no pleasure. In the midst of the flower garden stood a fountain where she, a newly arrived young girl, had once sought comfort in the sound of water rushing over its side. A great deal had changed since that first day at Neville Manor.

How could she enjoy anything about the place when it was at the root of all the pain, heartache, and abuse that she'd suffered at Roderick Neville's hands?

Her uncle had thought he'd done her a favor by

snatching her away from a life she loved and bringing her to England to "educate" her. She didn't want to be his heir, nor did she want the full charge of running all of the deceased man's holdings.

Had she asked for the responsibility? No. But she had been trained to handle it, and she would do her duty. What else could she do? There were people who lived and worked on her uncle's property, servants, and employees counting on her to keep the estate running smoothly.

The manor was beautiful, large, and built of stone, old England at its best. But Joanna could remember only the hurt she'd suffered there ... the pain of being unable to please her Uncle Roderick. Until Roderick Neville had sent for her, Joanna had been truly happy living among the Lenni Lenape Indians with her cousin Mary. When she had become severely ill, Elizabeth Neville, Joanna's mother, had sent for her niece Mary to care for her daughter. Orphaned at five, Joanna had lived with poverty-stricken neighbors until Mary had finally come for her. Only Mary hadn't come for a long time, not until after the death of Joanna's mother. Mary had been captured by Iroquois Indians during the journey to her aunt's Delaware home, then traded to the Lenape. She had not been freed for several months. When she did finally arrive, Mary had already married Rising Bird, a Lenape warrior.

Joanna had been fourteen when Roderick Neville had sent for her, his only niece. She'd wanted to live in the village forever, but the choice had been taken from her when Mary made the decision to send her back to England. Once there, she'd been forced to live with a man who was cold, unfeeling, and cruel in his efforts to tame the "savage" in her. For the next seven years, until his death, Roderick Neville had controlled her, shaping her into the lady he deemed suitable to be his heir.

"You are a Neville, Joanna," he'd told her on more than one occasion. "A Neville conducts herself in the proper manner. You will not wear those awful buckskins. You will get rid of those filthy moccasins and wear only the shoes that I bought for you." He'd pause, and his gaze would harden. "Do you understand?"

Joanna had been made to understand. Uncle Roderick did not tolerate her "heathen" ways. She had to obey him, or be severely punished for it. She'd hated England and despised her uncle. Once, she had tried to run away, but Roderick had caught her. Her punishment had been so severe that Joanna had not attempted another escape.

Joanna shuddered and tried not to recall her uncle's methods of punishment.

He's dead. He can't hurt you anymore.

Roderick Neville had been a hard man. Had Mary honestly thought him kind?

I hate this place, but it is mine now, Joanna thought. *All that is left me.*

Somehow she would find a way to ease the painful past, and bring joy to this cold, dark manor house. There were many who relied on her. Servants and employees who had also endured her uncle's cruelty.

Joanna shivered and hugged herself with her arms. She would make things better for all who lived and worked at Neville Manor.

"Joanna, you're shivering!" John's voice drew her from her dark thoughts, and she felt the weight of his coat as he draped it about her shoulders. The navy wool was warm with the heat of his body.

"Thank you," she murmured without meeting his gaze.

"Joanna?" He turned her to face him. "What's wrong? Tell me. Is it the letter?" John's expression held curiosity mingled with concern.

Joanna nodded. She gazed into blue eyes so kind

and gentle that for a brief second she wondered if she could fall in love with him someday.

"The letter is from my cousin Mary in the Colonies," she said.

Something flickered across John's face and was gone. "What does your cousin want?" He didn't seem surprised to hear that she had a cousin. Had he heard about her former Lenape life?

Her jaw tightened and, angry, she could feel the heat burn in her stomach. Joanna fought to keep her fury where it rightfully belonged—with her late uncle and not with John who had proven to be a good friend.

"Mary lives in the Pennsylvania colony. She wants me to come." She moved from the window to the sofa and sat.

John joined her, his gaze unreadable, but it didn't seem like he knew about the Indians. "Do you want to go?"

She nodded. "Someone I know, someone I care about a great deal, is ill and may be dying." She glanced down at the letter to find her hands in her lap, clutching the parchment tightly. Mary had written to tell her that Wild Squirrel, the *sachem* of the Lenni Lenape village of Little River, was very ill. Mary had thought that Joanna would want to know because the man had been like a grandfather to her.

Her throat felt tight as she met John's gaze. "I know it's been only a week since Uncle Roderick's death, but . . ."

She was torn . . . torn between her love for an old Indian chief who was ill in the Pennsylvania colony, a man she thought of as a grandfather, and her duty to her uncle's servants. Here she would have to wear the black of mourning for her uncle, and it would be a lie. Terrible or not, she didn't care that Roderick Neville was dead.

Joanna turned a beseeching gaze on her friend.

"John, I know 'tis a lot to ask . . . but I'd hoped that you would come and keep an eye on things here at Neville Manor."

"Me?"

She was relieved to see a pleased look enter John's gaze. She smiled as she nodded. John Burton was a second son with the skill of running an estate, but it was his twin brother, Michael, older by only three minutes, who had acquired his father's wealth. If John was bitter about Michael's legacy, he'd never shown it.

He was the perfect choice to oversee the property in her absence. John had the freedom to come to Neville Manor and the knowledge to run it properly. She trusted him. And now, judging by his reaction, she realized that he would enjoy himself while he worked.

"I'd be honored to look after things while you are away," he admitted. Then he frowned. "Who will escort you to the Colonies? 'Tis not a journey to be taken by a young woman alone."

"I'll bring servants with me," Joanna said. "When I get to the New World, I'll hire someone to take me the rest of the way." Would she make the trip only to learn that Wild Squirrel had died? She didn't tell John that she'd be going into the wilderness, or that her final destination was a Lenni Lenape village. He didn't have to know. She wasn't concerned for her safety, but she didn't expect John to understand that.

Just as she'd feared, John suddenly looked worried. "Joanna, what if it's not safe?"

Joanna smiled. Thoughtful as always, John wanted what was best for her, even while he looked forward to the challenge of running Neville Manor. "I'm not afraid," she said, meaning it. She relented on her decision to keep silent. "I once lived there."

A servant appeared in the parlor doorway before Joanna could judge John's reaction to the revelation. "Miss Neville, Miss Gordon is here to see you."

"Gillian!" she cried with genuine pleasure. " 'Tis good to see you!" She smiled with welcome as she approached her friend.

Gillian Gordon, a lovely woman with hair of midnight and eyes of violet, was dressed in the latest French fashion in a shade of lavender that became her. Joanna had been friends with Gillian since her uncle had introduced her to a group of young ladies of the same age, daughters of neighbors who were the "right kind of" families. Joanna and Gillian had bonded immediately, although Joanna had had more difficulty with the other girls.

Gillian's smile was as warm as Joanna's as the two women embraced then eyed each other with affection.

"You've come at the right time," Joanna murmured in her friend's ear. "I've much to tell you."

Gillian glanced at John before whispering to her friend. "With him here?"

Joanna shook her head as she smiled at John. "John, you've met my friend Gillian, haven't you?"

"Charmed," he mumbled distractedly, barely acknowledging Joanna's friend except for a brief glance at the neckline of her gown, which was low and exposed the upper swells of her young breasts. Blushing, he quickly returned his gaze to Joanna. "I'll call on you tomorrow to discuss details," he told her.

Knowing that he referred to his temporary position as overseer of the estate, Joanna nodded and followed him to the door. Once John was gone, she turned to her friend with a grin and an offer of tea.

Deep in the Pennsylvania wilderness
June 1727

"How much farther, Mr. Grace?" Joanna asked.

Her hired guide and Indian tracker, Mortimer Grace, crouched and fingered the dirt of the trail. He rose to his feet, looking thoughtful. He was a young bearded man with the wisdom of age in his gray eyes. He wore buckskins and looked more at home in the forest than in a town. "About a half day's journey," he replied as he brushed off his hands.

Joanna nodded. She thought as much herself. The surrounding forest looked familiar, but it had been years since she'd been to the area, and there were probably acres upon acres of woodland that she could have mistaken for the forest where she'd once lived. That's why she'd hired the Indian tracker. He was familiar with the Lenni Lenape people, and he knew their signs well. And he'd come highly recommended as a man she could trust. Her own gut instincts told her that what she'd learned about him was true.

As Mortimer continued through the woods, Joanna fell into step behind him. Following were her two servants from Neville Manor, silent and unhappy to be traipsing through the woods. Cara Jones, her personal maid, was a loyal servant girl, only too willing to go where Joanna led her. Harry Mett, the young man who had once worked with Patrick Williams, Roderick Neville's groom, was not only loyal to the new mistress of Neville Manor, but also smitten with Cara.

Conscious of their steadfast loyalty and presence behind her, Joanna made a silent promise that once back in England, she would reward her employees well.

She continued in Mr. Grace's wake, her thoughts nervously turning to her destination as they left the trail and Mr. Grace began to clear a path.

It had been years since she'd seen her cousin Mary.

Would she recognize her? The pain that had begun earlier in Joanna's stomach sharpened as she recalled the day she'd left her Indian family, the resentment she'd felt toward Mary. It had festered over the years, fueled by her uncle's cruel treatment of her. Didn't Mary realize what manner of man Roderick Neville had been?

Tears filled her eyes as she recalled all the nights she'd cried herself to sleep, wishing she were back in the New World, in the wigwam with Mary and Rising Bird.

I'm a grown woman now. I mustn't allow my memories to upset me. Uncle Roderick is dead, and I'm alive. I'll never suffer his abuse again.

Sunshine burst through the foliage overhead, brightening the day and lighting Joanna's path. Joanna felt the tension within her leave. The flaming knot in her stomach loosened.

She would be all right. She would visit the Lenni Lenape people, then return to England where she belonged.

She inhaled deeply of the fresh forest air, and felt her heart quicken as she detected the scent of roasting meat.

The Lenni Lenape village of Little River
The Pennsylvania colony

Fireheart entered the wigwam silently, unwilling to disturb the ailing man who lay on the sleeping pallet. Beside him on a rush mat sat the man's wife, Stormy Wind, embroidering a new set of moccasins. She rose when she saw Fireheart, as if waiting for him to come.

"Stormy Wind," he greeted her as she approached him.

Their gazes locked, hers tired and sad, his worried. "He does not wake, does not eat," she said gravely.

He gave a silent nod, and then Stormy Wind

touched her nephew's arm before leaving to allow Fireheart time alone with his uncle.

"How is he?" he asked the shaman who had remained, standing near the bed.

Raven Wing shook his head. "He sleeps uneasily." He studied his chief with concern. "This man worries."

A ball of tension formed in Fireheart's gut. The sick man was his uncle, and he had loved him for his entire life. As Wild Squirrel's health continued to fail, Fireheart felt an overwhelming fear.

Wild Squirrel was their leader, *sachem* of the Lenni Lenape. If the old man died, Fireheart would become the next *sachem.* It was destined to be, Fireheart knew, but he was in no hurry to become chief. He wanted his uncle to live long and prosper, and to be alive for the birth and marriage of Fireheart's sons.

Raven Wing left the wigwam, leaving Fireheart alone with his uncle. Approaching the sleeping pallet, Fireheart studied the sick man.

"Be well, Grandfather," he said, using the title of respect. "Fight your sickness and come back to us." His eyes glistened as he bent his head and began to pray.

As if the Great Spirit were listening, the old man stirred, drawing Fireheart's attention, at the moment he opened his eyes. The chief's gaze cleared as he focused, and lit up when he saw Fireheart.

"Fireheart," he rasped.

"Grandfather, it is good to see you awake. How are you feeling?" Fireheart could barely contain the rush of joy.

The old man grimaced as he shifted in bed. "I'm alive, but barely."

Fireheart experienced alarm. "Shall I get Raven Wing?"

Sighing, Wild Squirrel closed his eyes. "No." After

several seconds, he opened them again. "We must speak."

The young man nodded. "If you wish." But he feared what his *sachem* would say.

"You are the son of my sister, Doe at Play," the chief said. "When I leave this great white path, you will be *sachem.*"

"You must not talk of leaving—"

"I am an old man."

"Maata, you are not old, merely a man of experience. You have many years left as our leader."

"If the Great Spirit wills it," Wild Squirrel said.

"He must," Fireheart said forcefully. "He must!"

Wild Squirrel smiled faintly in acknowledgment of his nephew's loyalty and love for him. "You are a good man, Fireheart. A wise choice for *sachem.* I could not have picked a better chief for our people."

"Do not talk of me as chief!" Fireheart exclaimed, upset by the discussion. "You are chief! You are *sachem.* It is you our people need for wisdom and guidance."

"Fireheart." The *sachem* spoke quietly and with patience. "You must face the fact that someday I will pass from this life, and you will lead our people."

"I know this," the brave replied. "But the time is not now."

"I grow weaker by the day." The chief closed his eyes.

"Nay! You are awake. It is more than you did yesterday."

"Aye," Wild Squirrel admitted. "It is so."

"Then let us not continue such talk. Let us speak of other things instead."

"What shall we discuss?" the old man asked.

"I will tell you of Raining Sky and her latest antics."

The chief's eyes glowed at the mention of Fireheart's cousin. "Aye." A smile of amusement touched his lips. "Tell me what the girl is doing to make your life hard these days."

But as Fireheart began to tell tales, Wild Squirrel slept again.

Chapter 2

Memories assailed Joanna as she entered the Indian compound. A huge fire burned in the center square, and from the kettle hung over the flame came the delicious smell she'd detected while still in the forest.

Women and children came out of their lodges, eyeing the white people curiously, with a wariness that Joanna understood.

Young Indian maidens, each with their hair in two dark plaits, studied Joanna's clothes and blonde hair shyly. A small Lenape baby was content in a cradleboard strapped to his mother's back, perhaps sleeping. Small toddlers with honey-brown skin played in the dirt, naked, while their mothers stood by protectively, staring at Joanna, her servants, and her guide.

Were they in the right village? she wondered. Was it possible that one of these maidens had been her friend?

She recalled one Lenape girl in particular—Little Blossom. Little Blossom had been Joanna's confidante and closest friend.

As she waited for someone to approach them, Joanna studied her surroundings more closely. Some of the Lenape wigwams were domed while others were rectangular huts, all made of sticks and birch bark. Joanna was pleased as she recalled the pleasure of living inside. As she stared at one of the dome-shaped wigwams, she remembered how it felt to lie on her sleeping pallet in the warmth of a summer's eve. As she pictured the onslaught of winter, she distinctly recalled how it felt to huddle inside near the fire to ward off the winter's chill. Rising Bird used to tell stories as they sat by the warm fire, adventurous tales that had captured young Joanna's attention and kept it riveted.

"Miss Neville," Mortimer Grace's voice drew Joanna from her memories.

She followed the direction of the guide's gaze, and stiffened as she spied the approaching warrior. Everyone else had stepped back as if afraid to come closer.

"Talk with him," Joanna whispered.

Mortimer nodded, then greeted the warrior. The Indian wore his hair in two long dark braids with a tuft of hair that stuck up at the crown of his head. A breechclout and moccasins were his only clothing. His chest was tattooed, and his ears were pierced with strips of leather for earrings. A beautifully embroidered belt was slung about the waist-string that held the fringed cloth covering his loins.

The men exchanged words in the Lenape tongue. They spoke so quickly that Joanna couldn't follow them, and she wondered if she remembered how to speak the language. Aware of her servants standing in fear behind her, Joanna kept a respectful distance from the pair as Mortimer and the Indian continued their conversation.

"Dear heavens!" Cara exclaimed when she saw a bare-breasted Indian matron exit from a wigwam. "Don't any of them have morals?"

Joanna turned to her personal maid with a smile. It hadn't startled her that most of the women were bare-breasted. She had seen it before when she was a child.

"The Lenape see no shame in the female form," she explained. "They are a proud people, surrounded by everything that they love."

"You sound as if you've lived among them," Harry commented.

She frowned as she remembered those early days. "I did," she replied. "I lived here as a child, but my childhood seems like a distant memory."

Where is Mary? Joanna searched the sea of faces for one that looked familiar. Was her cousin among these people?

Where were Rising Bird and Wild Squirrel? What if they had come to the wrong village? What if the chief had died?

"Mr. Grace," she said when the two men paused in their conversation.

The Lenape warrior focused his attention on her with a narrowed gaze. She stared back at him without intimidation.

"Did you speak about Wild Squirrel?" she asked.

"Aye, Miss Neville, I did," Mortimer replied. "This is his village. They call it 'Little River.' "

"I see," Joanna said. The village might be in a different place, but it had the same name as when she'd been here last. The Indian frowned at her. "Ask him about Rising Bird."

The tracker asked the question in Lenape.

The warrior's brow cleared as he responded rapidly, nodding as he did so. He must have been telling Mortimer Rising Bird's whereabouts for the Indian was gesturing with his arm toward the opposite side of the village.

"The warrior's name is Turtle That Hops. He said

to tell you that Rising Bird lives over there," Mortimer said, pointing. "Nearer to the lake."

Turtle That Hops. Joanna tried to remember if she had known a brave by that name, but her memory didn't serve her. She followed the direction of the tracker's pointing hand with her gaze. "Tell him that I'd like to see Wild Squirrel before I visit Rising Bird."

"The white woman wants to see your *sachem,*" Mortimer said in the Indian's native tongue.

Turtle That Hops frowned. "Our *sachem* is ill. He cannot have visitors."

Mortimer glanced at Joanna with an apology in his expression. "He said that Wild Squirrel is ill and cannot be disturbed."

"Tell him I know this," Joanna said with impatience. "Never mind. Let me try to talk with him myself." She thought long and hard to find the Lenape word for "grandfather."

"*Nukuaa,*" she said, recalling the term for "father" instead. "*Nukuaa . . . Xan-eek-wh.*"

"What did you say to him?" Harry asked.

"I said "father" and "squirrel." I wanted to say that Wild Squirrel was my grandfather, but I couldn't remember the word for 'grandfather' or 'wild.' "

"Your grandfather!" Cara exclaimed. "I didn't know you had an Indian grandfather!"

"It is a title of affection or respect," Mortimer said. Cara blinked. "Oh."

A woman exited the nearest wigwam, and froze when she saw the newcomers. "Joanna?" she gasped.

Joanna narrowed her gaze. *Mary.*

Mary hurried forward to give Joanna a hug. She looked the same but slightly older, Joanna thought with dispassion. Dark hair worn pulled back at her nape, warm brown eyes, and the same sunny smile.

She didn't return the embrace or smile after Mary released her. She gazed at the older woman as she would a stranger. She didn't want to feel any love, any emotion at all. For the present, she was successful in tamping down her feelings.

"I didn't know you were coming," Mary said with a waver to her voice. "You must have received my letter."

"I did receive it. There wasn't time for me to write back," Joanna replied stiffly. "How is Wild Squirrel?"

"You haven't seen him?"

"I've been trying to learn where he is."

A grave look entered Mary's expression. "He is ill and very weak. I am afraid for him."

"May I see him?" Joanna felt a painful pang.

Mary stared at her a moment before answering. "I will ask the shaman." She started to leave.

Turtle That Hops followed her.

"Who is this woman?" he asked.

Mary halted. "It is Joanna—Autumn Wind. She has returned home to see our chief."

"Little Autumn Wind?" The Lenape brave turned to eye Joanna with amazement. He recalled a young girl with hair like the golden sun and smiling eyes like the forest trees. "This woman is too sad to be Autumn Wind," he said. He frowned. "She has changed."

"*Kihiila*. She has changed," Mary agreed. "I pray to the Great Spirit that she will find her smile here in the village." She looked back to find Joanna watching her intently. She gestured for her cousin to follow her. "Joanna! Come, and together we'll see if Wild Squirrel can have visitors."

Joanna hurried to catch up. As she accompanied Mary across the compound to the wigwam of the *sachem*, she continued to note the physical changes in her cousin. When she had left, Mary's skin had been smoother, unlined. Now Joanna saw the effects of age . . . the small laugh lines near Mary's eyes and mouth, the smattering of gray strands in her dark hair. But although age might have left its mark on her cousin, Mary still looked as beautiful as Joanna remembered.

Her cousin paused outside the wigwam doorway to glance at her. The tension between the two women was palpable. Joanna saw Mary's struggle for something to say to smooth over the moment's awkwardness. "Don't be upset by how he looks," she said finally. "He's been sick a long time."

Joanna swallowed against a lump in her throat as she nodded. She didn't know what to say to her cousin. She had loved Mary like a sister, even a mother, certainly more than as just a cousin. But their separation had changed their relationship. Joanna couldn't forget that it had been Mary who had sent her away, and she couldn't forgive her cousin so easily for all the pain Mary had caused her.

The two women gazed at each other for several seconds in silence. When Joanna had nothing to say, Mary's eyes took on a look of pain as she raised the wigwam's door flap and stepped inside.

Following closely, Joanna entered the dark interior with a pounding heart. Her attention immediately went to the ailing man who lay on the sleeping platform, his form highlighted in golden light. There was a banked fire in the wigwam's fire pit.

Joanna had recognized the old man as Wild Squirrel instantly although his illness had aged his features, which looked pale and drawn. The strong smiling *sachem*, who had patiently taught her how to use a knife, was a mere shadow of his former self.

Tears filled Joanna's eyes as she approached his bedside. She became oblivious to everyone in the room but the man who lay on his bed, a man who had shown her only kindness and love when she was a little girl. Wild Squirrel was the loving grandfather that Joanna had never known. It was her affection for this man that had prevailed upon her to leave

England and return to a place that she'd thought she'd never visit again.

The low murmur of voices drew Joanna's gaze to Mary and a man. *The shaman*, Joanna thought. She frowned when the shaman turned briefly and flashed her a look of displeasure before presenting her with his back.

Mary and the man appeared to be arguing. *About me*, Joanna thought. Ready to defend her right to visit, she glared at the brave, willing him to turn her away. It was too dark to see much of anything but the honey-brown skin of the man's naked back. Once her gaze fully focused in the dim interior of the wigwam, she was surprised by how muscular he was . . . his powerful back and arms and the muscled thickness of the back of his legs.

His dark hair fell past shoulders that were broad and as muscular as his arms and back. He was naked from the waist upward. He wore only a loincloth, and Joanna felt a flutter in her stomach as her gaze traveled down the back of his muscled calves.

The shaman's sinewy body looked like it should belong to a warrior rather than to a holy medicine man.

Where were his medicine man's tools? Joanna suddenly remembered another occasion when she had been living among the Lenape, and there had been an ill child within the village. The boy had been the brother of her best friend, Little Blossom. Walking Dog had been sick with fever, and Little Blossom's father had sent for the shaman. Joanna recalled the arrival of Raven Wing with his cloak of many colors, his turtle-shell rattles, and other implements of his position.

Raven Wing had chanted and sang, and worked his special magic on little Walking Dog. By the next afternoon Little Blossom's brother was up and running about the compound, once again a young healthy boy.

Joanna had always been amazed and in awe of the shaman's powers and ability to heal. She wondered now if it wasn't simply Raven Wing who had won her admiration. She had yet to speak with this new shaman, but she already doubted his abilities.

The man turned then, and Joanna experienced a jolt as she became the focus of the shaman's intense dark eyes. He gazed at her without kindness. She was startled by his animosity, wondering at its cause.

And then Mary drew her attention by speaking in English. "Joanna, the shaman is not here. Fireheart says that Raven Wing will return soon. I don't see why you can't visit with Wild Squirrel as long as you don't disturb him while he sleeps."

Joanna realized then that the man in the wigwam was not the village shaman. Apparently, Raven Wing was still the shaman.

Frowning, she studied the man before her. So this brave was called Fireheart, she realized. Who was he? And what right did he have to argue against her being here? Although Mary did not tell her of the reason for their argument, Joanna was certain that the subject was her and her desire to see Wild Squirrel.

To Joanna's disconcertment, Fireheart scowled as he continued to study her. Unwilling to be intimidated, she glared back at him while wondering what it was about her that irritated him.

After several seconds of tension between them, Joanna dismissed the angry brave and returned her attention to Wild Squirrel. She remained conscious of the warrior's presence as she went to the sachem's bedside. Studying her beloved adopted grandfather, she began to pray.

She felt the tension in the wigwam ease and guessed that Fireheart had left. She glanced back and sighed. She was right. Fireheart had departed, and only Mary remained, silently studying the changes in her young cousin.

He had never expected to see her again. Fireheart left the wigwam for the forest where he could be alone to think. The appearance of Joanna—Autumn Wind—had startled him speechless. It had been many years since he had seen the golden-haired beauty. Then he had had a wild love for the young girl, but she had wanted nothing to do with him.

Joanna had had many admirers. She had seemed most taken with Broken Bow, the eldest of his group of friends. He himself had been the youngest. He had been known as Yellow Deer then, before he had become a warrior, earning his present name.

Had Joanna guessed who he was? Her expression as she studied him suggested that she had for she had gazed at him with barely concealed hostility. He should not have been affected by it, but he realized with some dismay that he was.

Autumn Wind was as beautiful as he remembered. More so, in fact. But he must be immune to her beauty now. Maturity and distance had taught him to dismiss his feelings of admiration for her. He was no longer a child; he was a warrior. And he was the man expected to marry Moon Dove, a lovely village maiden.

He knew Joanna had chosen to return because of Wild Squirrel, but he had no intention of remembering what she had once been to him . . . nor would he allow his thoughts to linger on the woman she'd become.

"You'll stay with us, of course," said Mary.

After a short visit with Wild Squirrel, who did not awaken while Joanna was there, the cousins left the dark interior of the *sachem's* wigwam for the warmth of the summer sunshine outside. Mary made an effort to be friendly, but Joanna had difficulty responding in kind. The knowledge that Mary had been the one to send her away still hurt Joanna deeply. She wanted to ask Mary why, but she wasn't ready to hear the painful truth.

Now, as they stood within Mary's wigwam, Joanna wondered how she could share her cousin's lodge while feeling resentment. But to argue against Mary's generosity seemed churlish and rude. So Joanna made an effort to smile as Mary told her of the sleeping arrangements.

Joanna then recalled her servants and realized that Cara and Harry were the perfect excuse to stay elsewhere within the village. Before she had a chance to mention them, a light breeze created by the lifting and closing of the deer flap drew her attention to the door. Rising Bird, Mary's husband, had entered and stood by the door with a grin.

"It has been many summers since I have seen my Autumn Wind," Mary's husband said.

Joanna couldn't contain her joy. "You have not changed much, Rising Bird." She smiled at him as he approached. "It is good to see you, my father."

The warrior looked as magnificent and handsome as her young girl's memory had pictured him. He appeared pleased by her endearment. He had the kindest eyes, she thought. Those gentle dark eyes of his glistened with emotion as he studied her. A lump rose to Joanna's throat as her eyes filled with tears.

"You are a woman now," he said, his voice sad.

"Yet," she answered, "you recognized me."

"I will always know the young girl who came to us with sadness in her eyes but with great love in her heart." He looked at his wife who remained silent during the exchange. "She has come home to us, Mary."

"I hope she will stay," Mary said sincerely.

The conversation made Joanna uncomfortable. She had come only for a visit. Her life and her inheritance were in England. In a few short weeks, she would return there with only the memory of this visit in her heart. Unwilling to discuss the length of her stay, Joanna told Mary about her servants.

"And so you see," Joanna continued, "it would be wonderful if there were a lodge available for us to stay together."

"There is room in Red Dress's wigwam," Rising Bird said. "She has gone to visit her sister in the north."

Mary looked upset by the switch in Joanna's accommodations. "Cannot your friends stay in Red Dress's lodge alone?"

"Cara and Harry have never been to an Indian village before," Joanna said. "Cara is understandably nervous. Harry, although more confident, will be unable to calm the girl's fears." She looked to Rising Bird for understanding.

The brave nodded. "I see how much you wish to visit with Autumn Wind," he said to his wife, "but Joanna knows best. You will have time enough to spend with our little girl."

Rising Bird convinced Mary as no one else could. He smiled at both women before leaving the wigwam to see about Red Dress's lodge.

A smile lingered on Joanna's lips after Rising Bird had left. She had loved the brave like a father when she had lived here before. Now, as a woman, she could appreciate even more the warmth, affection, and friendship of such a kind warrior.

"Are you hungry?" Mary asked, trying to mask her disappointment with a smile.

Joanna turned to her cousin. "I'm famished. Can I help with the meal?"

Mary's expression lit up with pleasure, and Joanna

realized the direction of her cousin's thoughts. For a
brief moment, the two women smiled at each other as
they recalled an earlier time when Joanna had begged
Mary to teach her how to prepare hominy . . . and the
young girl's first attempt at preparing the dish.

  Joanna made an effort to put aside her resentment
toward Mary for the first evening of her brief return
visit to Lenape life.

Chapter 3

"This is where we'll be staying?" Cara appeared upset. "It's nothing more than a primitive hut!"

"Actually, Cara," Harry replied, "I imagine we'll be quite happy here."

"I've slept on a Lenape sleeping pallet." Joanna wandered about the wigwam, noting things that seemed familiar to her. "I've found it comfortable."

There were different structures that served as lodges or wigwams within the village. Some were long rectangular buildings with curved roofs. Intermingled with these larger wigwams were dome-shaped huts with just enough room for a single person or small family. All were made from sticks and birch-bark. Joanna and her servants had been given one of the small huts. Studying its interior, Joanna felt the wigwam would do nicely.

The wigwam held many provisions, no doubt left by Red Dress, the absent matron who owned the lodge. Dried corn known as *Xus'kwim* with its husks braided to form clusters hung from the roof rafters. Sacks of grain, dried beans, and dried berries lay against one wall near Lenape-fashioned pots, dishes, and cooking utensils. There was also dried meat. Joanna recognized a cloth bag as a container for bear grease, an ointment used by the Indians for many purposes. She saw an axe with a stone head and a birch-bark box filled with tree-sugar. The sleeping pallets were rush mats on the dirt floor, covered with deer skins and beaver pelts.

Joanna glanced at her servants and frowned. Back in England, it would be shocking for two unmarried women to share a room with an unattached man. She felt that the unusual circumstance of staying in an Indian village in the Pennsylvania wilderness was enough of an exception to forget society's standards.

Besides, she thought, *who else other than the Indians and us will know or care?*

"Harry, perhaps it is unseemly for you to share our wigwam," Joanna said, "but under the circumstances, I feel it would be best for Cara and me that you remain here." Her gaze went to her maid. "Is that all right with you, Cara?" She smiled at her servants. "You mustn't think that I feel we are unsafe here. The Lenape are a peaceful people. They will not harm you. But I think that you will both feel more at ease in a wigwam of our own."

The young woman nodded, looking relieved. "How long will we stay?"

Joanna became thoughtful. "A month . . . a few weeks at least."

"A month!" Cara breathed. She looked horrified. "Whatever you wish," she whispered uneasily.

"Life here isn't so terrible," Joanna told her. "Given time, you'll enjoy it, I think."

"If you say so, Miss." Cara appeared unconvinced.

Later that evening, Joanna once again headed toward Wild Squirrel's wigwam. As she walked across the village yard, she fervently prayed that the brave Fireheart would be nowhere in sight. The warrior's behavior toward her earlier had upset her. Why had the man been so hostile to her?

She didn't know him, and he certainly didn't know her! The memory of his glaring dark gaze made her shiver. She didn't deserve such treatment! She had come to see Wild Squirrel because she was concerned for the *sachem*'s well-being. What right did Fireheart have to forbid her to see him?

Mary did not have to translate her conversation with Fireheart for Joanna to understand what had been said. Fireheart's expression and gestures had spoken volumes.

Joanna paused outside the *sachem*'s wigwam before entering. Drawing a deep breath, she firmed her resolve to visit Wild Squirrel, despite the possibility of Fireheart's presence.

The fire in the center pit had been stoked to a hearty flame. Joanna looked quickly about the wigwam, relieved to see no sign of Fireheart. Her gaze went to Wild Squirrel on his sleeping platform. Beside him, Raven Wing stood with his head bowed as he chanted a prayer to the rhythm of his turtle-shell rattle. As Joanna moved farther into the wigwam, the shaman, sensing her presence, stopped chanting to identify the visitor.

Lowering his rattle, Raven Wing turned and approached. Joanna made an effort to smile at him. The shaman paused within three feet, his dark eyes narrowing as he studied her.

As she waited for some sign that the shaman remembered her, Joanna searched her memory for the proper greeting. As the words continued to elude her, she watched as Raven Wing's expression changed.

"Autumn Wind?" The shaman grinned when she nodded. "You have been gone a long time, my daughter."

Joanna returned his grin. "You know me, Raven Wing."

"You look the same yet brighter, like the moon on a clear night." Raven Wing's English was excellent.

"You are the only one besides Mary and Rising Bird who recognized me," Joanna said.

"My people said good-bye to a little girl. They did not expect to see that child become a woman." Raven Wing smiled at her with affection as he gestured toward Wild Squirrel's bed. "He would want to know that you have come to see him."

"Will he get well?" Joanna asked.

The shaman's expression sobered. "He is not fighting the sickness as he should. I do not know what else to do."

"May I speak to him?" Joanna's voice was soft.

Raven Wing studied the man on the bed. "Perhaps he will recognize your voice and awaken." He gave her a smile of encouragement. "Speak to our *Sahkeé-mah*. See if he will listen. Do not be afraid."

Despite the shaman's encouraging words, Joanna felt her heart flutter nervously as she moved closer to address Wild Squirrel.

She felt her stomach burn as she studied him. He looked even frailer than he had earlier. His skin, usually dark, appeared pale and translucent. His high cheekbones, which had once given him a look of authority and power, seemed too prominent in his thin drawn features. The sharp angles of his face, which gave him character when he was healthy, now added to his appearance as an ill man.

"Grandfather," Joanna whispered in Lenape. Her knowledge of the language was coming back to her. "I have come from far away to see you. Won't you please wake up and talk to me?"

Wild Squirrel seemed oblivious to Joanna's presence, but the young woman was unwilling to give up. She touched his cheek with light fingertips.

"Wake up, Grandfather! It is Autumn Wind. Do you remember me? You used to tell me stories when I visited your wigwam with my friend Little Blossom."

But Wild Squirrel lay without responding. Joanna attempted to wake him for several minutes before she decided to try again tomorrow. When the shaman learned of Joanna's intent to return the next day, Raven Wing smiled his approval.

He stood out in the yard and watched the woman leave the *sachem*'s wigwam. Fireheart scowled. Why did she have to come back? He had put her out of his mind and his heart. Why did she have to return to taunt him?

He couldn't deny that she looked lovely although there was something much changed about her. She seemed subdued. Where had the wild-spirited girl gone?

His memory was of a bare-breasted girl walking across the compound, teasing the boys with her smile. She hadn't noticed him, it was true, but he had adored her anyway.

Now Joanna wore an English gown of soft blue with a scooped neckline and large sleeves that billowed, trimmed with fabric just below her elbows. She was covered primly from the neck to her wrists down past her ankles, but the dress also outlined her breasts and small waist.

Fireheart found himself wondering what lay beneath the blue fabric. He scowled as he recalled how earlier he'd noticed the way the gown had outlined her womanly curves, and how the firelight in Wild Squirrel's wigwam had brightened the red-gold in her blonde hair.

She paused in mid-stride as she saw him. They stared at each other for several long seconds before she dismissed him to continue on toward her wigwam.

He should not be thinking of her, he thought. He was to marry Moon Dove. She would make him a good wife while Joanna never bothered to look his way before now.

We were children, he thought. And now they were not.

It was dusk. Fireheart watched as Joanna disappeared inside her wigwam. With a frown, he turned away and tried to force her from his mind.

Joanna wandered about the village the next morning, searching for familiar faces. Her servants were still asleep. They'd had a difficult time on their first night in the village. Unfounded fear, she was sure, was the reason for their sleeplessness as Joanna herself had slept quite cozily on her fur pelts. For propriety's sake, she had erected an animal-skin curtain to separate the women's quarters from Harry's, a simple arrangement that would be taken down during the day. Despite her servants' difficult first night, Joanna was sure that Cara and Harry would adjust after a few days in the encampment.

A young mother came out of one of the larger wigwams followed closely by a naked boy and girl. Joanna wasn't shocked by the children's lack of clothing. It wasn't unusual to see youngsters at an early age without garments. The Lenape saw nothing indecent or wrong about it, and Joanna, smiling at the grinning brother and sister, had to agree.

The threesome headed toward her, venturing onto a path that led out of the village, probably toward a lake or pond, Joanna surmised. The young woman nodded as she passed by her, then, with a word of scolding to hurry her children, she continued on her way.

The thought of refreshing cool water tempted

Joanna on this warm morning, and she fell into step behind the mother and her offspring.

The path narrowed, then widened as it reached a glistening lake. Joanna stopped to appreciate the natural beauty. When she'd been a child and lived among the Lenape, she had bathed in lakes and streams—not this one perhaps, but ones like it.

The mother and children were not the first at the waterside. A group of women were already there, but a short distance farther along the shore. They chatted and giggled as they washed and swam naked.

Joanna longed to take off all of her clothes and join them, but she was too self-conscious of her English white skin and undergarments. She was no longer the child who had bathed with the Lenape. She was a woman with a different form, and she was pale where these women were golden-brown. She had no desire to draw attention to her naked body.

She saw a boulder near the water's edge, away from where the Indian women cavorted. Moving toward the natural seat, Joanna decided to remove her shoes and stockings and be content with getting her feet wet.

Some of the matrons regarded Joanna curiously as she sat and dipped her bare feet in the cool water. Joanna smiled at them, then tried not to stare at the scene made by the naked women. She turned her gaze instead to a view of the lake and the land that she could just make out on the other side.

After a while, she turned her attention from the view to search for small pebbles to cast into the lake. She found a few and cupped them in her palm. She tossed first one tiny rock, then another into the water, enjoying the different sizes and shapes of the ripples made by the splash.

She became so engrossed in her actions and their effect on the lake that she sensed someone's presence only when it was within a few feet.

Joanna looked back and saw a woman. She frowned

for something about the Indian maiden looked familiar. The girl smiled, and Joanna felt a shock of surprised pleasure. "Little Blossom?"

Little Blossom nodded. "Autumn Wind," she said with a smile. "It is good to see you again." She spoke slowly as if she realized that it had been a long while since her friend had spoken Lenape.

Pleased to have understood, Joanna rose and gave her old friend a hug. It had been seven years since she'd seen Little Blossom, but the memories of their friendship came back to her sharply, moments of joy from a distant past.

"You have been too long in returning home," her friend said as the two young women released each other.

"I wasn't sure I'd be welcome," Joanna said.

Little Blossom raised her eyebrows. "You doubt you are a daughter of the Lenape?"

"It's been so long," Joanna whispered. "I'm not the same person as when I left."

"You are my friend," the Indian maiden said, gazing at her with concern. "That will never change."

Her words made Joanna smile. "It is good to see you, Little Blossom. How is She with a Smile?" she asked, recalling the sweet disposition of her friend's mother.

Sadness dulled Little Blossom's beautiful dark eyes. "She is no longer with us."

Joanna drew a sharp breath. "I am sorry," she said. The Lenape did not speak of their dead, and she was afraid she had offended her childhood friend.

"I have a daughter," Little Blossom told her. The mention of her child brightened her gaze.

"A daughter?" Joanna stared at her friend in stunned amazement. Little Blossom had a child! "You are married then?"

Little Blossom chuckled. "To Broken Bow. That is how I had my daughter, this is true." She patted her bare belly. "Soon there will be a son or daughter to join my Water Flower."

Joanna smiled with genuine pleasure. She suddenly recalled the brave Broken Bow. He had been a handsome warrior. She was glad Little Blossom had found happiness with him. "I am pleased for you."

"*Wa-neé-shih,*" her friend said, thanking her. Little Blossom glanced toward the group of women enjoying bathtime together. "Why do you not join the matrons?"

Joanna followed her gaze. "I don't know anyone . . . it's been a long time."

Little Blossom frowned. "You know many," she told her. "Come." She held out her hand. "I will tell you about each matron, each maiden."

Feeling self-conscious in her cambric gown, Joanna placed her hand in her friend's.

The two women approached the group enjoying their daily bath. Soon, Joanna was undressing to join them.

Fireheart dipped his paddle in the water rhythmically to propel his canoe. Feminine laughter drew his attention toward the lake's edge, and he smiled to see the Lenape women at play. He grinned and waved at Moon Dove who stood amidst a group of giggling maidens. Their giggling increased when the girls saw the direction of Moon Dove's returning wave.

Suddenly, he heard shouts of encouragement from the matrons to someone on the shore. Curiosity had him glancing to see the object of the women's focus, and his smile froze. A woman ran naked into the lake, and dived beneath the water's surface. Fireheart recognized the flash of red-gold hair.

Autumn Wind.

He found himself waiting with bated breath for her

to rise, then releasing a sigh when she rose up several feet from where she had gone under.

As she ran her hands back over her slick wet hair, she appeared all white and smooth and silky, and Fireheart felt an involuntary tightening in his loins. She turned to speak with Little Blossom, and he got a glimpse of her white shoulders and red-tipped breasts. Desire stole his breath. His whole body ached with it.

Then, as if she'd sensed that someone male was watching her, she spun, saw him in his canoe, and with a gasp, dipped her head below the water. There was much laughter as she came up sputtering. She rose to reveal only her shoulders, keeping those soft, womanly curves beneath the surface, much to Fireheart's chagrin.

He saw her talking excitedly with her friend, and saw Little Blossom glance his way before she replied to Joanna. Then, one of the matrons saw him and began to scold him to go away.

With a wave, Fireheart began paddling his canoe farther up the lake. His mind retained Joanna's image clearer than any of the other women, even Moon Dove's. He scowled and tried again to block her from his mind.

Chapter 4

"Is he gone?" Joanna asked, refusing to look.

Little Blossom nodded. "He has taken the canoe for fishing farther up the lake."

Joanna's sigh of relief drew her friend's curious glance.

"Autumn Wind." Mary Littleton, Joanna's cousin, known to the Lenape as Mary Wife, suddenly appeared at Joanna's side. She had been bathing with the matrons, and looked pleased to see Joanna join the group with Little Blossom. Surprised by Joanna's shyness, she smiled at the young woman. "It is good to see you among us again."

Startled by Mary's appearance, Joanna managed a cool nod. "The lake feels wonderful," she admitted.

"It has been a long time since you have enjoyed such a bath."

"Yes." Joanna frowned. "Too long," she said, feeling renewed anger at her cousin for having sent her away. She felt slightly guilty when Mary appeared taken aback by her hostile tone, more so when Mary excused herself to rejoin the matrons.

Joanna studied her cousin, battling with conflicting feelings of love and anger. After her cousin had found her as a child, Mary had been the center of her world. Now, they spoke as strangers. When she'd been sent to England onboard ship, fourteen-year-old Joanna had felt unloved and abandoned. She'd been terribly frightened to be traveling alone. Mary had placed her in the care of Mrs. Whitely, a stranger they'd met only minutes before the departure of the ship, but Joanna hadn't liked or trusted the old woman. The girl had kept to herself most of the time instead, frightened of the crew and other passengers, a difficult feat for a journey that seemed to go on forever.

By the time the *Nancy Kay* had reached port in England, Joanna had been anxious to get off the ship. She'd been optimistic about meeting her uncle who would surely treat her kindly since she was his only niece.

She had become disappointed and frightened once again to have been met, not by her uncle, but by his barrister—an ugly sinister little man who resembled a weasel.

Her uncle hadn't been much better, she recalled with a shudder. Was it any wonder she'd felt unloved and betrayed by Mary?

"Are you ill?" Little Blossom asked, stirring her from her thoughts.

Joanna forced a smile. "I'm well. Thank you."

"Come, let us talk with Woman with Eyes of Hawk."

Remembering the name, Joanna was able to give her friend a smile that was more genuine.

As she swam alongside her friend toward the woman Little Blossom wanted to see, Joanna looked down the lake for Fireheart. Her heart gave a thump when she saw his canoe, a small speck in the distance. Who was he? she wondered.

As she and Little Blossom visited with Woman with Eyes of Hawk, Joanna found her thoughts drifting to the Indian brave. She would learn more about him, she decided. She wanted to know why this man had the power to make her pulse race and her stomach flutter when it was obvious that he disliked her.

"She wants me to do what?" Cara exclaimed as she eyed the deer carcass that one of the braves had just brought in.

"Woman with Eyes of Hawk wishes to teach you how to tan the deer-hide," Joanna told the young woman.

"I don't want to learn how to tan a deer," the maid whined with a look of disgust.

"Cara," Joanna said patiently, "if you don't try to settle into village life, you'll never be happy here."

Cara gazed at her employer with horror. "Why do I have to be happy here? You said we'd be going home in another fortnight, didn't you?"

"Yes, yes, I did." But Joanna wasn't in any hurry to return to Neville Manor. She was enjoying her time in Little River despite the continuing tension between her and Mary, despite Fireheart's strange animosity toward her.

"Then why must I learn to tan doeskin?" Cara asked.

Joanna sighed as she studied her. The maid wore a gray muslin gown with a white V-neck collar that reached the white apron covering her skirts. Small ringlets of the girl's dark hair peeked out from beneath the edges of Cara's white mobcap with its matching gray ribbon. She was the portrait of a perfect servant at Neville Manor, but here in the Lenape village she looked uncomfortable and out of place.

She could understand Cara's reluctance to tan a deer. The job was an unpleasant one for someone who was not used to the work. In tanning animal skins, it was necessary to scrape the fur from the skin, then rub the brains of the beast into the hide to preserve it. The work was important to the Indian way of life. Animal skins were used to clothe the Lenape and as bedcovers and mantles to keep them warm. Still, Joanna took one hard look at Cara's white apron, slightly soiled but still white all the same, and knew she couldn't force Cara to do it.

"You run along, Cara," she said. "I'll explain to Woman with Eyes of Hawk that you have little stomach for such things." She paused to remember when she had learned how to skin and tan her first deerskin. "I'll help her." She had on a brown muslin gown that she'd never liked anyway. She didn't care if it became soiled or ruined as she had two or three other garments with her.

"You?" Cara asked with surprise.

Joanna smiled. "I've done the task before. 'Tis not so terrible."

The maid looked skeptical, but pleased that she wouldn't have to do the chore. "May I go find Harry?"

Joanna nodded, then turned thoughtful as she watched her maid scurry off in search of her friend. It had become more apparent with each new day that Cara and Harry were smitten with each other.

What was she going to do about the two of them? she wondered. She hadn't foreseen the couple's increasing unhappiness with village life. Perhaps she should think about sending them home.

She herself could stay, she thought. Wild Squirrel had awoken, but he was still weak, and she wanted to remain until he was better. She was also reluctant to leave because there was much unresolved about her past and present life. She hoped she would find answers here, in this village of her past, before she returned to the estate and the England of her future.

* * *

He saw her at the lake, fetching water. He knew he should stay away, but something about her drew him near. Fireheart approached on silent feet, remembering the last time that he'd seen Joanna in the lake, naked. He paused several yards from where she stood to study her unobtrusively.

He watched as she bent with the water-skin and dipped it into the lake, holding the neck of the vessel under for several seconds until the container was full. She straightened with the heavy skin, then set it down near the base of a tree before picking up another. After filling the second water-skin, Joanna retrieved both containers, then stumbled under the heavy weight.

Fireheart hurried forward and took one of the water-skins.

Joanna gasped as the brave took up one of the skins to help her. Heart thumping wildly, she stared at him, and he nodded without expression as he gestured toward the path with his free hand.

"*Wa-neé-shih*," she murmured gratefully. She studied him to gauge his reaction to her thanks, but his attention was elsewhere as he reached for the other water-skin.

"I can manage this one," she said, holding on to the container tightly.

"*Maata*," he said, tugging it from her grasp. No. "I will carry it. Why must you females be so stubborn?"

A flash of anger lit up her green gaze. "Because I wish to finish the job I set out to do?"

An amused smile curved his lips, but didn't quite reach his cool dark eyes. "Go, Autumn Wind. I have offered to help you. Take my offer and move along."

"You know who I am," she said, stunned that he knew her Indian name. She should be angry, but the fact that he knew her made her more curious than vexed.

Who is he? She narrowed her gaze as she studied

his hard-hewn features. Had she known this man as a child?

"I know you," he said.

"Who are you?" she asked, deciding to be bold.

He raised an eyebrow in reproach. "You do not remember me?"

Her cheeks flushed with embarrassment. His features seemed familiar. She should know him, she realized. He was about the same age or older than she. "I'm sorry."

He sighed. "It matters not. It was a long time ago."

"Yet, you remembered me," Joanna replied softly.

They headed back to the village in silence. Joanna was conscious of Fireheart's strength, his presence. She cast surreptitious glances at him, hoping to find something that would trigger her memory of him. It disturbed her that nothing did.

"Please," she said, "tell me who you are."

He turned to look down at her and shook his head.

Her breath caught as she gazed at him. He was taller than she was—and attractive. She couldn't keep her attention from focusing on his firm sensual mouth.

His dark eyes glistened in a masculine face that had chiseled features more appealing to her than the smooth cultured faces that belonged to most Englishmen.

Who was he? she wondered. "Fireheart—"

He looked at her expectantly. "It matters not," he told her softly. "It was many summers ago."

She recalled that Lenape boys were given new names when they became men.

"Broken Bow?" she guessed, wondering if this was Little Blossom's husband.

Hardness came to his dark eyes. "No, Broken Bow was already a warrior when you were here last."

"Then who—"

"Autumn Wind!" Little Blossom appeared on the path ahead as she crested a small hill.

Joanna waved and silently wished her friend away. She didn't want to end her time with Fireheart, and she could already feel him withdrawing . . . just at a time when she thought he might have unbent a little and told her his identity.

Why should she care if Fireheart liked her or not?

"Fireheart," Little Blossom gasped as she hurried toward the pair.

Fireheart's expression softened, and Joanna felt a flash of envy toward her friend at the affable change in the brave. What had she done to cause Fireheart to dislike her?

He had helped her, hadn't he? Maybe he didn't actually dislike her. Maybe he was simply indifferent to her.

Which didn't make Joanna feel any better.

"Wild Squirrel awakes," Little Blossom told Fireheart. "He asks for you."

Fireheart nodded before turning to Joanna. "I will carry these up to the lodge of Red Dress."

"I can take them."

"I will carry them," he insisted.

"*Wa-neé-shih,*" she said. She wouldn't argue with him.

He bowed slightly, then hurried away.

Joanna watched him leave with a flutter in her stomach. When she turned to her friend, it was to find Little Blossom studying her speculatively.

"You have made friends with Fireheart."

Joanna shook her head. "Not exactly."

"He is a handsome warrior, is he not?"

"Yes, yes, he is," Joanna admitted, blushing.

"He is expected to marry Moon Dove."

Joanna felt a burning ache. She had a sudden mental image of a lovely young Lenape maiden, whom she had met briefly at the lake, with long silken dark hair, lovely dark eyes, and a figure that matched in beauty. She felt a curious disappointment. "I understand."

"He is destined to be our chief," Little Blossom said.

"Little Blossom, he says I should know him. Who is he?"

"You do not remember the young boy who used to follow you with his gaze?"

Frowning, Joanna shook her head. Then, she recalled a face . . . an adoring look . . . and a feeling of irritation that the youngest of the braves seemed more impressed than the other boys. Could it be?

"Yellow Deer?" she gasped, her mind reeling from the possibility, the shock. The image of a young boy came to her clearly . . . dark eyes that followed her every move . . . his shy smiling greeting whenever she passed him.

"Fireheart is Yellow Deer?" She shook her head. She could hardly believe it. Guilt began to claw at her, making her remember things about her treatment of him that now seemed selfish and mean. She hadn't meant to hurt him, she thought defensively. She had simply been interested in the older boys.

Little Blossom looked at her sadly. "*Kihiila*, Autumn Wind. Fireheart was Yellow Deer until he became a man. Now he has earned the name Heart of Fire."

Fireheart is Yellow Deer, she thought with continued disbelief. When she returned to the wigwam, the two water-skins had been left inside the door flap. She did not see Fireheart again, and she wanted to thank him.

Later, well into the night, Joanna lay awake, marveling that the strong handsome warrior was the same boy who had been infatuated with her when she'd lived among the Lenape. She still had difficulty believing it to be true.

Her stomach burned as she recalled the way she'd

ignored him while she'd longed instead for the attention of the older boys . . . braves like Broken Bow and Flying Eagle, and their friends Big Cloud and Silver Fox.

Broken Bow is Little Blossom's husband. He was a handsome brave as he had been as a boy, but Joanna thought he paled in comparison to the one called Fireheart.

When she was fourteen, the older boys had made her feel special, watching her as she walked past them and smiled, pleased when they grinned back at her.

But the only one who had looked at her with the longing she'd wished to see in the others' expressions was Yellow Deer. But Yellow Deer had been too young, she'd decided all those years ago. She had treated him without regard to his tender feelings.

Fireheart was Yellow Deer!

Was it any wonder that the man disliked her? As she remembered the past, so did he.

He still thinks that I am the same thoughtless person, she mused.

Should she apologize for her childhood behavior? For injuring a boy without concern for his tender feelings?

I hurt him, she realized with remorse. She had been young and foolish then, before the receipt of her uncle's letter had turned her world upside down, before she'd been sent to England.

She was more cognizant of others' feelings now, she thought. Being manipulated and feeling unloved did that to a person. It stripped the joy and optimism from one's life. It had changed her forever.

She tossed and turned on her sleeping mat, conscious of Harry's snoring on the other side of the animal-skin curtain . . . of the soft murmuring and stirrings of her maid Cara as she slept.

I must talk with him and apologize, she thought. It

was the least she could do . . . to admit when she'd behaved badly.

With that resolved, she felt the tension leave her and her thoughts drift as she grew sleepy. She slept and began to dream. . . .

Joanna was feeling particularly grown-up this day. She had a new doeskin kilt on, made especially for her by Stormy Wind, Wild Squirrel's wife, and she wore it proudly.

Broken Bow and Big Cloud had recently returned from hunting. She was anxious for them to see her in her new garment. She had taken great pains with her appearance. First, she'd parted her hair down the middle, Lenape style, and braided it into two thick golden plaits. Then, as she'd seen the village women do when they dressed for ceremonies and special tribal days, Joanna had painted the part in her hair with vermillion.

The red in her hair and the red berry juice she'd used to paint her lips and cheeks gave her color. She liked having color. Next to the Lenape, she was pale, and it bothered her. The Lenape girls were dark with beautiful midnight hair and eyes. She would have darkened her hair as well, but she hadn't yet found a way. So she had to be content to use the stain on her face and hair to make her beautiful.

Convinced that she looked her best, Joanna left the wigwam.

"Mary?" She paused to wait for her cousin's reaction to her appearance. Mary had taken her handiwork outside. Today, the woman worked with clay to make a new baking pot. She was pounding the clay, grinding it to a fine meal, taking out all the rocks, stones, and sticks that had been dug up with it from the earth. Next, she would add water, and knead the mixture until it could be shaped and then dried.

At the sound of her call, Mary stopped pounding to glance up with a smile. Joanna waited a heartbeat as her cousin's face changed while she studied her.

"Are you going someplace special?" Mary asked quietly, without a hint of her thoughts.

Relieved that she hadn't immediately been scolded, Joanna shook her head. "No, I thought I'd make myself look pretty."

Mary nodded. "I see."

"May I visit Little Blossom?"

"Don't be long. I'll be needing help in the field."

Joanna happily agreed and left. She was hurrying across the yard to the wigwam of She-with-a-Smile, Little Blossom's mother, when someone called her name.

"Autumn Wind?"

She halted and turned. She scowled at the young boy who hoped to speak with her. "What do you want, Yellow Deer?"

He looked wounded by her sharp tone, and she sighed heavily.

"I made you this," he said, handing her a necklace.

She took the piece of jewelry and examined it. It was lovely, made of copper beads, shells, and animal teeth. "It's utiissa," she said sincerely. It was pretty, beautiful in fact.

He beamed, but she frowned and gave it back. "But I can't accept it."

A hurt look replaced the happiness in his dark gaze. "But it's for you."

"Yellow Deer—"

"A gift," he said, almost pleading.

He was a good-looking boy with long dark hair and beautiful dark eyes, but his chest was thin and scrawny, and his legs were like two sticks beneath his loincloth. A man barely formed. He was a kind boy who adored her, but she didn't like him in that way.

"I will take your gift," she said, annoyed when he looked pleased. She caught sight of Big Cloud, one of the older boys, watching her, watching them. She became embarrassed and angry with Yellow Deer for stopping her. "I must go. Do not make me another. It would not be right for me to take your things."

"I do not mind."

She all but snarled at him. "But I do!"

She stifled the barb of her conscience that made her feel guilty for treating Yellow Deer rudely and hurried to see

*Little Blossom to·tell her about Big Cloud and the brave's
notice of her in her new doeskin kilt.*

The next morning when Joanna woke up, her
thoughts returned with guilt and regret to Fireheart.
Her stomach filled with butterflies as she wondered
whether or not she could follow through with her
decision to apologize.

As she stepped outside the wigwam, the first thing
she saw was Moon Dove and Fireheart together, speaking quietly by the community cook-fire. They each
held a bowl with their share of food from the huge
kettle that had been heated over the flame. The Lenni
Lenape prepared two meals in their wigwams. At
other times during the day when they were hungry,
they took their meal from the community pot that
had been prepared by the village matrons.

Joanna felt an odd little pain in her chest as she
continued to observe the smiling couple.

Little Blossom's words returned to her. *Fireheart is
expected to marry Moon Dove.*

She turned away from the disturbing sight.

Chapter 5

Joanna still hadn't seen Fireheart when she went in to visit with Wild Squirrel the next day. To her delight, the chief was sitting up in bed, eating some thin corn gruel.

"Wild Squirrel, Grandfather, it is good to see you awake," she said softly as she approached his sleeping platform.

The old man frowned as he focused his gaze. She could tell he recognized her when he glanced at her reddish-blonde hair and smiled.

"Autumn Wind, could that be you?" he said in Lenape. "Is it possible that you have returned to us?"

She nodded. "It is Autumn Wind."

"Come. Sit and talk with this old man."

"You are not that old, Grandfather."

"I am a tired old man, little one," he said with such sadness that it made her heart ache.

"Don't talk like that. We need you. The Lenape people need you."

Wild Squirrel shook his head. "They have Fireheart. He will make our people a good leader."

"I'm sure he is in no hurry to become chief," she said although she didn't know Fireheart enough to be certain of anything.

The chief sighed. "This is true. He wants me to live a long life." He set his bowl of gruel aside without finishing it. "It is up to the Great Spirit to decide if I shall continue as chief, or join our brothers in the Spirit World."

"No," she whispered. "Don't say that."

"You sound like Fireheart."

If Fireheart felt half of what she felt when Wild Squirrel spoke that way, then Joanna realized that she and the brave had more in common than a childhood.

Silence reigned between them for a time, but it was a companionable quiet, marred only by the realization of the chief's failing health.

Joanna placed her fingers over his hand where it lay on the sleeping platform. "You must rest and take care of yourself," she said.

"I am tired of resting, almost as much as I am tired of living."

Joanna was alarmed by the old man's pessimism. Something was terribly wrong. Was he right? Had he guessed that his end was near? Was that why he was reluctant to get up and resume his chiefly duties?

"Are you in pain?" she asked him. "Shall I get Raven Wing?"

He shook his head. "Do not call the shaman. There is nothing he can do." He tried to sit taller and winced.

Joanna rose, anxious to find someone who could help. Fireheart? she wondered. "I shall get you fresh water to drink." Then she hurried from the wigwam before he could stop her. Her throat tight with tears, Joanna went to look for Fireheart.

* * *

It didn't take long for Joanna to find Fireheart. Grateful to learn he was so near, she hurried to his side and quickly got his attention. "Wild Squirrel needs you" was all she said.

Fireheart abruptly finished his conversation with another brave and hurried toward the chief's wigwam.

"I think he is in pain, but he won't say. There is something wrong," she said as she struggled to keep up with him. "I can feel it."

He flashed her an unreadable look and continued on. He tugged up the deer flap covering Wild Squirrel's doorway and stepped inside. Joanna stuck out her hand to catch the flap so it wouldn't shut behind him. As she entered the wigwam, her gaze went to the old man in bed.

Fireheart was speaking in low tones with the chief. Joanna couldn't make out the Lenape words. She stayed just inside the door, concerned but unwilling to intrude.

"I told her I was fine," Wild Squirrel said to his nephew.

"You don't look well." Fireheart studied his uncle critically. "What hurts?"

The chief scowled. "Nothing." Seeing Joanna by the door, he waved her forward. "You did not listen to me," he scolded affectionately.

She smiled at his tone. "You are stubborn, Grandfather. I thought Fireheart would make you listen as I could not."

Wild Squirrel eyed his nephew with fondness. "I am an old tired man. Leave me to rest in peace."

Fireheart felt a trickle of alarm. Glancing at Joanna, he saw that she shared his fear about the chief. "I—" He clasped Joanna's arm. "We," he corrected himself, "will leave once we know you are comfortable. I will have Raven Wing make you that special healing tea of his."

"I will drink it if you will let me be," Wild Squirrel promised.

Joanna's eyes met Fireheart's and sent a silent message. *Agree*, she urged him. She was conscious of the warmth of his fingers above her arm as he nodded in understanding. After he made his answer clear, he silently released her.

Joanna slipped from the wigwam to find the Lenape shaman, her concern with Wild Squirrel . . . but her skin still tingled where it had known Fireheart's touch.

Joanna waited outside Wild Squirrel's wigwam for Fireheart to emerge. It had been some time since the shaman had entered, and she wondered what was happening inside.

Finally, after what seemed a long while, the door flap was lifted, and Fireheart came out.

"How is he?" she asked with concern.

The brave looked at her blankly. As his expression cleared, he appeared surprised to see her.

"He is sleeping. Raven Wing has eased his pain."

Joanna felt relieved. She waited for Fireheart to say more, and was disappointed when he didn't. She wanted to talk with him. Was this the right time? she wondered.

Fireheart stared at her for a long moment, and the thundering of her own heartbeat filled the awkward silence.

"May I speak with you?" she asked.

He frowned. "There's nothing to say."

"I think there is," Joanna said softly.

"About Wild Squirrel?"

"*Maata*." No. "This isn't about Wild Squirrel. I have something to say to you. I owe you an apology."

The brave regarded her skeptically. "For what?"

"You don't like me, and I think I know why." Joanna wanted desperately to offer this man friendship.

"I do not dislike you." Fireheart turned as if to leave.

"Fireheart!"

But the brave kept walking.

"Fireheart," Joanna cried again. *"Yellow Deer!"*

Fireheart froze and slowly turned to face her. "You know who I am." He approached, his gaze narrowing, his lips a firm line.

Joanna studied the man before her, and tried to see the boy that he had been. But there was no hint of the adoring Yellow Deer in Fireheart's hardened gaze. Nor was his smile apparent on his sensual male lips. "Little Blossom told me," she confessed.

Her explanation seemed to darken his expression further. "You did not see for yourself," he said coldly.

She shook her head. "But you don't look the same!" she exclaimed when she saw his scowl.

His smile was grim. "That is because Yellow Deer and Fireheart are not the same brave."

"I must have hurt your feelings badly," Joanna said softly.

"You are mistaken. I have no feelings for you." Then, Fireheart walked away.

Stunned by his coldheartedness, Joanna could only watch him leave as tears filled her eyes.

Fireheart's open hostility toward her upset Joanna greatly. She was so disturbed that she decided to seek out Mary in the hope that her cousin would help her understand.

She had been in the village for over a fortnight.

Her relationship with Mary hadn't improved much since her arrival. Joanna felt torn. She was trapped between the past and the present. Her painful years with her uncle made it difficult for her to forgive Mary for sending her away, but her childhood memories made her long for the comfort of her cousin's love.

It was her childhood memories that were uppermost in her mind as she headed toward Mary and Rising Bird's lodge. She recalled the day that Mary had first come for her. Joanna's mother had died and she'd been given into the care of neighbors by the local Methodist minister. The Smiths had been good people, but they had had little enough money to raise their own five children. Joanna would never forget how Mary had appeared like an angel, sent by her own deceased mother to come and care for her.

With the image clear in her mind, Joanna paused outside of Mary's wigwam, hesitant about entering. Since her arrival, Joanna had treated her cousin as if she were an unwelcome stranger. How could she have forgotten how kind Mary had been?

Then why did she send me away? Joanna was confused. *Mary seemed to love me. Did I do something wrong to make her angry with me?*

Joanna called out her cousin's name without entering. When there was no answer from the other side of the deer-flap door, she left, disappointed. Either Mary was gone or she didn't want to see Joanna. Joanna thought that Mary had probably gone to work in the fields. Should she go there and see?

She felt a sudden nervous fluttering within her breast. Her visit with Wild Squirrel and her encounter with Fireheart had taken a toll on her. She'd lost all desire for confrontation that day. Joanna decided to return to her wigwam where she might have a few minutes alone.

Her head began to throb. Right now she couldn't deal with Mary or Fireheart. She attempted to banish

Fireheart from her mind. And Mary? Well, she would just have to talk with her cousin later.

She had another decision to make. There was the matter of when she'd return to England. Her servants were anxious to leave. Joanna, on the other hand, had a strange reluctance to go. But Neville Manor waited, and she couldn't expect her good friend John Burton to manage the estate forever when he had his own concerns. His brother Michael might need him.

She needed to go back to England, she thought, before John, in his caring concern, sent a search party after her.

Neville Manor
England

"Miss Gordon is here to see you, sir," the manservant announced.

John Burton stood. "Thank you, Charles. Would you show her in?"

Charles bowed, then left to do the man's bidding. Within seconds, Gillian Gordon stood in the library doorway.

"Hello, John. Have you heard from Joanna?"

"Gillian," he said softly, "come in." His gaze narrowed when he saw Charles hovering behind her. "You may go, Charles. I shall not need you for anything more this afternoon. Just have Ellen bring us a pot of tea."

"Yes, sir," Charles said, then left.

"Won't you sit down?" John invited, gesturing toward a leather chair.

"Thank you," she said sweetly as she carefully took a seat.

There was an awkward moment of silence between John and Gillian until the maid Ellen brought in the tea, and set it on the tea table within reach of Gillian.

John politely thanked Ellen, then told the servant

that she and the household staff had the rest of the afternoon free.

Surprised yet obviously pleased by the news, Ellen curtsied to the pair, then hurriedly left to enjoy her unexpected holiday.

Without being asked, Gillian poured the tea while John went to quietly close and lock the library door.

When he returned to Gillian, the young woman held out a cup of steaming fragrant tea. He accepted the cup and took a sip. "Delicious," he murmured, meeting her gaze. " 'Tis just how I like it."

She smiled and sipped from her own teacup. Both were quiet as they enjoyed their tea until John finished his cup and set it down on the tea table with a clatter.

Gillian, startled by the sound, glanced up at him. John studied her with a look that made her heart thunder within her breast. The thunder became a raging roar in her ears as John removed her unfinished cup from her hands, and set it carefully next to his.

"Gillian," he rasped, reaching for her hand.

She swallowed hard. She had waited with sweet anticipation for this moment, and now that it was here, she could scarcely contain her joy.

"Come here," he urged huskily. John jerked her from her chair and into his arms. He lowered his head. His mouth captured hers in a kiss of passion so hot that she moaned and sagged weakly against him.

When he released her mouth, there was a glazed look in his blue eyes. Her lips curved as Gillian held his gaze. Her smile became a gasp of pleasure as he settled his hands on her breasts, cupping the soft responsive mounds through the fabric of her bodice. When he fumbled to free her from her gown, Gillian cried out with encouragement and helped him. Then they struggled to undo his shirt.

Within minutes, they were on the floor, naked, their tea and pastries forgotten. Neither man nor woman gave any thought to Joanna, the woman who owned this room and this house. Amid harsh male grunts and soft feminine cries, the world around them faded as they sought to heighten and satisfy their sexual pleasures.

With the mistress of the house and her servants gone, the couple made love in the library first, then moved to start again in every room.

Chapter 6

Lenni Lenape Village
Pennsylvania Colony
June 1727

Joanna was startled awake by the sound of rhythmic, almost musical, thumping. She sat up and listened.

"What's that?" Cara's shaky voice came out of the darkness next to her.

"Lenape drums."

"War drums?" the frightened maid asked.

Joanna frowned and rose from her sleeping pallet. "I don't know." It was possible, she thought. Why else would they be playing their drums in the dead of night?

"Miss Neville?" Harry inquired from the other side of the curtain.

"Yes, Harry, we're awake." She'd been sleeping in her muslin shift. She reached for a plain calico gown and slipped it over her head.

"Miss?"

"Stay inside, Cara," Joanna told her. "I'll go and see what is happening."

"Would you like me to come with you?" Harry offered.

Joanna raised the door flap. "No, Harry, you stay here with Cara." She could sense his relief in his agreement. "I'll be back as soon as I learn something."

"Are we in danger?" she heard Cara ask Harry as she left the wigwam.

"No, surely not, dearest" was Harry's soft response.

With the sound of Harry's tender words for the maid in her ears, Joanna stepped into the night. Her gaze was immediately drawn to the gathering around a fire in the center yard. She headed in that direction.

She spied her cousin's husband first. Rising Bird stood on the fringe of the circle of men.

He turned in time to see her approach. "Autumn Wind," he greeted her.

"What's wrong?"

His expression was solemn. "Our brothers to the north have been attacked by the Cayuga."

Her stomach tightened. "Iroquois here?" The Iroquois were the enemy of the Lenape. They raided and tried to take over Lenape land. It had been a problem for years, and apparently it continued to be a problem.

He nodded.

"What are you going to do?"

"Fireheart is deciding that now."

"Fireheart?"

"Our chief has asked him to take care of this matter."

Her gaze sought and found Fireheart. He looked serious, concerned, as he spoke with the Lenape men. He glanced her way, and she stiffened. Moving away from the group, she spied a gathering and headed toward the women.

"Joanna!" Mary hurried to her side.

"Are they going to war?" she asked, a ball of fear lodging high in her stomach.

Mary sighed. "I don't know. Something must be done if it's true that the Cayuga have attacked Bear Paw's village."

Joanna nodded. "Bear Paw's village . . . Isn't that the village where Red Dress, the matron who owns our lodge, is visiting?"

"*Kihiila*, it's the same one."

"Have you heard of any injuries?"

"The Cayuga don't usually leave any injured behind. Whomever they don't kill, they kidnap and take as slaves."

"No," Joanna whispered. She didn't know any of Bear Paw's villagers, but it was as if they were her own kind. How could she not feel for them when she had lived among the Lenape for nine years? In many ways, these Indians were more her people than the English were.

"Is that what they've done?" she asked Mary.

"I wish I knew. Word about the raid arrived only a short time ago. Fireheart is organizing a party of men to go to the village."

Joanna heard a tremor in her cousin's voice and wondered if she feared that Rising Bird would be among them. "Do you think the Iroquois will still be there?"

Mary sighed and hugged herself with her arms. "I wish I knew."

Moved by Mary's worry, Joanna slipped her arm about her cousin's shoulders. Mary smiled at her and, for the first time, all tension faded between them.

The drums suddenly ceased, and the sound of Fireheart's voice filled the ensuing silence. Joanna listened with rapt amazement as the brave spoke confidently and seriously, his deep voice shivering along her spine. It dawned on her how much of a burden of responsibility now rested on Fireheart's shoulders. She didn't envy him his position.

Would he go with the war party? she wondered. Her heart tripped with fear at the thought. He was the acting chief. Surely, there was a war chief who would lead the men into possible battle.

She studied him as he addressed the men, and felt a tingling in her midsection. He was so handsome, so strong. It was hard to believe that he had been such a shy boy.

Or had he been that way only with her? Because he'd longed for her friendship? Her love? She thought of the necklace and was sorry.

Now she was in the same position as young Yellow Deer, wanting another's friendship and being rejected. Was he paying her back for the pain she'd caused him?

"You must not go with hate in your hearts," Fireheart was saying. "Hate clouds one's judgment. Look first, decide what must be done, then do it!"

Wise words from the chief, Joanna thought.

No, she realized, whatever reason Fireheart had for his hostility toward her, it wasn't to punish her for the past. He seemed too wise, too fair a man for that.

Why then? she wondered as she continued to watch him. Had she misread her treatment of him? Had she been cold when she'd thought she was friendly?

Why do I care what Fireheart thinks?

Because she was attracted to him.

He is expected to marry another.

It didn't matter, she thought. The heart ruled the head, and made one think and act illogically at times.

It is true that I have not seen Fireheart with Moon Dove often.

If they were in love, wouldn't they spend time together?

When he was done talking with the men, Fireheart

came to the women. His expression softening, he spoke again.

"When the sun rises in the morning sky, a group of our men—your husbands and fathers and sons—will go to Bear Paw's village to see how our brothers have fared in the attack by our enemy, the Iroquois. This is a dangerous task I have set our men to do, but we must help our Lenape brothers. And we must protect our own village from the dark enemy who threatens our lives."

Woman with Eyes of Hawk stepped forward from among the matrons. "How many of our braves must go?"

"I will send ten men from among us. The warriors who will go have volunteered to protect us."

The matron nodded. "This is a wise decision, Fireheart. You act as chief in Wild Squirrel's name. Your mother's brother will be proud of you."

Mary joined Woman with Eyes of Hawk. "Is there something we can do, Fireheart?"

Fireheart regarded the women with warm affection. "Protect our children, and be here when our men return. They will bring back any of our people who need our help."

All of the Lenape women nodded their approval. The men soon rejoined their families, and returned to their wigwams for the remaining night's sleep. Joanna lingered to speak with Mary.

Sensing her young cousin's need to speak with her, Mary talked briefly with her husband, then turned to take Joanna's arm.

"Let us walk for a while," she said.

Joanna was only too happy to comply. They walked toward the forest and onto the path toward the lake. She marveled at the way her cousin had read her thoughts. "Will Rising Bird go?"

"He will go," Mary told her. "He is a good warrior,

and the men respect him. Fireheart will put him in charge.''

''Are you scared for him?''

Mary's eyes filled with tears. ''I'm terrified.''

''How do you bear it?'' Joanna felt sympathy for her cousin. She stopped walking to give her cousin a hug.

Mary hugged her back hard. ''I fear for him as much as I feared for you when I left you on the *Nancy Kay*.''

Joanna stiffened, disturbed by the memory. ''Then why did you let me go?'' The air between them grew tense again.

''How could I make you stay when your uncle obviously had so much more to give you?''

''You were wrong! Roderick Neville was a hateful man who made me miserable!''

Her cousin looked stunned. ''Joanna . . .''

But Joanna, hurt again by the memories of her past, wanted to talk no longer. She left Mary gaping as she ran off into the darkness of the night.

Rising Bird saw his wife as she returned to the village yard from the forest. There was a blank, almost stunned look about her. Immediately concerned, he hurried to meet her.

''Mary Wife, what is wrong?'' He placed his arm around her shoulders to lead her back to their lodge.

She blinked back tears. ''I have done a terrible thing.''

Her husband looked skeptical. ''What could you have done?''

''I sent my Joanna away as a child, and now she has returned a bitter woman.'' She reached up to brush away a tear that escaped. ''Oh, Rising Bird! Roderick Neville was an awful man, and I sent her to him!''

Rising Bird frowned. ''Are you sure of this?''

''Joanna has told me so herself. She suffers still,

even after the man's death!'' Her tears fell harder and faster. "No wonder she never answered my letters."

"You must not blame yourself alone, wife. I helped you to make the decision."

Mary smiled through her tears as she cupped her husband's jaw tenderly. "I was afraid to be selfish and keep her," she said softly. "You did nothing but allow me to discuss my thoughts with you. You did not make the decision. I did."

"I will talk with her," Rising Bird said.

"You must sleep, my husband. You have a task ahead of you tomorrow. Tonight, we will think of you and your journey. I will speak with Joanna another time." She slipped her arm about Rising Bird's waist, and the two kissed before entering their wigwam.

Fireheart couldn't sleep. His first act as chief weighed heavily on him. The responsibility of sending men to meet the enemy was a great one. He hoped he'd made the right decision. It had seemed the only thing to do.

Tomorrow, a party of Lenape braves would leave Little River and head north to the village of Bear Paw, their Lenape brother. Rising Bird, he knew, expected to lead the group, but Fireheart couldn't send his men into battle without taking full responsibility for the deed. When the morning sun rose in the summer sky, Fireheart would be among the Lenape war party. He would fight alongside his brothers. He would fight and win, or die in the attempt.

It was warm that evening, and Fireheart headed toward the lake for a late swim. He would get little sleep that night. He would enjoy the refreshing water.

He followed the path over a rise then down to the water's edge, then untied the strings that fastened his loincloth. Naked, he waded into the water, sighing at its coolness. He dove beneath the surface, and began to swim fast and furiously to try to rid himself of this strange tension.

His arm cut cleanly through the water as he swam farther, into the deeper regions of the lake. He stopped to tread water, then lay on his back and floated. The night was clear, the sky filled to bursting with bright stars. He lay, studying the bright lights, then offering a silent prayer to the spirits of the stars and the sky for guidance. He prayed to all of the good spirits of the earth, asking for assistance in righting the wrong that had been done to his people.

He closed his eyes and began to swim on his back . . . with a stroke of each arm and a kick from each leg. The air, the water, and the peace of the night began to ease away the tension, and Fireheart felt at peace.

Joanna had fled to a sheltered spot in the forest where no one was about but the animals of the night and the song of summer insects. She sat on a fallen tree, and sobbed softly for the child she had been. Her uncle was dead, and she knew that she had no reason to cry now, but she clung to the past, unable to release it. The memory of her first day at Neville Manor haunted her still. It came back again with stark clarity. She allowed the images to come, hoping to face them and put them to rest. She recalled the first time she'd come downstairs to share supper with her Uncle Roderick. . . .

She had worn her new gown on the day she had arrived in England. Mary had seen that she had the new garment so that she would make a good impression on her uncle Roderick. But she saw Uncle Roderick only briefly that afternoon when she'd arrived at the house. Oh, and what a big house it was! Dark inside, but huge. She wondered if she'd get lost coming from her bedchamber to the dining room where she was to meet her uncle for dinner.

After bathing, Joanna slipped on her Lenape doeskin gown. She didn't want to wear her calico gown as it was stale. She had not been able to bathe often onboard ship. Her bedchamber on the second floor was pretty. The draperies and bed covers were in shades of blue, and the furniture, like the kind downstairs, was dark and heavy.

Clean from her bath and anxious to get to know her uncle, Joanna skipped lightly down the stairs and asked a maid the way to the dining room.

The maid looked at her strangely, opening and shutting her mouth, but she gave Joanna directions before nervously scurrying away.

The dining room, like the rest of the house, had walls of dark paneling and a long table with seats enough for ten, but with place settings for only two— one at the head of the table and the other at the opposite end. There was no sign of her uncle so Joanna studied both settings and chose the seat nearest to the door that she thought led to the kitchen.

She sat carefully with her hands folded neatly in her lap, waiting patiently for Uncle Roderick to come so she could talk with him.

A manservant entered the room, saw her, then shooed her from the chair. " 'Tis your uncle's seat you've taken, girl. Get up and away with ya. Roderick Neville likes things the way they is. Your seat is at the other end of the table."

She stood, and the man looked at her with disapproval. "Is that all ya have to don? Roderick isn't going to like yer garment any," he said. "Ah, but well, then, he can afford to buy ya some new ones what with his money and all." He narrowed his gaze. "Ye're a lucky girl, Miss Neville. You'd best remember that. It isn't every day that a man as rich as yer uncle comes to the rescue of an orphaned girl."

Joanna scowled. She didn't understand the word *orphaned.* She knew she was a girl, but she didn't think she liked him calling her "orphaned." She didn't like his tone that suggested that it was something unpleasant and unclean. And she had just had a bath!

She also didn't like the way he spoke of her garment. Her doeskin tunic had been lovingly crafted by her friend Little Blossom's mother. It was of the finest deer hide and was beautifully adorned with beads, embroidery, and porcupine quills. She was proud of her dress and thought her uncle would like it too, once she told him of the painstaking effort made by She with a Smile on her behalf.

The manservant had left the room, and Joanna was alone again.

A closed door along one wall of the dining room opened, and Roderick Neville came in. Joanna stood, remembering the way her cousin had taught her to curtsy, then tumbled to the floor in her poor attempt to execute it.

"Good God, girl!" her uncle exclaimed as she scrambled to her feet. "I can see you have a lot to learn!"

"Yes, uncle," she murmured, hanging her head.

"Look at me when I talk to you," he ordered, grabbing her by the chin and jerking her head upward.

Shocked by his rough treatment, Joanna looked up and stared.

His gaze treated her harshly as he studied her and apparently found her wanting.

"What in God's teeth are you wearing?"

"It's a Lenape tunic," she said in English but with an accent that told of the years she'd spent with the Indians.

"It's hideous," he said. "You are never to wear it again, do you hear me? You are in England now.

Leave your heathen things outside your bedchamber
door, and Charles will come get them."

Give up her Lenape things? she thought. Never!

"I'm warning you, young lady, if you don't do what
I say you shall pay the consequences. Do you understand?" He squeezed her jaw, making his message
clear. She fought not to wince and murmured in the
affirmative. . . .

A snap of a twig in the forest jerked Joanna to the
present. She glanced about the woods, fighting tears.
How she'd hated Roderick Neville, but she'd been
afraid to defy him. That first day was only a taste of
what was to come. Whenever she displeased him,
whether she didn't make the proper impression on
his friends or some other offense, he would backhand
her across the face, or take a strap to the back of her
legs. Joanna still had the scars where he had cut welts
into the fleshy part of her thighs with a leather strap.

This had occurred when he'd caught her wearing
her Lenape tunic for the second time. She had
thought he would be out for the day. She had put
on the dress for she'd been so miserable and wanted
to surround herself with memories of the village . . .
of love. She'd spent a happy afternoon in her room
with her Lenape things surrounding her, the things
she had refused to give up . . . and Charles hadn't
told on her.

When Roderick Neville had come home unexpect-
edly, Joanna had been in the kitchen, emerging from
her bedchamber for a brief bite to eat. Roderick's
eyes had widened when he saw her, then his face
had turned beet-red with rage. He had grabbed the
nearest weapon—his riding crop—and Joanna had
run to escape him.

She'd tripped on the stairs, and he'd caught her.
Dragging her by the hair to her room, he had hit her
with the crop across the back of the legs bared
beneath the Lenape tunic. She didn't cry. She had

learned early on that to cry only incited the man's lust for punishment. She bore the pain, sobbing in private only when he collected her Lenape things afterward. He took her tunic, her moccasins, and her string of beads. The only thing he didn't get was a medicine pouch given to her by Wild Squirrel.

As she listened to her uncle rant and rave about exorcising her of her "heathen" ways, she vowed that he would never learn where she'd hidden her precious medicine bag. She vowed, too, that while Roderick Neville might attempt to tame the "savage" in her, she would always have her memories.

Joanna stood in the darkened forest and realized as she began to walk that her cheeks were wet with tears. She wandered aimlessly and found herself on the path to the lake again, heading toward the water rather than the wigwam. The thought occurred to her that Cara and Harry waited anxiously for her return, but at that moment Joanna didn't care. She was hurting. Even from his grave, Roderick Neville had the power to bring pain.

The thought of the cool wetness of the lake appealed to her, and she continued on, anxious for a swim.

It was late. Everyone had gone back to their sleeping pallets. The shore was deserted as she'd expected. The moon was only a sliver in the night sky, but the clear clean air afforded a lovely view of the glistening water. Joanna slipped off her gown, and stood a moment in her shift, enjoying the light breeze that came in off the lake. She closed her eyes, and allowed the air to dry her tear-damp cheeks. She willed her mind to a calmer time, a more pleasant place than England and the manor she'd left behind. She hated the house for its darkness, its memories, and for everything it stood for in her life.

Her uncle had had such an effect on her that she'd been unable to don Lenape clothing since her return to the village. Now, she silently scoffed at herself for her silliness. Her uncle wasn't here. He was dead, and the choice was hers alone.

She unfastened the ties of her shift and held onto the fabric. At one time, she'd had no qualms about being naked. She'd been the first to take off her clothes at the bathing hole. She'd gone about with only a kilt, and she'd felt comfortable, happy, and free.

Don't allow him to hurt you still, an inner voice scolded. *Take off your shift. There is no one here to see you. Swim naked like the Lenape and the fish as it was meant to be.*

Joanna grabbed her shift and pulled it over her head. The breeze caressed her naked breasts, waist, and hips, brushing against her thighs and legs, stirring sensations within her that stimulated all of her senses.

"Yes," she whispered, closing her eyes. "Yes."

She lifted her lashes as she waded into the lake.

A head emerged from the water only a few feet away.

"No!" she gasped.

But it was too late. Fireheart had already seen her, and he approached her with a strange look in his eyes.

Chapter 7

"Fireheart!" Joanna gasped. She dove under the surface to hide her nakedness, then came up choking on a mouthful of water. She wheezed, sputtering, and had difficulty catching her breath.

Suddenly, Fireheart was there to help her, patting her on the back and soothing her.

Once she could breathe again, she became conscious of her bare breasts above the water, and she hugged them with her arms. She tingled where he had touched her naked back.

"You frightened me!" she scolded, backing away.

"I did not know I would see you here," he said softly. His dark eyes boldly eyed her breasts where the tops pushed up from her arms.

She turned away. "Why are you here?" she asked, averting her glance. She was shocked when she felt the water swirl around her as he came closer.

"I could not sleep."

Her skin tingled from his nearness. Her heart thumped hard in her breast. She bit her lip, then released it. "Are you worried about tomorrow?"

He didn't answer. The long moment of silence made her turn. She inhaled sharply as she felt the desire emanating from him. She swallowed hard. *For me?*

"Fireheart," she murmured.

He seemed to snap out of a daze. She felt his demeanor change.

"You should not be here," he said. "It is not safe for you."

"Have I a reason to fear you?"

"You might."

Joanna felt warmth in her stomach. She hadn't expected such an answer. "Why?"

"There are Iroquois about—"

"No," she said. "Why should I fear you?" Her breath slammed in her throat as he took a step closer. She could see his eyes clearly . . . the sudden gleam of desire.

"You have to ask why you should run from this man?" he whispered, reaching to cup her chin.

Warmth pulsed through her body. His fingers were gentle as they caressed her jaw, her cheek. She closed her eyes and leaned into his palm.

"You are the same," he said huskily, "yet you have changed."

She opened her eyes to gaze at him. "You are different," she said, "yet I see a gentleness that is Yellow Deer's." His features were anything but boyish; the gentleness had been in his eyes.

He frowned and released her. "Yellow Deer is a boy. I am not."

She nodded. He seemed offended. "I didn't mean—"

"You should go back to the wigwam."

"I've come here to swim." She needed this time to banish the memory of her uncle. Standing here with Fireheart certainly helped.

"Since it is not safe, you must swim with me."

Her heart tripped. "I thought I had reason to fear you."

He stared at her hard. "No," he said. "I will not harm you."

She had never thought he would, not even with the weight of responsibility on his shoulders, not even when he was angry.

"Come," he said. "Let us swim."

Joanna was reluctant to move. She was supremely conscious of him as a man. Her body pulsated with life at his nearness, and she was embarrassed. She wondered how she could swim without revealing more skin. "You go first," she said.

He lay back in the water, kicking out with his feet, stroking with his arms. He continued to watch her, which set her nerves on edge.

"Close your eyes," she said.

He looked amused. "When you were a child, you showed your breasts."

She felt herself flush. "I'm not a child anymore."

"*Kihiila,*" he agreed with such meaning in his tone that Joanna couldn't help but laugh. Her laughter made him smile. "Come, Autumn Wind, forget you are English. Be Lenape again."

His words and tone enticed her. Wasn't that what she wanted? To forget that she was a Neville and the niece to an awful man? To remember those times in the Lenape village when she had felt free, open, and loved?

Joanna slowly lowered her arms. The air was warm, but little bumps rose on her skin. The tips of her breasts hardened as a summer's breeze touched them.

She caught Fireheart's gaze, was unable to release it. It was dark, but she could make out the planes of his face in the shadows. There was enough light to see the glistening of his dark eyes.

Her pulse racing, she lay in the water, and began

to swim slowly, carefully, in Fireheart's direction. His teeth flashed in the darkness as he grinned. He swam backward with her following, stroke after leisurely stroke, kick after gentle kick.

"You swim like an otter," he told her.

She grinned. "You swim like *Kuikuenkuikiilat.*"

He chuckled. She had told him that he swam like a frog.

"Let us see who swims the fastest—the otter or the frog."

Taking up the challenge, Joanna shot through the water with her hands flat to her sides, kicking her feet to move quickly.

Fireheart moved like lightning, and as she fought to catch him, Joanna marveled at how playful their exchange had turned after moments of tension laced with a strange almost sexual anticipation.

She paused to see where he was, then laughed as she saw him disappear beneath the surface.

When he didn't immediately come up, Joanna became alarmed.

"Fireheart!" she cried. "Fireheart!"

She made a frantic search of the water for some sign of him. Beside herself with concern, she wondered what to do. Then a hand clamped onto her ankle and tugged her downward. Suddenly she was facing him in the water, and his hands fastened on her waist, drawing her close. To her shock, she felt his lips on her mouth, and might have drowned with the surprise of it, but then he was pulling her to the surface.

She had no time to utter a word, as he kissed her a second time, holding her up in the night air beneath her arms, while her head spun and her body pulsed with wild sensation.

The kiss seemed to go on and on. Joanna moaned softly as Fireheart raised his head and shifted his hands to cup her face.

"*Uitiissa,*" he murmured.

Pretty, she thought. He had called her pretty.

She smiled, pleased, and felt his lips press against hers once again, tenderly exploring then becoming hotter. Joanna whimpered, and started to sink beneath the water.

Fireheart released her mouth to tug her upward. He cradled her in his arms, and began to swim toward shore.

Lying within his arms, her head against his neck, Joanna breathed in his scent, and felt her head spin with desire.

Where was he taking her? Would he touch her, kiss her again?

She was conscious when his feet hit soil; then she became embarrassed when he rose from the water, carrying her naked body, his own male form bare.

The breeze caressed her damp skin, making it tingle. She burned wherever he touched her . . . along her back, under her arms, along her thighs . . . against one buttock.

She thought he would put her down once he was on dry land, but Fireheart held on to her as he continued along the shoreline to a clearing, free of rocks and sticks and lined with pine needles.

Here, he set her on her feet, releasing her slowly so that she brushed against him as she went down.

"Autumn Wind," he murmured.

She could hardly breathe as she cupped his face, ran her fingers over his features. He grabbed her hand, and pressed her palm to his mouth. She closed her eyes as Fireheart nibbled on her skin, then turned her hand to kiss her wrist before taking her fingers and placing them on his bare muscled chest.

His flesh was firm, wet, and warm from his body heat. Joanna began to touch him, loving the feel of him, the scent of his skin . . . the sound of his breathing as it deepened.

"Fireheart," she whispered. She was drawn to him as she'd never before been attracted to another. The awkwardness between them was gone. It had disappeared somewhere back at the lake. Here, in the forest clearing, they were man and woman. Fireheart and Autumn Wind . . . alone together in the night . . . and wanting.

She slid her hands over his chest up to his nape and pulled his head downward. She yearned for his kiss again. His kisses were intoxicating, tender, and sweet.

But the passionate meeting of mouths in no way resembled the previous kisses. It was a hot fusion of lips and tongue while hands fondled and stroked damp flesh and bare buttocks.

He kissed a path down her throat, pausing at the base before trailing lower to her breasts. She waited with breath held as he lifted his head before capturing a nipple with his mouth.

Joanna caught her breath in the sure joy of his suckling her. She cradled his head with her hands, wound her fingers in his long, wet hair, and arched closer.

Fireheart lifted his head and eased Joanna to the ground, while embracing her. The scent of pine and other forest vegetation filled Joanna's senses as Fireheart stretched out next to her. She lay open and vulnerable to his gaze and his touch, and she gloried in it.

He began to caress her, beginning with her hair, then her face, and lower. But Joanna wasn't content to be still. She stroked his chest, then reached to pull his head down once again for another kiss. As their lips touched, the fire of passion ignited between them.

"Joanna. Autumn Wind . . . you are soft and smooth and I want to touch all of you."

How could he be expected to marry another when

he clearly desired her? Joanna tried not to think about the Indian maiden Moon Dove whom Little Blossom had said he would marry.

Yet, how could he not marry Moon Dove when she herself had no future with Fireheart? When she must return to England and manage her estate?

His fingers brought her heaven. His lips coaxed her most passionate response. Joanna fought to banish the reasons for stopping, but the image of Moon Dove and the overwhelming responsibility of managing her late uncle's property hovered outside the haze of ecstasy, intruding.

She caught Fireheart's head and held him away from her. "Little Blossom said that you will marry Moon Dove. Is that true?"

He frowned and rose to his knees. "It is true that I must take a wife. It is possible that Moon Dove will be my mate, but that has not been decided."

Joanna experienced an odd little pain in the region of her heart. "Do you love her?"

Fireheart scowled, clearly reluctant to talk about his prospective wife. "She is a good Lenape maiden. This man cares for her."

"How do you feel about me?" she whispered.

"Joanna . . ." His face contorting with passion, he reached for her, lifting her into his arms. He touched her face and then kissed her. His lips tenderly worshiped her mouth and cheek before he buried his face in her neck and just held her.

Joanna was convinced that Fireheart felt something special for her. His tenderness, his caring, and his reluctance to declare his love for Moon Dove gave her hope that this time between them would be a cherished memory, if nothing more.

Suddenly, it became vital that she gave herself to this caring man.

Fireheart was all that was good and true, and Lenape. Joanna lay back against the rich forest carpet, and pulled Fireheart down so that she could lie with him . . . and love him.

The sun slanting in through the smoke-hole in the roof of the wigwam woke Joanna the next morning. She thought back on her time with Fireheart, reliving the memory with a smile.

Despite her willingness to lie with him, Joanna and Fireheart had not made love. As they'd kissed and caressed a while longer, both had sensed that the time was not right. Fireheart had risen from her side reluctantly, and strangely enough Joanna had been disappointed, but not hurt.

Her heart and her body still yearned to belong to him. But to lie with him when the future was still uncertain seemed more wrong then right. As he'd walked her back to the village, she'd silently thanked his source of strength that stopped him from taking what she so freely offered.

Cara and Harry had fallen asleep in each other's arms. As she'd entered the wigwam and seen them lying together, Joanna had felt an ache in her heart, and had experienced the strongest desire to return to Fireheart.

But Fireheart had enough on his mind. Within hours, he would be sending his men into battle, and Joanna sensed that his men wouldn't be going without him.

Unwilling to disturb her servants, Joanna had gone to sleep on the other side of the deer hide curtain. It was the warmth of the sun and the sound of the villagers moving about the encampment that urged her from her sleeping pallet.

She rose, still clad in the calico gown that she had worn the night before, peeked past the curtain to see that Cara and Harry still slept, then slipped outside into the morning air.

Her heart thumping in her chest, Joanna searched for Fireheart. She didn't want him to leave, hoped she was wrong that he would go, but knew it was his duty as chief. As she looked about the village, she prayed for Fireheart's safety. She wanted him to return so they could explore their feelings for each other. Her feelings for him were so new, so special, that she vowed to remain until she knew if it was love.

She left the vicinity of her wigwam and moved toward the village center. The men had already begun to gather. Joanna saw Rising Bird and Broken Bow conversing quietly near the huge kettle hung over the community cook-fire.

There was no sign of Fireheart. Determined to see him before he left, Joanna headed toward the lake in the hope that he had gone back there.

She saw only an Indian maiden down by the water. The girl turned, and Joanna tensed when she saw that it was Moon Dove. She hesitated before approaching. As she gave herself a moment's pause, she saw a figure emerge from behind trees and bushes, coming from the direction of the secluded forest clearing she had shared with Fireheart.

Her stomach gave a lurch when she recognized her warrior brave. With a sick heart, Joanna watched as Moon Dove hurried to greet and embrace Fireheart.

Joanna gasped with pain and hid behind a huge oak. From her hiding place, she observed the pair kissing, then talking in earnest. Devastated by the sight, she turned away to head blindly back toward the village.

Chapter 8

Burton Estate
England
June 1727

"Well?" Michael Burton rose from his seat when he saw his brother. "Are you going to go after her?"

John shook his head as he entered his late father's study, and sat down in a chair that faced Michael's desk. "It's too soon. She would have barely reached the New World."

"You've got to find her, John. You've got to marry her and soon." Michael came out from behind the desk to pace the room. "We need money, and we need it fast. You should have married her before she left. The Neville estate is worth a hefty sum, and it borders our property."

John nodded. The land would be a tidy bonus that would help them regain their losses and make them wealthy as well.

"What do you think I should do?" John asked. He didn't know how long Joanna would be gone. There were many factors that might determine the length of her absence . . . the ship voyage, whether or not the vessel made it in three months or four . . . her length of stay, whether or not she decided to stay a month with her cousin, or two. Then there was the return journey. She could be away for possibly ten months, or more. He said this to his brother.

Alarmed, Michael froze in the act of pacing. "Ten months! We can't wait much longer!" He went back to his seat and opened a ledger. "Our debts are mounting. We need money. Roderick's death has made this all the more difficult; you know that he wanted the girl to marry you."

John sighed. "Aye, I know." Joanna Neville was an attractive enough woman, but it was her fortune that lured him, nothing more. "I don't understand how you expect me to handle this. I'm here in England, and she's in the New World."

"Send someone to find her."

" 'Tis four months' journey by ship! Who?" John asked.

Michael scowled. "I don't know. You must know someone capable to do the deed. One of her own men?"

John looked thoughtful. "Perhaps." He rubbed his temple where his head had begun to throb. He hated to worry about such things. He had enjoyed managing Neville Manor these past months, and wondered if he would be allowed the same freedom at overseeing after his and Joanna's wedding. She could be a willful female, he thought. Would she agree?

It doesn't matter. She'll be my wife.

Tired of the conversation and the concern, John made a decision as he stood. "I'll see whom I can find." It wouldn't be easy to find someone willing to make that long journey to the Colonies. It wasn't a place any sane person, who wasn't desperate or a criminal, would want to go. Why hadn't he thought of this when Joanna had told him she was going? Because he'd been too happy to learn that he'd be taking over for her, he thought.

"Could you borrow some funds to tide us over?" Michael asked worriedly.

"Without chance of her suspecting?" John asked. His brother nodded.

"I'll see what I can do. How much do we need to get by?" John asked.

Michael named a figure, and John agreed to get the money and alter Joanna's books to hide the deed.

When Joanna returned to the village, she saw the men gathering in readiness to depart. After a brief look, she averted her glance and headed toward her wigwam, struggling to banish the painful image of Fireheart and Moon Dove.

The men had formed a circle; someone was in the center, talking quietly with them. They broke apart, drawing her attention as Joanna walked past them. She stopped, stunned, when she saw Fireheart talking with her cousin's husband Rising Bird.

She frowned and stared at the acting chief. If Fireheart was there, who was the brave at the lake?

It couldn't have been Fireheart.

Her spirits lifted. Joy swelled in her chest, and she stopped to gaze at him longingly. He noticed her presence as he finished the conversation, his dark gaze catching hers across the yard. As Rising Bird left, Fireheart approached.

"Autumn Wind."

His beloved face caused her to catch her breath. She beamed a smile at him. "Fireheart."

His brow furrowed as he studied her. "You have been crying." He reached out to touch her cheek.

She nodded. She didn't see any reason to deny it when the evidence was there. And it no longer seemed important, for she had been mistaken. It hadn't been Fireheart and Moon Dove kissing, embracing. . . . It had been Moon Dove and another brave. Who? That thought would be a matter to consider later. Right now she just wanted to enjoy her brief moment with Fireheart.

He continued to study her, his dark eyes intent on her expression, his finger tenderly tracing her jaw. "What is wrong?"

"Nothing," she answered. "Now." She placed her hand over his where it had settled on her cheek.

His brow cleared as if he sensed that she had spoken the truth. "I was just going to look for you. I leave with Rising Bird and the warriors for Bear Paw's village to the north."

"I thought you would go," she said without surprise.

He arched his eyebrows. "You know me this well?" He turned his hand, and captured her fingers to bring them to his lips.

Her expression was as soft as her smile. Her hand tingled as he kissed it. "I learned a lot about the man Fireheart last night. Fireheart, the chief, would not stay behind while his men ventured out alone." Her stomach quivered as she thought of him facing the enemy. She could not disguise the fact that she was worried about him.

He kissed her palm, before lowering it, still held between his hands. "You will be here when I return?"

"I will be here," she promised, knowing that she wouldn't leave until he had returned safely. She didn't want to leave at all.

He pulled her away from the village and into the forest, away from prying eyes. He paused when they were hidden. There, he released her hand and cupped her face. "You will think of me?"

"*Kihiila*," she murmured with feeling. "Yes, I will think of you."

"Joanna—" he began.

A sharp cry from the direction of the village drew Fireheart's attention. "They are calling for me. It is time."

Joanna's blood chilled. "Please be careful, Fireheart. I don't want anything bad to happen to you."

His lips curved. "To this warrior?"

She nodded.

"Fear not, little one. I will return to you."

His words thrilled her. He would return to her, she thought.

"Go now," she said gently, knowing that he could stay no longer. She wanted desperately to kiss him.

She could read it in his eyes; he wanted it, too.

With a harsh groan, Fireheart gave in to the urge first, bending to give her a kiss. Her pulse raced and her heart sang with joy.

He lifted his head. "Joanna—"

She grabbed him, pulling him down for one more kiss. "I will be here," she said, and pushed him on his way. If she didn't, she would likely detain him longer . . . and she wouldn't be responsible for her actions if he stayed.

The men left, and Joanna went about life in the village with a fear that overwhelmed her. She cared for Fireheart. She thought she might be falling in love with him, which was a ridiculous thing to do since she couldn't stay. She had to return to England.

Her servants had been urging her to go. In bed that night, Joanna lay, debating what to do until she realized that she had no choice in the matter. She would send Cara and Harry home, and she would stay longer. Cara and Harry could assure John that she would be returning soon. No doubt he was wondering, worrying about them after all this time.

The next morning when she told them the news,

Harry and Cara were overjoyed until they learned that she would be remaining.

"I'll be fine," Joanna assured them. "You've forgotten I spent my childhood here. My cousin is here, and many of my friends."

"But what shall we tell Master Burton?" Cara asked, obviously not looking forward to the meeting.

"Tell him that I will return in a few weeks." A few weeks after Cara and Harry arrived in London would give her plenty of time to wait for Fireheart, time enough, too, to spend days with him.

Fireheart must marry Moon Dove, she reminded herself.

She frowned. Would the marriage be Moon Dove's choice?

Joanna couldn't forget the sight of Moon Dove wrapped in another man's arms. Fireheart deserved a wife who loved him. Would Moon Dove give him the love he needed?

As if Joanna's thoughts had conjured her up from air, Moon Dove appeared from the doorway of a wigwam. Joanna debated whether or not to speak with her, then thought better of it. It wasn't her business, was it?

Studying the Indian maiden, Joanna felt a spurt of jealousy as she pictured the woman as Fireheart's wife.

She loved Fireheart, she realized. She must! It was too late to save her heart. Why else would she be concerned with Fireheart's future happiness? Whether or not he would be happy with Moon Dove?

I love him, she thought with awe. And she wanted only the best for him. . . .

The braves crept silently toward Bear Paw's village. Rising Bird held up a hand, and everyone stopped to listen to the forest sounds.

The sun was bright, and the smell of smoke was in the air. The Lenape braves kept low as they began to inch closer and closer with Rising Bird in the lead, and Fireheart behind him. Rising Bird was an experienced war chief; Fireheart trusted him, and wouldn't think of using his authority to take his position.

Rising Bird signaled to one of the braves, Turtle That Hops, and the warrior slipped past the others into the village.

Suddenly, there was a wild cry like an owl. It was Turtle That Hops calling to his friends.

Rising Bird glanced at Fireheart who nodded and waited for the man's lead.

The warrior signaled back with a birdcall, then the Lenape war party entered the village.

Four days later, they returned to Little River during the night with Red Dress and several women and children from Bear Paw's tribe. Hearing their call, the villagers came out of their wigwams to greet them.

Joanna emerged to see Mary run to embrace her husband. Heart thumping hard, she searched for Fireheart and couldn't find him. She saw Turtle That Hops being hugged by his wife. Then she realized that there were women and children in the village whom she'd never seen before.

People from Bear Paw's village? she wondered. Since the Iroquois seldom left survivors to tell about their raids, surely this was a good sign.

Although it was still dark, someone had stoked up the community cook-fire. Dogs barked and ran about the children. The kettle above the fire already emitted the scent of simmering meat.

After ensuring that their loved ones were safe, the women gathered with the visitors, chatting and talking in earnest. Joanna heard a burst of laughter from a group she could not see behind the women, and the merriment made her smile as she searched again for Fireheart.

Where is he? The smile fell from her lips when she didn't see him.

Her stomach contracted. Was he safe? The people wouldn't be in a celebratory mood if their chief had been killed or injured—even an acting chief. Some of the tension eased out of her at the thought.

Mary saw her and approached.

Joanna smiled a greeting. "I saw Rising Bird."

Her cousin grinned. "He is well. So are the others. The Iroquois raided the village, but Bear Paw's men were able to chase them away." Her expression became solemn. "Two warriors died. Bear Paw asked that the women and children of his village come to Little River for a time until the threat of the enemy is gone. He believes the Cayuga war chief will return soon with more men."

Fear had gripped Joanna when she heard about the two warriors' deaths. "The braves who died—"

Mary studied her with a knowing look. "They were not from our village, but Bear Paw's." Her gaze fastened on something behind Joanna. "If you are looking for Fireheart, look no farther, for he is behind you, speaking with Wild Squirrel."

"Wild Squirrel!" Joanna exclaimed. She spun, and set eyes on an incredible scene. The ailing chief had come out of his wigwam to greet his nephew. Happiness filtered through her at the sight of the chief, looking so well, and her beloved Fireheart who had returned to her safely as promised.

Fireheart glanced over to find Joanna studying him. She didn't move, didn't smile. The brief look he gave her was all she needed to wait patiently for him to come to her later.

She was in the forest picking berries when he finally sought her out.

"Autumn Wind."

She spun, gasping. "Fireheart, I didn't see you!"

He came to her, took her basket. He popped a plump blackberry into his mouth and chewed slowly. "Good." He smiled, reached for another berry, and held it to her lips.

Joanna grinned, then opened for his offering. The amusement left her face when she caught him staring at her mouth as she ate the berry. The fruit had never tasted so sweet. Warmth pooled in her abdomen as she gazed up at him with longing. It was if he'd kissed her without touching. "Fireheart," she whispered hoarsely.

"I came back safely."

She nodded. "I see."

"You are happy that I have returned?"

She swallowed against a throat that had suddenly become dry. "*Kihiila*. Was it terrible?"

He shook his head. "Bear Paw and his men fought bravely. They have forced the enemy away, but we must watch for the Cayuga's return."

He smiled. Still holding her basket, he took her hand. "Come. You have berries to pick."

She glanced into the basket. "I have enough."

"No," he said, "you need more." He gave her a look as he gently squeezed her hand. "I know a good place for berries."

She felt her insides melt as she stared into his gleaming dark gaze. His expression promised her untold sensual delights. Her heart began to pound as she followed him.

They were on a new path when they heard someone calling Fireheart's name.

He paused to see who it was, then released her hand as Moon Dove appeared at the crest of the hill and approached him. "I will see what she wants," he said, handing her the basket before walking way.

Joanna felt a burning in her stomach as she watched Fireheart and Moon Dove greet each other. She recalled Little Blossom's words and a buzzing filled her head.

Fireheart is expected to marry Moon Dove.

Had she been mistaken? Could it have been Fireheart down by the lake with Moon Dove after all?

She narrowed her gaze as she watched the pair. Moon Dove placed her hand on Fireheart's arm as she spoke with the brave. She saw Fireheart nod, then glance in her direction before centering his attention on the Lenape maiden again.

I feel like an intruder. She should leave before her heart was crushed any further.

If it had been Fireheart and Moon Dove embracing that morning, would she have foregone her time with Fireheart? Joanna wondered.

No. She wouldn't have given up that brief time for anything.

Which made her a what? A wanton? An adulteress of sorts?

They are not married, she reminded herself.

But it didn't matter. The idea was there, and it wouldn't leave her.

Fireheart separated from Moon Dove and approached. "I must go," he said, his words making her spirits sink. "Moon Dove's mother needs me."

With a lump rising in her throat, Joanna nodded.

He left her without a promise to return or to look for her later. Joanna watched him walk away with unshed tears stinging her eyes.

Chapter 9

With the return of the owner of her wigwam and the visiting guests within the village, Joanna vacated Red Dress's lodge and moved in with Mary and Rising Bird.

"I'm sorry," Joanna apologized to her cousin as she moved her belongings inside.

Mary appeared surprised. "For what? Have you forgotten that I wanted you here from the first?"

Joanna grinned. "I must have." Tears threatened as she stored her satchel of clothing beneath a sleeping platform. In her cousin's wigwam, the beds were built of sturdy sticks about a foot and a half off the ground. Personal possessions, cooking utensils, and food items were stored beneath the sleeping platforms.

As Joanna straightened, Mary tapped her arm. "Here," she said. She held something out toward her.

Joanna recognized the garment as a Lenape tunic, one similar but more beautiful than the one she'd taken with her to England. "What's this?" she whispered.

Her cousin's expression was soft. "It's something

I made for you. You must be tired of wearing those English gowns by now.''

Joanna was touched by Mary's gift. ''Thank you.'' Still, she hesitated in taking it. ''You shouldn't have spent all that time on me.''

Mary frowned. ''You're my cousin. I love you. Why shouldn't I make you a gift?''

''*Wa-nee-shih.*'' Blinking back tears, Joanna accepted the garment and turned away. She set it carefully on the sleeping pallet that Mary had said was hers.

''Why don't you put it on?'' Mary eyed her young cousin with concern. Since her return to the village, Joanna had slowly become more at ease, yet the girl was holding back her emotions. What had happened to the spirited young child who had lived among the Indians?

I did that to her, Mary thought. *I sent her to a life that tethered her happiness and spirit.*

''Perhaps I'll wear it later,'' Joanna said.

Mary kept her concern hidden as she nodded before setting out to prepare dinner.

The guests in the village were easily accommodated. The eight women and ten children had been taken into Lenape homes, many of them invited into the larger wigwams with a few settling into the small dome-shaped lodges like Mary's. Watching Mary gather the implements needed to prepare the main meal, Joanna began to wonder about her cousin's life.

Why didn't Mary have any children? There were too many years and too much that had happened between them for Joanna to ask.

Mary would have made a good mother, Joanna thought. Hadn't her cousin stepped into the role for her after her mother died?

She began to realize that while life had been terribly unpleasant for her, perhaps it hadn't been a cup filled with happiness for Mary either.

''May I help?'' Joanna asked as she bent to help

Mary move a large sack of ground corn from under a sleeping platform.

Their hands touched briefly as they dragged the sack to where they could reach it more easily. Mary glanced at her with such affection that Joanna felt the resurgence of tears.

"I would like that. Thank you," Mary said quietly.

Joanna nodded and asked what she could do to assist.

Fireheart entered the wigwam of Moon Dove's clan and followed Moon Dove to where the maiden's mother sat on a rush mat, shelling beans.

"I have brought him, mother," Moon Dove said.

The old woman looked up from her bowl of beans. "Fireheart, I must speak with you about my son White Cat."

Surprised, the brave inclined his head and took a seat on the mat that Moon Dove, on her mother's instructions, had set on the dirt floor for him.

"You may leave us, daughter," Berry Tree said.

Moon Dove appeared relieved before she went away.

Fireheart watched her leave before turning back to the girl's mother. He found himself the object of Berry Tree's intense scrutiny.

"You like Moon Dove?" she asked.

"*Kihiila*," he said, surprised by the question.

"Why have you not asked her to be your wife?" the woman demanded with a puzzled look.

"I do not wish to take a wife now."

Berry Tree made a derisive sound. "You are a good warrior. Soon Wild Squirrel will die and you will be chief."

"Wild Squirrel has many years as our chief."

The woman shoved a pile of beans in Fireheart's

direction, and with a nod of her head instructed him to shell them.

Fireheart did so, without thought, even though the job was women's work.

"Wild Squirrel is doing well. He will recover and be the leader of our people," the brave said.

Her expression filled with compassion, Berry Tree shook her head. "Wild Squirrel has been ill for much longer than he has shown. He grows tired of this life. The Spirit World calls him."

Fireheart scowled as he opened a bean pod and separated bean from shell before throwing the bean in with the others in Berry Tree's bowl. "Why do you say this?"

"It is something I know. Something I feel."

"Must we speak of our chief?" Fireheart frowned. "You wish to talk about White Cat, your son."

Berry Tree gazed at him a long time without answering. Fireheart shifted uncomfortably under her gaze, but continued to shell beans while waiting for her to speak. "My son wishes to know when his sister will marry," she said. "And he wishes the great warrior Fireheart to take him on a hunt."

Fireheart raised his eyebrows at the first, then smiled at the second statement. Despite the old age of Berry Tree, her son White Cat was a young boy who was anxious to become a man. Since Berry Tree's husband had died last winter, the task of helping to raise the boy fell on the other male members of the Lenape tribe. "I will take White Cat on a hunt when the area is safe from our Iroquois enemy."

"And Moon Dove?"

"Have the matrons decreed that Moon Dove and I must marry?" he asked. When the married women of the village made the decision, it would be announced at a gathering, and then it would be so.

"I wish to know your thoughts first," Berry Tree said.

"I must think on this."

"There is someone else you might take as wife?"

"There is no one else," Fireheart said with an odd little catch in his chest. No one except Autumn Wind, and she would leave soon to return to the land called England.

What did I tell you about that animal skin you're wearing!" Uncle Roderick said.

Joanna cringed as he raised his hand. "I'm not hurting anyone by wearing it. I'll stay in my room—"

She felt the crack of his hand as he slapped her across the face. "You are not a savage, do you hear me? You are my niece, and I will not tolerate your Indian ways!"

He hit her again, knocking her to the floor. Seeing the direction of his gaze, Joanna scrambled to cover her legs, but the tunic was too short.

"Come with me, young lady," he growled as he jerked her to her feet. "You will not listen to reason! I will make you listen in the one way you'll remember!"

"No!" Joanna cried as Uncle Roderick called for a servant.

"Get me my riding crop," he said to the frightened young maid who answered his summons. "Then see that we are not disturbed!"

The girl returned within minutes with the piece of leather, then with a look of sympathy toward Joanna, she hurriedly left.

He turned to Joanna with anger in his gaze, and, Joanna thought, a sense of satisfaction.

I hate you, *she thought as he shut the door to her room.* I hate you!

But she didn't utter the words nor did she cry out loud when the first slash of the leather strap hit her arms as she raised them in defense. She gasped as it found its target with the back of her legs.

He left her when her legs were a mass of red welts, and she lay facedown on the bed, vowing to be free of him.

She rolled over and gasped with pain. Wincing, she got up from the bed and her bedchamber door opened.

"No!" she cried as Roderick Neville reentered the room.

Joanna shot up in bed, gasping, her eyes wide but unseeing.

"Joanna!" Mary sat on the edge of the sleeping platform, gently shaking her younger cousin awake. "Joanna, 'tis just a dream. A terrible dream by the looks of you."

She nodded, still dazed by the horror of her nightmare. Her gaze fell on the lovely doeskin gown that Mary had made for her. It was that beautiful gift which had triggered the dream . . . terror from a childhood spent alone and afraid of a cruel man.

"Is she all right?" Rising Bird appeared by Mary's side, his concerned expression lit by the glowing embers in the fire-pit. Joanna gazed at him, unable to speak.

"She will be," Mary said, hugging her. "Would you like to tell me about it?"

Joanna vigorously shook her head. "No," she rasped. "Someday maybe, but not now."

Mary stood. "I understand."

And Joanna realized that she did. Something passed between them, a feeling of affection . . . of love.

"Will you be able to go back to sleep?"

Joanna shook her head. "I think I'll get up and go to the lake."

"I'll come with you—"

"No." She smiled at Mary to take the sting out of the rejection. "I need to be alone."

"But it's dangerous—"

"She will be fine, wife," Rising Bird said from his sleeping platform, surprisingly taking Joanna's side.

A look passed between the couple. Mary saw the tunic she'd made carefully draped over the end of Joanna's sleeping pallet. "Wear the doeskin," she urged her cousin. "You'll be an easy target in that gown."

The gown she was referring to was the yellow print that Joanna had worn the previous day.

Joanna felt a momentary qualm about donning the tunic. The memory of her dream still haunted her, making her heart race.

He is dead. He can't hurt you anymore.

She agreed and reached for the gown. She waited for Mary and Rising Bird to go back to bed before she took off her shift and put on the soft doeskin.

The tunic felt wonderful to her. Soft and supple, it fit her perfectly. Ignoring her leather shoes, she decided to go barefoot.

She slipped from the wigwam into the clear warm night. The sliver of moon was larger than it had been before Fireheart and the others had left. Joanna paused a moment to study it and the starry sky before venturing from the wigwam.

As she crossed the yard, it occurred to her that there might be guards now, with the threat of Iroquois. She saw a brave as she headed toward the path to the water. Waving, she hoped he recognized her and wouldn't stop her from leaving.

The warrior stared at her hard, and then he must have realized who it was, despite her Lenape garb. When she came abreast of him, he nodded and softly asked her where she was going. When she told him her destination, he signaled her to go, but with a warning to be careful of the enemy in the night.

Joanna felt a tingling at her nape as she followed the path up the rise in the land and down again toward the water. When she'd decided to come, she hadn't given a moment's thought to encountering Iroquois. Her mind had been filled with images of her past and her uncle . . . a nightmare that had seemed more real than her present situation.

The forest was filled with the night sounds. The

hum of summer insects, a rustle in the leaves as some frightened animal sensed her and took flight.

The ground felt hard to her feet, but she ignored the pain, recalling a time when she'd spend much of her days either barefoot, or wearing the soft leather soles of her moccasins.

She would ask Little Blossom or Mary to teach her how to make moccasins again. She must have known at one time she decided, for there was always someone about tanning hides or making clothing . . . sharpening arrowheads . . . or making tools for gardening or preparing food.

As she continued toward the lake without mishap or the sound of anything other than a small animal in the brush, Joanna felt the tension within her start to unwind. The image of her uncle's face began to fade as did the strange throbbing at the scars on the back of her legs, pain brought on by the memory of her punishment.

The path opened up onto a clearing at the lakeshore. Joanna gazed out over the calm water, and the painful past faded away.

I could have belonged here, she thought. If she hadn't gone to England, she would have been free to live out her remaining years with the peace and harmony of the Lenni Lenape Indians.

But she had gone to England and inherited her uncle's estate, and now there were people who depended on her, people she'd forced from her mind for a time.

She didn't have to worry about them at present, did she? There was her good friend John Burton to take care of things . . . although she feared that he might be anxious to get back to his own home, which he shared with his fraternal twin brother.

Joanna went to the rock she'd discovered on her first day at the lake and sat down. Swinging her legs over the edge, she dipped her feet in the cool water, sighing with pleasure as it soothed the soreness from her soles and lapped gently at her ankles.

There she sat for a long while, studying the water, the sky, and the stars ... and longing for things beyond reach.

As soon as Joanna left the wigwam, Rising Bird kissed his wife and left their bed to trail his wife's cousin. He would keep his distance so that she wouldn't know he had come. The night in the forest was a dangerous time and place. He would guard her, then return before she knew he'd followed.

He had reached the edge of the village when he saw Fireheart talking to the night guard. Fireheart signaled to Rising Bird to wait before leaving, and he halted, although he was anxious to get down to the lake.

Fireheart approached him with a curious expression. "Why do you leave your bed so late, Rising Bird?"

Rising Bird gestured toward the trail. "Autumn Wind has decided to take a walk. Although I don't want her to know it, I would not want her to leave unguarded."

"I will guard Autumn Wind," Fireheart said, unable to believe that the woman would be foolish enough to leave the safety of the village. "I was on my way to the lake when I saw Rain Cloud." Rain Cloud was the guard.

"You?" Rising Bird asked, his gaze narrowing.

Fireheart nodded. "I will protect her from the enemy with my life."

Something in the younger man's tone gave Rising Bird food for thought. "You will not let her know that my wife and I are concerned for her."

"She will not hear it from me." Fireheart held up

his bow and arrow. "I have a weapon to protect her." He eyed his friend with amusement. "What would you have used to defend against the enemy?" he asked.

Rising Bird realized with a sheepish grin that he had forgotten to bring a weapon. He'd been so concerned with leaving to follow her quickly. "My hands and feet are weapons."

Fireheart chuckled softly. "My arrow will fell a Cayuga more quickly."

The older man conceded the younger man's point. "Go then, Fireheart, and know this man is grateful for your protection of the one he considers daughter."

"I will guard her with my life," Fireheart repeated, meaning it.

Because he trusted that Fireheart could protect Joanna, Rising Bird thanked the brave and headed back to the wigwam and his waiting wife.

After ensuring that the area was safe, Fireheart paused in the forest and hid behind a stand of trees. He saw her immediately. Joanna was seated on a rock with her legs dangling in the water.

He crept closer for a better look. His breath slammed in his throat as he studied her. She was beautiful. Her blonde hair flowed, unbound, about her shoulders and back. She turned and there was enough light to see her features. Lovely. Tempting him . . . luring him nearer.

Fascinated, drawn, Fireheart slipped from one tree to another without making a sound. He was surprised to see her in Lenape clothing. She had been in the village for over a month and had never discarded her English gown. In the doeskin tunic, she seemed more like the young girl who had lived among his people.

Unable to help himself, he left the cover for the open and moved toward the lake. He wanted to touch her, kiss her.

He halted, unsure of his welcome.

The water felt good against Joanna's skin. She stood and waded out into the lake, raising the hem of her tunic as she moved into deeper water. A light breeze began to stir in the air, caressing her face and lifting the loose tendrils of her hair. She had not gone very far when she heard a noise behind her.

With the hair rising up the back of her neck, Joanna spun to see who was there. Visions of Iroquois Indians on the warpath invaded her mind, chilling her to the bone.

At first, she could see nothing. Then a shadow moved, and her heart began to pound as she focused her gaze near the edge of the woods where she thought she saw movement.

Joanna waited for what seemed like forever before she began to relax, certain that she had imagined things. She had started to turn when out of the corner of her eye she saw a figure step from the forest.

She gasped. Her body taut with fear, she carefully searched with her eyes for something to use as a weapon. The only thing she could see to defend herself with was a rock, but she would need to pick it up with two hands.

How would she do so without drawing the man's attention?

She moved casually back to her seat and found a smaller stone, one that would be less effective in the fight to defend, but less easily detected by the enemy.

Without turning to look again, she could tell he was a warrior. Iroquois?

Her chest tightening with terror, Joanna moved slowly to face him.

The thunder of her heart nearly drowned out the sound of her breathing. The man was indeed a warrior. He held a weapon of some sort in his right hand. She peered into the darkness and was able to see that he had a bow and arrow.

Fear kept her frozen as the figure approached. The moon slipped behind a cloud as the warrior came closer. She was so frightened that she didn't recognize the man before her.

"Autumn Wind."

The sound of his voice released something inside her, and she began to tremble as relief set in. She blinked. "Fireheart?" she called weakly.

"*Kihiila.* You are out here all alone. Are you not worried about our enemy?" He set his weapon on the shore, then covered the distance between them, wading through water until he reached her side.

Her body began to tremble violently. "You frightened me!"

He frowned. "You did not look frightened."

She turned to face him fully, allowing him to see the rock.

Fireheart looked startled. "You would fight with that small stone as weapon?" He grabbed it from her hands and tossed it into the lake. "Did you think you could kill with it?"

"Why are you here?" Joanna cried, embarrassed. "You should not be here!"

"It is good that I am," he said. "If I had been a Cayuga warrior, you would have been killed or kidnapped."

Furious with him, she backed away. "I don't need you to tell me what could have happened to me." She stopped to glare at him. "I am well aware that I could have been harmed!"

Fireheart saw then that Joanna was shaking. Con-

trite, he moved closer. "Are you all right?" he asked
softly. "I did not mean to frighten you."

"You did frighten me," she mumbled reproach-
fully.

When he was within a few feet of her, he reached
out and pulled her into his arms. "You should have
told me you wanted to swim." He kissed her forehead.
He felt the warmth through his being when she trem-
bled at his kiss.

He held her with her head tucked under his chin
and his arms wrapped tightly about her. They stood
in the lake, heedless of the water lapping against their
bare legs, wetting the hem of Joanna's Lenape dress.

"Fireheart?" Her soft voice was muffled against his
chest.

He loosened his hold on her and lifted her head
so he could see her face. "What is it, *Kitehi?*"

Joanna felt an infusion of warmth at the use of his
endearment. He had called her "my heart." "Is it
really unsafe for me to be here?"

He nodded, releasing her chin. "Until we are sure
that our enemy will not come."

"But won't they return to Bear Paw's village?"

"We do not know for certain," he said. "We must
be ready for them."

She moved her foot, watching the ripples her leg
made in the water. "I couldn't sleep."

"This man could not rest either," he admitted.

She glanced up at him. "Must we go back?"

Her tone suggested that she was reluctant to return.

Fireheart made a thorough study of their surroundings. He could sense no danger, saw no sign of the
enemy nor of dangerous wildlife in the night.

"We can stay for a while," he said, facing her with
a smile. "Would you like to swim?"

Joanna gazed at his wonderful handsome face, and
told him with a nod that she would like to swim.
The thought occurred to her that she would have to

undress. She knew she should be appalled at the idea, but he had seen her before, hadn't he? And he hadn't made her feel ashamed of her body. In fact, he had made her feel beautiful, special. She wanted to swim naked again with Fireheart. She shouldn't, but she wanted to. . . .

Without glancing his way, she waded back to shore, wondering if he would follow, glad when she heard the swish of water behind her that told her he had. After moving toward her rock, she caught the bottom edge of her tunic and tugged off the garment. She had her back toward Fireheart, and couldn't judge his reaction, or see what he was doing behind her.

She was naked beneath the doeskin, and she was immediately conscious of the summer breeze brushing against her bare skin. Joanna lifted the hair from the back of her neck, and allowed it to fall back against her nape. Turning, she encountered Fireheart's warm gaze studying her with a flame in his eyes that stole her breath.

Just as she had undressed, Fireheart had done so, too, having removed his loincloth. Joanna swallowed against a dry throat. He was magnificent, a prime example of a well-honed man—broad-shouldered, lean-hipped, muscular, and strong. Fireheart closed the gap between them. The glow in his dark eyes as he neared made her tingle and flush with heat.

She spun awkwardly and entered the water. She thought she heard his low chuckle as she splashed out into deeper water.

"Be careful that you don't drown, *Kitehi*," he said with soft laughter.

"I know how to swim!" she called back. She dipped below the cool surface to help banish the hot flush she felt rise in her cheeks.

As she swam beneath the water, she had a mental picture of Fireheart with Moon Dove. The heat within her suddenly chilled.

What was she doing swimming with a man who was promised to another?

Or was he?

She still wasn't sure whether or not their marriage had been formally arranged. She understood that these matters were often decided by the village matrons: mothers of the intended couple, aunts, grandmothers, and other wise women of the tribe.

She had come out here to forget her past and she had succeeded. But it was the present and the future that bothered her now . . . and her relationship with Fireheart. . . .

He promised to return to me, she thought with a measure of comfort. *Not Moon Dove. But me.*

She rose above the water, slicking back her wet hair with her hands. Joanna turned to look for Fireheart, and saw him a short distance away, floating with his head just above the water, studying her.

"The water is nice," she said.

He didn't reply; he just watched her. Her body tingling all over, she lay back and closed her eyes, pretending that his presence with her in the lake didn't disturb her.

Then she became aware of the way her nipples pebbled into hard little nubs, of the sensual feel of the water trickling into and caressing all her most secret intimate places. Gasping at the sensations, she spun on her stomach and sunk down.

She allowed her body to float freely, tried to get her mind to float freely as well, but her thoughts were anything but easy and free.

Fireheart had invaded her thoughts and her heart. She didn't know how to free herself from him.

She didn't know if she wanted to.

Fireheart watched her for a time, and his pulse quickened as she lay back in the lake, exposing her breasts. It wasn't that he hadn't seen a woman's breasts before, but there was something about Joanna's . . . everything about Joanna stirred his blood, invited him to touch and taste her . . . and crave for more.

He felt a soft groan well up in his throat, fought hard to suppress it, then found himself rising to his feet before swimming in her direction.

"Autumn Wind," he called out to her hoarsely. "Joanna! Wait until I come to you."

He slipped under the water, moving through the lake like an eel. Catching her by the arm, he pulled her toward him, rising up out of the lake to kiss her soundly.

She whimpered and clung, kissing him back with passion. He moaned, deepened the kiss, and felt his desire pulsate to new heights.

"Autumn Wind," he murmured.

She looked at him with water droplets sparkling on her eyelashes. Her eyes were bright, sad almost.

"What is it?" he asked.

She shook her head, as if unable to answer.

"Joanna," he said more sternly.

"We shouldn't," she whispered. "Moon Dove—"

He frowned. "What about Moon Dove?"

"This isn't right. You are going to marry her."

"She is not my wife," he said, annoyed by the suggestion. It hadn't been decided yet.

She appeared stung by his words. "And neither am I."

"Did you not tell Little Blossom that you must return to England?"

"Yes," she admitted. *He has spoken with Little Blossom.*

"And how is this different? You would kiss and make love and then leave me?"

"I don't know."

"You would stay?" His heart hammered with hope.

"I can't."

"Then why do you worry about Moon Dove when you have no wish to stay here in the Lenape village?"

At first, silence was her answer. "I'm sorry," she said. She broke from his hold and began to wade toward the shore.

He quickly followed her. "Wait."

She paused, but didn't turn around. "Please," she gasped. "Let me go."

He had caught her by the shoulder, his fingers caressing the damp curve. "I don't want to release you."

He felt her shiver. "I have to go!" she cried.

He stopped her flight. "Autumn Wind, stay."

She shook her head, but didn't leave. He stroked down her arm, caught her wrist, and raised her hand to kiss it.

As Joanna faced him, he could see her tears. Something knotted within him at this sign of her unhappiness. "I will not hurt you," he promised.

"You already have."

His stomach muscles tightened. "How?"

"You shouldn't touch me, kiss me," she said breathlessly.

"How can I not when it is all I want to do?"

Her gaze flew to meet his with wonder. "When you left earlier with Moon Dove, I thought—"

"Her mother asked to see me. Moon Dove said it was to talk about her brother White Cat."

"And was it?"

He shook his head. "It was to talk about Moon Dove."

"About your marriage?"

He inclined his head.

Joanna stared at the man before her, and felt a deep ache in the region of her heart.

"So, it is set," she mumbled, pulling away.

"I have cared for you since you were a child," he said stiffly, hurt.

She looked at him. "I know," she whispered. "And I didn't see you. How was it that I didn't see you?"

One corner of his mouth curved in a crooked smile. "You saw me," he said. "But I was not big enough or strong enough then."

"I am sorry."

He stroked a strand of wet hair back from her face. "Perhaps you want Fireheart because you cannot have him?"

She tensed, jerked away. "Is that what you think?"

Dropping his hand, he shrugged. "It is not true?"

Was it true? Joanna wondered, studying the man she loved. She wanted him to give up Moon Dove, yet she had no intention of staying. Was that fair to him?

No.

Would she have still wanted him if he declared that he would not marry Moon Dove? He had said that their marriage was not set, yet he didn't say that it wouldn't be soon.

Yes, she would still want him if he chose her over Moon Dove. But the matrons would never permit it. She had been too long away from the Lenni Lenape people. What kind of wife would she make their chief?

Not as good a Lenape wife as Moon Dove.

"Please," she begged, "let us go back."

He stared at her hard. "You have given me your answer," he said without feeling.

No, she thought. *No, I haven't, but I can't make promises to you. If I could stay, I might try, but I have to go back to my uncle's estate. Who would run it if I didn't? It was the reason I spent all those terrible years with him, wasn't it?*

They left the water and dressed silently. Joanna avoided looking at Fireheart while he dressed for she was sure she'd give in and plead with him to make love to her right there and then if she looked.

If only she hadn't had a taste of what it was like to kiss him, hold him . . . hear his labored breath and his soft groans of pleasure. But she already had that one night . . . a beginning, she'd thought.

But it hadn't been a beginning, she realized with sadness. It had been the end.

CHAPTER 4

Chapter 10

Neville Manor
England
June 1727

"You know I would marry you if I could," John whispered as he fondled his lover's bare breast. "But you know the condition of Burton Estates. I must marry Joanna."

Despite his touching her, arousing her, Gillian pouted. "But what of us? What will happen to us when you wed her? I'll die if I can't be with you!"

He smiled before he bent to lick her nipple. He laved the tiny bud with his tongue until he heard her gasp, then lifted his head to meet her gaze.

"We'll continue to see each other," he promised. "I'll set you up in a place of your own, a lovely cottage. And I'll slip away to you every opportunity that is afforded me."

The whole idea sounded sordid to Gillian. She didn't want to be his mistress. She wanted to be his wife.

And Joanna was her best friend. If Joanna did marry John, how could she betray her like that?

He belongs to me! she thought with conviction. *Me!*

Still she had her doubts as to the feasibility of his plan. "I don't know, John," she said. "Isn't there some other way to acquire the funds that you need? Perhaps I could ask Father—"

"No!" John, who had bent his head to kiss her throat, lifted his head and narrowed his gaze. "I'll not take a single copper from that man."

Gillian's eyes filled with tears. Why couldn't John and her father be friends? There had been a time when she held on to the hope that she and John would marry with her father's blessing. For some reason, though, her father had taken an instant disliking to the man of her heart. She'd been trying ever since to change her father's mind about him.

"I'm sorry," she whispered, reaching up to weave her fingers in his hair. "I know he wasn't polite to you."

His expression softened as she rubbed his scalp and ran her fingers over his face to his lips. His eyes glowing, he kissed the hand at his mouth, then grabbed it and her other hand, tugged her farther down in bed, then clamped her arms above her head, leaving her arched and open to him.

"John, no," she gasped when she saw the look in his gaze. She wasn't finished discussing his marriage to Joanna, and he was trying to make her forget.

"Yes." He laughed softly before, using his mouth, he began a journey from her face to her breasts, where he paused to suckle her, drawing deeply, hard, from each swollen twin.

Soon, Gillian was writhing on the bed, arching up and into his mouth, begging him to take her, as he released her hands to kiss lower. Her stomach quivered as he dipped his tongue in her navel. The area between her legs filled with liquid warmth as he slowly ventured a path past her hips.

"Now, John!" she begged, gasping.

He rose up to eye her with a vision that was clear, calculating almost, but Gillian was too aroused to see. "Say you will continue to be my lover," he demanded.

"Yes," she cried. "Yes! How could I give this up?"

He groaned harshly then, and gave into the spiraling ecstasy that so easily ignited between them.

As they lay, breathing heavily in the aftermath, their minds were already contemplating the next round of lovemaking.

Days went by, and Joanna kept her distance from Fireheart. How could she not, when to be with him was a reminder of what she could never have?

With the improvement of Wild Squirrel's health, she began to visit the *sachem* daily, spending an hour or more with him each time. His coloring was much better, and the sparkle had returned to his dark eyes. He smiled more and spent a lot of time outside his wigwam, sitting in the yard, watching the children, speaking with the villagers.

One morning, Joanna was in the yard with him. She sat on a rush mat beside him, helping the chief's wife shell corn. Stormy Wind smiled as she watched Joanna efficiently strip the cob of its kernels into a bowl from which they'd later be spread out and left in the sun to dry.

"I remember you as a little girl," the woman told her.

Wild Squirrel nodded. "She was always about, asking questions, offering to help with the work of the women."

"You were a beautiful child, and now you are a beautiful woman."

Joanna flushed. "*Wa-neé-shih.*"

"We wish you to remain in our village," said Wild Squirrel. "This is your home. You should never have gone to England across the great sea."

"I can't stay," Joanna said. "I have obligations in England. Now that you are better, Grandfather, I must think of returning."

The chief opened his mouth, but his wife's gentle hand on his arm stopped him from speaking his thoughts. "We must not force her, my husband," she said softly.

"But Fire—"

She silenced him with a finger over his lips. "She might want to leave before Fireheart's wedding," she said, glancing at him with meaning.

The old man blustered. "Why shouldn't she stay?"

So they are getting married, Joanna thought, feeling a terrible ache. Stormy Wind was right. The last thing she wanted was to watch as Fireheart and Moon Dove wed.

"It is true, Grandfather," she said. "I must go home. I cannot stay to see the wedding."

"It is a time for celebration," Wild Squirrel said.

"I know," Joanna murmured. But she couldn't bear to see the man she loved marrying another.

"When must you go?" he asked her.

"Soon," she said noncommittally. "Soon."

She searched for another topic of conversation. She didn't want to discuss Fireheart. Every time she heard his name she experienced a sharp pain.

She glanced up from her work, saw Fireheart and Moon Dove on the opposite side of the village yard, talking, touching.

Joanna gasped and abruptly stood. "Forgive me, Grandmother, Grandfather, but I have something I must do."

She fled, out of the village, away from the sight of the pair.

Wild Squirrel looked at his wife with a sly smile. "You are right, my Wind. She loves Fireheart."

The matron nodded. "I see the way she watches him. She is hurting, but will do nothing to stop it."

"But what of Moon Dove? What are her wishes in the marriage?"

Stormy Wind frowned. "I do not know, but I think there is someone more important to Moon Dove than Fireheart."

"Hmmm." Wild Squirrel was thoughtful.

"I will see what I can learn from her mother and the women of our village," said Stormy Wind.

"Yes," replied Wild Squirrel, pleased with his wife's suggestion. "See what you can find out." He gazed wistfully off in the direction that Joanna had taken. "She is white, but she is more Lenape."

"She was away from us a long time. She clings to her English ways as if she will be punished should she leave them."

"Yes," he said. "I saw the tunic that Mary Wife made her. I thought she would wear it instead of the white woman's gown."

"She will wear it," his wife promised him. "She will wear it because she is Lenape and will know this soon." She set a corn cob aside to reach for another fresh ear. "Have you thought why she has not said when she will leave us?"

Wild Squirrel looked at her expectantly.

Stormy Wind's smile was soft. "Because she does not want to go."

"I hope you are right, wife," he said.

She gave him a sly look. "I am always right, my husband."

"Moon Dove," Fireheart said, "you have heard our grandmothers talking. They want us to marry. What do you think of this?"

The Indian maiden glanced up to regard him shyly. She had lovely dark eyes with long lashes. Her skin was smooth, and she had all of her teeth. His gaze fell to her mouth, which was perfectly formed. But he felt no heat when he looked at her . . . none of the heat he'd experienced when he was with Autumn Wind.

"It is an honor to marry our future chief," she replied quietly.

He narrowed his gaze, searching her expression for some hidden meaning. "So you would marry me?"

"If it is your wish," she said without smiling. She kept her eyes cast downward, a strange thing for one who had known him since they were children. In all other matters, she could face him steadily. Why was the topic of their marriage so different?

Was it the prospective intimacy between them that seemed difficult for her?

"Is there someone else in your heart?"

She didn't reply, and Fireheart wondered if her affections lay elsewhere.

"Do not answer that," he said. For he had no right to ask it, not when his own heart was otherwise engaged.

She seemed surprised by his statement. "You do not think I would make you a good wife?" she asked, looking troubled.

He smiled and touched her arm. "I think you would make a good wife." It was his role as her husband that he doubted.

She grinned then, like the sunshine bursting forth from behind a cloud. "I will give you many sons."

Fireheart nodded, and hid the anguish he felt that his children would not come from the woman he loved.

Autumn Wind. It had always been Joanna.

Why did she have to come back now when he had

forgotten what it was to be hurt by her? Why couldn't he make himself forget how good she felt in his arms?

Such discussion between a man and woman contemplating marriage were unusual for his people, but Fireheart couldn't begin the courtship ritual until he was sure that Moon Dove wanted the match as well. It might be a decision for the village matrons, but it was his life, and he had too many responsibilities to worry about an unhappy wife.

But Moon Dove seemed content to marry him. He would marry her and make her happy. And she would make him a good Lenape wife.

Grave Point
England

"I want to go with you." Gillian sat naked on the bed, while John dressed for the day's work. They were discussing John's trip to the New World to fetch Joanna Neville.

"I don't think that is wise," he said.

She scowled. "Why not?"

"For 'tis a terribly long journey. People die onboard ship. I wouldn't want anything bad to happen to you." He stopped in the act of dressing to reach down toward the bed to brush the top of Gillian's head with his light fingertips.

"And because Joanna will be there," he added in a low husky voice, "and I don't know if I'll be able to keep my hands off you."

Her expression softened. "Please." She lay back on the bed, lowering the covers, arching upward, tempting him with the sight of her belly and breasts. He released her and straightened. She was mollified by the hot flash of desire in his gaze. "I'll not worry about the danger if I'm with you."

"Gillian—"

"If I promise to behave?" she asked softly, sliding her body up sensually on the sheets.

He swallowed hard. With his trousers on and his shirt unbuttoned, he moved toward the bed. The sex between them had been particularly good during the night. Lately, he had felt a need for her that surpassed his desire for any other woman.

It would be hard to leave her behind, he thought. But he should. And what of Joanna? Could he hide his desire for Gillian in front of the woman he planned to marry?

Gillian moved on the bed, shoving the bedcovers down farther, exposing the dark nest of curly hair between her legs. "Do you really have to work so early?"

They were in Gillian's bedroom. Her parents were away for the night. Gillian had sneaked him past the servants, but assured him that none of the help would tell if they saw him coming or leaving.

There had been an added thrill to their lovemaking, bolstered by the fact that they were doing something as illicit as having sex beneath her father's roof.

"Gillian," John rasped harshly as he reached out to stroke her leg.

"It's such a long day and I'll miss you," she purred, stretching her body languidly. "Come back to bed for a little while."

"I should go." She looked so warm, so lush . . . so inviting, he thought. Just another hour. What harm could there be if he stayed another hour? Her parents weren't expected home any time soon.

She opened her legs slightly, giving him a better view of her hidden secrets. Watching him closely, she touched herself briefly, drawing his attention to her actions, pleased to see the way the expression in his eyes changed.

"*Please, John.*"

His shaft was rock-hard beneath his breeches. John

wanted to take her, thrust deeply inside her warmth, until she cried out with release. She made him feel huge and tall and all man. She didn't want Michael. It wasn't the first twin she loved. She desired him, only him—John Burton, the second son to his father, but the one who came first in this incredibly lovely woman's affections.

She stared at him with beautiful violet eyes, blinked up at him with thick dark eyelashes. "John—"

But he was already pulling off his shirt, tugging down his breeches. He turned, and felt proud when she gasped at the size of his throbbing manhood. He grinned, preening for her.

"John, darling." She held out her arms to him, and with a laugh, he pounced onto the bed.

Their lovemaking was rough, frenzied. When it was over, and both were reeling from the sensual pleasure, Gillian rolled to her side with her head propped on her hand.

"John," she said softly, "let me go to the New World with you."

His breath laboring, he opened his eyes, and tried hard to stifle his impatience for she looked like a fairy queen, a beautiful sensual wood nymph. "Gillian—"

"Please, John." With her other hand, she traced a path from his chest to his stomach, then lower still. When she took his limp manhood into her fingers, his eyes glistened, and he hardened immediately.

"I'll be good, John," she promised softly, rubbing him. "See how good I can be." She bent her head and took all of him into her mouth.

He groaned as the ecstasy began to build again and so soon. She pleasured him until he was hot and throbbing and unfulfilled, but desperate for satiation. She straightened to smile at him, her violet eyes glistening with passion and promise. "Please?" she whispered.

"Yes, yes," John rasped, his body taut and throbbing

with passion. "You can go with me. Just finish what you started, damn it."

With a mewl of happiness, Gillian continued until they were both sated, exhausted, and immensely pleased with themselves.

Chapter 11

Joanna was convinced that, given her time away and her duty to Neville Manor, she should leave the village as soon as could be arranged. She couldn't travel alone. She sought out her cousin's husband, and asked Rising Bird to send word out to the nearest white settlement to find a suitable guide for her.

"I can take you," Rising Bird said.

But Joanna wouldn't hear of it.

"You are needed here," she told him. "What if the Iroquois return and attack not Bear Paw's village but Little River?"

And Joanna was concerned about Rising Bird's reception in the English settlement. She knew first-hand how the white man regarded the Lenape people. Rising Bird was a kind man. He didn't deserve to be treated badly, which she was sure would happen if he came with her into an English encampment.

Mary studied her cousin with sad eyes. "Must you go? We were just getting reacquainted."

"I think it's best," Joanna replied. "I've been away from England for too long. Neville Manor is mine now. I need to return to ensure that all of my employees are well cared for.''

Her cousin was quiet after that, and Joanna could tell that the advent of her departure bothered Mary.

Joanna wished she could stay, but she had responsibilities in England, duties she'd neglected for too long. John was no doubt doing a good job in her absence, but it wasn't fair to continue to burden the man with her affairs.

She frowned. Michael Burton would need his brother John at Burton Estates. Although John had looked forward to overseeing Neville Manor, she didn't suppose he'd expected her to be gone this long.

How long has it been? she wondered. In her mind, she tried counting the weeks. Had it really been seven months since she'd left England? Was it July? August? She couldn't be sure. Time seemed to stand still in Little River. There were no schedules to follow. People simply got up and ate, went about their chores as they wished, dined as they desired, and finished their day in the same way.

It was such a peaceful and easy life, marred only by intruders such as the Iroquois who wanted to reign in terror over the land. She hoped that the problem with the Cayuga was finished, that Bear Paw and Fireheart were wrong and the enemy had no intention of coming back, at least for now.

Rising Sun finally agreed that he should stay at the village. ''I will send someone to search for Mr. Grace.''

Joanna smiled. Mortimer Grace had been a wonderful guide on the journey here. She would be happy to travel again in his company. He knew the area well. She felt safe with him.

''*Wa-neé-shih,*'' she told him.

''You are most welcome,'' he said in perfect English, which made her grin.

Later, alone with her own thoughts, Joanna realized

the real reason she wanted to leave was due to Fireheart. She didn't want to wait until the matrons decreed that Fireheart and Moon Dove would wed. Her heart couldn't bear the pain. She didn't want to stay and listen as the village celebrated the announcement of Fireheart's upcoming marriage.

Why then did she feel so terrible about the prospect of leaving? Of not seeing Fireheart again? She couldn't stop envisioning him with Moon Dove . . . holding her . . . sleeping with her . . . their joining in the most intimate way possible. . . .

She wished she had lain with him that night. Joanna had wanted to feel him inside of her so badly, but reason had ruled for the both of them, and they'd decided to wait.

Wait for what? Now there would be no intimacy between them. She would be leaving soon and have nothing to sustain her throughout the long lonely years ahead but the memory of their brief time together.

Tears filled her eyes as she lay in the darkness, huddled within the beaver pelt lining her sleeping pallet. The night was cool for an August summer, but she suspected that the chill she felt was more from within. She knew that once she left, she might never again return, never again see Mary and Rising Bird. She would never again be able to spend time with Wild Squirrel, his wife Stormy Wind, or her good friend Little Blossom.

But the thing that most saddened her was that she knew her heart would remain in Little River forever, with her beloved Fireheart. When she returned to England, she would be but an empty shell, living in a dreary manor that had been left to her by her uncle.

"Will you walk with me?" Mary asked softly as Rising Bird left to arrange for a messenger. The brave had said he had an idea where Grace might be currently staying.

"If you'd like," Joanna said congenially. She followed her cousin from the village onto a path that led in the opposite direction from the lake. They walked in silence for a time until Joanna spied a stream ahead. "Oh, look! Does that feed from the lake?"

Mary shrugged. "I don't know for certain. There is a river before us. We had set up our village in a clearing near the river, and then we found the lake. Wild Squirrel thought the area near the lake a better place for the village, so we moved it."

They had continued walking as Mary spoke. There, through a break in the trees, Joanna spied the sparkle of water.

"Is that it? Over there?" she asked.

"Yes." Mary changed direction. "Come and I'll show you."

They left the path, cutting through the forest until they reached the river's edge. The river was lovely, adequate for the needs of the Lenape people, but Joanna could see why Wild Squirrel had decided to move his village to the larger lake. From the direction of the water flow, she realized that the river emptied into the lake. It probably fed the stream they'd passed as well.

The forest was beautiful at this time of year. There had been enough rainfall to keep the foliage a bright green. The ground was dry, but not dusty either. Joanna spied wildflowers growing near a clump of briars. She thought to pick one, but decided against it when she saw the number of thorns on their stems.

Mary was silent as they walked for a time along the river. Finally, she halted and gestured to a natural seat made by an unusually low limb of a tree.

Joanna had worn her doeskin tunic that day so she hopped onto the limb easily, settling herself next to Mary once her cousin was seated.

"Joanna," Mary began, sounding strange.

Joanna looked at her. "What's wrong?"

"We need to talk. I want to know about your life in England."

"No," Joanna said. "I don't want to talk about it."

"Joanna—"

"I can't," she said, her eyes filling with tears. She silently cursed her weakness. "I'm sorry." She climbed down from the tree. "If this is why you wanted me to come—"

Mary hopped down behind her. "Don't!" She hurried forward to clasp her young cousin's arm. "Joanna, stop, please." She was on the verge of tears herself as she turned Joanna to face her. "You told me that you were unhappy there," she said, her voice hoarse. "Don't you see? I have to know! I sent you there, and I need to know!"

Joanna stared at her cousin, and realized how upset she was. "It's all right, Mary. I'm here and I'm fine. Whatever happened years ago, it doesn't matter now."

"Are you certain?" Mary asked brokenly.

Filled with sympathy, something she hadn't expected to feel, Joanna smiled as she caught Mary's hand and gave it a squeeze. "*Kihiila.*" She tugged her hand as she started back toward the village. "Let's go."

"I don't want you to leave," Mary admitted.

A shudder went through Joanna. "Thank you. I needed to hear that although it doesn't change the fact that I must."

"Why?"

"I have property to care for now. People who rely on me."

"Will you come back?"

"I don't know." Joanna's voice was barely a whisper. She didn't think she could bear seeing Fireheart married to another, especially years from now when they'd have had children.

"How soon will you leave?"

"As soon as we hear from Mortimer Grace," Joanna said.

"Does your leaving have anything to do with Fireheart?"

Joanna felt a jolt. "I don't know what you mean—"

"You care for him. I've watched you." Mary smiled. "You love him, don't you?"

"No!" she denied. At her cousin's look, she lowered her gaze and admitted, "Yes."

"I understand."

Joanna blinked and looked at her. "You do?"

Mary nodded. "Come on. Let's go back and spend some time together in the village before you have to leave."

The Iroquois came in the night. They entered the village with shrill war cries, and tomahawks and war clubs raised to fight. Joanna heard the wild screams and jerked up in bed, gasping.

"Stay here," Rising Bird ordered as he grabbed his weapons and ran out into the night.

Mary and Joanna huddled together and listened to the fighting.

Dogs barked in the compound. Joanna heard a man shriek with pain and held Mary tighter. She heard the pain-filled squeal of an animal.

"How can we just stay here?" she whispered, terrified. Her mind raced with thoughts of the others within the village. Wild Squirrel, Little Blossom, the children . . . *Fireheart.*

"We must listen to Rising Bird," Mary answered. Joanna could feel her cousin's trembling.

Were they going to die? What had happened to the Lenape guards watching the village? Had they been taken by surprise and then murdered?

Joanna pulled herself from her cousin's arms.

"What are you doing?" Mary whispered.

"I'm going to see what's happening."

"No, Joanna! Stay inside," her cousin warned as she watched the younger woman move to the door.

"I'll just take a peek." She raised the deer flap just a little, using the small opening to peer outside. She saw nothing at first, and then there was movement between two wigwams.

Joanna felt her heart begin to pound hard as she spied an Iroquois warrior entering the lodge across the way, and heard the screams of its occupant.

"Quick, Mary!" Joanna cried. "Find us some weapons! An Iroquois has entered the lodge of Woman with Eyes of Hawk!"

"What!" Mary scrambled to her side after grabbing a knife and a tomahawk.

Joanna stared at the choice of weapons with horror. "Which one can you use?"

"The knife," Mary said. "You take the tomahawk, but be careful!"

Accepting the tomahawk, Joanna found the weapon to be lighter than she'd thought. She lifted it with one hand to test her strength. "Let's go!"

Mary caught her arm. "Where?"

"To see if we can help!"

"And get ourselves killed?"

Joanna flashed her a glance. "There is only one Iroquois, and there are two of us."

Despite Mary's objections, Joanna slipped from the wigwam and hurried to the next lodge. Her mouth dry with fear, she raised the door flap, and reared back in surprise at what she saw.

Woman with Eyes of Hawk stood over the prone body of the Iroquois warrior. The matron met Joanna's gaze and grinned. "Stupid Cayuga didn't know that this matron is good with a war club."

Joanna saw then that the woman had a war club of her own, one she'd apparently held in readiness should someone enter and attack. Her fear receding slightly, Joanna grinned at the older woman. Her grin became a chuckle.

"Is he dead?" Mary asked, coming in from behind.

Woman with Eyes of Hawk shook her head. Her eyes gleamed with satisfaction. "He is not dead. We will leave his death to our village men."

"Shouldn't we tie him up then?" Joanna asked.

The other women agreed. While they worked to bind the man with ropes made of sinew, the sounds of fighting within the village continued.

Joanna shivered when she heard a child's cry, followed by a woman's scream. She stood, after securing her piece of sinew on the Indian, and regarded the two women with wide eyes.

"We just can't wait here!" she said, hugging herself with her arms.

Woman with Eyes of Hawk rose and patted her shoulder. "It will be over soon."

"That is what scares me." Joanna picked up the tomahawk from where she had set it down earlier.

"Our men will win. They have prepared for this."

Mary and Joanna exchanged glances, each hoping that the old matron was right.

The village became silent suddenly, and Joanna felt the eerie quiet more than the noise. "What's happening?" she whispered, going to the door.

"No," Mary said. "Stay away from the doorway. We'll know the situation soon enough."

Suddenly, they heard a loud, keening wail right outside the door flap. It was the sound of a pain so deep that it raised the hair on Joanna's arms and neck. Startled, she hurried to look outside.

"Joanna!" She heard Mary's hushed warning cry, but Joanna refused to listen. She had to know who that was.

She moved the door flap, ready to spring to someone's defense, then halted. The sight before her shocked her. It was Rising Bird's wild cry she'd heard.

He stood peering into his wigwam, looking grief-stricken.

Joanna understood the situation immediately "Rising Bird!" she cried.

He spun at the sound, his expression frantic. Then he saw Joanna with his wife and the old matron behind her, and joy entered his features. "Mary!" he cried.

With a low moan of understanding, Mary swept past Joanna and into her husband's open arms.

Woman with Eyes of Hawk moved closer to Joanna. "He thought that you both had been kidnapped."

Joanna nodded, moved by the emotional display of love between Mary and her husband. "They love each other."

"*Kihiila*," the old woman said, moving to Joanna's side. "It is a bond such as this that you wish for your own."

Surprised, Joanna glanced over at Woman with Eyes of Hawk. She opened her mouth to protest, but found herself nodding instead. "It must be wonderful to be loved that much."

The matron's smile was gentle. "You are loved that much, Autumn Wind. You are daughter to the Lenape. You are much loved by all of us."

Joanna was deeply touched by the woman's words. It wasn't the type of love she'd meant, but Woman with Eyes of Hawk had pleased her.

"I have been gone a long time," she said.

"We are your people. You were gone, but now you've come home."

The younger woman sighed. "I wish it were that simple. I must go back. I have responsibilities there, people who depend on me."

"There is no one else to take your place?"

It was something to which Joanna had never really given much thought. She had been groomed, molded, and beaten into the position of Roderick

Neville's heiress. What would happen if she did choose not to return to Neville Manor? Who would manage the estate? Who would care about all who lived and worked there?

"I don't know," Joanna murmured. But it was something to think about . . . to stay here in the New World among the Lenape.

The thought made her happy until she remembered that it was possible, and probable, that Moon Dove would one day be Fireheart's wife.

Saddened, she shook her head. She couldn't stay. It would hurt too much to stay. Some physical force beyond understanding drew her to Fireheart. She couldn't remain and live each day when she might see Moon Dove and Fireheart happy together. She didn't want the pain of a broken heart.

My life is in England.

Joanna smiled as Rising Bird opened his arms to invite her into his hug. She moved toward him easily, needing the comfort of those fatherly arms.

It would have been wonderful if I could have stayed, she thought, hugging Rising Bird and Mary tightly. And she fought against tears.

Chapter 12

The Iroquois had been conquered. Everyone within the village had survived the attack. There were a few injuries during the fight, but nothing serious, nothing that the shaman's magic and healing powers couldn't cure.

As she milled about the village yard afterward, Joanna saw mothers comforting children, wives tending husbands with minor cuts. Several Cayuga braves lay dead, waiting for burial. The brave tied up in Woman with Eyes of Hawk's lodge would be dispensed with later in a manner Joanna didn't want to contemplate although she supposed the man deserved it.

It was dawn as she headed toward the lake, hoping to find Fireheart. There had been no sign of him in the village. She had checked the *sachem*'s wigwam and found Wild Squirrel awake and alert, and alone with his wife. After ensuring both were fine, she had wandered about the village, checking the lodge of Fireheart's clan, the Wolf, but he wasn't to be found there. Although she knew she should stay away from him, Joanna couldn't rest until she saw for herself that Fireheart was safe and uninjured.

Rising Bird had told her that their warriors were successful because of Fireheart. He had set up a plan in the event of an Iroquois attack, and the plan had been a smart one. Rising Bird had told her that Fireheart would make a good *sachem*.

There was no one on the path through the woods to the lake. As Joanna negotiated the trail, it occurred to her that if she did find Fireheart she might not find him alone. Since she had avoided his company, Fireheart might have sought out Moon Dove.

She felt a little ache inside at the thought, but it didn't stop her from continuing to the lake. Her need to see Fireheart was too great.

There were a few villagers at the water. Little Blossom was there, tending her husband Broken Bow's shoulder. Joanna stopped briefly to see how the two were faring before she walked along the lakeshore.

The sun was but a hint of light in the sky. A soft breeze tossed the surface of the lake, creating ripples. Joanna stopped to pick up a rock and toss it into the water. Disappointed that Fireheart was nowhere to be found, she picked up another and threw it in.

The fact that she hadn't seen Moon Dove didn't make her feel any better, Joanna realized. Were Fireheart and the Indian maiden together, comforting one another after such a terrible night?

She continued along the lakeshore, well away from the village and the area used most often by the Lenape. Soon, she was enmeshed in vegetation as she moved away from the water's edge and headed inland. It didn't matter where she was going. She just wanted to get away.

As she walked, she had the mental image of Fireheart with Moon Dove. The pain of her thoughts brought tears to her eyes. She walked on, uncaring of where she was going or whether or not she could find her way back. She saw a small clearing, and headed for a huge boulder on the edge. She sat down, wiped the tears from her eyes, then thought of Fireheart and cried harder.

She had to leave! How long had it been since Rising Bird had sent for Mortimer Grace? she wondered. A week? A fortnight?

It's only been a few days. She stood and began to pace the clearing. It suddenly became imperative that she get away. She didn't want to love Fireheart. She wanted to be happy without him.

Would she ever be happy without Fireheart? Could she go back to England and find a love of her own?

He is my love.

Little Blossom said that Fireheart was destined to marry Moon Dove, she thought.

"But it hasn't been decided yet by the matrons," she murmured.

But the announcement could be made soon, an inner voice taunted.

Sniffing, Joanna plunked herself down on the rock and gave in to tears.

Later, when her tears had stopped and she felt tired from crying, Joanna stood and started back the way she'd come. She had long since left the path, and she didn't recognize anything familiar as she started back. For the first time, she wondered if she was lost.

She paused to study her surroundings, and debated about which direction to go. She made a decision and started forward again. When she detected no sign of the village, she began to panic. She continued on, determined to find her way back. When exhausted, she stopped for a few minutes to rest.

You can't be far, she told herself. The sun had risen in the sky, and the sight cheered her. Once they discovered her missing, the villagers would search for her. They knew how to read the trail. They'd find signs of her travel, rescue her quickly, and bring her home.

Should she stay here and wait? she wondered. Her head began to throb, and she cradled it in her hands. She imagined her eyes were still red from crying, and her face was probably streaked from wiping her cheeks with her dirty hands.

A rustle in the brush brought Joanna's head up. Alert, she scanned the forest, her muscles tensed with fear.

Iroquois? Was it possible that one had escaped and was still in the area?

She tried hard to remember what she'd been told about the fight, but for the life of her she couldn't recall whether or not all the Cayuga had been killed or captured.

The sound came again, drawing her attention to the right. She saw the brush move, and she froze. Her mouth dry, she stared as the grass parted and an animal exited the forest, entering the clearing.

Joanna gaped. A dog? Was that a dog? She stood and moved closer. It looked like a puppy, one of those that lived in Little River, the offspring of one of the larger dogs. Pointy-eared, long-nosed, and with tiny legs, it was a little thing that could be dangerous, but was harmless.

She crouched low, calling to the dog softly. "Here, boy. Come here, boy."

A snap of a dry twig beneath someone's foot made her stand up in a hurry. She backed away, a lump of fear in her throat, as shrubs, trees, and other brush moved then parted, and a male figure stepped out.

Joanna gasped until her vision cleared and she recognized the man before her. "Fireheart!"

"Autumn Wind." He didn't seem surprised to see her as he followed the puppy's path and approached. He paused within several yards of her.

To Joanna's amazement, the puppy spied him and

trotted back to stand at his feet, whimpering. Fireheart bent to pick up the puppy, which he tucked in
one arm. He began to gently stroke the dog's head
with the other hand.

The picture of man and dog made Joanna's heart
melt with warmth and tenderness.

"What are you doing here?" she asked.

"I had something to do," he said.

What? she wondered, but didn't question him. "I'm
glad to see that you were not hurt in the attack."

He shook his head. "Mary told me you were not
injured. This is good."

They spoke as if strangers, not like they'd embraced
and kissed and swam naked together, and it saddened
her.

Fireheart glanced around the clearing and
frowned. "Why have you come here?"

"I didn't mean to. I got lost. I've been looking for
the village."

To her surprise, he smiled. "You are not lost." He
gestured in the direction she'd been traveling. "The
village is there." Then he showed her a few ways to
track her trail.

She sighed, relieved. "Who is your little friend?"
she asked, enchanted.

He glanced down at the puppy with a smile. "This
is Little Nose. She is daughter to Big Ear." He met
her gaze with a regretful look. "Big Ear died in the
attack. I came out into the forest to bury her."

"Poor dear," Joanna said, moving toward the man
and dog. She recalled the squeal of an animal's pain
and shivered.

Little Nose was an adorable little pup, she thought.
And now the dog had lost his mother. Tears pricked
behind Joanna's eyelids as she reached out to stroke
the puppy's head. She knew well what it was to love
and lose one's mother.

Her fingers collided briefly with Fireheart's before

she pulled them away, dropping them to her sides. She glanced up to find that Fireheart was watching her with an expression that caused her to ache inside.

"Little Nose is beautiful," she said.

"You are beautiful," he murmured, surprising her.

She wanted so badly to feel his embrace, but knew it mustn't happen. She couldn't allow her emotions to rule her head. "Fireheart—"

"I speak only the truth, Joanna. I will not be silent. My eyes see beauty, and so I must say it."

He bent and set the puppy down. The dog barked until Fireheart withdrew something from the pouch at his breechcloth, a piece of dried meat, which he gave to Little Nose.

He stood then and the look in his eyes made Joanna catch her breath. "During the attack, I was afraid for you. I feared that you were hurt or kidnapped. When I could leave Wild Squirrel, I hurried to find you, but you were nowhere to be found. Mary said you were fine so I had to believe it. But I wanted to see you with these eyes."

She nodded. "I worried about you, too."

Her admission made his gaze brighten. "What are we to do, Autumn Wind? You must leave, and I must stay. I want to touch you, and you want to touch me, I think." He paused as if to wait for her answer.

"Yes," she breathed.

"I want you."

Gladness swelled in her breast then dissipated with her next thought. "Yes, but what if the matrons decide that you should marry Moon Dove?"

"If you would stay—" he began, then stopped.

She felt a rush of hope. "Yes?"

He shook his head and averted his glance. She saw the way his broad, powerful shoulders slumped, and felt like she'd been kicked in the stomach. He looked vulnerable and defenseless. Unable to keep from offering comfort, she approached him, touched a spot beneath his right shoulder blade in his muscled back. She saw the ways his muscles tightened and relaxed beneath her touch.

He spun then, caught her arm, and tugged her against him. Cupping her face, he stared into her eyes, at her mouth. With a harsh groan, he kissed her hotly, deeply, until Joanna moaned softly and put her hands on his shoulders and clung.

He released her with a muffled curse and stepped away. "This man is sorry," he said huskily. There was regret in his dark eyes . . . yet there was something more. It was that other emotion simmering in the dark depths that captured her attention and her heart.

"Fireheart," she whispered.

He met her gaze, saw the invitation in her green eyes, and with a wild cry, he came back to her, embracing her once again.

They kissed passionately, then softly like two lovers learning to pleasure the other. Joanna gloried in the strength of his arms, in the warmth and joy of his kiss. She wanted to finish what they'd started. She wanted to be joined with this man.

"We should get back," she said against his chest as he held her.

He nodded. "*Kihiila.*"

"I don't want to go."

"Then let us stay."

"But Moon Dove—"

He frowned. "She wishes to marry the *sachem.*"

"And isn't that you?" She glanced up to read his expression.

He closed his eyes, tightened his hold on her. "No, Wild Squirrel is our *sachem.*"

"Yes, but someday—"

"Wild Squirrel will live many summers yet," he insisted.

Joanna, studying his beloved features, hoped he was right, but she'd wondered. . . .

When she had seen him today, she'd been surprised to see the return of an ailing old man.

"I'm sorry for what I did—when we were children," she said. She needed to say it before she left. She'd been horrid to Yellow Deer, and the young brave he'd been hadn't deserved such treatment. She wanted Fireheart to know that she regretted ignoring the tender feelings of a young boy.

He loosened his hold on her. "You were beautiful to a young boy's heart," he said softly, with a gentle smile. "You are more than beautiful to this grown man's. . . ." He tapped his chest, drawing her attention to the superb condition of his muscular flesh.

She looked at him with her heart in her eyes, and a lump rising in her throat. "You are the one who is beautiful," she murmured, giving in to the urge to touch his chest.

The warmth of his flesh burned beneath her fingers. She saw by his reaction that he enjoyed her touch. She trailed light fingertips to his nipple, and was surprised to see it rise into a tight bud, much like her response when he caressed her breasts.

They stood, facing each other. Fireheart remained still. Her breasts tingled and a curious sensation coursed through her as she continued to stroke him. He didn't have to touch her to make her ache and throb down below.

She saw him studying her with heavy-lidded eyes. As his heart began to pound harder, she felt the thunder beneath her fingertips.

This is dangerous, she thought. *I shouldn't be touching him. He belongs to Moon Dove.*

Not yet, he doesn't, she reminded herself.

Was it wrong to want him for just a little while? Moon Dove might have him forever while she would have him only for this one moment. . . .

Wrong. She dropped her hands, pulled away.

It isn't wrong for he is not betrothed.

Fireheart caught her shoulders, ran his hands down her arms. She shivered with pleasure, and all her doubts faded as she ceased to think past the point of the pleasure he evoked in her.

"No," she breathed, but she wasn't trying to stop him. She was telling him with soft moans where to touch, where to pleasure her best.

He caught her under the legs and lifted her. Clinging to his neck, she was aware of the daylight, but she didn't care. Her body tingled with anticipation and warmth as he carried her from the clearing to a more secluded bed of grass.

He had no sooner set her down, than he was lifting her tunic hem, raising it over her head so that she stood naked and trembling before him.

She didn't move as he undressed. Her flesh throbbed and was infused with fiery warmth as she watched with interest as Fireheart removed his loincloth.

They stood facing each other, naked, unmoving. Fireheart touched her breast, and she closed her eyes in enjoyment of his caress.

When Joanna lifted her eyelashes, it was to see adoration, such awe in his expression as he continued to stroke her that she felt humbled.

He began to fondle both breasts simultaneously, rubbing her nipples until she moaned softly, and arched up into his hands. He bent his head, and tasted first one bud then the other. She stroked his hair as he suckled her. He caught her around the waist, and lowered her to the ground.

His head blocked out the sun as he settled his weight on her form. He shifted to continue his pleasuring of her breasts. Joanna opened her legs, anxious to feel all of him.

Fireheart had waited a long time for this moment.

She was sweeter, more responsive then he'd ever imagined. He had loved her as a boy, but now he adored, loved, and desired her as a man.

He was not ignorant of the pleasure points of a woman. He raised himself up from her, and reached down to touch the tiny wet nub between her legs. She gasped, widening her eyes, and he kissed her, pleased that she had never been touched that way by a man.

He would be her first if not her last, he realized. The thought of another man kissing her, loving her, bothered him, and he vowed to put his mark on her. She might lie with someone else, but she would never forget Fireheart . . . just as he might marry another, but Joanna would always have his heart.

He slid his finger inside her moist cavern as he nipped on her breasts. Her innocent touches, the way her hands fluttered over his back and down his sides to his hips, incited his desire. Hers were the lightest of inexperienced touches, yet he felt as if she'd known exactly where and how to please him.

He was nearing the breaking point. She was wet and ready for him. He kissed her tenderly as he eased between her thighs, pressing his shaft to her moist opening. He pushed slightly, heard her gasp, and pulled back.

"I will try not to hurt you." The thought of giving her pain upset him. He wanted her only to experience pleasure, such ecstasy that she would soar. . . .

"Please," she begged, urging him with her hands on his hips. " 'Tis all right. I'll be fine. Please . . . love me."

She didn't have to ask for his love. She already had it although he had a feeling that she didn't believe herself worthy of such devotion.

So he set out to prove it to her. He entered her with one thrust. Then, when she had adjusted herself around him, he began to move. Sliding in and out of her moist warmth, he held himself back. He wanted her to climax first, then he would pleasure her again before he found his release.

But in her innocence, she grabbed hold of his buttocks. She squeezed his cheeks, urging him on with soft words until he was hot and throbbing and gritting his teeth with the pain of holding back his climax.

She kissed him with her soft mouth, nibbled on his ear, ran her hands down his back, then clutching his buttocks again, she arched up and tightened herself around him.

"No!" he groaned. He was losing himself in her.

"Yes," she cried, embracing him tightly.

Joanna gasped and stiffened as sensation pooled in her breasts and between her thighs. She lifted her head and buried her face in his neck, then on impulse she ran her fingers down over his thighs. She heard his harsh groan, and her pleasure intensified. Soon she was clinging to him and spiraling high in a world of delight unlike anything she'd ever experienced before.

Fireheart, she thought as he joined her in her world of sensual ecstasy.

"Joanna," he rasped as he finally found his release.

Chapter 13

They lay close, touching as their hearts slowed and their breathing eased. Joanna rolled onto her belly, and unable to resist caressing her, Fireheart stroked her back. Her skin was smooth and soft and very white. He studied the darkness of his hand against her pale back and enjoyed the difference. She was soft where he was hard. She was smooth where he was rough.

If only he could make her stay . . . he would marry her and make her his forever. She could be happy in the village; she had been before. Why not again?

Yet he knew she had changed. Something was different about her. There was much he didn't know about her life in England. She had suffered there. He wanted to know what had put that sadness in her beautiful green eyes.

He rose up on his elbow, and ran his hand over her buttocks to her legs. He saw tiny thin lines across the back of her thighs. *Scars*, he realized and frowned.

"What are these?" he asked softly, rubbing them gently with his fingers.

He felt her stiffen. "Nothing."

He became alert to her inner pain. "Where did you get them?" he pushed.

She rolled over, and scrambled to her knees. "It doesn't matter."

He caught her chin firmly, but not hurting. "Joanna, who hurt you?"

She pulled away, averted her glance, but not before he saw the tears glistening in her lovely green gaze.

"Why?" she asked. "Why do you want to know?"

He touched her cheek, then drew her gently to face him. "Someone hurt you," he said softly. "I do not like it that someone hurt you." He leaned in to briefly kiss her mouth. "Who did this to you?" His voice was soft, but he was seething inside toward the person responsible.

She shuddered, and hugged herself with her arms. "My uncle."

Joanna didn't look at him, afraid that he would guess the truth, that she wasn't the woman he thought she was. She was unlovely and unlovable. Fireheart had made her forget for a little while, but now . . .

He was silent for so long that she was afraid to meet his gaze. "Your uncle hit you?"

She nodded, but still didn't look.

"With what?"

She whispered her response. "A riding crop." Then, in a halting voice, she explained what that was and what her uncle had done.

His fury building toward her uncle, Fireheart mumbled an Indian curse beneath his breath.

She glanced at him. Seeing his anger, she cringed away from him until she realized by the way he was stroking her bare arm that his anger was directed at the pain she'd suffered, not at her.

"Your uncle beat you," he repeated.

She closed her eyes in shame. "Yes."

"Why?" Fireheart was furious. How could the man have hurt Joanna?

He could sense that she didn't want to tell him.

"Autumn Wind," he said gently. "Tell me."

"He didn't like me to have Lenape things."

Rage burned in his breast, threatening to erupt. "You wore your tunic, the one Little Blossom's mother made for you?" he asked gently.

She was surprised that he'd remembered. "Yes. First, he was angry because I wore my tunic. I loved that dress," she added, sounding like a child. She shied away from his glance. "Then it was my moccasins." She gave a soft sob and hugged herself tighter.

Fireheart pulled her arms away from her body and tugged her close. "Don't cry, *Kitehi*," he murmured, feeling her pain.

She snuggled against him, her lips against his breast. "He was a hateful man," she said, pulling away slightly. "I wanted to leave, but I couldn't." She shuddered within his arms.

"The one time I tried to escape him I was punished," she continued. She held up her arm and he saw a tiny scar near her wrist. "He hit me. He wore a ring on his hand . . . it cut me. I wasn't hurt as much as I was shocked by his cruelty."

As she felt the comfort of Fireheart's arms, Joanna didn't elaborate on Roderick Neville's cruelties. She could feel the tautness of Fireheart's muscles. He was angry and upset. Why shouldn't he be? She withdrew from his embrace.

He would be wondering about her, thinking her a horrible person for driving her uncle to punish her so severely.

She reached for Fireheart again and clung. "I'm sorry."

His arms closed about her. He was silent, but he continued to hold her so she took comfort in his nearness, his gentle embrace.

Still hugging her, Fireheart eased her to the ground. They lay together, unmoving except for his stroking her back and lower. She closed her eyes and enjoyed it all . . . his tenderness, his touch . . . his soothing whispers.

She would remember these moments always, she thought. They would warm her during the long cold lonely nights back in England.

She slept for a time, and Fireheart realized he must have dozed, too. When he woke up, he watched her sleep. He studied Joanna for a long time, frowning. She lay on her side with her back facing him. He eyed the long expanse of soft skin and feminine curves from her smooth back down her spine to her buttocks and lower.

She had lived through an ordeal greater than what she had confided in him, he suspected. He sat up, saw her leg scars, and bent his head to tenderly kiss each one. Joanna stirred and rolled over. Catching sight of him, she smiled and held out her arms.

"Fireheart," she murmured.

He returned her smile, then flowed into her arms.

They made love again, slowly, as if each wanted to savor every moment. When they were done, they fell asleep until a wild cry from the distance jerked Fireheart from a sound sleep.

He experienced a terrible sense of foreboding.

Wild Squirrel was dead. Joanna listened in numbed shock as her cousin told her of the beloved *sachem*'s death.

"He went quietly," Mary said. "Stormy Wind was with him. He was happy and at peace."

As the pain of loss hit her hard, she studied the villagers gathered in the yard for the news. Little Blossom, her face lined with sorrow, stood holding her daughter Water Flower. Her husband Broken

Bow stood at her friend's side, his arm around his young wife's shoulders.

Woman with Eyes of Hawk's eyes were red as if she'd been crying although her face was stoic while the matron Red Dress, Moon Dove, the maiden's brother White Cat, and her mother Berry Tree stared vacantly ahead.

Joanna had returned to the New World because of Wild Squirrel. The man was the grandfather she'd never known. He'd treated her kindly when as a child she'd visited him, asking endless questions that would have tried the most patient man.

But not Wild Squirrel, she thought with sorrow. He had enjoyed Joanna's visits, and she had loved him fiercely. Now the *sachem* was dead, and Joanna had again lost someone she loved.

When the cry had come, Fireheart and Joanna had returned to the village separately. Fireheart had raced on ahead, and Joanna had lagged behind, bringing the puppy. The sense that something was wrong had hit them both while they were still in the forest clearing, stealing away the joy of the hours they'd spent together making love.

Suddenly, they were again two people destined to be apart. Strangers.

While still holding the puppy, Joanna searched for Fireheart and found him standing among a group of Lenape men. He didn't look like the lover she'd lain with only a short time ago. That man had worn a carefree look and a smile that was almost boyish. The warrior she saw now bore the weight of his new responsibilities heavily. Wild Squirrel was dead. Fireheart was the new chief.

Tears filled her eyes as she studied him. He'd been so tender, so wonderful. She willed him to look her way, then when he did, she wished she hadn't. His glance at her was brief, unemotional ... like a stranger's.

Joanna stroked the puppy absently until the animal whimpered and wanted to be put down. She hugged him to her chin briefly, taking comfort in the dog's fur and warmth. Then she released him with a last pat, setting him carefully on his feet. She watched as he scurried off to comfort one of the children.

She stood and glanced in Fireheart's direction. He met her gaze briefly again, unemotionally, before he turned away to continue his conversation with the men.

There would be much to do, Joanna realized with an aching heart. Preparations for the funeral ceremony would begin immediately, she thought.

Joanna knew that she would stay until the funeral ceremony was over even if Mortimer Grace arrived today to take her away. She hoped that the guide would come by the time the ceremony was done, if not before. Once Mr. Grace came, she could pack up her belongings, and leave the Indian village and the pain. She didn't think she could bear more heartbreak. Wild Squirrel had been ill a long while. He had seemed much better. Why couldn't he have lived?

He had known, she realized. *He had known his time left in this world was short, but no one, especially me, wanted to believe it.*

"Joanna." She felt Mary's arm surround her shoulders.

Joanna glanced at her cousin with tears in her eyes. "I loved him."

Her throat worked as Mary shared her grief. "I know you did," she whispered. "That's why I wrote you. I thought that you would be interested in news about our chief."

"He seemed better, didn't he?" Joanna said, her voice thick with tears.

Mary nodded. "He did. Stormy Wind had said that his appetite had returned, and you saw him up and about." Her expression darkened. "Things seemed to change after the attack—"

Joanna agreed. After the Cayugas raided the village, Wild Squirrel had seemed older, frailer. And in less than a full day he was dead. *It isn't fair!* she thought.

"I know," Mary said, hugging Joanna, making her realize that she must have cried it out loud.

"How can I help?" Joanna wanted to assist in the funeral ceremony.

"There will be food to prepare," her cousin murmured. "Let me ask Woman with Eyes of Hawk."

The Port of Philadelphia
Pennsylvania
September 1727

"We are here," Gillian said, stating the obvious. "Now what shall we do?"

Ignoring her, John studied the milling crowd near the dock.

"John?"

He looked at her then. "Oh, we find someone to take us into Indian Territory," he said.

She shivered. "Won't that be dangerous?"

"Undoubtedly," he said with impatience. "Gillian, you know why I had to come. Did you think I'd check into a hotel, and wait for someone to bring Joanna to me?"

"I—" She bit her lip. "I guess I didn't really think about it."

He scowled. "Would you like to go home?"

She thought of the terrible ship's voyage they'd just endured, and she pulled herself together. "No, no, I'll be fine." She touched his cheek, and made an effort to smile. The only good thing about the voyage was that she'd been with John. "I'll go wherever you go. It will be interesting to see the wilderness."

John knew she was lying, but his expression softened. She might try his patience at times, but he was glad she'd come. The journey would have been lonely without her.

He glanced back and saw a fellow who wore fine clothes. "I'll wager that bloke knows whom I should hire." Capturing Gillian's arm, he started in the man's direction.

"But, John, what about our belongings!" Gillian cried.

"I've already arranged for them to be sent to an inn," he said. He flashed her a lascivious grin. "I never said we wouldn't be spending any nights in comfort."

The scent of roasting meat filled the air as the Lenape women prepared the food necessary for the funeral ceremony for Wild Squirrel. In the wigwam of the *sachem,* the body of Wild Squirrel was laid out and being mourned by a group of village matrons who wailed over the body loudly. Stormy Wind, the chief's wife, had already donned the garb of a mourning widow. She had chopped off her hair until it stood in short spikes over her head. An old ragged buckskin had replaced her lovely doeskin kilt. She had discarded her beads and ornamental jewelry, and scrubbed her face free from any vermilion and face powder frequently used by the Lenni Lenape women.

Joanna entered the wigwam to pay her respects as was the English custom. She had seen a Lenape funeral before, but she'd been young and she remembered little.

Her gaze went first to the women keening a mournful song in the room, then to the chief lying upon his sleeping pallet. She had put on her tunic and tied back her blonde hair. Head bowed, she approached the bed to silently acknowledge and pray for the deceased man, her grandfather.

As the women continued to chant and sing, Joanna finished her prayer, and then met Stormy Wind's gaze. The woman's expression was stoic. Joanna knew, though, that for Stormy Wind to cry, moan, or show emotion of any kind would incite the others' ridicule. The widow of the deceased must show her grief in the ways of the Lenape ... like the cutting of her hair, the discarding of fancy garb, and painting her face black. Later, once Wild Squirrel was buried, Stormy Wind would be allowed to go and weep over his grave in private.

Joanna wanted to go to her, hug her, tell her how sorry she was for the loss of her husband, but this wasn't the time or the place to do it.

She stayed a short while, then left with the intention of offering her help where needed. She headed toward the fields where she was sure she'd find Mary harvesting vegetables for the feast.

Word had been sent to the surrounding Lenape villages. Wild Squirrel's death would bring many guests, many chiefs, to pay their respects to the deceased's family.

As she left the village for the forest, she wondered where Wild Squirrel would be laid to rest. It would be a place far from the village, a secluded place, a beautiful setting where a man who was loved would find his final resting ground.

The forest opened up into the fields, divided plots owned and worked by the matrons. Joanna spied her cousin picking beans. A basket of freshly harvested squash lay on the ground near her feet.

"Mary."

She didn't see Joanna's approach. Mary looked up, startled. "Joanna!"

Joanna smiled. "Can I help?"

"I am almost finished. You may carry the basket of beans back to the village."

She nodded and took the full basket of beans.

Mary bent to retrieve the squash, and the two women headed back toward the village.

"Is there anything else I can do?" Joanna asked softly, noting her cousin's grief-stricken expression. If Wild Squirrel had meant a lot to a little girl, he must have meant even more to Mary who had known him much longer.

"Soon, we'll have visitors, then the funeral ceremony will begin. Turtle That Hops and some of the other braves have asked to do the dance. Rising Bird would like to, but he knows it is best if the others do it."

Joanna understood why. Those selected to do the funeral dance would dance to the beat of the drums and the rhythm of the gourd and turtleshell rattles nonstop for three days. Rising Bird might be needed elsewhere. The braves who danced would not leave the ceremonial circle.

When the *sachem* died, his people usually mourned his death for a full year before replacing him, but while he was still alive, Wild Squirrel had decreed differently. He had asked Fireheart to take his place. His people needed a chief, he'd told the villagers. Fireheart must become *sachem* upon his death.

Fireheart was the chief, Joanna thought, the realization truly sinking in for the first time. What a tremendous responsibility for him. She knew he would carry the weight well. She only hoped he would find the happiness he deserved.

The guests started to arrive that day. They came from Bear Paw's village, all of them—the men and the women and children who had returned to their homes shortly before this recent attack. The wigwams were filled to capacity. Some of those who had come to mourn and pay their respects brought wigwams with them that could be easily constructed, then taken down and moved again.

A tall platform had been built in the ceremonial

house for Wild Squirrel's body. He would lie there for others to see while the dancers performed the funeral dance. With the arrival of the guests and the completion of the platform, several braves carried Wild Squirrel's body to the top. Then everyone gathered into the ceremonial house except those women who continued to prepare food for the villagers and their guests.

As she entered the ceremony house, Joanna looked at the platform and fought back tears. She saw that the different Lenape tribes sat together in separate areas around the perimeter of the room. The dancers stood with their faces painted black and the rest of their bodies oiled with bear grease. The drummers sat together inside the circle along with those performers who would keep time with their rattles.

Joanna stood on the fringe of the circle near the door, debating whether or not to stay. She searched for a sign of Fireheart and was surprised to see him among the dancers. Fireheart would be doing the dance, she realized with surprise.

Everyone in the circle sat on rush mats, cross-legged. They had brought with them small items, which lay near their feet, gifts for the deceased's family.

The gathering in the ceremonial house quieted as Fireheart stepped into the inner circle.

"We have come to mourn the loss of our *sachem.* It is a sad time for us, but it is a cause for celebration, too, as he has gone to follow a different path . . . a path with the Great Spirit. We must give thanks to the Spirits of Life for giving him to us, and we pray that his journey to the next world will be a safe one."

He nodded toward the drummers who began to play. The dancers formed a line and began to dance about the circle, their feet stepping in time to the rhythm of the beat. Soon, the sound of the Lenape rattles joined the drums, and the Indians raised their voices in song.

Joanna watched for a time, noting that she'd been mistaken about Fireheart. He did not dance but sat against one wall. His features were drawn; he looked tired. Joanna wanted desperately to go to him and offer him comfort, but knew such actions would be inappropriate.

He watched the dancers with an intensity that displayed deep emotion, deep loss for his dead uncle compounded by the new weight of responsibility that rested on his shoulders.

He had donned the cloak of mourning. Black streaks of paint coated his handsome face. He wore only his breechclout, but his skin had been oiled to a fine sheen, and he wore a beaded headband.

As she studied him, she willed him to look her way. He stared at her almost as if unseeing, then focused his gaze elsewhere. Hurt, Joanna remained only a few more moments before leaving the building.

With the sound of the Lenape music in her ears, Joanna approached the women who worked in the center square. She approached Little Blossom who silently handed her a knife and a basket of squash. Joanna sat in the yard, slicing squash and fighting back tears, her mind on Wild Squirrel and the one who would replace him.

"What's that?" John asked as he heard the drums in the distance.

"Indian war drums," their guide said.

"War drums!" Gillian gasped, snuggling close to John's side.

"Or the savages could be having a feast," the man replied without concern.

"As long as the main meal isn't a man," John joked.

Thomas Brown shrugged. "Who's to say?" he said as he continued along the trail.

They had hired the man in Philadelphia. He had seemed capable enough at the time, but now John wondered. Studying the man's rifle, he hoped that Brown was as experienced a woodsman as he'd claimed, and as good a shot with his gun.

John touched the pistol at his side, fingering the handle until the cool metal gave him comfort. He, if not Brown, was an excellent marksman.

"John! John!" Gillian whispered anxiously, tugging his arm as they followed Brown. "Is it true? Do the savages eat people?"

John met her worried gaze with a concerned one of his own. "I don't know," he whispered back. " 'Tis possible, I suppose."

"Why isn't Mr. Brown scared then?"

She looked terrified. John placed a comforting arm about her. "Perhaps the savages know him," he said. "Perhaps they are his friends."

Gillian relaxed slightly beneath his hold. "Then we'll be safe."

"As long as we don't make an enemy of Thomas Brown," John said darkly as he released her.

"I've been polite enough to him, haven't I?" Gillian said with worry.

His expression softening, John clasped her hand. "Yes, love, you've been more than polite to him. Don't you worry. I'm sure we'll be fine."

Gillian studied her surroundings fearfully. "I can't believe that Joanna has been living out here alone."

"She's not alone," he pointed out. "She's with her cousin." *In the village of heathens!* he thought with a scowl.

They'd had a surprise encounter with Joanna's servants in Philadelphia. Cara and Harry had been delayed, waiting for a ship. John had been dismayed to find out that Joanna had sent her servants home while she'd elected to stay longer. And he'd been shocked to discover that she had been living, not at a country manor house as he'd believed, but with heathen savages somewhere in the Pennsylvania wilderness. His only relief came from having learned from Cara and Harry that when the servants had last seen their mistress, Joanna had apparently been happy and safe.

Gillian shivered and hugged herself. "I didn't realize that her cousin lived with savages!"

John frowned. "Neither did I."

A noise in the brush made them freeze. They breathed a collective sigh of relief when a deer exited from the forest onto the trail, then took off after one brief look in their direction.

"John, what if she wants to stay?"

He shook his head, refusing to entertain the possibility. "I've no doubt that by the time we find dear Joanna, she'll be more than ready to come home."

The young woman nodded. "This place is wild and dangerous."

The sudden clap of gunfire made her shriek and cling to John. When Thomas Brown turned to them with a rabbit in his hand and a grin, Gillian scowled.

"Supper," Brown announced.

She fought to control her temper. *I mustn't make the man angry*, Gillian reminded herself. "How nice, Mr. Brown," she said, hiding her dismay.

"Will we be stopping soon then?" John asked.

"Aye," the man said. "Over that rise is a small clearing. I've been through here a bit and again. We'll camp there for the night before continuing to the village at first light."

Chapter 14

The funeral ceremony continued into its second day, and the dancers kept up their steps. Joanna slipped in to watch on occasion, but she didn't stay long. Her help continued to be needed by the women who were kept busy watching the children and keeping everyone fed.

Joanna noticed that while he didn't dance, Fireheart, too, did not eat, and she worried about him. When she mentioned the fact to her cousin, Mary suggested that Joanna prepare a plate and take it to him.

"He may feel that as chief he can't leave," she said.

Joanna hadn't thought of that. Her heart began to thrum in her chest as she ladled out a bowl of venison and rabbit stew. She grabbed a corn cake as well, thinking that he would enjoy it also.

She felt a bit awkward entering with the stew until she saw others within the building eating and passing around food. She wondered then if someone else had thought to make Fireheart eat. Then she saw him as he'd been before, seated on the dirt floor cross-legged, his eyes closed, no sign of food or drink anywhere.

Drink! Once she'd brought him the stew, she would find him some fresh water.

Fireheart was on the other side of the structure. Joanna carefully negotiated past mourners to get to the area where he sat. She murmured an apology when she accidentally bumped someone along the way.

Soon, she was near the far wall, and she was able to edge along close to it and approach Fireheart.

There was a space, but no one directly behind him. Joanna ventured into that space and waited for him to sense her. But Fireheart didn't move, didn't look over his shoulder, or say a word. She knew she would have to gain his attention if she were to get him to eat.

"Fireheart," she said softly. His back glistened in the light from the fires that lit up the room. "Fireheart, you must eat."

But he still didn't turn.

Frustrated, concerned, Joanna moved to his side and crouched down. She looked at him, expecting him to meet her gaze, but his eyes remained closed. He seemed to be in a trance almost. Frightened now, she set down the food, and placed her hand on his shoulder. "Fireheart—"

His eyelids flew open. He stared at her, unseeing, until his vision focused, cleared. Then his gaze narrowed.

His dark look made her swallow hard. "I've brought you some food. You need to eat. To keep up your strength."

He glanced down at the stew and corn cake, then stared straight ahead. "I do not need food," he said, closing his eyes again.

Alarmed by his demeanor, Joanna remained determined to get him to eat. She grabbed hold of his arm, squeezed it lightly. "Please, Fireheart. You are our *sachem*. You need to eat and keep up your strength. Everyone else is eating," she said. Everyone else but the dancers, she knew. Had Fireheart longed to do the dance, too?

She studied him, hoping to read something in his expression, but he kept his thoughts, his emotions, secrets locked up tight.

"Fireheart? Fireheart!" she cried.

But he refused to look at her, to open his eyes.

She left him then, taking the stew with her because she knew that he wouldn't eat it. As she negotiated her way out, she met Moon Dove near the doorway.

Joanna stiffened as she met the young maiden's gaze. Moon Dove was beautiful with lovely dark hair and eyes, and she was Lenape, everything that Joanna was not. "I tried to get him to eat," she said defensively. "He won't eat."

There was no censure in Moon Dove's expression as the maiden looked at her. She glanced at Fireheart, then back to Joanna with a frown. "He is to be my husband. I will get him to eat," she said, holding out her hand for the food.

Stunned by the maiden's words, Joanna could only nod and give the girl the stew and corn cake. She waited and watched as Moon Dove made her way to Fireheart's side.

Had it been decided then? That Moon Dove and Fireheart would indeed marry? The maiden acted as if it had already been announced.

Joanna saw Moon Dove stop at Fireheart's side, and bend to speak with him. The brave looked at the food, flashed Joanna a glance across the room, then nodded to Moon Dove and took the food.

Joanna felt the sharp shaft of pain when Fireheart looked at her, then at Moon Dove, and began eating. *He didn't want food from me, but he took it from Moon Dove,* she thought.

"The matrons have decided that Fireheart must marry," a feminine voice said from close by.

She turned to find the one who had spoken, Woman with Eyes of Hawk. "I didn't know. When did they announce it?" How could she have missed such an important announcement, words that she'd been dreading to hear?

"It was said last night. Late," the woman said softly. "This is not how we would celebrate a union, but it was made known that the decision of Fireheart's marriage could not wait. Fireheart is *sachem*. He needs a wife. His wife will be Moon Dove."

"I see." Joanna fought back tears, then turned away from the sympathy in the matron's dark eyes, her gaze returning to the newly engaged couple.

Fireheart was eating the food that Moon Dove had given him while rejecting an offer that Joanna had made.

But wasn't that how it should be? Moon Dove was going to be his wife while she was . . . what? His former lover?

She was nothing to him now that the matrons had made their decision.

Her pain intensifying, Joanna battled back tears as she hurriedly left the Big House. Outside, she raced toward the forest to be alone. Fireheart had rejected the food she had brought him because he had been making it clear to her that he was no longer free. He took the same food from Moon Dove because he was showing his approval of his future wife.

John Burton and his traveling party arrived at the Lenape encampment during the final day of the funeral ceremony. They entered the village, strangers but for Thomas Brown whom one of the Indian matrons recognized.

"Who are these people?" Woman with Eyes of Hawk asked.

"The man is from England. He is called John Burton," Thomas said. "The woman is Gillian." Brown studied the female whom he'd led through the woods. She had acted like Burton's woman, but according to Burton, he was looking for his future wife. He eyed the pair speculatively, wondering if the two were lovers.

"Why have they come?" Another matron entered the discussion. "This is a sad time. These people should not be here."

"Do you know a young woman called Joanna Neville?" the guide asked. "The man searches for her."

The second matron opened her mouth to speak until Woman with Eyes of Hawk bumped her arm.

"What does he want with this white woman?" Woman with Eyes of Hawk asked.

"He says she is to marry him." The guide didn't miss the flicker of surprise in the two women's gazes. He realized that they knew where Joanna Neville was, but he didn't press the issue. They would tell him what he needed to know when they were ready.

"Mr. Burton," Thomas said, waving the man to approach. "What other information can you give me? Anything about your fiancée that might help our search."

John looked at the Indian women's bared breasts and stared until he became aware of Gillian's displeasure. Averting his gaze, he turned his attention to the fur trapper. "She has a cousin . . . her name is Mary. Mary lives among the Lenape."

"Mary?" Brown asked. "Just Mary?" His tone was derisive.

John's cheeks turned bright red with anger. "I don't know her English surname, and it wouldn't matter if I did because she probably has some Indian name."

John listened while Brown spoke to the women in their native tongue. They replied, talking rapidly, and John decided he couldn't possibly have understood them whether they'd spoken English or not.

As they continued their discussion, John studied his surroundings. The heavy beat of drums permeated the air, accompanied by other foreign sounds. He could smell whatever was simmering in the large kettle over that big fire. He stared at the pot. He doubted that the meat flavoring the stew was human. He took a small measure of comfort from that.

Where were all the men? he wondered, relaxing as he noticed there were none around.

Gillian was nervous. She clung to him, her fingers digging into his side, breathing heavily. He looked at her, feeling annoyed. Why was she afraid? Didn't she realize that there were no men in sight?

"John, I'm scared."

"Gillian, there are no warriors here."

She stiffened with surprise and looked around. "There aren't?"

His lips firmed. "Do you see any?"

"They are here," Thomas Brown said, interrupting. "The villagers are gathered in the Big House. Their chief has died. Today is his funeral."

Gillian's eyes grew round as saucers. "Oh."

John noticed then that there were wigwams ahead as far as his eye could see. *There are men here,* he realized with dismay. *Lots of warriors.*

"Do we have the right village?" he asked Brown.

"These ladies wouldn't say, but my guess is yes."

"They wouldn't tell you?"

The guide shook his head. "But I could tell by their expression that they recognized Joanna's name."

"So you think we've come to the right place—"

"I think we'll know soon enough," he said, glancing around. He saw the door flap of a wigwam raised from the inside, and a blonde woman in Lenape clothing exit the structure.

"Your Joanna," he said. "Does she have blonde hair . . . kind of red and golden like the sun?"

John stared at him. "Why, yes . . ."

"Then we may have just found her. Turn around."

John turned, cautiously, slowly. He spied Joanna crossing to another wigwam and was stunned at her appearance. She was dressed as one of them—like a savage. "Joanna!"

She halted as she was about to enter the other wigwam. Joanna turned, saw him standing in the middle of the yard, and her eyes went wide with surprise for a moment. Then her expression brightened. She approached them.

"John!" she said, her green eyes warm. She held out her hand to him.

Smoothly, John took her fingers and brought them to his lips.

"Joanna?" a soft hesitant voice said from another direction.

Joanna turned and stared. "Gillian?" Her eyes grew round with surprised pleasure. "Gillian!" She hurried forward to give her friend a hug. "I can't believe you are here!" She glanced from one of her friends to the other. "I can't believe you're both here. Why have you come?"

"For you," John said, trying not to show his displeasure at how well she'd apparently adapted to the Indian way of life.

"We were worried about you," Gillian added softly. Her violet gaze, as she studied Joanna, was filled with concern.

Puzzled, Joanna looked from one to the other again. "You must have left when I'd been gone for only a couple of months." Her frown disappeared. "I was thinking about going back. Perhaps you read my mind."

"You were?" Gillian asked. She flashed John a meaningful glance.

John narrowed his gaze at his lover, then smiled at Joanna. "That's wonderful. We can travel together then."

Joanna nodded. "I had planned to go back days ago, but then Wild Squirrel died, and . . ." Her voice dropped off and her eyes filled with tears. "He is the reason I came," she said in the softest murmur. "The chief—he was like a grandfather to me."

Gillian's eyes filled with tears in instant sympathy. "Oh, Joanna, I'm so sorry."

"Joanna?" Mary crossed the yard, having seen the newcomers. She eyed the man and woman warily as she approached. The second man had left the group and was conversing with one of the braves.

"Mary," Joanna said, "these are my friends. John and Gillian. They came here from England because they were worried about me."

Mary studied the two and gave a solemn nod.

"We were hoping that Joanna would be ready to return with us. When we mentioned it to her, we learned that she is."

"I see," Mary said.

Joanna felt her cousin's gaze. She saw Mary's tense smile of welcome.

"You will stay awhile with us, though, won't you?" Mary invited.

Joanna gazed at her cousin with understanding. She knew that Mary was upset by the talk of her leaving. She knew her cousin wanted her to stay, just as Mary had known that she would have to leave someday.

"Yes, John, you must stay awhile," Joanna said, wanting to banish the new pain from Mary's expression. Mary already had enough sadness at this time in her life. Perhaps if they stayed a little longer . . . "This is a sad time for the Lenape," she explained, "but after today the funeral ceremony will be over, and everyone from the other villages will leave Little River."

Gillian looked horrified. "There are sav—*people,*" she amended quickly, "from other villages here?"

"Yes, there are people from several Lenape villages and from the Shawnee, too," Mary said. "They have come to pay their respects. Our *sachem* was a good leader. Many loved him. They are here for him and his family."

"If there are so many people here, where will we sleep?" Gillian asked.

"You can stay with my husband and me," Mary said. "Joanna is with us. There is room for two more."

"Thank you, Mrs.—" Gillian began.

"Mary," she said. "Just Mary. Or you may call me Mary Wife as the Lenape do."

Even though she looked puzzled by the Indian name, Gillian nevertheless agreed.

Thomas Brown returned, having finished his conversation with Big Cloud, a Lenape brave. "Woman with Eyes of Hawk has invited me to stay in that big house over there with other members of her clan."

"We'll be staying with Joanna and her cousin," John said. He gave Brown a meaningful look. He didn't want to stay in the village long, despite Joanna and Mary's invitation to do so.

"We can discuss when to leave later," Brown said, interpreting John's look correctly.

"Fine."

The fur trapper addressed Mary. "Any chance of getting a taste of the food in that pot over there?"

Mary smiled slightly. "Most certainly," she said. Then she gestured for them to follow her.

Still reeling from the hurt of being rejected by Fireheart, Joanna was more than glad that John and

Gillian had come. As she'd told them, it seemed as if they had read her mind and then appeared. Their arrival was like an answer to her prayers for leaving. Thank goodness Cara and Harry had been delayed in Philadelphia. She wanted to leave this place of pain, and now her friends were here to take her away from it.

The last one she'd expected to see with John was Gillian, however. She was so pleased that Gillian had braved the voyage. She hated the time spent onboard ship herself. She could imagine how difficult it must have been for her friend. At the first opportunity, she would thank Gillian for caring for a friend so much that she would come all this way just to make sure she was all right.

That opportunity came later that day, the last day of the ceremonies, before the Indian guests had left, when Joanna finally found the time to ask Gillian to walk alone with her. Gillian, who seemed a little lost in the Indian village, was only too happy to have something to do.

As they started down the path toward the lake, Joanna was silent. There was much that she needed to tell Gillian. Where should she start?

With Fireheart, she decided. While her and Mary's relationship had vastly improved, she found it easier to confide in Gillian about her feelings for the handsome brave. It was easy to talk with her friend. From the first day of their meeting, they had become instant friends. They had told each other secrets, encouraged each other when one wanted to do something daring or bold. Their friendship had endured over the years from the time they'd met when they were fifteen until the present. It was a friendship that Joanna valued highly.

As the dancers danced their final steps and some of the villagers ventured out to eat, Joanna and Gillian went to the lake where Joanna suggested they take off their shoes to wade in the clear water.

Studying her friend as Gillian removed one shoe, Joanna realized that Gillian wasn't just uncomfortable in the wilderness, she seemed terrified of it. It was as if her friend expected a warrior or a beast to jump out at them at any moment.

"Gillian, relax. It's safe here," she told her. *For the time being,* she could have added but didn't.

"But the Indians—"

"Harmless," Joanna assured. "Oh, not all of them are." She was forced then to explain about the Iroquois and their attack on the village. She was sorry she'd said anything at all about them when she saw her friend's rising fear. "Don't look so alarmed, Gilly. The Cayuga won't be back," she quickly assured her. "Our Lenape men took care of them."

"They killed them?"

Joanna nodded. "Yes, all of them." All but one, she thought, but soon he too would be a dead man.

"How can you stand it?" Gillian's face looked white, as if the thought of the battle had made her ill.

"What?"

"This life?" She glanced back. "Living in huts. Eating who knows what?" She caught Joanna's arm. "They don't eat people, do they? Tell me I don't have to worry about that."

Joanna laughed softly. "No. At least, not lately. Now, I don't think I can say the same for the Iroquois—especially the Mohawks."

Gillian glanced around with fear. "Are there any of them here?"

With an amused smile, Joanna shook her head, then chuckled out loud when she heard her friend's sigh of relief.

Joanna was glad that no one else was at the lake. She preferred this time alone with her friend. Hoping to help Gillian to relax, she sat down on her favorite rock, and invited Gillian to join her.

Once seated on the rock with her feet kicking lightly in the lake, Gillian seemed to relax as she watched the play of the water against her feet. It was late afternoon, and the sun was an orange glow in the sky. The orange orb lit up the sky, and shimmered on the lake's surface. It was peaceful and lovely, and the drums that had seemed so sinister before were less so now, coming from farther in the distance.

The two women were quiet for a time, each content simply to be in each other's company. *It has always been like this with us,* Joanna thought. *Good friends, willing to wait for the other one to speak.*

"Gillian, there is something I have to tell you. It's about a Lenape brave. His name is Fireheart. . . ."

Then Joanna began to tell Gillian about the man she loved. She told her about the warrior who was now chief, and about the woman he intended to marry.

The funeral ceremony ended, and Wild Squirrel's body was taken to his burial place, a grave hollowed out of the ground in the forest. The gravesite was a lovely place surrounded by ferns and wildflowers.

The hole in the ground that would serve as the chief's resting place had been lined with planks of wood along the sides and on the bottom. After the body was lowered inside, the men would lower boards to cover the top, too.

The braves who carried Wild Squirrel set the chief's body in his grave. His nephew Fireheart placed Wild Squirrel's bow and arrow at his side while a matron put in a supply of food. These items and those that another warrior included would be things necessary to the *sachem* during his long journey from this life to the next one. They were items that would ensure Wild Squirrel's comfort and safety.

The chief's face and exposed body parts had been painted red by his clansmen. He was dressed in the finest clothing: a new breechcloth, beautifully adorned moccasins, and his feathered headdress. He wore an embroidered sash with beads and porcupine quills. He lay curled on one side, a position he'd been laid in shortly after his death. He looked like a gentle old man sleeping the sleep of peace. Only his people knew that he had a battle still to fight, and a journey to make to the Spirit World.

Those at the gravesite remained for a few minutes while the *shaman* sang a prayer, made an offering of tobacco to the spirits, and then laid the first piece of birch wood over the dead man's grave. The other pieces of wood followed, laid over the body by friends and relatives saying farewell. Then one last prayer was said, and the funeral post was placed at the head of the grave to mark the site. With that done, Fireheart and the others said their silent good-byes and returned to the village.

Fireheart felt the emptiness of having lost someone dear as he entered the village yard. Seeking comfort, he searched for Joanna and saw instead two strange white men. His body became seized with a chill as he wondered who they were, what they were doing here in Little River.

Was one of them Joanna's guide? Rising Bird had told him that Autumn Wind wanted to go home to England. Had this man come to take her across the sea, home to the house of her uncle?

He tensed, recalling Joanna's scars. Why would she want to go back to that place? The place which held bad memories for her, a place of tears?

He sensed Joanna's presence before he saw her coming up the path. She wasn't alone. She had someone with her. A white woman.

The white woman was someone she knew, he thought. A friend. From England?

Fireheart studied the dark-haired woman and found her wanting in comparison to the woman he loved. She wasn't as vibrant or as beautiful as Autumn Wind. Still, this woman was Joanna's friend, so she must have been good and kind to her.

Fireheart didn't move, but waited for Joanna to see him. When she did, she stopped, and he still fought the urge to go to her. It wouldn't be right if he looked too anxious to talk with her. He wanted her, but she would never belong to him. And he had to remember. . . .

"Moon Dove," he murmured.

As if to taunt him, to incite his guilt, the Indian maiden came up from behind him and touched his arm.

"Fireheart, I have brought you a cool drink," she said with a soft smile.

He returned her smile as he accepted the cup she offered him. "*Wa-neé-shih,*" he murmured before taking a sip.

Drinking thirstily of the cool water, he thanked her again, told her he had had enough, and gave her back the drinking vessel. She seemed pleased as she nodded and took it away.

Moon Dove will be a good wife, he reminded himself.

And wouldn't Joanna? an inner voice taunted him.

He knew the answer, but he refused to listen to it. He couldn't accept what his heart and his mind were telling him. If he did, there would be no chance for his future happiness with Moon Dove.

"*Kihiila,*" his heart and thoughts said anyway.

Yes, Autumn Wind would make me a good wife.

Chapter 15

"Joanna, there is something I need to discuss with you."

She frowned at John's tone. She had never before seen him looking this serious. "What is it, John?"

He glanced around, scowling. "Is there someplace where we can be alone?"

Joanna nodded, and led him from the village toward the river, not the lake. It was morning, the time of day when there would be others at the lake, bathing, washing dishes, or fetching water.

They walked for a time, and then Joanna turned to him. "What is it? Has something happened to Neville Manor?" she asked. Strangely, the thought of a calamity there didn't particularly upset her.

"No, no," he assured her. "Nothing like that."

"Who is overseeing the estate?"

"My brother Michael's man. He's very good actually, but not as good as your uncle, I'm afraid. That's why I wanted to speak with you." He took off his vest, and laid it on the ground, then gestured for her to sit.

Joanna did so, studying him with curious eyes. "Joanna . . ."

His reluctance to continue puzzled her. "Yes, John?" she encouraged him.

"You are returning home with us, aren't you? You didn't just say that you were when we got here because you were happy to see old friends."

She looked away. "Of course, I'll be returning home with you. It's time I go back. There are things to do there, affairs to take care of—"

"Marry me, Joanna," he urged.

Her eyes widened as she stared at him. "John—"

"I think you know where my heart has been all along, and when your uncle died, I didn't want to push the issue. But it would work out for the best, don't you see? I can handle all those business matters for you—"

"That's a generous offer, John, but—"

"Oh, I know that you don't love me." He smiled. "But I hope to change your mind in time. I have a great deal of affection for you. We are good friends, aren't we?"

"Yes, of course, we are—"

"Then won't you give us a chance? There are worse things than two friends marrying. It seems like a wise decision to me. I know people who have married with far less between them."

Joanna knew such people, too. Those who married for money, or for an English title. Those who married because their parents had made an arrangement when they were children, or just born.

John was right, she'd always suspected he wanted to marry her, and she understood why. He was a twin. It was his brother Michael who had inherited Burton Estates, not John, yet John had worked beside his brother loyally as if the property belonged as much to him.

She didn't doubt that he cared for her. He had

shown it in many ways over the years. But would friendship be enough? she wondered.

Her heart gave a lurch as she thought of Fireheart. When she had tasted heaven, would she be satisfied with earth?

It was on the tip of her tongue to refuse him.

"Don't give me your answer immediately, Joanna," he said. "Think about it for a while. You will, at least, do that for me, won't you?"

She gazed into the blue eyes of her good friend and nodded. Of course, she would think on it for a while. She owed him that much. "I'll think about it."

John smiled. "I'll not rush you. I promise." He extended a hand to help her to her feet.

"John, I can't promise to give you the answer you want to hear."

His expression sobered. "I know." His voice had grown soft.

She smiled as she inclined her head. "Fine, then." She caught his arm, and together they headed toward the village. "Have you tried the Indians' corn cakes yet, John?"

He shook his head. He had tried, though, some of their other dishes and had found them surprisingly palatable—and even sweet, considering savages had made them. But he didn't tell her that. These savages were her friends, family even.

He nodded appropriately as she chatted with him on the return journey to the Indian town. He understood, though, why Roderick Neville had felt it necessary to rescue her from this savage place. When they were married, he'd ensure that she never again felt the need to visit the Indians.

"Fireheart, there is word that the Cayuga are joining with their Seneca brothers in the north."

The chief and several of his men were in the *sachem*'s

wigwam. Stormy Wind had moved out and into the Lenape longhouse of her clan, the Turtle. Reluctantly, Fireheart had left the wigwam of the Wolf clan and moved in.

The new *sachem* was thoughtful after listening to the words of Turtle That Hops. "Where is the Cayuga?"

"The prisoner is being held in the longhouse of my mother," the brave said.

"Bring him to me."

The warrior agreed and left.

The Iroquois captive had been kept alive during Wild Squirrel's funeral ceremony. There had been no time to take care of him. Fireheart wondered if the occasion was right to kill him, or whether it would be wiser to release him.

Several of the braves offered suggestions on what to do with the enemy prisoner, their tones laced with satisfaction as they envisioned the mental images. Turtle That Hops returned moments later, shoving the bound prisoner into the wigwam before him.

The Cayuga tumbled to the ground at Fireheart's feet. The captive raised his head to glare at him.

"What was the name of your *sachem*?" Fireheart demanded.

With the help of Turtle That Hops, the Iroquois climbed to his knees. Fireheart queried him again, and the Cayuga stared at him without answering.

"I asked you a question," Fireheart said easily.

Turtle That Hops grabbed the Indian's bound arms and pulled them upward. The Cayuga gasped with pain and fell to the ground. With a nod from the chief, Turtle That Hops helped him up again.

"Who is your chief?"

The brave mumbled something beneath his breath.

"He said it is Great Thunder," Rising Bird said. He sat nearest to the Cayuga, on Fireheart's right side.

"Was Great Thunder," Fireheart corrected. "Your chief is dead."

"My people will come and seek vengeance!" the Cayuga spat.

"We did not attack your people. We are a peaceful nation. We fight when we are threatened. We kill when we must defend ourselves. Untie him," Fireheart said.

Several of the Lenape braves looked surprised while others looked pleased as they anticipated the Cayuga's torture. Turtle That Hops undid the sinew strips binding the man's wrists, and then the ties that bound his ankles.

When he was free, the Cayuga stood before Fireheart, his head held high, unafraid.

Studying the man, Fireheart had to admire his courage. "You are free to go," he said.

There was a chorus of low murmurs among the Lenape war chiefs as Fireheart offered the prisoner his freedom.

The Cayuga stared at Fireheart distrustfully.

"Go. We will not harm you," he said. His dark eyes narrowed in warning and his voice deepened as he continued. "But tell your brothers that we will be ready for them if they come to us again. Keep your brothers to their longhouses. Next time, we will kill you. Not one of you will escape."

The Iroquois looked around him at each Lenape warrior with fear.

"They will not harm you. No one will harm you."

"This is so," Rising Bird said in support of his chief.

"We will not hurt you," echoed Black Fox.

Each of Fireheart's men assured the Cayuga that he would not be harmed.

The Iroquois started to back out the doorway.

Turtle That Hops briefly held out his hand. "Come," he said. "I will take you to the edge of the forest so that no one within the village will be afraid and kill you.''

His eyes fluttering nervously, the Cayuga nodded.

When the enemy had gone, all eyes turned to the new chief.

Fireheart's gaze went to the war chief, Black Fox. ''Take some men and follow him. Don't let him know you are there. Learn where he goes and if our enemy prepares for a new battle. Learn this and return here so that we shall know.''

The sound of approval swept about the *sachem's* wigwam.

''This is a wise thing, Fireheart,'' Rising Bird said as the others started to leave.

''It is the only way we will know what we must fight,'' Fireheart said, his features solemn. ''It is the only way we can protect the Lenape people from our Iroquois enemy.''

John's proposal of marriage gave Joanna something to think about in the days that followed. *I don't have to make a decision now,* she thought. There would be plenty of time for that when they returned to England.

John and Gillian had been urging her to go. She wanted to leave, she told herself, but not yet. She wanted to talk with Fireheart one more time. . . .

She saw him exiting his wigwam with Rising Bird and another brave. Something was happening, she realized. A problem?

During the Iroquois attack, the Lenape had taken a prisoner. Perhaps the meeting had been about the captive.

Fireheart separated from the other men, and crossed the yard toward the longhouse of his clan. Joanna, seeing her opportunity, hurriedly approached him.

''Fireheart,'' she called softly.

He halted and faced her. "Autumn Wind," he said without a smile.

"Are you all right?" she asked.

Was that a slight softening in his expression? "I am well."

"Is something wrong? I saw Rising Bird and the others."

He frowned. "You must not be concerned."

She had every faith in his ability as chief. "I'm not worried—"

But he was already turning away. "I must go—"

She experienced a tightening in her throat. "But—"

"Fireheart!" Moon Dove approached the pair with a smile for her husband-to-be.

"Moon Dove." His smile for the lovely Lenape maiden was soft, genuine. Joanna had never felt such pain.

"I must help Mary," Joanna said, leaving quickly, her heart breaking into pieces.

She had to leave the village and soon!

She encountered John as she headed toward the lake. His hair was wet as if he'd been swimming.

"John," she said impulsively, "I'll marry you."

Hie expression brightened. "You will?"

She nodded, anxious to be free of the village . . . of Fireheart.

"I'll take good care of you, Joanna," John promised.

No talk of love for there wasn't any. But there was friendship, she reminded herself. And affection. Her chest tightening, she managed to smile at him. "I know you will, John."

He found her alone at night while everyone congregated in the community square, sharing stories, eating food. Fireheart left the yard, and headed toward the lake. When he didn't see her there, he went to the secluded glade where they had first kissed and held each other.

He couldn't stay away. He knew he should avoid her, to turn away and head back to the village, but something deep within him pressed him on.

He didn't expect to find her at the clearing, but his heart pumped hard when he did. "Autumn Wind."

She rose to her feet with a gasp. "Fireheart!" Her blonde hair looked silver in the moonlight.

"I want to talk with you."

She averted her gaze as he approached. "You didn't want to speak earlier."

And he had regretted the moment instantly, he thought, as he'd watched her walk away. "I know this."

He sat down on the bed of grass, tugging her down to sit at his side. For a long moment, he studied her. The moon was full, casting a soft glow through the trees and into the clearing. He could see her face cast in the shadows and light . . . the glistening of her green gaze . . . the trembling of her sweet mouth. He wanted to hold her, kiss her. He wanted to make her stay. But she was leaving. Her friends were here, and her visit was near its end. And he was to marry Moon Dove.

"Then why are you here now?" she asked suddenly, her voice weak.

"I had to talk with you again. I want you to be happy."

"I see." She stared at her hands, which lay in her lap. She played with her fingers, pretending great interest in their movements. But her thoughts were not on her actions, he knew. She was thinking of what to say.

He fought the urge to touch her hair, which lay unbound past her shoulders. She had donned her English gown again as if she was ready to go. He wanted to see her wear her tunic . . . to see her free and happy with her smile ready to tease. This changed woman was so different from the young girl he'd known that he was afraid for her. He knew she was there somewhere beneath the surface of cool politeness. If only he could see the real Joanna again. . . .

"It seems that we have nothing more to say to each other," she said as she rose to her feet.

He caught her arm, pulled her down again. He heard her sharp little intake of breath as he turned her to fully face him.

"This man will miss you," he said huskily.

She blinked against tears and shook her head. "You will have a wife . . . someone who will make you forget you ever knew Autumn Wind."

"*Maata*," he murmured, unable to keep from wanting to kiss her. His head bent lower. "I will never forget you, Joanna."

She stared as if mesmerized as he dipped his head and took her mouth. She groaned softly as he kissed her sweetly, tenderly.

"Fireheart." She breathed when he lifted his head. With a startled look she pushed him away. "I am going to marry John."

He stiffened, experiencing a pain like he'd been kicked in his midsection. "You will take the white man for your husband?"

She nodded.

"Do you love him?" he asked.

She didn't answer him, and his heart began to soar. "I respect him and care for him," she said.

He placed his hand on her bodice where her right breast pushed against the fabric of her gown. "Does John Burton make your heart beat faster than the way Fireheart does?"

Joanna reached up to grab his hand, wanting to pull it away, but holding it in place instead. The warmth of his touch burned her, creating a longing within her to undress and invite him to lie with her. She fought her feelings for him.

"I'm going to marry John." She tugged Fireheart's hand from her breast, set it to his side. "I'm sorry," she said.

His features contorted, but she felt that he understood. "It is I who am sorry. I should not have touched you. It was not right."

"It's all right," she murmured for she had liked having his hands on her. If only . . .

"Tomorrow," he said, "I will leave Little River to journey to the north. Will you go before I return?"

"You are leaving? Why?"

"We have learned where the enemy is camped. We go to avenge our people. We must go to protect the Lenape from Iroquois attack."

Joanna sensed that there was much he wasn't telling her. "They are planning to attack again," she guessed.

He didn't answer as she studied him in the moonlight. His face was highlighted in the white glow, sharp angles and rugged planes. She wanted so desperately to stroke him, to kiss his lips, his chin . . . his jaw.

He seemed to close off his thoughts as she gazed at him. It would be a dangerous journey, she realized. Perhaps one during which his people would be killed.

A cold dark dread filled Joanna with fear. She didn't want him to go! But how was she to stop him? He might desire her, but he didn't love her. She had no claim on him.

He was silent for so long she wondered why he stayed. This meeting had done nothing to steal away her love for him. It had only deepened her pain.

Why had he come? she wondered. Because he felt guilty for making love to her, a virgin?

She frowned. No, she thought, such things were not viewed in the same way here as they were by the English. Neither was marriage, she realized. A brave could have more than one wife if he wanted. She had known of few relationships in which this was so, but they existed nevertheless.

"I hope you find your enemy," she whispered. "But don't get killed."

He captured her chin, lifted her head, and studied her with an intensity that was unnerving.

"You are beautiful, Autumn Wind," he murmured. "It will be a long time until this man will forget you."

"I will never forget you," she said, staring at his mouth. The memory of his kiss made her ache inside. She wanted those male lips pressed against hers. She wanted his arms around her, and more.

But it was more than physical attraction that drew her to him. She had seen his tenderness, his fairness and understanding when dealing with the Lenape people.

He will make a good husband, she thought. *A good father*.

She closed her eyes, withdrew from his hold. She rose, anxious to put distance between them.

"Be careful, Fireheart," she said softly.

He nodded and allowed her to leave him.

She said a silent good-bye for, although she did not tell him, she would not be there when he returned to the village.

Chapter 16

"No, John, stop! Someone may see us!"

John glanced about the forest then back at the woman before him. They had slipped away from the Lenape village to be alone. And from what he could see they had succeeded. "There is no one here, Gillian," he said. "And it's been too long." He backed her against a tree. "Kiss me."

"John—"

"Now!" he ordered. He leaned in to take her lips, but she turned her head away.

"Joanna—"

"Joanna isn't here." He scowled with frustration. He had been hard and aching for her for days now. It had been weeks since he'd lain with her, suckled her breasts. He spanned her waist with his hands.

"But this isn't right—"

"Gillian," John said with great patience, "are you willing to give up what we have just because I am marrying Joanna?"

Shaking her head, she closed her eyes. "No," she whispered.

"Then why are you hesitating when Joanna and I are not even man and wife yet?" He raised a hand to stroke her face. "Now kiss me, love," he urged.

With a shuddering sigh, she complied, kissing him with all the pent-up passion that had been simmering below the surface since they'd left the inn in Philadelphia. "Oh, John," she moaned after he'd nibbled on her lips and devoured the inside of her mouth.

"Yes, Gillian," he rasped. Her breasts pushed up from the neckline of her gown. He reached inside her bodice and freed a plump ripe mound. As he cupped the soft swell, the nipple hardened, begging for his lips. He bent his head to capture the red bud between this teeth. Gillian gasped, arching, and caught his head with her hands.

"Oh, John . . ."

"Say it, Gilly," he said. "Tell me it's been too long and you want me."

"Yes," she replied.

"Say it." His lips released her breast and he fondled her, one mound in each hand.

She whimpered. "Yes, yes! Take me! It's been too long. . . ."

He held up her breasts and nuzzled in the cleavage before sucking each one until she wriggled against him. He stepped back to free himself quickly, then he was lifting her skirts, pressing her against the tree, and plunging into her.

Gillian alternately moaned and gasped, and made little cries of pleasure deep in her throat as John thrust into her again and again. She screamed out her release, and his harsh cry joined hers within seconds.

When they were done, Gillian looked down at herself, saw her breasts lying above her gown, and felt the air about her bare legs and the dampness between her legs as he pulled out of her.

"There," John said with a grin. "That wasn't so bad, was it?"

She gazed at him with her heart in her eyes and a lump of yearning in her throat. She loved him. She wanted to marry him, but he was to wed her best friend.

Heat burned in her belly as she thought of Joanna. She felt terribly guilty although John told her she shouldn't. *She doesn't love him like I do*, she thought.

"Gillian?" he said, perhaps reading the concern in her face. "Are you all right?"

"Yes," she assured him, nodding vigorously. She slipped first one breast then the other back into her gown bodice. "I'm fine."

"You still love me, don't you?" he asked, sounding unsure.

Gillian's eyes met his, and her heart melted. He looked boyish, uncertain. She had to reassure him. "Yes, I love you," she said softly.

He beamed a smile at her. "Don't," he said, as she began to lower and straighten her skirts. "I'm not done."

Her eyes flashed with surprise as his hand snaked under her petticoats and found the most secret part of her, still pulsating. She gasped and stiffened as he began to stroke and worry the tiny nub of hidden pleasure. Gasping, she slid down the base of the tree, and he followed her down. As she lay on the ground with her skirts raised, and his hand caressing her, arousing her to the point of pain, John smiled and kissed her, then sent her over the pinnacle.

He heard the woman's cries and the man's grunt of pleasure. The brave saw the pair against the tree, and there was no doubt in his mind what the two were doing.

The Indian frowned. If what Little Blossom said was true, John Burton was to be Autumn Wind's husband. But the woman with him was the other one, Gillian Gordon, Joanna's friend.

Anger burned hotly in his chest as he turned away from the fornicating couple.

Joanna and her friends left the village the next day. Fireheart was gone. Black Fox had returned with the information Fireheart had requested about the enemy, and Fireheart had accompanied his party of men to the Iroquois encampment to the far north.

Although she longed to stay for Fireheart's return, Joanna realized that now was the best time to leave. Her departure would be more painful if she waited to see the chief again.

She said good-bye to Mary and to Rising Bird who had stayed behind this time. Tears filled her eyes as she hugged her cousin.

"I'll write," she promised Mary.

Mary nodded. "I'll write, too," she said. "Every month, just like I did before."

"You sent me other letters?" Joanna asked, puzzled.

"Yes." Mary looked confused, and then anger brightened her expression. "He kept them from you, didn't he? Roderick Neville took my letters and got rid of them before you knew they'd come."

Joanna felt a sudden happiness. "You didn't forget me when you sent me away," she said. "You didn't forget about me."

"No. No!" Mary's face crumbled as she gave way to tears. "I love you. I didn't want you to go. I'd hoped you would want to return, but—"

John shifted impatiently behind her.

"Joanna, we need to go," Gillian said, urging her friend.

Joanna glanced at her best friend and nodded. "I'll write, and if I can, I'll come back for a visit. I don't know how soon it will be. . . ."

Mary nodded, her eyes bright. "Be safe."

Rising Bird embraced his adopted daughter. "We will miss you, Autumn Wind," he whispered.

"Don't," she said, aching, willing him not to cry. If he did, he would open up her floodgates, and she would be unable to stop sobbing. Her throat felt so tight that the lump at its base hurt her.

"Farewell, daughter," Woman with Eyes of Hawk said.

Words were exchanged between her and her friends. There was Stormy Wind—her grandmother. Little Blossom with her husband Broken Bow and her daughter Water Flower. Even Moon Dove was there to see her off.

She smiled at all of them, then turned to John and Gillian. "I'm ready," she murmured.

"Let's go, then," John said.

Joanna waved to her Lenape friends and left with John and Gillian, accompanied by Thomas Brown who had waited to take them back to the nearest white settlement.

Good-bye, Fireheart, she thought, hurting.

Drums began to play shortly after the village was out of sight. The music was for her, Joanna realized, a farewell song. And it was then that she surrendered to tears.

Night had fallen. As Fireheart waited with his men, he could see the guards posted about the Iroquois encampment. A tall fence surrounded the village. They would have to get past the guards and the stockade to capture the Cayuga *sachem* in his longhouse.

The feat wouldn't be an easy one. The Iroquois lived in structures large enough for many families. How could a few Lenape venture inside, kidnap the leader, and then escape without harm or capture?

Fireheart knew the risk he and his men were taking

that evening. If the Cayuga caught them, they would be put to death or worse. The Iroquois delighted in torture. He had seen the remains of one of their victims, a sight that would forever be embedded in his memory.

There were fourteen warriors with Fireheart. He had asked Rising Bird to stay behind. If something happened to him, the warrior would avenge his death and see to his replacement.

They waited in the forest for the night to deepen. The best chance they had was while the villagers slept. They could easily dispose of the four guards near the gate and the stockade's perimeter.

The plan had been clear to Fireheart: kidnap the Cayuga chief and make him talk of peace. Perhaps when he realized how vulnerable he was, Flaming Sky would be swayed. He could be made to understand that the Lenape people had killed his brothers not in aggression but in self-defense.

His men were spread out about the woods. As he lay in his own hiding place, Fireheart longed for Joanna. Had she left? Would he ever see her again?

His heart continued to beat with the sound of her name. *Autumn Wind.* He closed his eyes, then abruptly shook himself back to the present. He forced her from his mind because he had to. *Autumn Wind.*

An owl cry captured his attention, and Fireheart's last thoughts were of the woman he loved as he crept toward an Iroquois guard with raised tomahawk.

Joanna, Gillian, and John followed Thomas Brown through the forest on trails, occasionally veering from the path in whatever direction the fur trapper decided. Their departure day was beautiful. The weather was warm, but not humid, and the sun burned in a clear sky, its light filtering past the trees to brighten their travels.

"We'll stop here for a brief rest," Brown said.

Joanna was more than happy to stop. They'd been journeying since first light. The sun was directly overhead. She was hungry, having eaten only a corn cake in the village before they'd left.

They halted, and their guide rummaged through the pouch he had secured at his waist. Withdrawing several strips of dried venison, he handed each of them a piece.

"Eat up. We'll not be stopping again until nightfall."

Gillian groaned softly, but Joanna nodded.

John glared at the man as he chewed off a piece of meat. "How long before we reach the nearest settlement?" he asked. They had come a different way. The area looked unfamiliar to him.

Brown shrugged. "A couple of days or so. It depends on how quickly the ladies can travel."

"We'll be able to keep up," Joanna said, speaking for both of them. The farther away from the village they'd come the more dispirited she'd felt. She missed Mary and Rising Bird. She missed the Lenape people . . . and she especially longed to see Fireheart.

"May I have some water?" Gillian asked, her voice sounding small.

Joanna gave her friend the water-skin she'd been carrying. She explained how to drink from it without spilling, and watched as Gillian quenched her thirst. When Gillian was done, Joanna took back the skin, drank some of the water herself, and set the container down on the ground beside her.

Her first thought before leaving was to wear her doeskin tunic for the garment would be the best for traveling, better than the blue calico gown she had finally chosen to wear. But she had realized that she would look out of place once they'd reached the settlement.

Her feet hurt, but she hadn't complained. She had discarded her comfortable moccasins for her old leather shoes.

Flashing her friend a glance, Joanna saw that Gillian fared no better. She looked tired. Her midnight hair was disheveled, and her features were drawn. She had come through the wilderness because she'd been worried about her friend. Grateful, Joanna smiled at the young woman, and touched her arm in sympathy for her discomfort.

She turned her attention to her other friend, now her fiancé, John. He was handsome, she thought with affection. But would she—could she—be happy as his wife?

For not the first time since she'd accepted his proposal, Joanna experienced doubts. She and John were friends. He loved her in his own way, he'd said. She could be happy with someone who loved her, she thought. She closed her eyes on a wave of pain. She could be happy with Fireheart. Would she be happy with John? Would she make him a good wife?

Fireheart was marrying another. She would be happy with John, she told herself. Very happy.

Joanna ignored the tiny voice inside her that said she would be more miserable in England with John than she would be in the village, even with Fireheart married to another.

Chapter 17

The Lenape braves returned to their village, triumphant. They had entered the camp of the enemy war party, and they had kidnapped their chief. Although the encampment hadn't housed a village of Iroquois families like they'd first thought, it had been a nasty battle for the Lenape band of men. The stockade had protected a band of Cayuga and Seneca warriors. Two Lenape warriors had been wounded in the fight. Three Iroquois were dead, and countless others injured.

The only reason that Fireheart and his men had been successful was that they, unlike the enemy, had had the advantage of surprise. They had taken the Iroquois unawares, and had been successful. The Lenape men had Flaming Sky as their captive. Fireheart hoped to win the peace the Indian people of the area needed.

Entering the village ahead of his men, Fireheart searched the compound, clutching his right shoulder. He had been slightly injured during the raid when an Iroquois warrior and he had tussled with knives drawn. A hard smile formed on his lips at the memory.

He had fared much better than the Seneca. He was alive with only a scratched shoulder while the Iroquois was dead.

Women and children greeted them. Fireheart looked for Joanna, and found Moon Dove instead. It was how it should be, he thought.

"Moon Dove," he said with a smile.

Her concerned gaze studied his shoulder. "You must let me bathe you and bandage your wound."

He nodded, and she looked relieved. "Come," she said. He studied her with amusement as she grabbed his other arm, and pulled him across the yard to his own wigwam. She tugged him inside, and instructed him to sit. He complied, surprised and not displeased at this new display of spirit.

"If you do not have it cleaned, it will become filled with bad spirits," she murmured as she poured water into a bowl and found a piece of soft doeskin. As she rinsed the area around his injury, she clucked her tongue, and asked about the raid.

"We accomplished what we went for," he said darkly.

She paused, her hand poised over the wound, and looked at him. "It was bad?"

He saw her worry and shook his head. "None of our people were killed. Some Iroquois, but no Lenape."

Releasing a relieved sigh, Moon Dove continued to wash his arm. Watching her, Fireheart wondered why she would display such relief then decided it was because she cared deeply for her warrior friends who had gone.

When the wound was bathed, Moon Dove set down the water. "I shall return with medicine for your injury." She scurried out the door.

While she was gone, Fireheart thought how nice it was to have a woman provide care for him. He thought of Joanna, and felt a shaft of pain. Better to think of Moon Dove and the comfort she would offer him as his wife. And if he felt no passion, no burning desire for Moon Dove, who was to say it wouldn't come in time?

Never, an inner voice said. *Your soul is pledged to Autumn Wind.*

Yet where was Joanna? She had not come to greet him as Moon Dove and the others had.

Fireheart forced the voice from his head, and concentrated instead on the woman who would return soon to bandage his wound.

A brave stepped from the shadows, intercepting Moon Dove's path as she crossed from her wigwam to the *sachem*'s.

"Moon Dove."

She gasped, and clutched the medicine bundle to her breast. "Black Fox! You frightened me."

His expression softening, he took her hand. "Come, I must talk with you."

She shook her head and pulled away. "I cannot talk now. Fireheart is injured. I must tend to his wounds."

Emotion worked across the warrior's features. "Fireheart has suffered only a scratch."

"He was cut with a knife!"

He scowled. "He will heal. He does not need your medicine to make him well."

A hurt look entered her dark eyes. "Why are you saying this? You know my medicine will help him."

The warrior sighed. "I am jealous. I wish to have you for my own, and you will belong to our *sachem*."

Moon Dove's eyes filled with tears. "We must not speak of this—"

"Your love for me?" he challenged.

She closed her eyes, shook her head. "I must go." She started to leave him.

"Wait!"

She froze and faced him, her heart beating wildly within her breast.

"Say that you love me, and I will be content."

"I can't."

"Tell me you don't love me then."

Her features contorted with emotion. "I cannot do that either." She was bound to the chief, but her heart belonged to Black Fox.

He nodded then, and a small smile came to his lips. "This man loves you as well," he said.

They stopped for the night, camping under some trees, but where a clearing allowed them a campfire. As Thomas Brown worked to ignite a flame, Joanna wondered if there were Iroquois in the area. If there were, she thought, the fire would alert the Indians that there were white men about.

She offered a silent prayer for their safety, and sat down on a blanket the fur trapper had also thoughtfully provided. Gillian sat beside her.

"How are you faring?" Joanna asked her friend.

Gillian smiled weakly. "I'm fine. A bit tired, but I'll live."

"That's the spirit," Joanna said, making Gillian grin.

They sat companionably for a time, sharing a container of water, watching Brown and John build their campfire into a roaring flame.

"John said that the fire would keep away wild animals," Gillian commented.

"Which ones?" Joanna said. "The four-legged or two-legged kind?"

Fear flashed across her friend's face, and Joanna instantly regretted her teasing remark.

"Oh, Gillian," she said, "I'm sorry. I was joking. Don't worry. We'll be fine."

Gillian nodded, but hugged herself with her arms.

The blanket was large enough for both women to share. Fortunately, with the warm night there was no need for a top cover. Each man had his own sleeping pallet, and John settled down on his while Brown took his rifle to hunt dinner.

Joanna turned her gaze from Brown as he entered the dark regions of the forest, disappearing from view, and found John studying her.

"We'll be on our way back to England in no time," he said with a smile.

She nodded. The thought gave her no pleasure. She had not missed the comforts of Neville Manor. She had been raised among the Lenape, and found she had adjusted quite well upon her return. And she didn't relish the idea of getting on another sailing ship.

"Come here," John said. "I'd like to talk with you."

She frowned. She could hear him very well from where she sat. But, she supposed, so could Gillian. Why shouldn't Gillian hear what he had to say?

Reluctantly, she rose, and moved over to his sleeping pallet. When he patted the blanket next to him, she sat down.

He touched her hair, and she stiffened, then lifted her face to him with a forced smile. Perhaps sensing her tension, he released her hair, and placed his hands on his raised knees.

Joanna glanced down at his breeches, and imagined a different man's bare knees. Fireheart's.

"We're to be married, Joanna," John said softly.

"Yes, yes, I know," she replied.

"You must learn to relax with me, or how are we to be man and wife?"

She inclined her head. "The idea is still new to me, John. We've been friends for so long, it seems strange to think of us as more."

She studied him in the firelight. He had discarded his powdered wig for his own hair. His dark tresses were thick and shiny, worn back in a queue. She wondered why men like John chose to cover up their locks when it was obvious that their own hair looked better.

Something dark flashed in his blue eyes as she gazed at him. The emotion, whatever it was, disappeared quickly. Startled, Joanna could only stare at him, and wonder what was going on inside John's thoughts.

"What did you want to talk about?" she asked.

"About the wedding—"

"We're not even on England's soil yet," she said, feeling dismay. "There will be time enough to think about such things."

He looked hurt. "I just thought—"

She sighed heavily, and apologized. "John, I'm sorry, but I'm tired, and I can't think of anything other than sleep."

His expression softened. "It has been a long day," he said with obvious relief.

"Yes, it has." She glanced at Gillian. "Gillian is tired, too. She's been a real friend through all of this." She shook her head with amazement. "How on earth did she manage to convince you to let her come?"

A smile curved her fiancé's lips. "She pleaded her case, and though I was reluctant at first, I relented." A gleam lit his blue eyes as he looked at the woman on the other blanket. "She can be very persuasive."

Joanna knew that Gillian could be stubborn and extremely convincing when she wanted to be. She had seen the young woman in action among the daughters of her uncle's peers. When Joanna had first come to England, she'd been ostracized, labeled "that heathen niece of Roderick Neville." It had been Gillian who had come to her defense, befriending Joanna when the other girls kept their distance. Finally, through Gillian's persistence, some of the other girls started being friendly. In Gillian's own quiet way, she had seen that Joanna was accepted.

Gillian had lain down on the blanket. She opened her eyes to find both John and Joanna staring at her. She seemed to blanch until Joanna got up, and approached her with a smile.

"John was telling me that you can be persuasive when you want," she said. "I asked him how you managed to come along on this journey."

Gillian flashed John a nervous glance. Some of the tension left her features as she faced her friend. "I threatened to release all of your horses should I be left behind. It would have caused quite a stir."

"Gillian!" Joanna exclaimed with a laugh. "You wouldn't!"

Gillian lowered her voice conspiratorially. "I know that, but he didn't."

The two women exchanged grins.

Joanna gazed at her friend, and felt a rush of affection. "I'm glad you're here," she admitted.

Gillian glanced away, looking uneasy. "I'm glad, too."

"Where is Autumn Wind?" Fireheart asked.

Little Blossom seemed surprised by the question. "She has gone, Fireheart. She and her English friends left after you went to kidnap the enemy chief."

"Gone?" His chest tightened with pain, making it difficult to breathe. "Gone to England?"

"*Kihiila*," the young matron said softly. "Perhaps you should speak with Mary Wife. She will know more about Autumn Wind."

Although she'd talked about going soon, he hadn't really expected her to leave before his return, he realized. He had wanted to say good-bye. Now she was gone, and he would never see her again.

Little Blossom was right. He must speak with Mary Wife. Fireheart started across the yard toward Mary's wigwam.

"Fireheart!"

He halted as he saw Turtle That Hops crossing to meet him.

"I must talk with you," the brave began.

"Autumn Wind is gone," the *sachem* said as if he'd explained something, but he hadn't.

"Aye!" the brave exclaimed. "I do not trust that John Burton. I saw him with that woman—Gillian. They were joined in the forest like two dogs stuck together."

Fireheart stiffened. "John and Gillian have joined as a man would with his wife?"

"*Kihiila*, this is so."

"Autumn Wind must have decided not to marry him."

Turtle That Hops shook his head. "She has not changed her mind. She does not know that John and her friend sneak off to lie with each other." The brave grabbed his chief's arm. "But I fear there is more. I think the white man is not an honorable man. I think he would steal and kill easily for what he wants."

Fireheart shrugged. What could the man possibly want from Joanna? he wondered. His blood chilled. *Her uncle's property.*

"How do you know this John would kill?"

"Little Cloud," the brave mentioned his son. "He saw the white man's gun. It was a small gun, but Little Cloud saw this John kill a rabbit, then let it be."

"He didn't take the fur, or bring back the meat?" Fireheart frowned. This showed a disregard for the spirit of the animal and the gifts of this earthly life.

"He did not touch it. He killed it, and laughed before he put away his gun."

Fireheart began to fear for Joanna's safety. What manner of a man was this English John, one who would lie with his wife-to-be's friend? he wondered. One who would kill for no reason.

"I must talk with Mary Wife," Fireheart said. "I must know if this English John would take Autumn Wind away to harm her." He looked at his friend who looked relieved. "*Wa-neé-shih*," he said.

Turtle That Hops acknowledged the *sachem*'s thanks, and left Fireheart who continued on to see Joanna's cousin.

Joanna began to have doubts during the second day of traveling. She wasn't ready to go back to England, wasn't ready to marry John. She wanted to talk with her cousin again, say all of the things she'd never taken the time to say. She wanted to know what Mary had written in all those letters.

If she waited much longer, it would be too far for her to return. She could go back, spend a few more days, then seriously consider what to do with the rest of her life.

Recalling her time with Fireheart, Joanna realized that Fireheart must care for her. He had made exquisite love to her. She was no expert on relationships, having lost her mother and father at a young age before being torn from her cousin Mary to live with the monster who was her uncle. But surely a man whose only motive had been lust wouldn't have been such a tender thoughtful lover.

She wanted to go back. She had to stop John and the others now before it was too late.

"John!" she cried, hurrying past Gillian toward him and Thomas Brown, her heart pounding with excitement. "I need to speak with you and Mr. Brown immediately."

Chapter 18

"You can't go back!" John argued. "We've wasted too much time, and we are too far along. Returning to the village will only delay us further. If we don't get to port soon, we'll have to travel during the winter months."

"I have to go back, John," Joanna said. She didn't care whether they had to travel during the winter or not, or if she had to endure rough seas. "I may never get back to the village again. There are things I have to say to Mary and the others. Things I have to do."

She needed to see Fireheart again, she decided. Confess her feelings for him. She wanted to ask him if there was a chance they could be together if she stayed.

"No," John said. "Gillian and I are not going back, and neither are you." John placed his arm around Gillian who looked exhausted. There were shadows under the young woman's eyes. "Look at her, Joanna. This journey is hard for her."

Joanna had noticed a strange tension about her friend, and she had attributed it to the hardships of the journey. Studying her more carefully, she wondered if her friend was ill.

If she were, Joanna thought, Gillian would benefit from a trip back to the village. They could stay for a few days until Gillian felt rested and well enough to travel. Perhaps the Lenape shaman, Raven Wing, would be able to help her.

"I'm sorry, Joanna," John said, his voice softer, apologetic. "You understand why we can't go back, don't you?"

"But Raven Wing can help Gillian if she isn't feeling well," Joanna replied.

"Joanna," he said, losing patience. "We've been too long from Neville Manor as it is."

She stifled the guilt that came from knowing that she had neglected her responsibility to her uncle's property, and to the people who had worked for him.

Joanna firmed her lips, determined to return. She had left the village once before against her will. She would not do so again.

"I'll return alone if you're so dead set against it. You can wait for me in Philadelphia. I promise I'll only be a few days, and no longer. Gillian will be rested and ready for the next ship by the time I get there. If I don't come when the ship is in port, don't wait for me. Just go." She had to add that in the event that Fireheart wanted her to stay.

"Joanna, love," John said. He released Gillian to reach for her. "Be reasonable. 'Tis too dangerous a journey for you to go back on your own. And how would you find your way?"

She smiled. She knew a few things more about the woods than she had when she'd first come. Fireheart had taught her what to look for when one was lost and needed to backtrack a trail.

She could do it, she thought with confidence. She had come to know the area well since her return to the New World. Time spent with Woman with Eyes of Hawk and Little Blossom had taught her even more techniques for finding her way through the forest. She would discover the signs for the path they'd taken to come this far. She would make it back to the village; she was sure of it! She was not in the least worried that she would be in danger or lose her way.

And it wouldn't matter if I were afraid, she thought. She wanted to go that badly.

Confident and sure of her plans, Joanna gazed at John, and decided that even if she did return to England, she would not be marrying him. Marriage between her and John would never work, she realized. Not when her heart belonged to Fireheart.

Joanna knew better than to tell John at this time. She would keep her decision a secret until the right occasion came along.

"I'm going, John," she said, gathering her satchel of belongings. "I have to go. Nothing you can say or do will convince me that I shouldn't return. You can't stop me."

"You'd best think again, Joanna." John's voice was cold.

She halted, and heard Gillian's gasp of shocked surprise as Joanna hefted her satchel into a more comfortable position, and turned to face him.

Her blood chilled as she saw the pistol. He was aiming the barrel of his gun directly at her. "John, no—"

"I don't want it to be this way," he said calmly. "But I can't let you do this. 'Tis for your own good that I stop you. Someday you'll thank me. I just can't let you leave, and be killed."

"You'll not kill me—"

"Nay, but I will injure you enough to keep you from doing further harm to yourself. I'd rather carry you to port than see you travel back through these woods."

Joanna gaped at him. Was the man insane? She

stared at his face, and the glitter in his blue eyes disturbed her. This wasn't John Burton, her friend!

She transferred her gaze to Gillian who stared at the gun in a stupor as if she, too, couldn't believe he'd pulled his weapon on her friend.

"You wouldn't shoot me," Joanna said with a gasp.

John smiled grimly. "I would." He threw a glance toward the fur trapper who stood off to the side, watching the whole scene. "Mr. Brown," he said. "Don't you agree that this territory is too dangerous for a lone woman to travel unprotected?"

"Certain enough," the gruff man said without apology.

"John," Gillian cried, having found her voice at last. "This is Joanna. Your friend and fiancée! Surely, you wouldn't use that pistol on her?"

"This isn't any of your concern, Gillian," John said darkly. He ignored the young woman's stricken face. He softened his expression as he turned back to Joanna. "You understand, love, don't you?" he said gently.

Her heart skittering with fear, Joanna could only nod.

"Then let's stop for a bite to eat, shall we?" he said. He nodded toward Brown as he spread a blanket on the ground for the ladies.

John captured Joanna's arm firmly, and escorted her to the blanket to sit. "Here you go, dear."

Joanna sat, more certain than ever that she'd made the right decision not to marry John. Her eyes met Gillian who had taken a seat on the edge of the blanket. Her friend's face was white, her hands trembling as she lifted fingers to tuck back a lock of escaped midnight-dark hair.

When John handed her something to eat, Joanna wanted to tear it from his hands, and throw the hard tack into his face, but she accepted it with gracious thanks instead. The man was crazy, she decided, and she would find a way to escape him.

But what about Gillian? She couldn't escape quickly without leaving Gillian behind, yet how could she manage to flee successfully with her friend?

Joanna ate the hard dry biscuit only because she needed the nourishment for strength. She would get away somehow. Somehow, she would find a way.

After talking with Mary, Fireheart left the village in search of Joanna. He explained what he'd learned about John Burton, and Mary had been as concerned as he about her cousin's safety. She had wanted to come. It had taken all of his persistence to keep her within the village. Finally, when Rising Bird had insisted on accompanying him, Mary had relented, knowing that, together with her husband's help, Fireheart would find Joanna, and bring her back.

"I didn't want her to go," Mary had said.

Fireheart had nodded. "I drove her away."

"You?"

"*Kihiila*. She is unhappy that I am to marry Moon Dove."

Mary didn't seem surprised by the revelation. "She cares for you."

"I care for Autumn Wind," he said, his dark eyes bright.

"Bring her back to me," Mary pleaded to her husband and the chief.

"We will find her, and bring her back," Fireheart vowed. "There are things I must say to her."

"*Kihiila*," Mary had said. "I have many things to tell her, too."

Hours later, Fireheart halted to examine the dirt of the trail. "They left the path here," he said, pointing in one direction.

Rising Bird bent to check the same sign. "Let us go that way then."

His thoughts wild with images of Joanna, Fireheart left the trail, and continued into the woods as night fell, darkening the forest.

"John," Gillian whispered, "you weren't really going to shoot Joanna, were you?"

It was night. With Brown and Joanna asleep, the couple had left the campsite a short distance for a few moments alone together.

John gently cupped the woman's cheek. He smiled. "No."

She shuddered with relief. "Thank God."

He lifted an eyebrow. "You doubted me?"

"I—" Her violet eyes filled with tears. "I'm sorry, but I've not been feeling well. A bit queasy mostly."

"Queasy?" he asked, his mind working quickly.

"Nothing too terrible," she assured him. "I'll be all right."

A cold knot formed in his belly. Was she with child? he wondered. Could Gillian be carrying his babe?

The thought gave him no pleasure. A swollen belly on his fiancée's friend would only complicate matters between him and Joanna.

Joanna. He had frightened her, but he thought she understood why. Since that unfortunate incident when he'd been forced to pull his gun, she had listened carefully, and obeyed him. *She will make an excellent wife,* he thought, pleased.

But before him was a woman who aroused him to the point of pain. He wanted her as he'd never wanted Joanna. His cock had been hot and throbbing since night had fallen, and he'd imagined doing all sort of delicious things to her. With Joanna and Brown only yards away, they would have to be quiet. His excitement grew.

"John, did you hear what I said?" Gillian whispered. "Why are we here?"

He looked at her without hiding his lust for her.

"No," she whispered, appalled. "We can't. We're too close to them."

He grinned. She could see his face clearly in the glow cast by the campfire. Too close, Gillian thought. They were too close. Joanna and the fur trapper would hear them. The thought unnerved her even while she felt a tiny spark of arousal.

John was pushing her to the ground. She drew a sharp intake of breath as he ran his hand beneath her skirts, slipping his fingers along her thigh.

"John—"

"Hush!" he ordered her before he plunged his fingers into her opening, making her stiffen and arch up. "Let me touch you, but don't make a sound."

"I don't know if I can be quiet," she gasped as he began to expertly rub her. He tortured her pleasure point until she was writhing on the ground, trying hard to stifle the moan that formed on her lips.

It slipped out—a soft groan of pleasure as he spread her legs, and used two hands to send her soaring, flying. . . .

The cry came to her mouth as she climaxed, but John quickly stifled it with his kiss so the sound that escaped was barely a whimper.

She lay there, shuddering with ecstasy, gazing up at the man she adored. "I'm sorry," she whispered apologetically.

His gaze glistened as a small smile played upon his mouth. "Now it's your turn to touch me," he said, grabbing her hand and placing it on his erection.

She was startled for she hadn't realized that he'd freed himself from his breeches; she'd been so caught up in the spiraling whirl of sensation that he'd woven like a pleasure web around her.

Happy now, trusting the man she loved, Gillian gripped her lover's staff and stroked him.

"More," he ordered.

She rose up, rolled him over, and bent her head between his legs.

Something woke Joanna, a strange sound in the night. She lay for a time, listening, then became aware that Gillian wasn't asleep beside her. Where was Gillian? Had she left the campsite to relieve herself in a place more private?

She sat up, saw Thomas Brown lying on his sleeping pallet, and turned toward the glowing embers, all that was left of the fire. The man slept with his mouth open, a trickle of drool running from the corner of his lips into his beard, and onto the blanket.

Her first thought was to escape as she turned toward the spot where John's sleeping pallet had been spread out the previous evening. The pallet was empty. John and Gillian were gone. Perhaps Gillian had awoken and needed John to escort her some distance from camp.

She pictured John as a gentleman with his back toward Gillian while Gillian lifted her skirts and relieved herself in as ladylike a manner as possible.

Joanna stood, and decided that she needed to relieve herself, too. Then she heard a sound like a harsh groan, and then a light whimper. She froze. An animal? Then the noise came again, and she recognized it as human.

Curious, concerned that Gillian might be ill with John comforting her, Joanna moved in the direction of the sound . . . and that's when she saw them. Gillian and John lay on the ground, rutting like two animals.

Joanna stared in shock at Gillian with her skirts raised, her legs spread-eagle while John with his arse bare, his breeches down about his ankles, humped and ground his hips against Gillian's. The two of them were clearly in the throes of building ecstasy, oblivious to the woman who stood nearby.

Joanna struggled with the hurt of being betrayed not only by John, but by her friend Gillian as well. If, at first, she had thought for one moment that Gillian was being ravished against her will, the notion was quickly gone as she saw the way her friend clutched John and moaned his name. She was not pushing him away.

She thought of her own love for Fireheart, how she had fought to keep from surrendering to her passion for him because he was promised to another. Yet Gillian, her best friend, had not bothered to consider her feelings. Gillian had wanted John, and had surrendered to her lust for him. It hadn't mattered that Joanna had agreed to marry him. Gillian hadn't bothered to fight her feelings for Joanna's fiancé.

Joanna stood frozen for a heartbeat longer, and then she realized that this could be her only chance for escape.

Gillian be damned, she thought with anger. Gillian could stay with John. They deserved each other.

Joanna turned from the mating pair, and quietly made her escape.

Chapter 19

"What was that?" Gillian gasped as John rolled off her, satiated, spent.

"It's nothing, Gillian." He reached to fondle her breast, but she evaded him.

"No," she insisted. "I heard something. Like an animal in the brush." She bit her lip as she sat up, and looked around nervously. "Or the sound of someone running away."

"Joanna." His heart beating hard, John scrambled to his feet, and tugged up his breeches.

"No," she whispered as she, too, rose, and quickly put herself to rights.

They moved toward the campsite, and within seconds saw the empty sleeping pallet. Joanna Neville was gone.

"Oh, God, no," Gillian cried. "I wonder if she saw us."

Teeth clamped shut, John strode over to the sleeping fur trapper. He scowled down at him. "Brown!" He kicked the man in the side. "Brown!"

"What?" The fur trapper awoke groggily as he was

kicked a second time. "What the hell are you doing, Burton?" he growled.

"Where is she?" John demanded. "Where is Joanna?"

The man seemed startled as he glanced toward the empty sleeping pallet. "I don't know." He looked at the couple, and narrowed his gaze. "Where have you been that you didn't hear her leave?"

"I heard her," John said, "but it was too late to do anything about it."

"Is that so?" Brown said. "Then which way did she go?" He saw the red staining the woman's cheeks and smirked. "Seems to me that if you'd been in your bed instead of swivin' the dear lady's friend, your Joanna would be still asleep, safe and sound."

"Why, you—" John launched himself at the fur trapper. Gillian screamed as he felt the satisfaction of his fist hitting flesh. He heard her wild shriek just before he felt the blow to his face that knocked him on his buttocks.

John gazed up at the man, stunned by the power behind the old man's punch.

"I'm not responsible for your lady friends," Brown spat, glaring. He cast a disdainful look at Gillian. "Neither one of them."

"John, no!" Gillian cried as John lumbered to his feet, and put up his hands in a fighting stance. "What about Joanna? She couldn't have gone very far."

John froze as if what she had said made sense. He lowered his fists, and stepped backward. "Sorry, Brown. Guess I got carried away." His apology was clumsy, oafish. He extended his hand in friendship toward the guide.

Brown stared at the man's hand a long moment before accepting the handshake. "If we leave now, we'll be able to find her," he said gruffly.

The young man nodded. He needed the old fur trapper or else he'd have done away with him when he'd first realized that Joanna had gone. He refused to believe that he himself had anything to do with Joanna's disappearance. She'd been determined to go, he thought. He should have been more alert, more wary of her apparent humility. How could he have forgotten Joanna's stubborn pride?

"Let's go then," he said as he bent to roll up his own sleeping pallet. He didn't bother to help Gillian who struggled to fold up her own. "Hurry, Gillian," he snapped.

Gillian paused with tears in her eyes. Then she obeyed him while she silently cursed the day she'd decided that John Burton was the only man for her.

Joanna ran, but her skirts hindered her. Gasping, she halted, struggled out of her gown, then started to run in only her shift. It was warm; she wasn't worried about taking a chill. The insects of the night might bite her, but earlier she had used some of the Indians' bear grease to protect her exposed skin. The only parts of her that might get bitten were the areas she'd been unable to reach under her clothes.

She didn't know if she was going the right way. She didn't care; her only concern was to escape.

Gillian and John are lovers! she thought. She felt a sharp pain as she recalled what she'd seen. *Gillian, how could you?*

She swept past brush and trees, tangling in sticker bushes, but she kept going as fear settled in her breast. No doubt John and Gillian would have discovered her absence. Would they come after her?

She recalled John's actions with the gun. *He'll come after me*, she thought.

She began to run faster, tripping once over a fallen tree branch, picking herself up, and continuing on.

And then she heard it . . . the sound of someone in the forest, slashing through brush and leaves.

She changed direction in the hope that she could trick her pursuer. Then she slunk low in the midst of forest foliage.

Her breath coming hard, she waited, listening; the only sounds were her heart thumping wildly in her chest and her lungs struggling for air.

"Come out, Joanna." John's voice so close startled her. Fearful, she rose, backed into some thorn bushes, and gasped with pain.

He was suddenly there, reaching in to grab her arm, dragging her from the briars, heedless or uncaring of the barbs that pierced her.

She struggled to get away, but he was too strong for her. Then Thomas Brown was behind her, holding her arms while John scolded and glared at her.

"You shouldn't have tried to leave," John said, his voice soft. Too soft. "I told you there are dangerous things in the forest." He raised his hand, and she cringed, expecting to be slapped. She was amazed when he ordered Thomas to release her arms . . . and she was free . . . free!

She rubbed her arms where the fur trapper had gripped her tightly, and studied John.

"You saw us—Gillian and me," John said quietly.

She nodded, glaring.

"That's unfortunate. We didn't mean to hurt you. I wouldn't hurt you for the world . . . only a man has certain needs. I didn't expect you to fill them . . . not before our wedding."

"I can't marry you," she said, throwing caution to the wind.

"Yes, you can and you will. You'll realize that once again I was only thinking of you . . . of protecting you, keeping you safe."

"Please, John, you don't want to marry me." She heard movement as Gillian came out of the forest to join them in the tiny clearing. "You should marry *her*," she snapped.

"Joanna," Gillian began, contrite.

"Silence!" John barked at her, making her blanch.

The first light of dawn had broken the dense darkness of the night sky. Joanna stared at the three people she had foolishly left the Lenape village with, and felt ill.

"Let me go back to the village, John. If you can lie with Gillian, you can't possibly have any affection for me."

He laughed. "I care for you. What more do you want?" He shook his head as he pulled out his pistol.

"No, John," Gillian gasped.

He ignored her. "If you don't come with us easily, peacefully, I'll have to kill you. 'Tis for your own good. You could die a worse death. You could get eaten by a bear, or be ravished by savages. . . ."

She snorted. The Indians didn't rape women. They believed that to do so would conjure up bad spirits, and give the women an unwelcome evil power over them. "The Lenape would never hurt me."

"Let's go," John ordered everyone, pointing the way back to camp with his gun. "Move!"

Thomas and Gillian went first with Joanna following. John with his gun was behind her.

Joanna stared at her former best friend, and felt bitter acid rise up to clog her throat. Gillian's betrayal hurt worst of all. She had loved and trusted Gillian since she was a child. She had thought they shared a special bond . . . the bond of friendship and love.

But Gillian had eyes and love for only a madman. For John Burton was mad, Joanna realized. Why hadn't she seen it before? Or had it just happened? Had something occurred onboard ship that had changed him, something that she didn't know about?

She trudged before him because she had no other choice. He had a gun at her back and her life in his hands, but she would be free of him. Somehow, someway, she'd be gone. Soon.

When they reached the campsite, the sleeping pallets had been rolled in readiness for traveling. The fire had been put out, and, as she watched, Thomas Brown wiped out all signs of evidence of their presence.

Fireheart, Joanna thought, silently calling his name. *I need you.*

But Fireheart wouldn't come, she mused, dispirited. He would be getting ready to marry his new bride. His attention would be on Moon Dove.

Fireheart and Rising Bird found a campsite the next day. They had traveled for hours, not stopping to rest, continuing on during the night and day. They halted when they reached the clearing where they had been led by trail marks.

Someone had tried to erase all signs of their stay. Fireheart, studying the campsite, thought what a poor job they'd done . . . or had someone done it intentionally?

Joanna? His breath lodged in his throat as he pictured her frightened and alone with an abusive and evil man. *A man like her uncle,* he thought.

Mary had learned the true nature of Joanna's life with Roderick Neville. From the things Joanna had told her cousin combined with the secrets she'd confided to him, Fireheart and Mary had learned the true extent of the young girl's suffering in England. Joanna had been ripped from her home and sent to another world, a world of unhappiness.

Mary had cried as they'd spoken. Fireheart had tried to comfort her, but she wouldn't be consoled. She stopped sobbing only when she'd learned about Fireheart's plan to go after Joanna. He told her that he would bring Joanna back to the village. Then they could give Autumn Wind the choice of staying or going.

Fireheart found tiny particles of ashes in the dry dust of the forest floor. He held them to his nose and sniffed, then dropped the handful of dirt and ash.

Rising Bird had left the main area of the camp to wander outside the site, looking for clues to the traveling party's direction.

The brave returned with his features tight with anxiety, his expression grave. "Someone tried to run from this place," he said. "There are signs of an escape. I followed it for some time, and found this."

He lifted his arm, and Fireheart felt the air whoosh from his chest as he saw the garment. Joanna's gown.

Fireheart crossed to take the dress and examine it. The gown wasn't torn, which meant that Joanna might have removed it willingly . . . unless someone had held a gun to her.

He scowled, tensing. He fisted a hand at his side as he passed the gown back to Rising Bird.

"Where did they go?" Fireheart said.

Rising Bird narrowed his gaze, and approached an area outside the immediate clearing. "This way, I think," he said, pointing.

Fireheart agreed. He led with Rising Bird following. He didn't offer to carry Joanna's gown nor did the other warrior expect it. They didn't leave it behind for Joanna might need it when they found her.

"Joanna, I'm sorry."

Joanna glared at her former friend. "You're a fool to trust him, Gillian. He's an evil man. I don't know why he is acting horrible except that he is crazy."

"He is not crazy!" Gillian defended with the naivete of someone blinded by love. "You don't know him the way I do."

"Obviously not," Joanna said with sarcasm.

Her friend blushed. "You saw us."

She nodded. "It wasn't a pretty sight."

Gillian was mortified. "I love him," she explained.

"And what of his marriage proposal to me? What were you going to do after we wed?" Joanna narrowed her gaze as she studied the young woman. "You were going to continue to see him behind my back." She felt deeply hurt by Gillian's betrayal. She had trusted Gillian. Where was the loyalty, the love?

"John said—"

She held up her hand. "Don't say it! I can imagine what John said."

"No, it's not like that. Our love is not sordid!" Gillian cried.

"Did he tell you he loved you, Gillian?"

Her eyes misting, she opened her mouth to answer. "I think so."

"You think?"

"I cannot remember! But he has shown me in many ways."

"I'll wager he did," Joanna mumbled sarcastically. Her tone grew serious. "Gillian, it's not losing John that bothers me, it's losing you for a friend. Friends don't betray each other!"

"I know," her friend whispered. "But I mean it sincerely when I say I'm sorry. I never wanted to hurt you."

"If John cares for you, why does he want to marry me?"

The two women were alone while Thomas Brown and John searched the nearby woods for food. Joanna knew she could be frank without incurring John's wrath—"Mad John," as she now thought of him.

"Burton Estates is in trouble. With your late uncle's assets, the brothers' livelihood and land would be saved."

"And you found that to be a suitable reason for him to marry your best friend?"

"He said we could still be together—"

"In a little cottage of your own perhaps?" Joanna taunted. Clicking her tongue, she shook her head. "What will your dear father think of all this?"

Twin red spots of anger appeared on each of Gillian's cheeks. "Leave my father out of this!"

"You aren't concerned what he will think of your being John Burton's mistress, and not his wife?" Joanna saw the way Gillian's hands balled into fists in her lap. "Or doesn't he like John?"

Gillian gasped as if Joanna had hit an open wound. "Father doesn't understand him."

"I think he does. He recognized John's kind." Joanna continued to taunt her former friend. "I must admit I myself was fooled into believing him my friend. No wonder he was happy to watch over Neville Manor for me."

"Stop!" Gillian cried. "I don't want to hear any more of this!"

"Well, you will hear it often, and you will listen," Joanna badgered, "unless you'll help me to leave." She sat up straighter, and placed a hand on Gillian's arm. "Help me escape, and you'll have John to yourself if you actually still want him."

"I cannot!"

"Now, Gillian. Go and distract him. Give me a chance to get away. Or let us plan another time, a better place . . . when it's dark perhaps."

Gillian rose stiffly, refusing to look at her former friend. "I will not listen to this. I will not betray John."

"Only your best friend," Joanna said coldly. Hearing Gillian's gasp, she no longer felt anger for the young woman who had been like a sister to her. She was filled with pity for her.

John saw the two women talking, and smiled with satisfaction as Gillian walked off, looking angry. He left the forest, and approached Joanna where she sat on a large rock. "What were you and Gillian discussing?" he asked.

Joanna looked at him and glared. "You."

He raised his eyebrows, making no secret of his amusement. "What did she say?" He was certain of her answer.

"She cares for you," she said with loathing.

John's amusement vanished. "And you find that inconceivable."

Joanna nodded. "She's a fool to care for a cruel madman."

"You had best watch your words and your behavior. I could kill you now and no one would care." He paused a moment to allow his threat to sink in. By her white face, he realized that he had succeeded in frightening her. *Good.*

"I'll not marry you."

"You may want to rethink that decision, for one way or another I will acquire Neville Manor. I prefer it to be the simple way—"

"Never!"

He dragged her up by the arm, pressed his face close to hers. "I can shoot you, and no one will know or care."

"Thomas Brown will," she said.

"Thomas Brown is dead," he replied, shocking her. He tossed her to the ground, and she landed with a thump. "I killed him. For some reason, he thought what we were doing to you was wrong. He told me I should let you go." John's smile turned evil. "I refused, then shot him when it looked like he was going to become a nuisance."

Joanna shivered as she stared into the face of a man she had once considered a friend. "I don't believe you," she said.

"Come," he ordered.

She rose reluctantly, fear lodged in her throat for what she would see. He took her to a place in the

woods where Brown's body lay with a bullet hole in
his head, between the eyes.

Staring at the dead man, Joanna felt physically ill.
She turned from the sight, and threw up her stomach
contents.

John chuckled as he grabbed her arm, and forcibly
led her back to camp.

Mad John, she thought with horror clawing inside
of her. He was mad enough to kill once. He would
be mad enough to kill again.

As she sat down on her rock seat, Joanna realized
that she would be wise to hold her tongue, and pre-
tend to go along with his plans for her. Only then
might she find an opportunity to escape.

She decided to try a different tactic first. "You want
Neville Manor. You can have it. Let me go, and I'll
return to the Indians. You can go back to England,
and make Roderick's estate yours."

John's blue eyes flashed briefly with pleasure until
he seemed to find some fault in Joanna's suggestion.
"I'll not get possession legally without marriage to
you or a sale. I've not the funds for a sale so you'll
have to return and marry me."

"You expect me to marry you?" she said with disbelief.

He inclined his head. He regarded her with a smile
filled with satisfaction. "After our marriage, I don't
care what you do. Return to this savage place if you
want. Once I have Neville Manor, your whereabouts
or well-being will no longer be of concern to me."

"You'll let me go?" she said, pretending that she
might be convinced. He would never let her go. He'd
kill her first, she thought.

"You have my word."

But Joanna knew that anyone foolish enough to
trust the word of a madman would soon be dead.

Chapter 20

With the horror of Thomas Brown's death lingering in her mind, Joanna knew she had to escape from John Burton—and escape him soon. Earlier, when Gillian had asked the whereabouts of Thomas Brown, John had explained to her that the fur trapper had been killed in a fatal hunting accident.

"How?" she'd gasped.

"He saw a deer, got excited, tripped, and fell, landing on his gun that was primed and ready. He died instantly."

"But how will we get home?" she cried.

"I'll lead the way, Gillian," he said calmly. "You do trust me, don't you?"

She nodded. "Yes, I trust you." She touched his shoulder, and smiled when he placed his hands at her waist.

Foolish girl, Joanna thought, as she studied her friend for some time afterward. If she had asked to see the body, Gillian would have known that someone wasn't killed by accident with a gunshot between the eyes.

How could she fight a woman whose only loyalty was to the madman she loved?

How could Gillian have forgotten their friendship, the good times they'd had together as children?

If she reminded Gillian of what they'd shared perhaps she could convince Gillian to help her. But how to do that without Gillian feeling like she was betraying John?

"Gillian," Joanna called softly as she stopped for the midday meal.

John glanced their way briefly, then turned his attention to finding food. "Watch her," he told Gillian before he slipped from camp with Thomas Brown's rifle.

"Gillian!" Joanna called again.

"I'm not going to listen to you talk ill of John, Joanna," she said.

"I'm not going to speak badly of him. I needed to talk with someone. Remember when we went to see your Aunt Martha together?" Joanna asked as if she were just reminiscing. "She was such a nice old lady. Whatever happened to her?" It had been a lovely afternoon, Joanna recalled. They had drunk tea with Aunt Martha, listened to her stories. It had been a time away from Uncle Roderick, an escape from the dark manor that held only unhappiness for her.

Gillian's expression softened slightly. "Aunt Martha was well the last time I saw her."

"It was a wonderful day," Joanna said softly.

"Yes," Gillian murmured with a reminiscent smile. "She is a special lady."

Joanna nodded. She began to remind Gillian of other times, of their friendship, the shared tears and laughter. She knew Gillian was beginning to remember the fond memories as tears sparkled on her dark lashes. Tears of guilt, Joanna hoped.

"Gillian, I think you should marry John. I told him

he could have Neville Manor, if only he'd let me go.
I want to go back to—"

"Fireheart," Gillian said.

"Yes. I told you how I felt about him so I understand
how you feel about John. Fireheart is expected to
marry Moon Dove."

"Oh, Joanna . . ."

"Please, Gillian, help me leave. I need to go."

"I can't betray John." She looked as if she were
weakening.

"You won't be betraying him," Joanna said. "You'll
be righting a wrong before it happens. I'll write you
a letter giving John ownership of Neville Manor."

Gillian's eyes widened. "You will?"

"Yes."

She blinked, shook her head. She closed off her
expression. "No, I can't."

"John, no," Gillian said when John came up from
behind her and slipped one hand around her waist,
the other over her breast. "Joanna—"

John smiled when he saw that Joanna was watching
them. It didn't dampen his desire; it enhanced it.
"Don't look at her. I want you, not her. You're the
one I love."

Gillian sighed. "You do love me," she murmured,
pleased.

"Of course, I do," he said, palming her breast,
and he kissed her until she could only think of the
pleasure he gave her.

"Joanna?" Gillian whispered, sounding scared.
"John is sleeping. You need to escape now!"

Night had fallen and John was asleep. He hadn't
bothered to tie Joanna up, believing her too frightened of his threats to disobey him.

Heart racing, Joanna gazed at her with gratitude. "Gillian—"

"No, don't," she said with tears glistening in her lovely gaze. "Please believe me when I say I'm sorry. I didn't mean to hurt you. You will write that letter, though? The one that gives John Neville Manor?"

Disappointment burned in her breast as Joanna nodded. "I promise I'll send it."

Gillian looked relieved. "Go," she said. She cast a fearful glance over her shoulder. When she looked back, she appeared terrified. "Hurry! Before he awakens!" She handed Joanna John's flintlock pistol and some ammunition she must have found. "He has Brown's gun."

Thanking her, Joanna took the pistol and extra shot, saw that the gun was loaded, and left without looking back.

Joanna ran and ran, her thoughts with Gillian, the woman she'd left behind. Gillian had proven to be her friend after all. She had defied John, taken his weapon, and freed her friend.

Joanna hoped that Gillian wouldn't suffer too gravely for the deed.

John woke up, stretching. He smelled something cooking on the campfire. He smiled when Gillian handed him a clay bowl of rabbit stew. "Thank you, love," he said. The rabbit he had shot the night before. Gillian had prepared the leftover meat well.

She beamed. "Did you sleep well?"

He nodded. "Like a babe."

"John—" Gillian got a worried look on her face. "Joanna is missing," she said. "Gone!"

He threw the bowl of stew to the ground, and came up off his sleeping pallet with a roar. "Gone! Where? How could she escape?"

"Well, you did not bind her," she said. "I woke

up and she was missing. I was going to wake you immediately, but you looked so peaceful. . . ."

He lowered his eyelids as he studied her. "Where is Joanna, Gillian? Did you help her escape?" A muscle ticked along his jaw.

Seeing it, Gillian tensed. "I don't know where she is."

He grabbed her arms hard. "You helped her escape!"

"No, John," she protested, trembling.

"Then why are you so afraid?"

"You're hurting me!"

John released her, and scrambled among his belongings. Gillian's heart tripped. Was he searching for his pistol?

"Where is it?" he bellowed. His eyes burned with anger as he rose to glare at her. "Did you give her my gun?" He stalked her. Gillian was afraid.

"No," she whispered, backing away. "Why would you think that, John? I love you. You know I do."

"But Joanna is your friend."

"I betrayed her, though, didn't I? I slept with the man she was going to marry."

"*Is* going to marry!" he raged.

He caught her again, squeezing her arms hard, making her wince, then pressing her harder so that she cried out with pain.

"Let go of me!" she cried.

"Tell me the truth," he shouted. "Did you help her escape? Did you give her my pistol?"

She shook her head. *Dear God, don't let him believe that I am lying!*

He stared at her hard, then his features softened. "Forgive me, love. I didn't mean to become angry with you. It's she who deserves my fury, not you, the woman I love."

She eyed him warily as she felt herself slowly relax. "Yes," she murmured.

"But you know I wouldn't hurt you, Gillian."

She didn't know that—not now. He was a different man than the lover she'd known.

What had happened to make him change? She rubbed her arms where he'd squeezed tightly. She knew she would have dark bruises there later that day. Would he be sorry when he saw them? Or would he not bother to see if she was all right?

"I should have awakened you," she said. "I'm sorry."

He nodded, still watching her closely. "Let me see your arm," he said, causing her heart to melt.

She went to him, a rush of love replacing her fear. This kind caring man who wanted to ensure that she was all right was the man she'd fallen in love with . . . not the raging man who'd grabbed and shook her and threatened to kill.

He tenderly pushed up the sleeve of her gown, and exclaimed softly over the red marks his finger had left on her upper arms. "I'm sorry, Gillian." He breathed, then he kissed each reddening spot.

" 'Tis all right," she said, enjoying his gentle touch.

"I wouldn't have gotten so angry, if I was not worried about the financial security of Burton Estates."

His family property again, she thought bitterly. Didn't he realize that the land belonged to Michael, that if their positions were reversed, his brother Michael wouldn't think twice about helping him out in his hour of need?

She did not like Michael Burton. He was John's twin, and although they looked like siblings, the resemblance ended there. Michael was selfish, greedy, and a rogue. John was the more handsome and gentlest of the two. Michael expected John to dance attendance on him, and unfortunately, John gave him the time and the attention.

John began to kiss his way up to Gillian's shoulder, past fabric to her neck where he nibbled at the sensitive area below ear and chin. Gillian became caught up in the pleasure of his touch, and sagged against him.

"Oh, John . . ."

"We've got time," he rasped, surprising her with his desire.

She nodded, relieved that he didn't mention trailing Joanna. Perhaps he'd realized that he didn't need or want her.

"She doesn't want Neville Manor, John. When we return to England, you can lay claim to the house and land."

She thought he tensed, but she couldn't be sure for the next moment he was relaxed again, kissing her ear, her throat, tugging down her gown bodice, and burying his lips in the cleavage between her breasts.

She cupped his head, anxious for him to love her. He had frightened her; she wanted to be reassured that this man was her John . . . the tender considerate man whom she loved.

He began to show her what it was to be loved, kissing her, touching her, making her cry out with need. After fumbling out of their clothes, somehow they both became joined, and John was plunging inside of her, rocking her, until she screamed her release.

Gasping, reeling in the aftermath of ecstasy, Gillian stroked his back, and lay with her eyes closed, content. He shifted slightly, and she opened her eyes to smile at him. It took her a few seconds to realize that he wasn't gazing at her with tenderness and love but with suspicion and anger.

"You helped her escape."

She shook her head.

He placed his hands about her throat. "You helped her. Tell me, Gillian. There shouldn't be any secrets between us."

"I . . ." She hugged herself with her arms. "All right, so I told her you were asleep—"

He gazed at her, stroking her throat before releasing her, and nodded. Encouraged, she went on, "And she needed a weapon to protect herself. As you said yourself, the forest is a dangerous place."

"Gillian—"

"She promised to sign Neville Manor over to you, John. She doesn't want the property. She wants to stay here in this savage place with her Indian friends."

John rose, and began to quietly dress. His silence disturbed Gillian who had half expected him to rant and rage, and tell her how foolish she'd been.

Perhaps he had seen the error of his ways? Perhaps he realized that he would get the land without marrying Joanna.

"John?"

He looked at her then, and smiled with regret. Relieved, she smiled back, glad that he finally understood.

"We'd better get moving," he said as he stooped to roll up his sleeping pallet.

"All right." She bent and began to fold up her blanket.

Happy for the first time, she began to plan her life with John. Since Neville Manor would belong to him, they could live there happily. Her father would have to accept John as her husband then . . . a gentleman with property.

"Gillian?" John's voice came softly, loving.

She stood and faced him. She had barely a second's time to become alarmed as John pulled the trigger on Brown's rifle, hitting her in the heart and killing her instantly.

John studied Gillian's bleeding body, and shook his head. "Such a waste, dear Gilly. We could have been happy, you and I, but you ruined everything.

You had to betray me. Well, I cannot live with a traitor. And I need Joanna to get Neville Manor."

He picked up her blanket, and unfolded it to cover her prone body.

"Sorry, love. You weren't so good a lover that I'd forgive your betrayal and live with your deceit."

Chapter 21

Joanna curled her body into a ball as she lay on the ground in a hidden hollow, hoping for a short sleep. She was exhausted. When she'd left the campsite, she'd run without stopping, fearful that John would wake up and discover her disappearance too soon for her to make a successful escape.

She was going to get farther this time, she'd decided. He would never catch her. And so she went on until her legs felt like jelly, and she was ready to drop.

As she struggled to get into a more comfortable position, Joanna thought about continuing. She hadn't wanted to rest, but was forced to. She prayed that after a short nap she'd have the energy to race on.

She wasn't sure where she was going, and for now she didn't care. The only thing on her mind was being free. If she could be sure that John Burton had given up the chase and gone home, she would breathe easier. She knew she should be afraid. There were wild animals about, Indians who were not Lenni Lenape, and the danger of exposure should the air temperature turn cold or the weather nasty. But it wasn't the forest that frightened her; she was afraid of the cold hard murderer who pursued her.

Joanna shivered. She was feeling chilled in only her shift despite the warmth of the late summer sun, but she thought the cold in her bones would pass once she was rested.

A wind kicked up, rustling the trees overhead and the brush around her. Her body trembling, Joanna huddled into a tighter ball, and tried to sleep. Her eyes closed, then flashed open when she heard a sound, but it was nothing . . . a squirrel or some other animal scurrying through the woods.

It happened several times that she heard something, thought it was John, and became alert just as she was about to doze off, only to discover that it was the wind or an animal.

Finally, she ignored the noise, shut her eyes and kept them closed, and felt the weightlessness of drifting. Vulnerable, exposed, yet exhausted beyond measure, Joanna finally slept.

"Bloody woman!" John raged and fumed as he crashed through the forest in his search for Joanna Neville. He had to find her! Marriage was the only way to save his home in England . . . to save his own neck now that he'd stolen money from her. If she got back to England, and learned that he'd taken some of the Manor's funds, he would be arrested. And he could easily hang for his crimes.

"Joanna!" he called. "Joanna."

He stood listening to the silence. The only sound was the increasing wind and the foliage it shook. There wasn't a man or woman or beast in sight.

"Joanna! Love, don't be afraid. I won't hurt you!"

But the silence after the sound of his voice lengthened.

Where the devil was she? he wondered. She shouldn't have run away! He thought of all the precious time that was being wasted because the woman had chosen to escape him.

His arms were aching. Brown's rifle was weightier than his own gun. The pistol would be ideal for the chase, but Joanna had it, not he!

He snarled as he eyed the gun. Furious, he aimed his rifle at a bird and fired off a shot, but missed it.

Enraged, he hefted the unloaded rifle, and slammed the butt of the handle against the tree, cursing. "I want my pistol!" he growled. "Bloody rifle is heavy and clumsy!"

With jerky movements, he reloaded the gun, pouring in black powder and dropping in shot, reminding himself that he'd best not waste any more ammunition.

He hated the rifle, but he couldn't let it go. It was his only weapon in a wilderness fraught with danger.

"Cursed woman has caused me nothing but grief!" He glanced down at his ruined garments, and cursed again.

She was shocked when she saw him. He looked magnificent in his breechclout and leggings. He wore a deerskin vest and a copper band that encircled his upper muscular arm. A bead- and bear-claw necklace hung about his neck, and his earrings were strips of sinew with tiny beads threaded through small holes in each ear. Joanna stared, and her mouth went dry with longing. His muscled arms and chest gleaming beneath the summer sun had drawn her attention, but it was the look in his eyes that made her heart begin to race.

"Fireheart," she gasped. She wanted him. Every inch of her stirred to life as she studied him.

"Autumn Wind." He smiled at her tenderly, and she caught her breath with anticipation at the burning look in his eyes. She had always wanted him to look at her that way . . . as if he desired her and more. As if he loved her.

"I have been searching for you a long time," he told her.

"You have?" Her heart began to pound harder. "You found me. I'm glad you did."

His smile widened into a grin. "I am glad, too. Come here." He held out his arms to her. With a soft cry, she ran to him willingly, hugging him about the waist, pressing her face against his muscled hardness. When he encircled her with his strong arms, she sighed with contentment.

He shifted. She looked up, and felt the heated passion of his kiss. Her knees weakened, but he held her up with his strong arms. She murmured his name when he raised his head, and he laughed softly and held her close.

"Fireheart," she whispered joyfully.

"I love you, Autumn Wind."

She was home where she wanted to be. Home . . .

Joanna sat up with a jerk, her pulse racing wildly. The smile on her face died as she realized that it had only been a dream. She was still in the forest. Fireheart wasn't there. He hadn't come for her, or searched for her for a long time.

Tears filled her eyes and she lay down again. Rain began to fall, and she pulled her knees up to her chest, trying to protect herself from the cold wetness.

She began to shiver. Then she scooped up some of the dead dry leaves that carpeted the ground between the live growth, hoping to shield and warm herself.

Joanna knew she should get up and move to a better place, but she didn't have the strength, and finally it didn't matter, as sleep overtook her once again, making her oblivious to the bad weather.

* * *

She stood along the edge of the lake, gazing over the water. A breeze blew onshore, teasing her hair and giving her a chill. She hugged herself with her arms for warmth, but was reluctant to leave. The sun was setting, and the view was beautiful. She didn't want to miss seeing the sight.

And then she felt him. He approached from behind, and her neck tingled as he stopped at her side.

"Fireheart." She faced him. The male beauty of him in the glow of the setting sun stole her breath.

She reached out to touch him, to see if he was real, and the heat of his bare muscled chest warmed her.

He breathed her name as he pulled her close. She shut her eyes, and moaned when he bent to capture her mouth.

His lips were firm and warm and loving. She moaned low in her throat as he deepened the kiss.

"Yes . . ."

"Lie with me, Autumn Wind. Let me love you." He touched her breast, palming the tip until she shuddered and captured his hand.

When he picked her up, and laid her on a bed of scented pine needles, she opened her arms and her legs to love him. And he gave her the gift of himself.

"We are near," Fireheart called as he came to a small clearing. It was raining, and the rain had wiped out some of the signs. Some but not all.

"How do you know this?" Rising Bird said, still in the forest.

The chief waved his friend over to his spot. "This."

Rising Bird stared down at the blanketclad body with mounting horror. He and Fireheart exchanged glances before he reached down to lift the blanket. He felt Fireheart's fear, perhaps because he shared it. He swept off the cover and stared.

"Gillian," he said, his chest tightening.

"It is not Autumn Wind," Fireheart said gratefully, "but someone did this to Gillian, and we know it was not she."

The warrior nodded. "There is a killer about, and he may kill Joanna."

"We must find her quickly." The cold dread that filled his heart made him shiver.

"*Kihiila*, before he kills her, too."

Rising Bird covered up Gillian's body. Then he and Fireheart continued into the forest, their knives drawn, their gazes alert.

"This way," Fireheart said as he noted a low broken bush limb. "They've gone this way."

"Do you think they are still together?" Rising Bird asked.

"This man does not know. We can only hope and pray to the Great Spirit that Autumn Wind has managed to escape him."

The old warrior frowned. "Then we must hurry, for John Burton will be chasing her."

Fireheart's chest tightened as he agreed.

Chapter 22

"Get up!" A kick in her side jerked Joanna from a sound sleep. When the foot caught her hard in the stomach, she gasped and scrambled to her feet.

"John!" She stood, paralyzed with fear, her thoughts and heart racing.

Rain fell heavily from the sky, drenching both of them. Joanna stared at him. John's dark hair was plastered to his scalp; his clothes were wet and clinging to him. He wore a white shirt that was soiled and torn, knee breeches, and black shoes with silver buckles and ripped stockings. Seeing the glimpse of his nipple through his soaked shirt, Joanna realized that she was more exposed than he was.

Just as the thought came, his look at her breasts confirmed it, and she covered herself as best she could with her arms. She could do nothing to cover her most private area, and when he glanced below her waist, she shuddered.

"You thought you could get away," he said, his blue eyes burning, evil. There were cuts and scratches on his face as if, while wandering from the path, he'd had a battle with some bushes. The thought might have otherwise made her smile if circumstances were different, but his expression terrified her.

Joanna felt a knot form in her stomach when she saw no sign of her friend. "Where's Gillian?"

His smile was grim. "She had a slight accident, I'm afraid." He fingered the trigger of the gun. "She had the misfortune of learning that those who betray me don't live."

She tightened her arms around herself as she felt a mix of horror and burning anger. "You killed her?" She couldn't believe what he'd said, that he had murdered her best friend.

He laughed as if the fact amused him. "Yes, I killed her! I shot her, my dear future wife, in the heart where all conniving lovers should earn their due."

Then he began to describe exactly what they'd been doing before he'd killed her, how it felt to pull the trigger, and how she looked when he'd done the deed.

Joanna felt sick. He had made love to her, then coldbloodedly killed her!

"You monster!" she hissed.

"I? I most certainly am not! If I were a monster, Joanna, I would be pulling this trigger instead of just touching it. But I'm a generous man. I'm giving you—us—a chance to talk about this." He gestured toward the ground. "Sit," he ordered.

She shook her head, but decided to relent when she saw his expression. She realized, too, that by sitting she could better conceal herself from his lecherous gaze. She sat, uncaring of the cold rain that continued to pour over her body. She began to shiver, her body's natural reaction to the chill and the man's nearness.

"What are you going to do with me?"

He gave her a soft smile. "That depends entirely on you, dear Joanna." He chortled when her answer was just to stare at him. "You don't understand, do you? You see, I still want you for my wife. As I said, I can be a generous man. Consent to wed me and be a good wife, and I'll allow you to live."

"And if I don't?" she dared to ask.

"Then I'll have to kill you, just like I murdered poor Gillian. Only your death will not be as nice and as quick as Gillian's for you, my dear Joanna, have betrayed me not once but twice."

Grief contorted Joanna's features as she pictured her friend's horrible death. "She loved you!"

"And I loved her," he said. "However, we don't always get to live with the one we love, do we?" She relaxed slightly when he lowered the gun. "I'll be perfectly content with you as my wife."

"I wouldn't lie with you if you were the last man on earth!" she said with vehemence.

He tried to look amused, but failed. Joanna saw that she had more than annoyed him. The spark that briefly lit up his eyes, which he was quick to conceal, was anger.

"And who would you allow to touch you and lie with you?" he asked. His mouth curved at an idea he thought preposterous. "A savage?" His voice, thick with sarcasm, was aimed to taunt.

A mental image of Fireheart making love to her made Joanna blush and look away.

"A savage!" he exploded, enraged to see her reaction. "Don't tell me that you care for a savage! Dear God in heaven, your uncle would die from an attack if he learned the truth, if he weren't already dead." He eyed her with contempt. "No wonder you wanted to go back to the village!"

She glared at him. "Fireheart is a better man than you will ever be!" she snapped. "And if my uncle were alive, I'd be happy if it killed him!" She fisted her hands at her sides. "Bastard! You are a sorry bastard, John Burton. I hope you rot in hell!"

With a soft laugh, he smoothed his face free of all expression. "Now is that any way to talk about your loving fiancé?" His voice was silky, sensual. Joanna thought she'd be sick.

"You are not my fiancé!" she argued.

She didn't care what he did to her, she thought. She wouldn't marry him!

And then she remembered the danger. And the flintlock pistol. She had buried the gun in some leaves. He must have read her thoughts for suddenly he narrowed his gaze at her. He lifted his arm and pointed the gun at her.

"Where is my pistol?" he asked, watching her like a hawk.

"I lost it," she lied, straight-faced. "It was dark and rainy and cold. I meant to keep it. It was my only weapon." She raised her hands. "I can't very well hide it on my person, can I?"

She allowed him the indignity of gawking at her . . . at her scantily clad breasts and bare legs. It didn't matter how he looked as long as he believed that she'd lost the gun.

"Well, can I?" she asked. "I've no pockets, no hiding places."

John stared. "True enough, I suppose." The arm propping the rifle up wavered.

Joanna willed him to lower the gun so that she could have a better chance of retrieving the pistol. Could she shoot him? she wondered. She must, or die trying.

"Get up," he ordered.

Her mind raced as she thought quickly. If she got up without getting the gun, her one chance would be lost.

"I'm tired," she said. "Can't we rest for a bit more? You woke me up!" she accused.

The whole scene seemed unreal to Joanna. She sat on the ground, getting soaked by the rain while the man whom she had once considered a friend held a gun on her and ordered her to rise.

"You'll have plenty of time for sleep later."

"John—"

"Now!" he barked.

His harsh command made her jump. Her hand fumbled beneath the leaves in search for the pistol as she slowly shifted while starting to rise.

"Joanna!"

Her heart pounded as she heard him move closer.

Her hand closed over steel. Triumphant, she gripped the pistol, turned as she rose, then spun and stuck it in the middle of his chest. "Bastard!" she hissed, poking him.

With a roar, he swung his arms with the rifle, and she felt the pain of the rifle connecting with her temple.

She cried out with pain before he hit her again, and the edges of her world began to darken. She breathed deeply, reeling with the painful throbbing, then fighting a feeling of desperation as she lunged at him.

She heard the air gush from his lungs as he was taken by surprise. Pleased, she began to hit and kick him. She felt a glimmer of satisfaction when her knee made contact between his legs and he bent over gasping with pain.

His weak moment gave her time to reach for the pistol and the rifle, but he was on her before she could retrieve both. And the two began to struggle again.

"Bitch!" he cried. Enraged now, he tried to grab her throat, but she evaded him. She tried to knee-kick him in the groin again, but he caught her arms and twisted them behind her back.

She cried with pain, and he laughed and shook her, causing her to whimper as he wrenched her limbs higher.

"I'm going to have to tie you up now," he said. "What a pity ... although it does give a man the chance to touch where he wants."

She cringed at the thought of his touching her. The only man who had touched her intimately had been Fireheart, and she had welcomed his caresses, gloried in them. She wouldn't—couldn't—allow John to tarnish the memory of a lover's touch.

She slumped against him in the hope that he would think her too exhausted to keep up the fight. She wasn't sure it was going to work at first. But when he had to drag her sagging body back to the spot where the fight had begun, he must have decided to believe it.

Joanna waited until he set her down. She couldn't let him tie her, or she'd be defenseless. *Where will he find rope to bind me?*

He threw her to the ground, pointed the pistol at her, which he had somehow managed to retrieve, and cocked the gun. "One move and I'll kill you!" he snarled.

And she froze for she knew he meant it.

Just when she thought she'd be safe from being bound, she saw John reach for his shirt hem and tear off a cloth strip.

He was going to use fabric from his garment to tie her she realized with a shudder.

"John," she said, "I'll not try to escape again. You don't have to tie me."

He glanced at her with disdain. "I'll not believe you again, Joanna. How can I when you've taken every opportunity to try to defy me?"

As he managed to start ripping a second strip, Joanna panicked. "I told you I'd give you Neville Manor," she cried. "I never wanted it anyway."

He paused in the middle of tearing. "You're joking."

She shook her head. "I didn't want to go to England. I was a young girl, perfectly content with my life here in the New World."

His look was disbelieving, then ugly. "Your uncle gave you everything, and this is the gratitude you have toward him?"

"He was a cruel man. I hated him."

John tore off a second strip. "He was a good man. He was never anything but kind to me and Michael."

"Perhaps you were the sons he never had."

"He had a son," John surprised her by saying. "Kenneth. But Kenneth Neville was a fool so Roderick disowned him."

Roderick had a son? She was stunned. Never again would she call Roderick Neville uncle. He didn't deserve the title or her affection. Now it seemed that he didn't deserve his only son.

"What was wrong with Kenneth?" she asked, curious, hoping to distract John from the thought of tying her up.

"Kenneth?" He looked thoughtful. The rain had slowed to a fine drizzle, less drenching, but no less cold. John, however, seemed totally unaffected by the chill.

"Kenneth was a weak bloke," he said. "He wasn't a bad fellow actually, but when Roderick's wife left him, Kenneth was foolish enough to leave with her. Roderick never forgave his wife or his son for abandoning him."

"He probably abused her as he did his servants and his niece."

John tensed. "He didn't abuse you."

"Oh, no?" She raised the hem of her tattered shift, and turned to draw his attention to the back of her thighs. "What are these scars from then?"

"The Indians," he said, but his voice lacked conviction. And then Joanna saw that he wasn't looking at her scars so much as at the small amount of silken flesh that she had unintentionally displayed of her buttocks.

She quickly lowered her shift and rolled over.

"You will be a better lover than Gillian. I'm sure of it," he said, making her nervous. She didn't like his look.

"John, no—"

"I would have waited until we wed, but now you've spoiled it. It will work to my best advantage to take you. If I ruin your innocence, we will have to wed."

She swallowed against a suddenly dry throat. "And what if I'm not a virgin?"

His features contorted with anger. "If you're not pure, I'll not have to be gentle with you." He stroked the fabric strips as one would caress a lover's skin. Joanna shivered as she was consumed by a cold dread.

"I'm pure," she said, hoping that he would believe the lie.

The slight softening of his features told her he did. She breathed an inward sigh of relief until she saw his approach . . . and his intent. He was coming to render her helpless with wrist and ankle bonds.

No, I won't allow him to touch me. If he ties me up, I'll never be able to get free!

She froze as he came to her, unable to move, unable to breathe. He settled a length of fabric about her neck, and her terror became centered in a new concern. He was going to strangle her. Right here and now, it was all going to end.

But he didn't tighten the noose. He rubbed the wet fabric against her skin, sliding it back and forth as if he wanted to arouse the sensitive area on her nape. John was titillated, she realized. She was appalled, and the longer he continued, she grew irritated, then angry.

Where were the guns? She looked and saw the rifle on the ground where he'd stood and pulled off pieces of his shirt. The pistol she couldn't see. Did he have it against her back? Would he take her by surprise as he had Gillian, or would he move around her, watch

her face as he slowly choked her then shot the life
from her.

Dear God, please help me.

Just as she wondered about the pistol, she saw his
hands on either side of her, pulling the fabric. It was
almost as if he was caught up in the sensual pull and
tug of cloth . . . as if it excited him although he had
wanted to stimulate her desire.

She grimaced. Disgusting. But she knew now that
his pistol was either tucked in the waist of his
breeches, or lying on the ground beside him.

He slid the cloth this way and that, moving it to
stroke her throat. When he began to murmur dirty
things in her ear, she knew she'd been right, John
Burton was becoming sexually, dangerously, aroused.

She offered up a silent prayer for guidance. She
acted on the thought that came to her, grabbing the
cloth strip, giving it a yank and rolling with it at the
same time.

She felt John's weight settle on her briefly as they
both fell to their sides. His grunt of pain was quickly
followed by his heavy breathing in her ear . . . as he
rolled back to her.

Joanna began to struggle in earnest.

Rising Bird saw the pair first and sprang to help.
Startled, unaware, Fireheart could only stare until he
realized what Rising Bird had seen. He waited with
weapon ready to spring into action should the warrior
need his assistance. To jump into the fight now would
only complicate things and put Joanna in further
danger.

Joanna screamed when John grabbed hold of her
breast and squeezed. She fought him, but he was
stronger than she was, and her strength was going

quickly. Just as she thought he would rape her, she was suddenly free of his weight. Startled, she watched as John's body was tossed into the air before it crashed against a bush. As John got up to fight, Joanna saw that her savior was Rising Bird, her cousin's beloved husband.

"Rising Bird!" she cried when she saw John locate his gun. "His pistol!"

Rising Bird lunged just as John dashed down to retrieve the weapon, and then the struggle began, a desperate fight for the gun.

A shot rang out, chilling Joanna. When she saw Rising Bird fall, she screamed with rage and charged John.

Uncaring of his gun, she beat at him with her hands, striking his face and neck, hoping to render him unconscious.

Although stunned by the suddenness of her attack, John regained his balance and his ability to subdue her.

He struck Joanna across the face, knocking her to the ground. When John raised his foot to give her a swift kick, his body was wrenched into the air. Fireheart had rushed in to help, grabbed his leg and jerked it upward. John screamed with pain as the limb was brutally pulled from the socket and he flew through the air to land with a thud against a tree.

Joanna barely had time to perceive the fact that not only Rising Bird had come, but Fireheart as well.

Fear clawed at her as she watched and worried about Fireheart. She loved him. Should anything happen to him . . .

He was a fierce warrior, her Fireheart. Strong, capable, he was a fighting man while John was not. But John was a madman. Would Fireheart's skill be any match for a man who murdered without reason?

A groan from Rising Bird had her focusing her

attention on her surrogate father. Rising Bird! *Dear God, is he all right?*

Fireheart will win, she thought as she rushed to check on Rising Bird. He was stronger than John was, and John had to be weakening now.

As the two men continued to fight, Joanna crouched over Rising Bird, checking his wound. But the warrior didn't move; fear clawed at her, making her check for signs of life.

"Rising Bird!" she cried, gently shaking him. "Don't die! Don't die!"

He had suffered a bullet wound to an area above his heart. Blood poured from the injury, flowing into the misty rain, creating a red rivulet of life that ran down the area between his chest and underarms.

She remembered all the times when she was a child and he'd been kind to her. "No," she gasped.

She tore fabric from her shift, which left her almost naked. She pressed the fabric into the wound, praying that she could staunch the flow of his blood.

Several yards away, Fireheart plowed his fist into John's face, and felt the satisfaction of hearing bone breaking. Blood poured from facial and body cuts. He wanted to beat him to a bloody pulp, but he wouldn't. There were worse ways to make this man pay, and he would bring him back alive so he could endure pain the Indian way.

Beaten, John staggered on his feet. Fireheart grabbed him by the shirt one more time and tossed him onto the ground. As the white man slumped backward, the warrior chief found the strips from John's linen shirt, and used the fabric to bind John's wrists and ankles.

Then he went to check on Joanna and his friend.

Chapter 23

Joanna began to sob as she pressed the cloth against Rising Bird's wound. The fabric was wet from the rain so it did little to stop the flow of blood. "Don't die," she cried. "Please don't die!"

"He's not going to die, Autumn Wind. Rising Bird is a strong warrior."

She gasped and looked up at Fireheart, dear Fireheart who looked healthy and alive, and was the love of her life.

"Oh, Fireheart!" she cried, rising. "You're all right!"

Like in her dream, he held open his arms, and she rushed into his embrace. Wrapping her arms about him, she held him tightly, absorbing his warmth, his strength. He allowed her to remain in his tender hold for several minutes; then he put her away from him. He cupped her face, inspected it from all angles. "Are you all right?" he asked roughly.

She bobbed her head. "I'm fine." Tears filled her eyes as she thought about her ordeal . . . about what she'd learned of Gillian . . . of seeing the men she loved fight the madman who would have murdered her. "Gillian—"

"*Kihiila*. I know. I saw her." Fireheart stroked her cheek. "I do not think she suffered, little one."

Skin tingling with pleasure, Joanna looked down, feeling guilt. He released her. "I hope not. She was my friend." She glanced up when he didn't comment.

"She loved him. She loved him, and so he could manipulate her into betraying me." Her tears spilled from her lashes to trail down her cheeks. The rain had stopped, but it was still cloudy. "She helped me in the end. She helped me escape, but then he killed her and came after me. She only wanted to be his wife, but he wanted more. . . . He wants Roderick's property, Neville Manor."

She wondered whether or not John was dead. The man had deserved to die, but it always troubled her when a human life was lost. "Is he . . . ?"

Fireheart, who studied her intently, shook his head. "No, the white man lives." He did not tell her that John Burton would not live to see the winter. It would be up to his people, especially Rising Bird and Mary Wife, but in the end John Burton would discover death.

He couldn't tell whether she was relieved or upset, and decided she was probably both. She looked so beautiful, even in her torn, wet, and dirty muslin shift. His gaze was drawn to her breasts and the skin exposed by a particular tear. His loins tightened as he caught a glimpse of white flesh and a rosy pink nipple.

"Rising Bird," she said, sounding breathless. He looked into her eyes and knew she felt it too . . . the attraction between them . . . the desire . . . the aching pain. "Are you sure he will be all right?"

He brushed past her to examine his friend's body. Rising Bird had been shot in the shoulder, but from the dwindling flow of blood, Fireheart knew that nothing had been severed that would cut Rising Bird's lifeline. "He will live. We must bandage his arm, and get him back to the village."

Joanna gazed at her cousin's husband with fear. "The journey will kill him." She raised her face to look at the man she loved to see him shake his head.

"I will make a stretcher to drag him behind me through the forest."

"But it will take us forever along the trails!" she cried with dismay.

"He will live," Fireheart said strongly as if by his will alone Rising Bird would make it. He retrieved the pistol, and handed it to Joanna. "You must watch John Burton along the way. He must not escape. He will be angry, but too weak to fight." He grinned suddenly. "Stupid white man does not know how to fight fair."

Joanna stared at his smile, and found her own lips curving. They had come through a terrible time; they had a reason to be happy. She took the gun. "You've tied him up?"

The brave nodded. "He will not go anywhere until we let him, and then we will change his bonds so that he can take little steps, but not touch or hit."

The idea of keeping John Burton tied was appealing to Joanna. She wished, though, that the man would just disappear so she wouldn't have to look at his horrible face, and be reminded of the pain he'd caused and the murders he'd committed.

Joanna glanced toward the clearing where John lay, unconscious. Then she turned back to Rising Bird only to find him gazing at her with eyes glazed with pain. "Rising Bird."

He managed to smile at her. "Autumn Wind, my daughter. You are well. Mary Wife will be so pleased."

She bent down to kiss his cheek. "*Wa-neé-shih.*"

"This man did not help you," he said, dismissing

her thanks. "Our *sachem* did. Fireheart." His eyes turned to his friend. "*Wa-neé-shih.*"

Fireheart nodded silently, then moved to help Rising Bird to stand. "You will sit here until I can make a stretcher."

Rising Bird scowled. "I do not need a stretcher."

"You will use one!" Joanna said stubbornly. "Mary will never forgive any of us if you do not return to her alive."

The warrior seemed about to argue until he saw Joanna's face . . . the combined fear and love sent his heart hammering. He would use a stretcher because this daughter of his heart wanted it. When he had seen Gillian, her friend, he thought that Autumn Wind was gone, dead at the hands of the white man. She was alive, and he would show his gratitude to the Great Spirit by listening to the second woman who had stolen his heart . . . Autumn Wind, his daughter. He sighed heavily, but agreed. "I will use the stretcher, but I must walk for short periods until we reach the village. If I tire or feel pain, I will lie down quickly."

Fireheart gazed at the two people whom he loved and saw the private war of emotions going on inside each of them. He knew for he battled his own. He was to marry another, but he wanted Joanna. He prayed to the spirits for a way to make all within the village happy without hurting another.

As Fireheart worked to fashion a stretcher out of pine branches and other brush, Joanna heard John moan as he started to stir. Her stomach roiling with anger, she approached him. "John."

He opened a swollen eye to peer at her, wincing as he focused his gaze. "Joanna."

"You'll never get it," she said, viewing his beaten body with satisfaction. She had never enjoyed seeing a person's pain, but then John Burton had pushed her past the limit of endurance. "Neville Manor. Your brother and Burton Estates be damned, you'll never see a shilling from Neville Manor."

To her surprise, he managed a lopsided grin, although he gasped as he formed it. "I've already taken coin, Miss Neville. In fact, I've taken several. I'm sure Michael will find a way to save our family home."

She sniffed and turned her nose up at him. "As long as you know that you'll not be the one doing the saving, John. After the authorities get done with you, you'll be lucky to ever see the sun shine."

"Is he upsetting you, Autumn Wind?" Fireheart had come up behind Joanna on silent feet.

She turned to smile at him. "He is not worthy of another thought, Fireheart." She touched his arm, ignoring the sound of John's snort.

"Savage lover!" he spat.

She spun to glare at him. "At least, he is someone worthy, while you—you're not fit for anything!"

They began the journey back to Little River once the stretcher was made, and Rising Bird felt ready. Joanna didn't care about John Burton's comfort. It might be an uncharitable way to feel, but he was a murderer! How could she feel anything but contempt for the murderer who had killed her best friend?

As she walked behind John Burton, prodding him with a gun while Fireheart followed with Rising Bird, Joanna thought of Gillian and fought back tears. Poor love-struck Gillian. If she herself had been fooled, for Gillian it had been worse. She had not only believed in John's web of lies, she had become ensnared by her love for him . . . and, in the end, he had killed her.

Recalling her friend, Joanna turned her thoughts to the two men who had rescued her. She had apologized to both men for putting them in danger. Both had dismissed her apology, telling her that they had come searching for her because they loved her and feared for her safety.

Joanna knew that Rising Bird loved her like a daughter, but what of Fireheart? He had included himself in that love. Yet, he was to marry another. How did he truly feel about her? Like a sister? Like a lover? Like a friend?

Her knowledge of John and Gillian made her realize that not everyone considered physical intimacy between two adults binding with love. Gillian had been in love, most certainly, but John . . . he had used Gillian just as he had wanted to use Joanna. She had satisfied a sexual need, and so he'd taken. From Joanna, his need was material. And it seemed that he'd already taken a bit of that in monetary gain.

She began to wonder about the state of Roderick Neville's estate. How much did John steal? Not enough to ruin it, she was certain, or else he wouldn't have been so adamant about marriage. He had probably just taken enough to help Michael manage to keep Burton Estate's creditors at bay.

Dear God, when she thought about how she had consented to be his wife! She shuddered and, for good measure and a great deal of satisfaction, prodded John particularly hard with the gun. She had traded the pistol for the rifle, preferring to keep her distance from him. Fireheart carried the pistol tucked into the string of his loincloth. She knew he would use it if he had to so she wasn't afraid.

As she thought about her impulsive agreement to John's proposal of marriage, she recalled why she'd agreed. Fireheart had hurt her. Seeing him and Moon Dove together had caused her heartache. She had decided that she had to get away. And there had been John offering her a new life, like a gift.

She didn't want Fireheart to think of her as a sister. She wanted him to look at her as his wife. She closed her eyes briefly, for just a second, and the images of their lovemaking came so fast, so clear, that she nearly cried out with the surprise of it.

He doesn't think of me as his sister, but then neither does he regard me as a lover anymore, which makes me his what? His friend?

She didn't want to be just his friend either, but she would take that for now for she had nearly lost the chance to see him forever. She would accept this new opportunity to find happiness in small simple measures.

The cry of welcome that they had been longing to hear came two days later. *"He!"*

They had stopped to rest for the night, then continued their trek. Rising Bird looked pale, but he had managed to walk quite a distance on his own. John was a mass of bruises and red welts, and Joanna didn't care that she had added a few dark sore spots of her own to his person. Although she was slightly ashamed of the fact, she took great delight every time he grunted with pain when she poked him.

She heard Fireheart give the answering cry, "Oho!" to the Lenape greeting someone had called out to them.

Rising Bird grinned as he got up from the stretcher, which Fireheart dropped to walk with him, side by side. Joanna turned to smile at Fireheart.

He came up beside her and took the rifle. "I'll watch John Burton," he said.

"All right." She was more than happy to relinquish the chore.

As they entered the village, family and friends immediately surrounded them. Mary, spying Joanna first, ran to embrace her cousin.

"I'm glad you're all right!" she exclaimed as she held Joanna. "I was frightened for you."

Joanna pulled away, but kept hold of Mary's hands. "With good reason." Tears filled her eyes as she lovingly squeezed her cousin's fingers. "He murdered Gillian, Mary. Killed her in cold blood."

Mary gasped and whitened, then glared at the bound white man.

"Go to Rising Bird," Joanna told her. "He's been injured." She saw the leap of fear that entered Mary's expression. "Fireheart said he'll be all right, but we've come a long way."

Mary gave her cousin one final hug before she ran to her husband whom she had just spied entering the village, trailing behind the others.

"Rising Bird!" she cried as she rushed to his side.

Joanna watched the tearful reunion between Mary and Rising Bird, and felt her throat tighten with emotion. She saw her cousin hug and kiss her husband before examining and exclaiming over his injuries. Rising Bird must have said something because Mary glanced her way again. Joanna's face became infused with guilty heat until she realized that Mary wasn't angry with her. . . . She looked relieved.

A rush of love for her family overwhelmed her. She didn't want to go back to England. She needed to find a way to stay with the Lenape people.

The weight of responsibility for Roderick Neville's property was heavy on her shoulders. And then she remembered John's claim that Roderick had had a son.

Kenneth Neville, Joanna thought. Could she trace the man's whereabouts? Kenneth was Roderick's rightful heir, she decided, not she.

"Autumn Wind." Fireheart's gentle voice drew her attention to the warrior *sachem.* "You must see to your injuries."

Injuries? She thought blankly. Then she looked down to find her legs covered with scratches and a small cut across her breast that would have been hidden but for the gaping of the remaining fabric of her ruined shift. She gasped, suddenly becoming aware of her state of undress. Her wounds were of no consequence; in her fury toward John Burton she hadn't even noticed them. Neither had she thought about her lack of clothes . . . until Fireheart's attention had reminded her.

"I'll be all right," she said, turning away as she became self-conscious of her breasts, her exposed legs and thighs. She'd had her satchel, but hadn't thought to change.

"I will call someone to help," he insisted. "Moon Dove is good with healing. I will get her—"

"No!" Joanna cried, probably more loudly than was warranted, but she didn't want to be attended by Fireheart's future wife. The fact of Moon Dove's role in Fireheart's life was already too painful.

"Then I will bathe your wounds," he said, grabbing her arm and tugging her toward the lake.

"Mary will care for them," she insisted, trying to pull from his grasp.

"Mary will be busy with Rising Bird."

Unable to argue that point, Joanna slumped with defeat and allowed Fireheart to escort her past villagers who stared at them, down the trail to the large body of glistening water.

"Sit," he said, helping her to rest comfortably on her favorite rock.

She started to rise as he dipped a small clay bowl into the water. "Fireheart, I can tend to my—"

"Sit!" he ordered, turning to push her down. "I am the *sachem*. You will listen to me!"

Aghast that he would use his authority that way, she obeyed him, more because she was so surprised by his commanding display than for any other reason. As she watched him refill the bowl with water, she slowly came to her senses and her temper began a slow boil.

She felt a fiery heat that tightened her stomach

and brought a hot flush to her cheeks. "How dare you—"

His expression as he faced her was tender, caring, and the diatribe she was about to deliver died before it left her lips. He looked as if he . . . loved her.

She closed her eyes as he began to wash first the scratches on her arm. Loved her? She shivered as he raised her head to wipe a soft piece of cloth over a small scratch on the underside of her chin.

"You were a brave *Hokuaa,*" he murmured huskily. "This man was proud of Rising Bird's Lenape daughter."

She opened her eyes to meet his gaze, but still felt the tingling of his touch. "I wasn't brave. I was frightened."

He paused in the act of washing the particularly sensitive area behind one ear where she must have been cut during her first struggle with John. "A good warrior must always be fearful. To escape fear makes a Lenape careless. Back there, you were a good warrior woman, Autumn Wind."

She flushed with pleasure at his praise. "Thank you."

He stared at her lips. "Do not thank me, Joanna. I let you leave the village, and I should not have done this. If you had stayed, your friend Gillian might still be alive, and you would not need someone to tend to your injuries."

He looked regretful as if he blamed himself for all that had happened to her. She knew that the opposite was true. She had acted impulsively, irrationally, anxious to flee without regard for her own or anyone's safety.

She grabbed his hand, halting him as he moved to cleanse the tiny gouge on her breast. "The fault is mine alone, Fireheart. You must not take the guilt. I won't allow it."

Then, unable to bear having him touch her intimately but with dispassion, Joanna took away the cloth and stood.

"*Wa-neé-shih*, Fireheart. I am able to take care of the rest of my injuries."

Chapter 24

Joanna came into the wigwam as Mary was tending Rising Bird's wound. The warrior was stretched out on his sleeping pallet with his wife seated on the edge, bathing his injury.

"How are you feeling?" she asked her cousin's husband.

He grinned, and the smile reached his eyes. "This man is well. It is good to have you back with us, daughter."

She returned the smile before meeting Mary's gaze. "I'm sorry," she said.

Her cousin waved her concern away. "You have nothing to apologize for."

"But Rising Bird would not be injured if not for me."

"Nonsense!" she exclaimed. "It is John Burton who did this, not you." She shuddered as she set down the water bowl and the piece of doeskin that she was using to tend her husband's shoulder. "Every time I think of what he could have done to you—"

Joanna didn't want to remember her time with John

Burton. She wanted only to forget the man and what he had done.

"Did you get the bullet out?" she asked in an effort to redirect the conversation.

Mary showed her the bloodcovered slug. "*Kihiila.* It came out easily enough. I used these." She held up a tool made of deer bone. "Fortunately, he's suffered no serious damage."

Rising Bird grunted. "That is what you say, woman," he grumbled, holding the arm beneath the wounded shoulder. But Joanna saw a twinkle in his midnight-dark eyes.

Smirking, Mary shook her head. "You'll live, husband."

"If I can live through your medicine," he grumbled, smiling.

Mary bent her head again as she continued to work on Rising Bird's injury. "Joanna, we'd like you to stay," she said without looking up.

Joanna thought she seemed tense as if afraid that if she looked at Joanna she wouldn't receive the answer she wanted.

"I'd like to stay in the village," Joanna admitted softly, "but—"

"What is it that upsets you, daughter?" Rising Bird asked. "Is it the property in England?"

"*Kihiila.* I am responsible for so many people there, and I've neglected my duty to them since Roderick's death." She sat down on her sleeping platform. She couldn't neglect her duties any longer because people needed her. It wasn't right to punish them for her uncle's deeds.

"When I received Mary's letter, I couldn't remain," she continued hoarsely, remembering. "I wanted so badly to come. But I was torn. I didn't know if I'd be welcome."

Mary looked at her, her eyes filling with tears. "I know," she said quietly. "We are glad you came."

Joanna gave a soft smile. "I am, too. I thought," she went on as if she hadn't been interrupted, "that I'd left the estate in good hands, but—"

"But?" Mary prompted.

" 'Twas John Burton I left in charge," she said with regret. "I left that madman to run Neville Manor."

"You do not sound like you wish to return to that place," Rising Bird said, moving to sit despite his wife's protests.

Joanna shook her head.

"Isn't there anyone else who can run the property?" Mary asked.

"I thought not . . . until recently. Now I believe there may be someone. Roderick Neville's rightful heir. But I don't know where he is, or if he'd want the property."

When husband and wife looked at her with questioning gazes, Joanna explained. "Kenneth Neville," she said. "After we'd left the village, John Burton told me that Roderick Neville had a son. Roderick disowned the boy when the child left with his mother." She became thoughtful. "I imagine that the wife left him because he was cruel to her. . . ."

She didn't finish speaking aloud her thoughts. Mary already had an inkling of the abuse Joanna had suffered at her uncle's hands. If he'd been cruel to his niece, he had probably been cruel to his wife and child. Why else would mother and son have left him?

"I should go back," Joanna said with a sigh. "If only to put my affairs in order, and find someone to take over the estate."

"But you will return to us?" Mary looked hopeful.

Joanna studied her cousin with sadness. "I don't know, Mary. I'd rather not go at all. I love it here. I think you know that now." She smiled at each of them with affection. "And I love both of you, but I've been away so long. I'm not sure I belong here with the Lenape people."

She wasn't sure she could endure watching as Fireheart and Moon Dove built a life together.

Mary opened her mouth to speak her thoughts, but Rising Bird must have guessed what his wife would say for he stopped her with a look and a touch on her arm.

"I don't know what to do," Joanna said.

"Whatever you wish to do," Mary replied. "You must do whatever you choose. But please, Joanna, know always that you belong here with us, with the Lenape People. You are the daughter of the Lenni Lenape. You are Autumn Wind, the daughter of our hearts."

Joanna was touched by Mary's words. "*Wa-neé-shih,*" she whispered, her eyes filling with tears.

Fireheart discovered her alone in the forest where she'd been gathering herbs and plants. "You are going to leave again."

Joanna jumped up when she heard him. She spun to find him only a few feet away from her.

"Fireheart!" she gasped. "I didn't hear you come!"

The sight of the chief stole her breath. Fireheart was the perfect image of a Lenni Lenape warrior with his glistening dark eyes, long shiny dark hair, and honey-brown skin. He was bare-chested, muscled, and without a single body hair on his breast area or stomach. She saw his strength reflected throughout his form, in his powerful chest, arms, and muscled calves and thighs. His copper armband gleamed in the summer sun.

"Joanna?" he said softly.

"Yes, yes, I think I must," she replied. She swallowed hard as she looked away, conscious that she'd been staring at him.

"Will you come back?"

"I know not."

"Your home is with the Lenape," he said. "Mary Wife and Rising Bird will miss you if you go."

And you? she thought. *Would you miss me at all?* Or would Moon Dove help him to forget her?

She wanted to know. Had to know. "Will you miss me?"

He didn't immediately answer. His silence drew her gaze to him. "This man will miss you, as will my people—*your people.*"

It wasn't the answer she'd hoped for. Joanna hid her disappointment.

"You will not miss me." She walked several feet to gaze out into the forest and the water that bubbled along in the stream just ahead of her.

"Autumn Wind." He was suddenly beside her, his breath in her ear, his nearness sending tiny tingles down her neck and spine.

She turned to face him expectantly.

"I will miss you. Must you go?"

She thought of the land, the people, Neville Manor. She nodded.

"What if this man asks you to stay?"

Her heart gave a lurch before it started to pump harder. "Moon Dove—"

"I ask about you, not Moon Dove."

What was he implying? she wondered. That he would give up Moon Dove, and marry her if she stayed?

"What are you telling me? That you will not marry Moon Dove?"

He touched her cheek, stared at her so long that she became uncomfortable.

Fireheart gazed at the woman he loved, and struggled with his conscience. He had already promised to wed Moon Dove. His heart belonged to Autumn Wind, but Moon Dove was his people's choice. He couldn't tell Joanna that he wasn't going to marry Moon Dove for he must wed the Indian maiden.

She gazed up at him with imploring green eyes. He loved her eyes, the color of the forest in the bright light of day. Her hair was golden like the sun with a splash of red like the coat of the fox. Drawn back in a knot at her nape, it was still beautiful. He couldn't help himself; he lifted a hand to touch her hair.

She closed his eyes as he stroked the shiny strands from her forehead to her crown. He felt his fingers tremble when she moved her head slightly so that his hand found her cheek.

"Fireheart," she whispered. She raised thick eyelashes to meet his gaze.

He struggled with his need to touch her, love her, and with his sense of duty and honor to his people and his wife-to-be.

"*Uitiisaa*," he murmured as he caressed her soft cheek.

She smiled at him and touched his face as well. "And so are you." He had called her pretty, and she felt he was, too.

"I want to kiss you."

She nodded. "*Kihiila*. Kiss me. I want it, too."

With his heart hammering in his chest, he lowered his head to take her mouth, and felt the ground shift beneath his feet as her lips softened and opened.

The contact of their lips was like making love. Slowly, hesitating at first, they dipped their tongues into each other's mouths. Then with a groan that came from deep in his throat, he couldn't hold back any longer, and the duel of tongues grew fiercer. They held each other, their bodies pressed close, straining to be nearer while their mouths mated in glorious wonder.

His manhood was hard and throbbing beneath his loincloth. Fireheart wanted to press her to the cloth and join with her. But as he pulled away to cup her face, he realized that it would be wrong. She expected promises that he couldn't give her.

She said she had to leave, to go back to England across the sea. It had been many summers before she'd returned. If she left again, she might not come back . . . and if she did, it could be many summers that passed again.

"Joanna," he said.

Something in his tone alerted Joanna, stealing her from the pleasurable haze created by their kissing. She saw the conflict in his expression, the pain, and felt a cold dread seep into her bones.

He wasn't going to ask her to be his wife. He would wed Moon Dove. "You are going to marry her."

He released her and nodded.

"Why?" she cried. "Why do you kiss me and marry her?"

"I am already promised to her."

"You are the *sachem!*" she cried. "The chief! You should marry whom you wish."

"You are going to England," he said simply.

"But I can come back!"

"Like you returned after seven summers?" he accused.

"I wouldn't be gone that long! I just have to find Ken—" She halted. What if she couldn't find Roderick's son immediately? What if it took months, years to find him? She couldn't leave England until he was found. If he wasn't located, what else could she to do but stay in England?

A glint came into Fireheart's eyes as he studied her. "You know this, too. You may not come back. I must have a wife. Children. You cannot be this wife. You must go back to your uncle's home."

"He is not my uncle!" she cried, refusing to be connected to that man any longer.

"Then why must you leave?"

How could she explain about the people there who needed her? About those who had suffered as she had suffered at Roderick Neville's hands? How she felt it was her mission to make up for their suffering, their pain?

Wasn't that the reason she wanted to find Kenneth? To right a wrong by giving a son his father's property, land that had been denied him, but should rightfully be his?

Kenneth Neville's birthright, she thought. *Neville Manor belongs to Kenneth.*

"I have to go," she said hoarsely, her throat tight with emotion. "I don't expect you to understand."

"As this man does not expect you to see why I will marry Moon Dove."

She understood all right. He couldn't possibly love her as she did him if he could marry another. Why couldn't he just wait for a few months?

Gazing up into his handsome face, she knew that was impossible. Fireheart was a Lenni Lenape chief. There would be many things over the months that took his attention. The Iroquois were still a problem. The Lenape people would move their village elsewhere when the time came that their fields here would produce no crops, and the weather changed, forcing them to seek a more sheltered place.

She smiled at him wistfully, battling tears. "I guess this is good-bye then," she said.

He nodded, his expression taut, stern. Perhaps he too was fighting to conceal emotion. She only wished he loved her as she loved him.

The crime of it all would be if he did love her, but his responsibility as the chief kept him from following his heart.

"Good-bye, Yellow Deer," she said, using his childhood name.

He did not protest for he seemed to understand that she was acknowledging her feelings for the boy he'd been as well as the man he was now.

"May the Great Spirit protect and guide you in your journey home," he said.

"*Wa-neé-shih,*" she whispered, and turned away. From now until the time she left—be it days or weeks—they would be as strangers.

She had come back to tell him of her love yet she had kept silent. Why had she kept silent?

She spun to tell him. "I love you!" she cried, but he had gone, disappearing into the forest and from her life. It was probably for the best that he hadn't heard her words, she thought. Fate had determined both of their paths . . . paths that went in different directions.

"I love you, Fireheart," she whispered, but only the forest listened.

Her throat aching, her chest tight, Joanna crumpled to the ground and gave in to tears.

Chapter 25

John Burton sat in a wigwam with his hands bound behind his back and his legs tied at the ankles. He had a mouth gag for he wouldn't be quiet, and the Lenape people grew tired of listening to his complaints. As he glared silently at the door flap, it lifted, and an Indian maiden stepped inside followed by a warrior.

John scowled at the brave as the warrior approached to remove his gag.

"You will eat," the Indian said in stilted English.

"Bloody hell, I will," he snapped once the gag was gone. When the warrior started to replace his mouth gag, he felt a prickle of alarm. "I'll eat! I'll eat! But untie these blasted ropes on my hands, would you?"

The Indian shook his head. "Stream That Runs will feed you."

John cursed, then shut his mouth when the warrior glared at him, and the maiden backed away. He was hungry, and wanted to eat. He would need his strength if he were to find a way out of this hellish place. He apologized, then smiled at the maiden when she approached again.

The food was adequate: corn cakes, hominy, and a small bowl of beans and corn that was surprisingly tasty cooked together in the Lenape way. Stream That Runs fed him without rushing him, giving him time to chew and swallow before offering him another bite.

As he ate, he couldn't help but watch her. The warrior remained to guard her, but John gazed at her nevertheless. At first, he noticed only a pair of dark eyes, a nose, and a pair of Indian lips. Then, as he continued to chew and swallow, his eyes fell to her firm bare breasts and the necklace of bird feathers and claws that hung about her neck and nestled between those sweet fleshy mounds.

He felt himself harden beneath his breeches, then silently cursed himself. The woman was a savage, and he didn't want to feel anything for the heathen, including lust.

He turned his head and concentrated on the one person he wanted to punish . . . the woman responsible for his captivity. Joanna Neville. He would escape this place, and take her with him . . . and he would make her pay for her sins.

"You are no longer hungry?" the warrior asked when it became obvious that John had finished all of the food that Stream That Runs offered him.

"Yes." *What did he expect me to say?* John thought. The savage could see he was done, couldn't he?

"Then you will come," the brave said. He bent and cut his ankle bindings.

John felt a flutter in his stomach. "Where are you taking me?" He wondered if he had eaten his last meal like a man about to be condemned to die.

The warrior didn't answer him. John would have struck out at the heathen bastard if he could, but his hands were still tied.

The Indian looked at him, and John had the impression that the savage could tell what he was thinking and was happy that John was tied, helpless, and at the mercy of all the savages in the village.

Where were they taking him? he wondered.

The warrior pushed him forward, then prodded him across the yard until they came to a domed wigwam. The *sachem*'s wigwam. John tried to control his fear as the brave lifted the door flap, then shoved him inside.

The darkness of the structure blinded him for a moment after the brightness of the daylight. As his eyes adjusted to the dim lighting, the fear in his belly grew. The place seemed to be filled with savages circling the wigwam.

Directly ahead sat Fireheart, the bastard who had beat him, captured him. Fireheart stared at him without expression, and it was the blank look in his eyes that forced John's heart to beat faster.

"Sit, John Burton," the chief said in English.

John wanted to refuse, but he looked around him, and sat, his pulse racing with terror.

No one said a word after he sat. It was as if they were waiting for something. Or someone. *Who?* John wondered.

Then he heard the rustle of the door flap behind him, and felt the tension of the men seated in the room.

A commotion had him turning as the warrior who had brought him shoved another man into the wigwam. An Indian. A prisoner.

As the prisoner shouted in a tongue that was different from the sounds made by the Lenni Lenape, John knew that the man was Iroquois.

When the Iroquois was shoved to his knees and then instructed to sit beside him, John felt a bone-chilling horror.

The Lenape were here to decide their fate. He and the Iroquois were going to die.

* * *

She didn't want to leave Little River, but there was nothing else she could do. Joanna wasn't foolish enough to think she could manage on her own. It had been different when she'd been escaping John and determined to return here.

Philadelphia was over a week's journey away; she'd never make it that long through the wilderness without a guide to take her. And after her experiences with John, she wasn't looking to find danger again.

It was her turn to help with the community cooking-pot. She sat outside on a rush mat, cutting chunks of deer meat into smaller pieces. When she had completed a bowlful, she rose and crossed the yard to dump the meat into the simmering broth. Then she went back to the mat to cut up more meat and some vegetables.

She wore her Lenape tunic for comfort. She had only two gowns that were decent enough to see her across the ocean. She had coin safeguarded in Philadelphia for her passage back to England, but she didn't know if she would have enough for a new gown. She didn't know if there would be time for garments to be made for her anyway, so she put on the tunic, which she loved, intending to enjoy her remaining moments within the village.

She was torn between her desire to stay and her desire to go. She had already said good-bye to Fireheart. Since that time there had been little talk between them but for a murmured greeting if they happened to pass by one another. The distance between her and Fireheart disturbed her greatly, but she didn't end it for to do so would be foolish. He spent much of his time with Moon Dove, she imagined, although she herself hadn't seen them together but for a few times.

As if her thought had conjured the maiden to taunt

her, Moon Dove appeared, going to the kettle with
her own offering of food. Joanna watched the girl
dump a basket of shelled beans into the pot, then
disappear from sight. Joanna suspected that Moon
Dove had left to find other food items.

Joanna had tensed when she'd first seen her, and
after Moon Dove left, her tension wouldn't go away.
I must leave!

It was during these times when she wanted to go
most. When she watched Moon Dove, and envisioned
the girl's life with Fireheart. When she realized that
she would never compare favorably to the lovely Lenape maiden with her beautiful dark eyes and honey-
brown skin.

Then the feeling would pass, and she would enjoy
the wonderful moments of village life. The quiet. The
smiles and joy of the Lenape people. And she would
think of the dark imposing structure that waited for
her in England, and she wanted only to stay.

Stay. Go. It was an increasing battle within her that
made her long for the arrival of Mortimer Grace. She
wondered if she would ever be happy wherever she
went, wherever she lived, or if life without Fireheart
would make it impossible to enjoy happiness again.

Joanna went back to cutting the meat with misty
eyes.

"Autumn Wind."

She looked up, and smiled at her friend. "Little
Blossom." She grinned at the little girl Little Blossom
held in her arms. "Would you like to sit for a while?"
she asked.

Little Blossom glanced toward her wigwam briefly,
then gave a nod. Joanna went inside Mary Wife's
wigwam for a rush mat, and returned to spread it on
the ground for her friend. Little Blossom sat, and
positioned her daughter next to her, then gave the
child a toy to keep her busy while the friends talked.

Joanna's friend pulled up a basket of vegetables that awaited someone's attention.

"The men are in council," Little Blossom said as she started to cut up some squash. "They have brought in the Iroquois." She hesitated. "And John Burton."

Joanna looked up from her work. "John?"

Her friend nodded. "It is said that this day the prisoner's fate will be determined."

Shuddering, Joanna continued to chop meat. Until now, she'd managed to put John Burton out of mind for she hadn't seen him. The Lenape had put him in a place where he couldn't get free.

She tried not to think what the Lenape would do to the men. The Indians were a kind people, but they could be merciless to their enemies. The English didn't understand how they could be so savage and cruel, but the Lenape were cruel only when it was justified.

As she continued to cut meat, Joanna had a distant memory of a man's screams in the night. She recalled those wild shrieks, and a time when Mary refused to allow her to leave the wigwam. She'd been able to leave after the light of the new day had arrived, when everything was as it had been before the enemy had been taken and she'd been forced to stay inside.

Joanna didn't know what had happened to the Indian who had screamed with pain that faraway night, but she could imagine if she tried. She simply chose not to. When the images came, she forced them away for she had never seen, and she believed her mind would make them greater than they truly were.

But the flash of memory showed John Burton as he had been before he'd come to America. He'd been a kind friend. A gentleman. She couldn't help but think, remember, and imagine. . . .

"So it is not only the Iroquois whose fate will be sealed this day," she said.

"This is true," Little Blossom replied. "The white man has been brought before the council with the enemy."

"The white authorities should handle John Burton."

"And who is going to take him there?" Little Blossom questioned. "You? Rising Bird? Which one of us would you want to endanger to bring John Burton to his own people? We are Lenni Lenape," she continued. "John Burton is white. Which one will the white man believe? The savage, or the white man?"

"The Lenape are not savages!" Joanna said, immediately coming to the tribe's defense.

Little Blossom's expression softened. "I know you believe this, Autumn Wind, for you are truly one of us. But you know that the white man looks upon us as such."

Joanna sighed. "*Kihiila.* They do. They are wrong, but they do. And you are right. The Lenape must see to the justice of John Burton. I would not trust John with a terrible beast." When her friend looked at her questioningly, she added, "I'd not want John Burton to triumph over the beast so that we would all be in danger again."

Little Blossom nodded solemnly, but there was a twinkle in her dark eyes. "Today, we start preparation for the *Gamwing*. You will stay until then? Even if your white man guide comes, you will stay and celebrate our good harvest?"

Joanna stared at her full bowl of meat a long time before replying. "Little Blossom—"

"It begins three days from now, Autumn Wind," her friend said. "Stay with us. Eat well. Say farewell with celebration not with death."

Joanna smiled. Little Blossom referred to the last gathering they'd had, Wild Squirrel's funeral. This upcoming feast would be a celebration of not only a good harvest but the coming of a new *sachem*, Fireheart.

Her heart tripped again as she thought of him. *I should leave.*

But she wanted to stay.

"I will stay," she said, wondering if she wouldn't live to regret her decision.

"Good."

And the two women worked side by side while the child Water Blossom played contentedly with her Indian doll. Joanna, glancing at the little girl, felt a small tinge of envy toward her friend for the love and life she had.

Chapter 26

The village was gathered in the Big House used for celebrations and ceremonies. The mood was festive. Guests had arrived from other tribes. All had come together for the *Gamwing*, their annual time of worship. It was a time when the Lenape thanked the spirits for the summer and fall harvests, and for many things.

Joanna sat in the huge circle next to Mary and Woman with Eyes of Hawk. She, like the others, had dressed for this special occasion. After she had gone to the lake for her morning bath with the other women, she had put on a new doeskin kilt that Mary had given her. It was a bold move for Joanna, for she now appeared like the rest of the women, bare-breasted. Strangely enough, Joanna no longer felt self-conscious of her half-nudity.

Around her neck, Joanna wore jewelry given to her by her friend Little Blossom. When her hair had dried, she'd braided it in to one long plait, then rolled it up and secured it with an *ah-see-pe-la-wan*, a hair ornament made of slate. Next, she had painted the

center part red as she had as a child, just as the other
women had done on this day. She wore face powder
made from finely ground dried corn, and her lips
and cheeks were red, too, stained with berry juice
that Mary had used as well.

She glanced over at her cousin, and smiled as their
gazes met. This day she no longer felt like a young
girl playing at being a woman. She was a woman true,
and to the People, the Lenape, she was the Indian
maiden Autumn Wind.

Food was being passed around from a table, bowls
of hominy sweetened with tree-sugar, one of Joanna's
favorite Lenape dishes.

Young Lenape braves sat in a row with their drums
and rattles, waiting for the cue that would start the
music.

In the center of the structure was a huge pillar with
a face carved into the wood, painted half-red and
half-black. Each post that supported the house had
face carvings. Joanna and her Lenape friends sat on
dried sweet grass that had been spread out on the
ground along each wall earlier by some of the village
women.

Despite the warmth of the autumn night, fires had
been lit in the two huge fire-pits at each end of the
hall. The flames were fueled from the stack of logs
brought in early by the men. The room smelled of
food, wood-smoke, grass, and the bear grease that
the Indians and Joanna used to coat the exposed
areas of their bodies.

Fireheart, as chief, stepped out into the center
between the two fire-pits. The shaman, Raven Wind,
came forward to stand behind him.

Joanna's heart started to race as she gazed longingly
at Fireheart. When she became conscious of her cousin's gaze, she pulled her emotions under control, and
attempted to conceal her feelings.

The *Gamwing* would take twelve days and nights.

Joanna wondered how she would get through it while suffering with the pain of heartbreak.

I will endure, she thought. Because she had her whole life ahead of her, a life without Fireheart. If she didn't learn to come to terms with it now, she would never learn to cope. And so she smiled, and attempted to enjoy herself as the drummers and rattlers began playing their song. Soon her smile felt genuine and her spirits lifted. The next twelve days would be filled with worship, food, games, music, and dancing. She would have a good time, or die trying.

"Good Lenape people," Fireheart said loudly for all to hear. The music softened as he continued to speak. "Welcome! Welcome to the *Gamwing*. This night we begin to celebrate our Lenape life. We start by giving thanks to *Gishelamu-kong*, the Creator. He has given us life, and we offer up this sacrifice of tobacco for him."

With that, the shaman moved to one of the fire-pits, and lit a handful of dried tobacco leaves. Everyone watched with respect as the tobacco caught flame and burned. Raven Wing held up the burning tobacco for all to see; then he set it down on the dirt floor in the center of the room. As the tobacco continued to burn, the shaman began to chant.

"Oh, Creator, we thank you for all that you have given us. We thank you for our sons and daughters . . . for the blessings you have given us in this life. Listen to us, hear our song and our music. Know that we are grateful."

Raven Wind shook his gourd rattle twice, then stepped back.

There were different ways for the Lenape to show their thanks and respect, Joanna knew. The words, the ceremony, might be different each year, but the sentiment and sincerity were the same.

Next, Fireheart, who had his face painted red and black, his hair unbound, and his head circled only with a feathered headband, addressed the gathering again. He spoke against a background of music while the drums and turtle-shell and gourd rattles played.

"During the *Gamwing*, we will thank the *manit'to* for many things. We thank the spirits of the Three Sisters: Mother Corn, Mother Squash, and Mother Bean for they have provided us with food to nourish our bodies and keep us healthy. Thank you, Spirits of the Three Sisters, for the gifts you have given us. This year we have had a good harvest."

Once again, Raven Wind lit an offering of tobacco leaves, and chanted a prayer as the leaves burned.

The prayers went on that way for a while with the subject of thanks being other *manit'to*, other spirits. There was the Spirit of the Wood that gave them the animals and the Spirit of the Sky that gave them the rain, the sun, and the wind. After a time, the prayers stopped. The villagers and guests left the Big House to continue the festivities outside.

There the games would start, and there would be many competitions. All night and day for the next twelve days, there would be feasting, prayers, games, and other activities. When the time finally drew to a close, the Lenape people would be exhausted, and the spirits would be appeased.

Unlike some of the Indians within the encampment, Joanna couldn't stay awake for the long hours of the first night. She slipped away from the others once the community moved outside. The drums would continue all night, but she would sleep for the sound was comforting, and the drums were not war drums, but the music of peace.

As she undressed in the dark, slipping off her kilt and lying naked on her sleeping pallet, Joanna thought of the night with a great deal of satisfaction. She pulled up the beaver pelt to cover herself from the waist down. She had found something of her past self this night. She no longer felt immoral for baring her breasts and wearing only a kilt. She felt like an equal, a Lenape woman with light skin, but her fairness no longer seemed to matter.

Mary and Rising Bird would stay up all night, Joanna knew. The next night they would sleep, and perhaps she might try to stay awake. She could alternate nights of sleeping and wakefulness, depending on the activities or her physical state. She didn't want to get too depleted for she wanted to be ready in case Mortimer Grace arrived to take her away.

The thought of her departure reminded her of John Burton and the last time she'd left the village. This time would be different. She'd be safe in the care of the tracker, and back in Philadelphia before the month turned cold.

She closed her eyes, and became conscious that she was a woman with her breasts bared above a beaver pelt. She was keenly aware of the soft plush fur against her abdomen and thighs.

Her senses were tingling and alive as her mind and body longed for Fireheart, remembering.

"Fireheart," she whispered into the darkness of the wigwam. "Fireheart . . ."

Her heartbeat seemed to echo the drums. Her breathing quickened, laboring as little fingers of sensation frissoned out from her spine titillating every throbbing inch of her. As she drifted off to sleep, she imagined the air on her breasts was Fireheart's caress . . . and the heat of the beaver pelt was actually Fireheart's body warming her, covering her.

But only in her dreams did he make love to her again.

"Moon Dove," the man whispered.

The maiden gasped. "Black Fox! You should not have followed me here!" She had left the public square to enjoy the cool waters of the lake. The yard was full of activity as the villagers and guests gathered to watch *tat-gusk*, a game with hoops and spears. While the drums continued playing and the people watched the players, Moon Dove had slipped away unnoticed. She was tired. Last night she had stayed away from her sleeping mat, and now with the day late, she wanted only to sleep. But first she had wanted a few minutes alone.

Black Fox came out of the shadows and into the moonlight that lit the shoreline. Moon Dove, already waist-deep in the soothing water, caught her breath, and her skin flushed with heat as he approached her. "Why have you left the *Gaṁwing?*" he asked.

"I wanted to be alone before I settled on my sleeping mat."

"I wish to stay with you," he said, his voice deep.

"*Maata!*" she cried. She was afraid to be alone with him, scared of her feelings for him, worried that she'd betray Fireheart. "You must go."

"I will not stay long." He came to her side, wading into the lake waters until he was next to her. "This man sees a woman who is not happy. She is as beautiful as the moon above, but there is no light in her eyes and no smile on her lips." He turned her to face him, and touched her mouth with a fingertip. "Then she meets my gaze, and the fire in her eyes is a bright flame for this man to see."

His touch raised the tiny hairs at the back of her neck. "*Maata*, Black Fox," Moon Dove whispered. *No!*

"Why do you not tell the *sachem* that it is Black Fox you wish. Tell him that you will wed Black Fox, give him many daughters? Many sons?"

Moon Dove felt her cheeks heat. "You must not speak of this. I will marry Fireheart."

"Because you wish it, or because Berry Tree has wanted it?" he asked stiffly.

"My mother wishes me only happiness," she defended.

"Then why do you not tell her about me . . . about us?"

"We are not destined to be mates."

His eyes gleamed brighter in the moonlight. "I can make it so," he said, reaching for her. He bent his head to kiss her, and she gasped, struggling until his warmth, his magic, wrapped around her, making her whimper and cling to his shoulders.

"Black Fox," she gasped when he lifted his head.

"I want you to be my wife. I want to share your sleeping mat. I wish to kiss these lips often. And touch you . . ." He cupped her bare breast. "Touch and taste this woman's fruit until you cry out with pleasure, and want to feel me deep inside you."

His words made Moon Dove tremble. Her nipple hardened beneath Black Fox's palm, her breast swelled to throbbing life. "You must go," she said weakly, not meaning it.

"I must stay," he said. He bent his head, and captured her nipple with his mouth.

"Black Fox!" She gasped, then moaned as she clung to him, weaving her fingers into his hair, holding him against her tighter.

When he lifted his head, he wore a smile of satisfaction at the passion he saw in her dark eyes. He cupped her face, and kissed her sweet mouth with longing.

Black Fox straightened and stared at her. "Tell him, Moon Dove. Tell him, or I will go to him and tell."

"No!" she cried. "You would shame me in this way?"

He scowled. "How is it that I shame you? I want only to take you as my bride. In what manner does that cause you shame?"

"I have been selected to be our *sachem's* bride."

"You have been selected for Fireheart," Black Fox said coldly. "Do you think that Fireheart will make you forget this man's lips? His touch? Will you be a full woman on his sleeping mat? Or will you wed him and wish it were not so?'' His voice thickened with passion. ''With me, you will find happiness because this man loves you. He loves and desires you above all else, and he will kill any man who questions this truth. I am bound to you by something that is above this life. Berry Tree and the matrons might wish you to wed Fireheart, but it is the spirits who have bound our hearts and our bodies. Why do you fight this when you know it is so?''

''Oh, Black Fox,'' she whispered as he opened his arms to her. She dared at this moment to surrender to her feelings for him for she loved him as she would never love Fireheart.

''Marry me, Moon Dove,'' Black Fox said as he bent to nibble on her mouth.

She drew a sharp breath as he caressed her. ''I cannot.''

''*Kitehi,* feel this man's body,'' He placed her fingers on his breast. ''Feel the way this heart beats for you and only you.'' He slid her fingers up along his throat, over his chin to his lips where he tasted her thumb then her forefinger.

Moon Dove's world spun. ''Black Fox . . .''

He had come to the lake to immerse his body in the cool water. Last night had been long, and the day following had been longer.

Fireheart left the path from the village to visit the clearing where he and Joanna had made love. He had only his memories of her now. She was still in the village, but she was gone from him. And he had gone to the clearing to remember before taking his swim.

He found the clearing as they'd left it. The only change was that the wildflowers that had been grow-

ing here had died away. The glow of the moon was
bright, casting its white light onto the bed of pine
needles through the trees.

After a time, Fireheart headed toward the place
where the villagers swam, bathed, and washed their
dishes.

A sound drew his attention as he found the path
again. He paused, drew his knife, then sighed with
relief when he saw the shadows of two figures.

Like himself, they must have left the festivities to
be alone, but while he had only his thoughts for
company, the man and woman had each other.

Suddenly, he thought of Joanna, and he became
alert and tense as he moved forward. He couldn't
have her; would she turn to another? Would another
man give her the love, the comfort she needed?

The couple moved into the moonlight, and Fireheart sighed with relief when he saw that the woman
had the dark hair of a Lenape maiden. The man bent
and kissed the woman deeply.

Fireheart felt relief that the woman wasn't Joanna
until she turned, and he saw Moon Dove silhouetted
in the light.

Chapter 27

He walked with his hands tied and his ankles bound just enough for him to take small steps. The Indian with him struck him with his club when John didn't go quickly enough.

To John's shock and dismay, the Lenape had set their Iroquois prisoner free and given him John as his captive. John was furious, and not just a little scared. There had been some discussion of honor and of giving the Iroquois a replacement for the dead. John didn't understand except that he had been given to the Iroquois people as a prisoner, in the hands of their chief, Flaming Sky.

John shuddered. Did a fate await him that was worse than his time with the Lenni Lenape? The only thing that John cared about was that soon he could be free. Only one Iroquois chief would take him to the Cayuga village, one chief while before many Lenape braves had guarded him. Surely, he could escape from only one warrior!

He didn't know the Iroquois language. When the warrior babbled in his strange native tongue, John nodded but didn't understand a single word. He was tired and hungry, and he tried to tell the Indian as they walked.

Flaming Sky glared at him. "*Haht-deh-gah-yeh-ee.*"

John wasn't sure, but took that to mean he was to keep going. He tried to explain what he wanted again. The Lenape had at least fed him and allowed him to rest. Would the Iroquois keep him plodding along forever?

He needed the food and sleep to keep up his strength. He needed it soon before he was too far from the Lenape village to find his way back . . . before they reached the Iroquois village and he became trapped.

"Food," he said, trying to show the Indian what he wanted while continuing to move. "Eat!"

The chief scowled. "*Te-ah!*"

John halted, refusing to move. "Food," he insisted.

The Indian stopped, and John breathed a sigh of relief. Apparently, he had some control over the Indian. He hid a smile. This might work to his advantage.

The warrior pulled his knife and ran the sharp edge down John's cheek, cutting him, making him bleed. John cried out, then became frightened.

"*Ey-on-di-ko-ni!*" Flaming Sky exclaimed. "*Te-ah!*"

Unable to clutch his throbbing cheek, John continued to walk the trail, cursing beneath his breath at the Indian. The heathen had cut him! He made a silent vow to kill the Iroquois before he escaped. *Savage bastard!*

During the third day of the *Gamwing*, Fireheart called Moon Dove into his wigwam.

"You wish to see me?" she asked as she followed him inside.

"*Kihiila*," he said, gesturing for her to sit. "I must talk with you."

Moon Dove lowered herself to the rush mat.

"The matrons have decreed that we should marry," he began, watching her face closely. "But they are wrong. We will not marry."

Alarm flickered across her features. "Have I displeased you?" she asked, her eyes filling with tears.

"You love another."

She gasped, turning pale. "I have not shamed you!"

Fireheart's expression softened. "Did I say I would punish you? Hurt you? *Maata*, I wish only for you to be happy. We talked of this before. Remember? You assured me that you wish for us to wed, but if this were so, you would not kiss another, or enjoy the moonlight with him."

Terror flashed in her dark eyes. "You saw us?" He inclined his head. "I am sorry," she whispered, hanging her head.

He reached to cup her jaw, urging her to meet his gaze. "Moon Dove. I am not angry with you for, truth be told, I do not love you. I love another."

A tiny ray of hope shone in her dark eyes. "You are not angry?"

Smiling, he shook his head. "I am disappointed that you would not be honest with me. But I understand, too." The smile left his face as he thought of Joanna. He was relieved that he would not have to marry Moon Dove, but sad that Autumn Wind was not his to wed.

"I wished only to be a good wife to the *sachem*."

Fireheart frowned. "I am Fireheart first before I am *sachem*."

She flushed, looking embarrassed. "I know this. And this was what Black Fox said. He wanted me to tell you."

"Black Fox said this?" he asked, and she nodded. "I wish to see him."

He felt her fear. "You will not punish him?"

Fireheart sighed. "I would not punish a good warrior for loving you. It is what you deserve. Why do you not take his gift with both hands?"

"I didn't think I could," she admitted.

His smile was grim with understanding. "I will talk with Berry Tree. She will not object to your choice. Black Fox is a good warrior. A powerful war chief. Any mother would be glad if her daughter took one such as he for a husband."

"But if the matrons don't approve—"

"They will approve," Fireheart said. He tapped her on the nose and grinned. "This man is still *sachem*."

"But they will want you to marry."

"I will handle finding my own bride. I will speak to Woman with Eyes of Hawk and Mary Wife. They will understand and convince the others."

"*Wa-neé-shih*," she murmured, her eyes sparkling with happy tears. "You are truly a great chief."

"Do not tell Black Fox of our meeting. I would frighten the great warrior some before I tell him the good news."

Her eyes widened, and she looked uncertain.

"I would not hurt him, Moon Dove, but I wish him to know that it is not wise to defy the chief." His smile must have convinced her because she returned it. Fireheart followed her outside, then kissed her lightly. "Now go, and tell your brother White Cat to find Black Fox and send the brave warrior to me."

Mortimer Grace arrived with a married couple who wanted to get to the white settlement at Fort Dobbs. Joanna was outside, watching a group of children at play when she spied the newcomers. Recognizing the tracker, she hurried to greet him.

"Mr. Grace!" She smiled. "Thank you for returning. I've been waiting for you."

The young man returned her grin with a smile of apology. "I'm sorry I took so long. I had only gotten word of your need a few weeks ago." He glanced at his friends. "I came as soon as I could." Noting the couple's curious gazes, he introduced Joanna to them.

Joanna smiled at each of them as she greeted them. Then she explained about the occasion as they entered the village yard, and invited them to join the feast. The woman, Abigail Weatherby, looked scared while her husband, Richard, looked merely nervous. They eyed Joanna's doeskin garment strangely, apparently surprised to see a white woman dressed like the savages.

"The Lenape are a peaceful people," she assured them. "You don't have to be worried or frightened here."

Her words had the desired effect, she saw, for both the man and the woman looked more relaxed.

Joanna introduced Abigail and Richard to her cousin, Mary, and they seemed happy to see another white woman within the village, a woman who obviously belonged, for with her was her Indian husband, Rising Bird.

With the couple safely in Mary's hands, Joanna drew Mortimer aside to speak briefly with him. "You can stay for a while, can't you?" She had promised Little Blossom she would stay until the *Gaḿwing* was done, but twelve days seem a long time to her now.

"Are you in a hurry to go?" he asked. "The Weatherbys are exhausted. They wouldn't mind spending a night or two, I suspect. Is there a place for them to stay?"

Joanna nodded. "If they don't mind sharing. There is always plenty of room for guests in Little River."

She left Mortimer with Turtle That Hops, the two of them having been acquainted before, and went in search of Little Blossom. She was going to have to explain why she felt the need to leave early. There were other people to be considered now. Little Blossom would just have to understand.

When she couldn't find her friend, Joanna left the public square to search for her, heading first to the long wigwam of the Turtle clan, Little Blossom's family. Crossing the yard to another cluster of wigwams, Joanna hesitated when the door flap on the *sachem*'s hut lifted, and Moon Dove and Fireheart left the birch bark structure together. She watched with an ache as the couple spoke briefly, quietly, then with a sharp shaft of pain as Fireheart kissed the Indian maiden, touching her hand briefly before she left.

Her stomach churned as Joanna turned away from the sight. Her mind screamed with pain, and she fought to escape it. How could Little Blossom expect her to stay when to see such a sight would be too painful for her? She couldn't remain, couldn't be forced to watch again the man she loved kissing another woman.

I want to leave now, she thought. She would talk with Mortimer Grace, and if the Weatherbys were willing, they would leave tonight, or first thing in the morning.

As luck or fate would have it, the Weatherbys, despite the Lenape people's warm hospitality, were still uncomfortable in the Indian village. They had been ready to leave almost as soon as they'd stepped into the compound.

Joanna hated farewells, but she couldn't leave without talking with Mary, saying good-bye. It wouldn't be fair. And Little Blossom would be upset with her if she didn't explain her change of plans.

She said a brief farewell to all who mattered to her, all but Fireheart for she had already said good-bye to him days ago. She wouldn't suffer the moment again. It was bad enough she had to leave with the lingering image of him with Moon Dove.

That night, while the villagers were gathered in the Big House, Joanna left with Mortimer Grace and the

Weatherbys. Their first stop would be the white settlement at Fort Dobbs where the Weatherbys were expected by Mrs. Weatherby's father.

Once again, as the drum music was swallowed up by the distance and the night, Joanna left with tears in her eyes and the knowledge that she would never be back again

John stood over the dead body of the Iroquois chief and gloated. He had slashed the man's throat, using the savage's own knife. It had been easy. He had followed the fool obediently until the chief had lowered his guard and untied him. Even then, John had continued to be the model prisoner.

Then, after night came and the savage slept, John had been able to steal the chief's knife. It had almost been too easy. He had slipped the blade from the sheath that the Indian had set on the ground beside him. Then, with one swipe of the sharp edge, he'd slid it across the man's neck.

"Stupid savage," John said with a grin.

The sight of the blood pooling on the ground made him feel competent, important . . . powerful. He had outmaneuvered all of his Indian captors. He was a free man again.

John grabbed the war club, the Cayuga's other weapon, and tucked the knife behind the waist strip of his breeches.

Joanna. His smile turned grim. It was time to kidnap her and teach her a lesson she would never forget.

Chapter 28

Fireheart received word on the fourth morning of the *Gamwing* that John Burton had escaped. The Iroquois, Flaming Sky, was found dead.

He felt cold seep into his bones as he thought of Joanna. Burton would be back, he realized. Fortunately, Joanna was here within the village where he could protect her.

He nodded a greeting at Woman with Eyes of Hawk as he passed her on his way to the Big House. Later this day, he would find Joanna, talk with her, and let her know that he was not going to marry Moon Dove. He would then tell her that he would wait many moons for her return.

His heart lightened as he entered the ceremonial house, and joined the shaman in the center between the fire-pits. As he stood readying to address the group, he searched for Joanna, but couldn't find her.

He would find her later, he thought. And he would kiss her breathless so that she would know that he loved her. And he would make her admit that she loved him.

* * *

The trail was mostly clear, and the journey this day was an easy one. Joanna lifted her skirts to avoid a twig and kept moving. The air was cooler than the previous morning's. A bird's song sweetened the soft breeze, making her smile as she looked up to see the warbler high in a treetop. Mortimer was ahead, and the Weatherbys were behind her. Joanna paused to wait as Richard Weatherby helped his wife to hurry forward.

"I'm sorry," he apologized as he and Abigail joined her.

" 'Tis no problem," Joanna assured him. " 'Tis a lovely day, and we'll not be reaching the settlement until tomorrow. Why not take time and enjoy the lovely scenery until we arrive?"

Abigail looked at her as if Joanna had sprouted two horns. "You call this 'lovely?' " she snapped.

"Now, darling," her husband scolded.

"I'm sorry," Abigail apologized. "I'm not feeling well." She leaned close to Joanna to exchange womanly secrets. "I've come upon my courses."

Joanna patted her arm consolingly. "I understand. Perhaps we should rest a while."

Abigail looked grateful, but Richard would hear none of it. "If we stop to rest every hour, we'll never get to Fort Dobbs."

At his brusqueness, his wife appeared crestfallen.

"Mr. Weatherby—"

"Richard," he invited with approval from his wife.

"Richard, Mrs. Weatherby—Abigail," she corrected when she saw the woman's face, "is feeling poorly. Surely we'll be able to make better time if we allow her to rest through this difficult time. If you don't allow this, 'tis likely she'll be feeling worse tomorrow. Then we won't reach the settlement until the day after tomorrow."

Mortimer Grace had stopped ahead once he'd noticed the others had not kept up. He returned now to see what the problem was.

"We were just discussing the need to stop and rest," Joanna explained. "Abigail isn't feeling well, and I told Richard that we need to take care of his wife, or she'll be feeling too poorly to travel."

Mortimer caught Joanna's meaningful look and nodded. "Ya'd best listen to Miss Neville," he said. "She knows the ways of women, being one herself and all."

Joanna's lips curved with amusement. "Why, thank you, Mr. Grace."

The man's cheek turned a bright shade of red. He brusquely ordered a stop for rest and food, then quickly excused himself and walked away. Richard, muttering about the burdens of females, followed him, leaving Abigail and Joanna alone together.

"Thank you," Abigail whispered, her brown eyes shining with gratitude.

Joanna's smile was compassionate. "Do you have something for the pain?" she asked in a gentle voice.

Abigail shook her head. "Mum would have given me chamomile tea, but I've not had a drop of tea since I left England two months past."

"I've got a remedy for you, but 'tis Lenape so you must trust me that it works for pain."

The woman looked uncertain. "Have you used it?"

"Yes. The first time I had it I was but a child who lived among the Lenape."

"*You* lived among the Indians?" She appeared startled.

"Yes, from the time I was five years old until I was sent to England at fourteen."

"You must have been glad when you left," Abigail said. "For England, I mean. 'Tis a better place than this wilderness."

"On the contrary," Joanna said stiffly, "my time

here was a much happier life." She reached into the small pocket sewn inside her skirts, and pulled out a handful of dried herbs. "I can make you a tea. We've no sugar to sweeten it, but it's palatable just the same."

The woman eyed the dried leaves in Joanna's extended palm, wincing when she was seized by a menstrual cramp. "This will work?" She sounded desperate.

"As sure as my name is Joanna Neville," Joanna told her. "I'll ask Mortimer if we can have a fire. If we can, I'll brew you the tea. All right?"

Abigail nodded. "Aye. Thank you," she said sincerely, trying to smile past her pain.

"You're welcome, Abigail." She leaned close to whisper. "We females have to stand together," she said in a tone much like the one that Richard Weatherby had used just minutes before.

Then Joanna saw that the woman was seated before she went to discuss the length of their stay with Mortimer. She also wanted to talk with him about the possibility of having a small campfire.

John knew he had to be careful as he headed back to the Lenape village. He and the Iroquois hadn't traveled far. It wouldn't take him long to go back, find Joanna, and take her away.

I should be able to get in and out easily, he thought. The *Gamwing* had brought guests from other Indian villages. He could slip in and out of the village during the night while the Indians were busy feasting and playing their silly games.

As he'd expected, he found the village of Little River with no problem, drawn by the sound of the drums. As he approached, he could hear the shouts and laughter of the Indians at the games.

John stayed in the forest. He found an area near the lake from which to watch. He decided to look for Joanna there first, in the hope that she would come to the water to bathe or swim.

He waited a time, and then became impatient when she didn't appear. Where was she? he wondered.

He dared to move closer to the activities, and found a spot high in a tree from where he could easily observe the village below. He searched for a time for Joanna's blonde hair, but still he couldn't find her.

As John debated whether or not to get down from the tree, a thought occurred to him. Was it possible that Joanna had left? Could the guide she'd been awaiting have arrived to take her away? Was she on her way, as he sat on his tree limb, bound for Philadelphia? It would explain why he hadn't spotted her.

Damn! John cursed the time he'd wasted, but how was he to have known?

A sudden smile curved his lips. Away from the savages, Joanna would be easier to abduct once he'd found her. With only a lone man to defend her, he'd be able to kidnap her from under the tracker's nose. She'd be helpless and at his mercy.

John's smile widened into a grin. He didn't know when she'd left, but it couldn't have been long ago. He and the Indian had left before her, and he'd retraced his steps to the village quickly enough. *Joanna*, he thought, *you'll not escape me now.*

The tea worked wonders for Mrs. Weatherby who was smiling gratefully at Joanna while feeling no pain. "Wonderful medicine," she said, slurring her words lightly.

Joanna smiled. "I told you it would work."

"Aye, ya did." Abigail grinned at her husband. "She did, ya know, Richard. Joanna said I would feel all better, and I do." She turned back to Joanna. "You must tell me how to get more."

Mortimer met Joanna's gaze with a lift of his eyebrows. Joanna grinned back, then watched with amusement as Richard Weatherby patted his wife's shoulder awkwardly.

"You are well enough to travel, love?" he asked.

"Cer-tain-ly!" Abigail quipped as if she were intoxicated. She stood up, and teetered drunkenly on her feet. "We can leave now. I can walk for hours so we can make up for lost time."

"We'll not be going anywhere this night," Mortimer said with a twinkle in his eyes. "We'll move out at first light. Mr. Weatherby, you'd best get your wife to bed so that she'll be well rested in the morning."

When Richard looked as he were about to object, Mortimer flashed him a telling glance. His decision to stay was final. They would sleep here in this sheltered clearing for the night, then set out at first light.

Joanna was more than happy to remain there for the night. Despite her belief, Abigail would not have gone far before she needed to stop to sleep. The tea was a powerful elixir for pain. The woman was already feeling light-headed. In a half hour, she'd be fast asleep. By the next morning, Abigail would be better, and more capable of journeying through the woods.

Joanna dug into her satchel for the blanket she'd managed to fold up small enough to fit in. It had been a gift from Mary, another generous offering like Joanna's doeskin tunic and kilt.

Her eyes filled with tears as a wave of longing came over her. Joanna had had to leave the tunic behind for the journey through the forest would be long, and she'd needed to keep her pack light. Still the memory of Mary's gift made her wish she were back in the village. She wanted to see her cousin again. She yearned to see everyone . . . especially Fireheart.

She managed a small smile through her tears. At least, she was able to bring the kilt. As she envisioned her late uncle, a small defiant grin curved her mouth. With Roderick's death, she could don the kilt whenever she felt like it. Whenever she wanted to feel bold and daring and free, she would put on the kilt in the privacy of her bedchamber, and dance half-naked in the candlelight before the mirror.

Joanna had to stifle the bubble of laughter that rose up in her throat. *I can dance naked as a Lenape under the stars if I like, Roderick Neville!*

Chapter 29

A cold hand clamped over Joanna's mouth in the night, waking her. It was dark. Unable to focus her gaze at first, she struggled against the hold until a low male voice whispered in her ear to keep quiet, or be killed.

Joanna froze, and waited for the man's next move. He shifted his hand slightly, and in a gruff whisper warned her again to be silent.

"I'll kill them, every one of them if you make so much as a whimper," he said in a more familiar voice.

John! Joanna nodded in answer. He released her mouth, and straightened to grin down at her wickedly.

"Get up, Joanna," he ordered.

She obeyed him because she saw that he had a knife and another weapon—an Indian war club. She shuddered. Why hadn't she asked Fireheart what had been done to John?

"I thought you were dead," she hissed as he grabbed her arm, and dragged her from the campsite out of Mortimer Grace's and the others' earshot.

"Disappointed to see me alive?" he taunted.

She glared at him. "Extremely."

Anger flashed in his blue eyes. "Too bad, darling Joanna. I'm here, alive and well, and I've come to collect what's mine."

He reached out and cupped the section of her skirts that covered her femininity. Joanna gasped, and batted his hand away only to have her arm taken into his grip and wrenched upward brutally. When she cried out with the pain, he ordered her to silence.

He released her arm, shoving her away so hard that she fell on the ground, winded. As she glared up at him, she felt her bones turn to jelly as her courage startled to falter.

He's going to kill me, she thought. But not before he had a chance to play some of his sick games with her.

It would be rape and death for her if she didn't get away. John had been injured recently. As she stared at his cut cheek, Joanna vowed to accept death over rape. He wouldn't have the chance to defile her. She would kill herself first before she'd allow his hands on her.

"Let's go." He jerked her to her feet, then shoved her before him.

"Where are we going?"

"Fort Dobbs," he said. "Did you think I'd be foolish enough to take ya to Philadelphia right off when your man and the others will be headed there, too?"

Joanna hid her relief. John didn't know that the Weatherbys were on their way to Fort Dobbs. If she were lucky, Mortimer would get there before her and John. If she saw him, she could gain his attention and ask for help.

She held on to that hope, small as it was, and followed John's commands so he wouldn't hurt her. Joanna hid a smile. They were traveling a different way than Mortimer had chosen. They were not likely to meet up with Mortimer before reaching the fort. She hadn't lost all chances for escape.

She fought the urge to grin until she reminded herself that there was still a full day's journey to the settlement. Much could happen in that length of time. She must keep her wits about her, and figure out a way to be alone.

It would be a difficult feat to accomplish. With Gillian dead, John wanted her now, but unlike Gillian, Joanna wasn't willing. That fact, unfortunately, didn't seem to concern John Burton, but then what did a murderer have to lose when his hanging death was already imminent?

"Where is Autumn Wind?" Fireheart asked Mary Wife. "I have not seen her for two days. Is she ill?"

With the knowledge of John Burton's escape weighing on him, he wanted to see Joanna, to ensure that she was unharmed and well, safe in her cousin's wigwam.

"You don't know?" Mary said, surprise mirrored in her eyes. "Joanna is not here. She left on the third day of the *Gamwing*."

"She left!" Fireheart's blood froze. "Why did she not come to say good-bye."

Mary's face softened. "She told me that she had already said good-bye to you, Fireheart."

"But I had something more to say—"

"Well, it cannot be said," she replied. "Joanna has gone to England. She left with Mortimer Grace. She'll be coming up on Fort Dobbs first. About now, I'd say."

"John Burton has escaped," he said quietly.

"No!" Mary said. "She'll be in danger."

"*Kihiila*. I'm going after her—" He turned to leave.

"Fireheart!" Mary cried, grabbing his arm. "Bring her back safely. I don't care what you have to do, but bring her back to us."

"If she will come," he said.

"What will you be telling her when you see her?" she asked. "That you love her? That you'll not be marrying Moon Dove?"

His face grim, he inclined his head.

"Then she'll come," Mary said with conviction. "The girl loves you. She will come if you but ask her."

She smelled the smoke from the chimneys at Fort Dobbs and knew the settlement was close. Joanna tried to contain her joy that soon she would be around others, people who might be able to help.

It had been a challenge to keep John from touching her. She avoided his touch whenever she could, and for some strange reason, he didn't carry out his threat and try something more. He must have a plan for her. She only wished she knew what it was.

At present, the thought of a real bed in a cabin excited her. Sleep, she thought. Real sleep . . . unless John insisted they share a room. Then she would be back where she was before, nervous, alert, and afraid to sleep.

When the first sight of the settlement rose before them, John grabbed her arm to halt her. "You're my wife while we're here. Do you understand? My wife, and no one is to know otherwise."

She frowned. "What if they don't believe us?"

He scowled at her. "You'd best do a good job of playacting, or else you and anyone who learns the truth will die. Would you like someone's death on your conscience?"

"No," she murmured, glaring at him with hate.

He squeezed her arm hard. "Is that any way for you to gaze at your beloved husband?"

She gasped at the pain, and forced a smile on her face. He eased his grip. "Not good enough," he said. "Try again." Joanna gave him a sappy grin. "Better." He chuckled. "But try to look a little more loving."

"I'll do it," she promised. "When I'm in there and forced to, but not before. Do you hear me?"

"Don't make threats or tell me what to do, bitch!" Tugging her arm, he wrenched her forward. "Move!"

The settlement was on a huge plot of land that had been cleared of lumber and fenced in. Joanna's heart started to pound as she and John entered through the gate, and greeted the first person they encountered.

The man looked at them suspiciously for a long moment until John became his old charming self. Joanna nearly gasped aloud at the change in him.

He was the best actor she'd ever seen, she thought. Had he always been devious? Had they all misjudged him these past years? Or had something within him just snapped? How could he have fooled both Gillian and herself so easily?

"Would you have a room where we could stay for the night?" John asked the man who called himself Bernard Coker.

"Aye, there'd be a room somewhere in the settlement," Bernard replied. "Mrs. Brenner might have one."

One room, Joanna thought, disappointed. She would be forced to share a room with John.

"Thank you," John said pleasantly. "We'd be obliged." Mrs. Brenner's place turned out to be a nice log cabin with three bedrooms, only one of which she used. John and Joanna were given another one. For a moment, Joanna wondered what excuse she could give to occupy the third room, but then she remembered John's threat and kept silent.

The room had one large bed, a washstand with ewer and basin, and a chest of drawers with a mirror. Near the window was a high-backed chair upholstered with brocade. The same brocade fabric curtained the window. Joanna stared at the bed, and fought the urge to flee.

"There be fresh linens on the mattress," Mrs. Brenner was saying. "The drawers are empty if you need them." She took a hard look at the two of them. "Then mayhap you won't."

"Thank you, Mrs. Brenner," John said with a winning smile.

The woman beamed, and Joanna cursed her own first foolish impression of him. The man was a murderer, a liar, and a cheat, and she had trusted him. He'd had everyone, including Roderick Neville, fooled.

Once the woman had left the two of them, Joanna went to the window, and hugged herself with her arms. John came up to stand behind her, putting his hands on her shoulders. She moved away from him. He narrowed his gaze, but didn't scold her.

"How many people do you suppose live in the settlement?" she asked.

"What does it matter?" John said with a careless shrug. "You'll not be speaking to any of them. We'll be leaving at first light."

Joanna concealed her burning anger. "I was just curious."

"I'll be seeing if there is a general store for supplies to get us the rest of the way to Philadelphia," John told her. "Don't you be leaving this room."

She gazed at him and gave a reluctant nod.

"I mean what I say, Joanna. I'll find and kill you. No second chances. And I'll kill anyone who helps you escape me."

Joanna sighed. "I just agreed to stay, didn't I? I'll not have another's bloodstain on my soul." Although she secretly thought he was the one responsible for murdering her friend, she couldn't help feeling guilty over Gillian's death. It was her escape that had aroused John's anger enough to kill.

"Lock the bedchamber door when you leave," he ordered. "I'll not have that busybody Mrs. Brenner coming in and asking questions."

"I'll lock the door if you promise me one thing," she dared.

He raised an eyebrow. "Bold 'tis that you're being for someone who is at my mercy."

"Are you unwilling to listen to what I have to say?"

His blue eyes lit up with curiosity. "Go on then and say it. What is it that's on your mind?"

"If I promise to stay in the room and avoid other people, except when you are with me, will you vow to sleep somewhere else?"

"No, I'll promise no such thing,"

She began to feel desperate. "Will you, at least, allow me to sleep in that chair, or on the floor? I won't sleep in the same bed as you."

"Are you saying that you don't like me?" he taunted. "I'm hurt."

"John, I'll not have you shaming me."

He looked intrigued. "You mean no other has touched you? Not even the Indian?"

She shook her head, hoping he couldn't see the lie.

"I'll allow you to sleep either on the floor, or in the chair," he said. "It makes no matter to me."

"And you won't touch me," she added.

"No. Touch you I will, but lie with you?" He stared at her breasts. "I suppose I could wait for a time." His eyes narrowed as he stared at her. "But heed me, and heed me well. You will share my bed, now or later. I understand your desire to wait until after we're wed."

"I'll not marry you, John Burton. I've already told you."

"We'll see," he said. "We'll see." He went to the door and opened it. "Lock it when I'm gone."

She nodded and John left. Joanna hurried to turn the key in the lock.

Joanna stared at the key in her hand, and wondered why John hadn't just locked her in the room. *Unless he wants me to try to escape so he can kill me.* He was, after all, mad.

The thought gave her gooseflesh as she went back to the window, and stared outside. As she looked, she hoped that someone would see her . . . someone who could help her.

Chapter 30

Fireheart and his band of men met up with Mortimer Grace and the Weatherbys along the trail. Abigail Weatherby shrieked when she saw them.

"Fireheart!" Mortimer Grace called out in greeting. "Mrs. Weatherby, please stop that screaming! This is Fireheart, chief of the Lenape at Little River. He is not the enemy! Stop your caterwauling."

"Joanna's Lenape friends?" she said in a high squeaky voice.

Mortimer nodded. "Fireheart, we've not seen hide nor hair of Joanna since yesterday. I'm afraid something dreadful has happened to her. We searched the area surrounding our campsite, but there was no sign that she was still around. I know we should have continued the search, but—"

"John Burton has escaped," Fireheart told him.

"Burton?" the man questioned, then Fireheart realized that Grace had never met the man. "The man followed her here from England. He's a dangerous murderer with revenge on his mind. He's after Joanna."

"Oh, dear Lord!" Abigail wailed.

And for once, both her husband and Mortimer agreed with her.

"What can we do to help?" Mortimer asked.

"We will go to the white man's fort first to look for Autumn Wind."

"Autumn Wind?" Richard asked.

"It is what we call the woman you know as Joanna Neville. To us she is like the autumn wind."

"That's lovely," Abigail said, sounding surprised.

Fireheart nodded. "John Burton might be looking for someone to take them to the place where ships come and go." He waved his men to follow. "Come," he said to the white people. "We will go ahead if we must. We must go quickly."

"We'll be able to keep up," Richard said with a glance at his wife. "Won't you, darling?"

Abigail nodded. "I'm fine. I can keep up." And it was thanks to Joannna—and to the Lenape people—for their powerful medicine that she felt well enough to travel.

"Come," Fireheart said. "Let us go then."

John stroked the woman's breast, then nuzzled his face between both firm, fleshy mounds. "You are an understanding woman, Mistress Goldsboro," he said as he lifted his head. "My wife—well, I love her, I do, but she is feeling poorly. She's with child, and, truth be told, she is not one to enjoy the pleasures of the marriage bed. Not like one such as yourself does." He bent again to gently bite her nipple.

She moaned and encouraged him to take a nibble of the other breast. "I don't understand the way of your wife then, Master Bartley," she said, using the name he'd given her. "You've a magic touch, you have."

"Ah, you're the magic one, Nan," he purred before

he kissed her. He tongued her mouth, then rose up to gauge her reaction.

He had found the widow at the trading post within the settlement. He'd heard of her widowed state from the shop keeper who happened to mention that the widow was lovely, and willing to any man with a cock between his legs and the stamina to endure her. John had immediately become intrigued. He'd been hot and aching for Joanna since he'd stumbled upon the campsite, and found her sleeping.

Despite his threats, he wasn't a man to force women. He'd rather seduce them until they were willing. And before he was through with Joanna Neville, she would not only be willing, she'd be begging him to take her hard and fast. At the present time, she was still playing reluctant and so he'd decided to humor her ... another part of his plan. But this part had left him stiff and throbbing until he'd discovered a way to satisfy his lust ... and now he was in her cabin lying in bed ... and Nan was proving to be a pleasurable diversion.

"You're a sweet young thing," he said, his eyes glowing, his voice thick with passion.

"Ah, Joseph you say the nicest things." She slipped her hand down his back to his buttocks and moved them in a way that was entirely new and exciting to him ... and apparently to her if her labored breath were any indication.

"Do ya like it hard and fast, or soft and easy?" he said as she took hold of his cock, then stroked him tenderly.

"Love, I like it any way you'd like to give it."

"Dear God," he gasped as she did something to arouse him to the point of pain.

Near to bursting, he shoved her legs open wide, mounted her, and gave it to her hard and rough, pounding between her thighs, spurred on by her cries of pleasure.

He fell over the edge, spilling his seed into her after he heard her scream out with the ecstasy he'd given her. Stiffening, he felt his surging climax last longer than any he'd ever had before.

Pleased, sated, he lay heavily on top of her, even more pleased when she didn't object to his weight but seemed to relish it.

"That was a good first try, lover," she said, startling him to raise himself up to gaze down at her.

There was a gleam of wicked pleasure in her glorious hazel eyes.

"You want more?" he asked gruffly, his manhood already hardening again.

"Let's do it slow and easy, shall we?" Then she touched him, and he gasped, wondering how he would ever be able to go slow with this woman who had so much experience.

He battled to get himself under control. He knew something of sex. She might have showed him a thing or two, but he had a few tricks of his own up his sleeve.

As he reached for that magic spot between Mistress Goldsboro's legs, John decided that he wouldn't be returning to Joanna this night.

He smiled as Nan whimpered and shivered as he began to manipulate her. Joanna wouldn't be escaping, he thought as he slid down her body to find her pleasure point with his tongue. She'd be too frightened to leave. It was safe for him to enjoy the rest of his stay at Fort Dobbs here, in this woman's bed . . . discovering new ways to pleasure and control her.

He didn't return to the room, and Joanna was grateful, but worried. Was he playing a game with her? Or had he found someplace to sip ale with the men?

She didn't sleep but for short dozes. The thought

remained that John could be somewhere getting drunk. Drunk, he could return to her, and he'd be more difficult to handle.

At one point during the night, exhausted, she had moved the dresser in front of the door, making up some excuse to Mrs. Brenner who had heard the scrape of wood against wood. Fortunately, the woman didn't demand that Joanna open the door for she'd have had more explaining to do. Why would she do such a thing as barricade the door to keep her husband from entering? If Mrs. Brenner asked, and she told her the truth, the woman's life would be in danger.

Joanna believed that John would kill anyone who learned the truth, or tried to help her. The previous murders he'd committed had shown that he was capable.

When the dawn lit up the sky, brightening the room between the open window curtains, Joanna got up from the bed, and went to move the dresser away from the door. If she hadn't moved the furniture there in the first place, she wouldn't have been able to doze. She would have stared at the door all night, waiting for the exact moment of John's appearance.

As she slid the piece of furniture the remaining inches, she thought of the night and had another thought. What if John had found a willing woman?

God, she hoped so. It would help matters greatly for her if John weren't so overly aroused and staring at her breasts all the time. Wherever John was, Joanna thought, he'd be back soon. Should she try to leave?

Seconds later, she opened the bedchamber door with the intention of going, but Mrs. Brenner was in the Great Room, preparing breakfast.

"Sit down and eat," the woman invited. "Where be your husband?"

Joanna feigned tears. "I don't know," she said. "He left last evening and didn't return. Do you think he's been hurt, or killed?'' She hoped he would never come back, but couldn't say so without arousing the woman's suspicions.

Mrs. Brenner, who had been eyeing Joanna suspiciously, softened her expression. ''Now, now, missy. Don't ya be worrying. I'm sure the Master found Pete Drummer's place. The fellows often go there to indulge. He probably got to sipping and playing a bit of cards.''

''Oh, I see. Thank you for telling me,'' Joanna said, pretending gratitude while calculating how much time she might have to escape the settlement before John returned. ''You're welcome for certain, Missy,'' the woman said.

Joanna stared at her and sighed. She couldn't leave and allow this friendly woman to brave John's anger. He'd kill her, and kill her for sure.

John returned while Joanna was eating breakfast. ''Good morn', wife.'' He sounded unusually cheerful.

Joanna stared at him. ''You were gone all night.''

He seemed pleased. ''Jealous?''

Aware that Mrs. Brenner was watching them, she bobbed her head.

''Now, don't ya be worrying the girl that way again, Mr. Bartley. She cares for ya and deserves better.''

Expecting his anger, Joanna was stunned to see John nod respectfully and agree. She fought the urge to cringe when he touched her cheek, then bent to kiss her lips. He smelled of flowers and something else that wasn't ale. Fighting the urge to wipe off her lips, Joanna decided that John hadn't spent the night at Pete's, but with a woman. And now Joanna was pleased.

Still, she wasn't in a hurry to leave.

''Joseph,'' she said, using his fictitious name. ''Can't

we stay another day? I've barely had a moment to visit with Mrs. Brenner.''

"No, dearest, we must go," John said with a warning glance. "You know we've a ship to meet."

"Oh, are some relatives of yours coming in on the *Elizabeth Mary*?" Mrs. Brenner asked.

"Aye, aye, that they are," John said.

"Well, then you can stay awhile for the vessel isn't expected for a fortnight yet."

Joanna beamed, thinking that John would be forced to concede. Only she'd forgotten how devious he could be.

"I've been wanting to buy my wife some new garments. It will take most of that time to find a seamstress in Philadelphia, and for the woman to make them."

"Then you'd best be moving along," Mrs. Brenner said, looking sad but resigned to losing her guests and the coin they'd brought with them.

John stood. "Thank you for your kind hospitality, Mrs. Brenner," he said.

The woman nodded. "Godspeed," she wished.

As Joanna preceded John out the door, she sincerely hoped that God would stay with her.

"What did you think you were doing back there?"

"I wanted to enjoy another night in a bed is all," Joanna said.

He studied her a long time. "I thought perhaps you'd hoped to find someone to help you." His smile made her feel cold. "There is no help for you, Joanna. I kept my promise, and left you alone last night. Don't expect me to continue such generosity." He touched her neck.

Horrified, she could only gaze at him.

"I've not noticed until recently, but you're an enticing wench," he said huskily. "I'll have you, and soon."

*   *   *

Fireheart, his men, and Mortimer Grace's party arrived at Fort Dobbs shortly after Joanna and John had left. Fireheart discovered that they'd missed the pair only by hours when Mortimer spoke to a woman named Mrs. Brenner. It seemed that Joanna and her husband Joseph Bartley had rented a room for the night.

"Handsome bloke, dark hair, blue eyes. He wore knee breeches that were a bit worse for the wear."

Fireheart nodded. "He called himself Joseph Bartley."

"Yes," Mortimer said, "but it's for certain that the woman with him is Miss Neville. The description fits her."

"I must go find her," the warrior said with fear in his heart.

"How can I help?"

"You have done enough. You have allowed me to come into the white man's settlement without fear."

"Good luck," Mortimer said.

"Luck?"

The man explained, then said, "Let me ask some of the others here before you go. They may know something that may help you."

"*Wa-neé-shih*," Fireheart said. "But I must leave soon."

Chapter 31

Joanna was afraid as she and John left the settlement. She'd thought John would hire someone to take them to Philadelphia. When he hadn't, she'd wondered how he intended to see them there, or if he had plans to go at all.

She watched him out of the corner of her eye as she negotiated the forest trail. The path was clear and well-traveled. Would it take them directly to Philadelphia, or to some other place?

Her thoughts in a whirl, she fought back the desire to panic. *Fireheart, if only you loved me, then I would never have left you.*

She couldn't get Fireheart out of her mind. In the room back at Mrs. Brenner's cabin, she had thought of Fireheart during those waking hours. When she'd dozed, she'd dreamt of him . . . until John's face had loomed up in her dream, destroying the fantasy, stealing her from the world of sleep.

She felt like a fool. She'd been in this position before, and she'd promised herself that she'd return to the village, and tell Fireheart of her feelings. The

sight of him and Moon Dove together had been hurt-
ful, but still she should have stayed. What would he
have said if she'd promised to stay to love him?

I'll never know. She had set herself on a path from
which she couldn't turn back.

What she wouldn't give to have Fireheart here,
watching her with that incredibly intense dark gaze
of his. If she closed her eyes, she'd be able to see
him clearly. But she couldn't for she was not in a safe
place. Not with John Burton only inches away from
her.

She was so wrapped up in her thoughts of the brave
that it was a second before she realized that John had
veered off the path. "We'll stop here," he said.

She studied him. His face was a mess. There were
bug bites on his nose and forehead, and a stubble of
dark whiskers covered his chin and jaw. The cut on
his cheek had begun to fester. He didn't look at all
handsome. She wondered what Gillian had ever seen
in him until she remembered how she'd also been
fooled by his boyish charm back in England when
he'd pretended to be her friend.

She stood by stiffly, watching as he gathered wood
and pine needles. He was going to build a fire! How
long did he plan to stay?

They'd been traveling for just a couple of hours!
It seemed too early to rest, and they'd eaten breakfast
just before they'd left.

Joanna frowned. She didn't like the feeling she was
getting. Maybe she should run, make her escape now.

"I wouldn't think about it if I were you," he said
suddenly, again drawing her gaze. He had carried a
pack of supplies from the settlement, and his head
was bent over the satchel as he rummaged through
the contents.

"About what?" she asked innocently.

"Escaping." He made a sound of satisfaction,
apparently having found what he'd been looking for.

Then he stood, facing her with a gun in his right hand.

She gasped. Where had he obtained that pistol?

"The trading post had more than just food supplies. Imagine, they carry weapons and ammunition, too. The shopkeeper assures me that this gun is quite suitable for protection on our journey north."

Her heart thumped hard. "North? I thought we were going to Philadelphia."

His eyelashes flickered. "We are." He frowned. "East, I mean."

She didn't feel the relief his words should have brought her. He was a madman with a gun, and every moment with him spelled danger. Now she would have to find a way to steal his gun before she could escape.

"Are we making a campfire?" she asked, hoping to sound unconcerned.

"Aye. We're going to stay here for the night."

"But we've only left a short while ago—"

"Business," he quipped. "We are meeting someone."

"Who?"

His eyes dropped to her breasts, and she was sorry she'd asked him. "Jealous?"

A woman? she wondered. Was he meeting the woman with whom he'd spent the night? Good God! Was he planning to bring her on their journey so that he could fornicate with the woman? In her presence?

As she stared at him, she realized with horror that she couldn't put aside the notion. It would be just like a madman to do such a thing.

She began to feel sick to her stomach. What if he'd have similar thoughts involving her?

Trembling, ill, Joanna slumped to the ground, and John smiled at her before preparing the campfire. He was not efficient with flint and tinder. Finally, he thrust the fire tools at her, and angrily ordered her to finish the job.

Glad to have something to do, Joanna took the flint and tinder box, and went to work until a spark came to life in a blaze of burning pine needles, dried leaves, and sticks.

"Burton didn't hire a guide," Mortimer Grace said as he returned to Fireheart. He had asked around, accompanied by Fireheart, finally finding an excellent source of information in the owner of the trading post. A man fitting John Burton's description, but again calling himself Joseph Bartley, had purchased food supplies, bedding, and a gun. Where he'd acquired the money neither one could say.

The shopkeeper had been reluctant to speak. He had looked at the Lenape warrior, and there had been fear and objection in his brown eyes . . . until Mortimer Grace told the man that the Indian had been hired by Grace to act as guide. Then the man had viewed Fireheart with thinly veiled contempt.

Still, he had told them what they'd needed to know.

"And he has the white man's gun," Fireheart said darkly.

"I'm afraid so."

"*Wa-neé-shih*, Mortimer Grace," Fireheart said, offering his hand. "This man is grateful for your help."

The two men shook hands. "I hope you find her soon, Fireheart," Mortimer said with sincerity. "She is a nice lady, and deserves to be treated as such."

She was more than a nice lady, Fireheart thought, as he agreed aloud. She was his love, and he needed her. When he found her, he wasn't going to be as willing to let her go. He would tell her he loved her, make her understand that she would be happier with the Lenape than in any other place.

Fireheart and his men left shortly afterward, taking the path that led from the village to the north. It was the wrong way to Philadelphia, but John Burton would assume that the cleared road would take them to the English place by the water.

John stared at Joanna, and felt his manhood harden against his breeches. She was right, they hadn't come very far, but he wanted to see Nan one more time. He couldn't forget the incredible sex they'd had. Joanna made him throb with desire for her, but it was Nan who had brought his pleasure to fulfillment. He and Nan were going to do it while Joanna watched. When he'd told Nan of his plan to help his frigid wife, she'd been startled, but then he'd seen how the idea had appealed to her. And he'd used all of his charm to press her into agreeing.

He had come to a place Nan had chosen. Less than an hour from the settlement, Nan had told him to find a clearing.

"Light a fire, love, and I'll find you with the smoke," Nan had said.

When he'd mentioned that anyone else could find them as well, she'd laughed. "Don't be silly, Joseph. Who would be searching for anyone out here when there is a settlement within distance?"

There had been a strange logic to her reasoning, but he hadn't cared. The only thing he cared about, dreamed about, was her coming. And Joanna's reaction to the two of them as they fornicated in the grass.

Of course, he would have to tie Joanna up, or she might try to escape rather than watch, but that would only make it all the more exciting.

He envisioned Joanna becoming aroused by watching him and Nan. She would see what she was missing by denying him; and when he released her, after Nan had left sated and smiling, Joanna would be hot and ready for him.

John sat, observing Joanna as she added fuel to the fire she had started. He felt the pulsating heat spread from his cock to all parts of him.

Joanna, he thought, smiling, dreaming, and trying to ignore the aching hardness in his breeches. He would have her just before he killed her.

Just like he had done with Gillian.

Chapter 32

Joanna stared at the woman with horror. She had come out of nowhere, sidling up to John as if they'd been lovers.

She approached Joanna to critically eye her from head to toe. "So you are Joseph's little wife," she purred, stroking her hand down Joanna's cheek.

Appalled at her touch, Joanna jumped back.

She flashed Joanna a smile. "Oh, Joseph, you didn't tell me she'd be a frightened little thing."

John eyed the two women with glee. "I didn't realize it myself." He went to Joanna and patted her shoulder. "You've nothing to worry about, love," he said, pretending to soothe her when it was obvious he found her discomfort amusing. "Nan and I are going to instruct you on the finer points of making love. You'll learn to enjoy it when we've finished our show for you."

Joanna turned away. "I don't want to watch!"

"Of course, you do, dear," Nan said. " 'Tis for your own good and that of your marriage."

"We're not—" She gasped when John grabbed her

arm, then quickly secured the other hand before she had time to react. The next thing she knew he had tied her wrists. She struggled, kicking back at him with her feet until she felt the solid end of his gun barrel at her back. Forced to submit, she was helpless as he made her sit so he could bind her feet.

Ropes, she thought, feeling dizzy, *he must have bought rope, too.* What else had he purchased that was in that sack? Why hadn't she looked?

"Now, Joseph, why the bonds?" Nan asked.

"She'll be too shy to stay if I don't tie her."

Nan pouted prettily. "Ah, too bad. I thought perhaps you had a taste for bondage."

Joanna was horrified to see a spark light up John's gaze, and to hear him murmur, "Hmmm, bondage?" as if he were giving it some serious thought.

Not on your life, bastard! Joanna thought before she started to pray.

She saw John stand a moment to gaze down at her. She glared up at him, murdering him with her eyes, but he only chuckled.

"You'll thank me for this, Joanna," he said, sounding confident. "I'm only thinking of your pleasure."

She grunted and looked away. Then she was foolish enough to glance back in time to see John reach for Nan's bodice and rip it open to expose lush breasts, which he grabbed and kissed. When Nan swayed and moaned, clutching him to her, Joanna turned away.

She didn't watch them. She couldn't watch them, but she could envision what they were doing. They were making enough noise, moaning, whimpering, gasping obscenities to make Joanna's heart race and her face burn.

Whatever John was doing, Nan sounded as if she loved it. She made mewling sounds like a newborn kitten, then keening sounds like a woman gasping in the throes of pain, or ecstasy.

Suddenly, the keening stopped and all was quiet.

Joanna chanced a peek and wished she hadn't. Looking away, she couldn't forget the image she'd seen, Nan sprawled on the ground with John riding her. She shuddered, and vowed to get free before they decided to include her in their little games.

She prayed harder, and tried to rub the rope binding her wrists against the tree at her back, hoping to break it. She winced as the bark abraded her skin, but kept working at it. She had to get free.

"Joseph," she heard Nan say. "She didn't watch. We did it for nothing."

"Not nothing, love," came John's thick voice. He sounded satisfied.

"Make her watch."

"I will."

Dear Lord, Joanna thought and continued to pray.

He made her watch. He had tied her head to the tree so that she had to face them. Then he'd threatened to shoot her if she closed her eyes.

Joanna watched, sickened, appalled by what she saw.

Then John did the unthinkable. He smiled at his lover, and rose to his feet to tug on his breeches. While Nan lay naked, her smile trying to seduce him to come back to her, he picked up his gun and shot her. It happened so fast and was so totally unexpected that Nan died with a smile on her lips.

Joanna screamed at the sound of the gun. When John turned to her with a look in his eyes that terrified her, she fainted into blessed oblivion.

Fireheart heard the shot and began to run toward the sound. His heart pounding, he knew instinctively that it was Burton, and that the man had killed again.

Joanna! he cried silently as his feet flew over the uneven ground.

His men followed behind him easily as he raced toward the scene, his direction led by the new scent of wood-smoke.

She woke up to find that she'd been released from her ropes, and was lying flat with John bending over her. She shrank back in horror as she realized that John was touching her, fondling her breast through the gown. She slapped away his hand, and rolled over to scramble to her feet.

"Joanna." John smiled. "You're awake. I'm so glad."

She gaped at him. He was the charming gentleman again. It was as if the lecherous murderer and he were not one and the same man. But they were. Joanna's gaze flashed to Nan's nude dead body.

Following her gaze, John studied the deceased woman with regret flickering in his blue eyes. "Unfortunate, but necessary. Nan was a wonderful woman, but she would have told. She would have told that I stole from Neville Manor."

Joanna's insides froze to ice. Nan wouldn't have known about Neville Manor! The only thing she would have known is how to make John come.

"But she's probably never been to England," Joanna said in a husky voice. "You didn't have to kill her."

A blank look entered John's expression, a look that clearly told her that she was observing the confusion of a madman, God help her.

"John, you must sit with her. She must be lonely lying there."

The man was mad, Joanna thought. In his confusion he might turn his attention back to his lover to comfort her.

And Joanna could escape.

"Yes, I suppose," John said.

"I'll get help. Maybe there's a physician at the settlement who can save her," Joanna said, backing away.

He stared blankly for a moment, and Joanna saw her chance to leave. She started to run.

"No! Stop!" John's cries preceded the sound of his footsteps crashing through the brush behind her.

He caught her when her skirts became tangled in a thorn bush. She tripped and fell to the ground with him on top of her.

He lay, winded for a long moment; then he grinned. But she saw anger not amusement in the curve of his lips.

"You are going to enjoy this," he purred, fingering her collar. "Just like Nan did. You saw the way Nan liked it, didn't you?"

She shook her head.

He looked annoyed. "Yes, yes, you did."

"No. She didn't enjoy it. I won't enjoy it either. If you touch me, it will be against my will."

He appeared upset by her words. Then his expression brightened. "I'll make you change your mind." He shifted, and his hand settled on her breast and squeezed.

Joanna struggled and screamed.

Suddenly the weight of John's body was gone. Curling herself into a little ball, Joanna began to sob softly.

Shivering, sobbing, she lay there until she realized that someone had come to save her. Who? She opened her eyes, and cried out with mixed joy and horror.

"Fireheart." She breathed as she watched the warrior ram his fist into John's face, then toss him like a rag doll against a tree.

John lay without moving, and Joanna saw Fireheart turn to face her. Their gazes met, and Joanna's heart fluttered. The man she loved was here. He had saved her.

"Fireheart," she cried, more loudly this time.

He smiled, and the light of love in his eyes stunned her. He opened his arms to her, and she rushed to have him envelop her in a tight embrace.

"I love you," she said, saying it with a rush.

"I know," he answered, his face nestled in her hair. "This man loves you, Autumn Wind. He will not let you go again."

John Burton roused himself, and staggered to his feet, swaying. His gaze searched for the gun, and he found it lying on the ground within a few feet of him. Seeing the warrior and Joanna otherwise engaged, John picked up the pistol and aimed it at the warrior's back. He pulled back the trigger. The sound of the gun going off startled Fireheart and Joanna who sprang apart, and spun around.

John Burton lay dead with an arrow through his heart, and a smoking gun in his hand. The gun must have gone off when he fell.

"He was going to kill you, Fireheart," a brave said as he approached. Other warriors came out of the forest behind him.

Fireheart smiled at his friend, Moon Dove's husband-to-be. "*Wa-neé-shih*, Black Fox."

Epilogue

The young girl crossed the yard, drawing her parents' attention. She was a lovely child with dark hair, light honey skin, and dark eyes. Her features were her mother's although her coloring was Lenape.

"Already she draws the attention of the young braves," Fireheart said darkly.

Joanna grasped her husband's hand, squeezed it lovingly, and smiled. "I am not worried about her. She has you to protect her. As you did me." She gazed longingly at his mouth, then looked up to see a flash of burning heat enter his dark eyes. "Fireheart." She gasped, letting go of his hand.

He looked amused as he encircled her shoulders with his arm, and they turned back toward the yard.

Joanna sighed, gloriously happy at her choice, her life. She'd never regretted not returning to England, not for one moment. She had more happiness than any one woman deserved, and she thanked the Creator every day for it.

With Mortimer Grace's help, Joanna had arranged

for someone to return in her place to oversee Neville Manor until her barrister could trace Kenneth Neville's whereabouts.

After Mortimer's assurance that he would find someone in Philadelphia capable of the job, she had promptly forgotten the unknown man, Neville Manor, and Kenneth Neville until a year later when Kenneth had actually been found.

Happy within the Lenni Lenape village, Joanna had married her beloved and bore him three children. It was their oldest child who currently caused Fireheart the most concern. But Joanna had meant what she'd said; she wasn't worried about their only daughter. Fireheart was there to protect Morning Sun just as he was there to protect her, their other two children, and everyone else within Little River. He was the *sachem*, but he was her husband first, and Joanna had enjoyed every living breathing moment of their last twelve years together.

Joanna's gaze continued to follow her daughter as the girl entered the wigwam of her best friend Water Flower. Water Flower, Little Blossom's daughter, was four years older than Morning Sun, but the age difference didn't seem to bother the older girl.

Seconds after her daughter went inside, Joanna watched as the door flap lifted, and Water Blossom exited the structure with her hair and face painted and wearing an abundance of jewelry. At fifteen, she was of an age when the braves within the village interested her. Joanna, with her husband by her side, studied the girl as she crossed the yard toward the community cook-fire to speak with Little Arrow, a young man Water Blossom had seemed particularly fond of lately.

Joanna and Fireheart stood outside of their wigwam, having just left the confines of their lodge. They had been inside kissing, making love. The children had gone out to play earlier, and the couple had been confident that none of their children would return soon.

Satisfied, feeling particularly happy at that moment with her husband's arm around her shoulders, Joanna slipped her arm about his waist.

Minutes later, she saw the door flap across the way open. Her eyes widened as her daughter stepped outside, having painted herself like the older Water Blossom. Morning Sun, her eleven-year-old daughter, was dressed like a maiden in search of a warrior husband.

Fireheart, too, had seen his daughter. And he knew his wife was gaping at Morning Sun. He felt Autumn Wind tense at the exact moment she had seen what Morning Sun had done.

He smiled for he knew that Autumn Wind was no longer the calm one. She shared his concern.

Joanna looked up, saw the amusement in her husband's dark gaze, and lightly pinched him. "I must have a talk with our young daughter," she said.

"*We* will have a talk with Morning Sun," Fireheart replied, showing her with a look and a kiss that he understood her worry. "I love you, Autumn Wind."

Her frown melted away. "I love you, husband."

From another wigwam within the village, Mary Wife and Rising Sun watched the couple studying their daughter and exchanged smiles. They had once looked upon Autumn Wind and shared the same concern.

And look at the woman she had become. Autumn Wind was in love, happy, and able to put the past behind her.

"Morning Sun will be fine," Rising Bird said.

Mary Wife nodded. "She is Lenape. She has her mother and father to watch over and protect her."

And it was true. Like her mother before her, Morning Sun would find happiness living within the village. But unlike her mother before her, she would be allowed to stay within the village always, without the pain of having known another life.

About the Author

Candace McCarthy lives in Delaware with her husband of twenty-five years and has a grown son. She is the author of fourteen Zebra historical romances, including *Irish Linen, Heaven's Fire,* and the tales of two sisters—*Sweet Possession* and *Wild Innocence.*

Candace has won numerous awards for her work. She was extremely pleased to have received the National Readers' Choice Award for her book *White Bear's Woman.* She loves to read and garden, and she enjoys music and doing crafts. It was her enjoyment of books that prompted her to first put pen to paper. *Fireheart* is her sixteenth book.

You may write to her at P.O. Box 58, Magnolia, Delaware 19962. Candace enjoys hearing from her readers.

Check out her Web site at:

http://members.aol.com/candacelmc/index.htm
or
http://www.candacemccarthy.homepage.com